"If you'll please step aside, Sheriff," Honey said stiffly.

Luke shifted enough for her to slip by sideways. As she attempted to pass him, he put his palms on the door frame, trapping her in the circle between his outstretched arms.

"You have exactly half an hour to get ready, Miss Honey Behr." Moving closer, he taunted, "Is it still Honey Behr this morning, or did you dream up a new name overnight?"

"Now, how could I do that, Sheriff, when all my dreams were about you?" Smiling up into his eyes, she reached down and yanked the waistband of his jeans so hard that the pants started to slide off his hips. He grabbed for them with both hands, and Honey stepped quickly past him.

Without a backward glance, she continued down the hall. "I suggest you put some clothes on, Sheriff MacKenzie, or the U.S. Marshal may have to arrest you for indecent exposure."

THE MACKENZIES
LUKE

ANA LEIGH

AVON BOOKS ◆ NEW YORK

THE MACKENZIES: LUKE is an original publication of Avon Books.
This work has never before appeared in book form. This work is a novel.
Any similarity to actual persons or events is purely coincidental.

AVON BOOKS
A division of
The Hearst Corporation
1350 Avenue of the Americas
New York, New York 10019

Copyright © 1996 by Ana Leigh
Published by arrangement with the author
Library of Congress Catalog Card Number: 95-95107
ISBN: 0-380-78098-4

First Avon Books Printing: May 1996

AVON TRADEMARK REG. U.S. PAT. OFF. AND IN OTHER COUNTRIES, MARCA
REGISTRADA, HECHO EN U.S.A.

Printed in the U.S.A.

RA   10   9   8   7   6   5   4   3   2   1

This book is dedicated to those sweet flowers at Steins:

Linda
Lori M.
Cookie
Lori G.
Pat
Marisa

And the rose by any other name,

Liz

Prologue

Missouri
April 1868

Honey Behr had to find an easy mark fast.

She had spent her last dollar buying a ticket on the riverboat *Delta Princess*, headed downriver to St. Louis. Now she didn't have one coin to rub against another. And she was hungry. She feared the rumblings of her empty stomach would be heard above the Mozart sonata being played by a string quartet seated in the alcove of the boat's salon.

Nonchalantly, she stopped near an abandoned table still cluttered with the remains of a recent lunch. She swept her blue-eyed gaze around the room. Most of the diners were engaged in conversation and appeared to be ignoring her. At the far end of the long salon, a dozen gaming tables were filled with card players. Thick clouds of gray smoke spiraled above their heads, dulling the crystal pendants that dangled from opulent chandeliers.

Daintily, she raised a lace-tipped handkerchief to her nose. For the past two days, the doors and windows of the room had been closed due to a steady

1

rain, and the salon reeked of the pungent blend of damp clothing and stale cigar smoke.

After another casual glance around her, Honey lowered the handkerchief to a plate on the abandoned table and deftly palmed an uneaten croissant. Thanking the gods for the slight-of-hand tricks she had mastered during her years with the carnival show, she popped roll and hanky into the drawstring purse suspended from her wrist.

Observing a waiter headed toward the table, she offered him a dimpled smile and slowly began to stroll toward the gaming tables.

As soon as she noticed a huge bankroll in front of one particular player, she selected him as her gull. When her steady gaze and demure smile easily detracted his attention from the card game, Honey knew the portly man would be an easy mark. Within minutes, he left the table and approached her.

"Sheldon Peters is the name, lovely lady," he said, doffing his black silk stovepipe to reveal a full head of gray hair. "Perhaps you will allow me to buy you a refreshing drink?"

Honey flashed a coquettish smile. "Why, that's most generous of you, sir. I think a refreshing drink would be most satisfying." She would have preferred a succulent chicken leg dripping with butter, but at the moment, she settled for what she could get.

Peters ordered a bourbon for himself, and by the time Honey finished her lemonade, she had agreed to join him for dinner.

She returned to her cabin to freshen up for dinner and was startled when a tall, dark-haired man forced his way into the cabin behind her and closed the door. She instantly recognized the pockmarked face of a player who had been seated at the poker table with Sheldon Peters.

Honey had been on her own too long to panic. "Get out of here or I'll scream for help."

"You're not fooling me, sister," he snorted, curling his thin lips into a smirk. "I've seen your kind before.

We're in the same business. Before you get the old man's last dollar out of him, I intend to get my share."

"I don't know what you're talking about," she protested.

"You're wasting your time, sister. Save your act for the old man." His black, beady eyes gleamed with malevolence.

Honey had survived by trusting her instincts, and she sensed a quality of evil about the slender man. Feeling uneasy, she decided not to tangle with him. "All right." She sighed. "I'll leave him to you."

"I've got a better idea. There's a lot of tables working this trip. You make sure he sits down at mine, and I'll cut you in on the take."

"I work alone, mister, so forget it. I'll just find another mark. Now get out of here." She turned away.

His long, bony fingers cut into her flesh as he grabbed her arm. "Not so fast, sister. You do what I say, or this whole boat's gonna know you're just a whore working the river."

"I doubt that bit of news would distress any man here," she quickly retorted.

"Yeah? Well this line don't want no whores fleecing their passengers."

"And what's to stop me from letting them know that you're a crooked gambler?" she challenged in a bluff. "You'll get tossed off the boat."

"Along with you, sister."

He could be right—and she had no desire to be abandoned on a sand bar in the middle of the river in the company of this river rat. "How much will you give me if I agree to help you?"

"Half the take."

"All right, after dinner I'll make sure Peters sits down at your table. But remember, I get half of whatever you win."

"Sure, sister," he said, "Jake Simmons keeps his promises. I'll even seal the bargain."

Appalled but resigned, she stood stiffly as he pulled her into his arms and covered her mouth with a wet, sloppy kiss. Honey tottered with dizziness from sheer hunger and the crushing assault of revulsion and fear she felt at the hands of this horrible man. By the time he released her, she was close to gagging.

"Yeah, you do what you're told, sister, and you and me'll get along just fine," Simmons said, adding a painful pinch to her cheek. He left with a confident sneer.

Desolate, Honey sank down on the bunk. *Whatever happened to honor among thieves?* She groped in her purse for the roll, chewed on the stale bread, and started to formulate a plan. Clearly, she wanted nothing to do with this Jake Simmons, but at the moment, the scum had enough of an upper hand to push her into a corner. She was penniless, and even though she wanted to cut and run, how could she? She was on a boat in the middle of the Missouri River!

Honey stood up and began to dress for dinner. For the time being, there was nothing she could do except go along with Simmons's plan for Sheldon Peters. But whatever plan Mr. Jake Simmons had in mind for her, he would be in for a big surprise.

As previously agreed, she entered the salon promptly at seven o'clock. Sheldon Peters awaited her at a dinner table. Honey tried to appear reserved as she devoured her first decent meal in two days.

While they finished dinner, the velocity of the storm increased. The ship was rocked and pitched by the force of the fury. As they waited for the squall to pass, she led Peters to Simmons's gaming table.

Watching the game, Honey's resentment toward the gambler steadily increased. *Dammit!* she cursed silently when she saw Simmons palm the aces. He was getting ready to make his move. She quickly shifted her glance to Sheldon Peters, who appeared not to have observed the covert action.

Simmons didn't fool her for a moment. She knew he had no intention of paying her off. If she didn't do something soon, nothing would remain of Peters's bankroll. She felt desperate—desperate enough to attempt something outrageous.

The opportunity she hoped for presented itself in the next moment. The captain announced that due to the force of the storm, he had tied up at the dock at Independence, Missouri.

Leaning down, Honey breathed into Peters's ear. "I'm bored, Sheldon. Let's get out of here," she suggested in a provocative whisper.

Undecided, Peters glanced at his cards, then looked up at Honey. "Well, ah, my dear . . ."

Honey arched a delicate brow. "You can always play cards . . . later." Her seductive smile seemed to promise delights that would far exceed any won at a poker table.

Hastily, Peters began to scoop up his money. "Mr. Simmons, you'll have to excuse me. I have some pressing business."

"Where do you think you're goin'?" Simmons growled. "You ain't just leavin' without givin' me a chance to win back my money." He glanced up at Honey, his dark eyes narrowed in a wary slit.

The cardsharper had used the ploy of letting Peters win a few hands before cleaning out the old man, and Honey knew she had interfered with his scheme.

She grabbed the cards. "He folds," she said lightly and tossed the cards into the middle of the pot. "Let's go, sugar."

"I'll see you later, sister. That's a promise," Simmons said ominously. He looked up at her with a glare as portentous as the warning in his voice.

Honey was unperturbed by the threat. She already had her bag packed. Once she bilked Peters, rain or not, she could get off the *Delta Princess* and be gone before the boat left the wharf.

"Oh, he'll be back soon. Won't you, sugar?" she said lightly in an attempt to ward off any further anger on the part of Simmons.

"Not too soon, I hope," Peters replied with a lewd smile.

He took her arm, and huddled against the storm, they hurried to her cabin. After helping her off with her wet cloak, he removed his own coat and hung the dripping garments on wall pegs. Seeing the complimentary decanter of liquor on the table, he rubbed his hands together with pleasure. "Aha, is that brandy?" At her nod, he quickly added, "You sit down, my dear. I'll pour us a drink."

Honey sat down on the edge of the bunk. With a wolfish smile, Peters handed her a glass of brandy. "Here you are, lovely lady. This should warm you."

Smiling shyly, Honey hesitantly put the glass to her lips. She hated any kind of alcohol.

He hurriedly gulped down his drink, then set his glass aside and eyed her like a cat about to pounce. She took a sip of the brandy before he grabbed her glass and set it next to his. Then, pulling her into his arms, he covered her mouth with a moist kiss and started to fumble with the buttons on her bodice.

"Why, Mr. Peters, slow down. The night is young," she added hastily.

"I've thought about this all day," he whispered as he parted the front of her bodice. Licking his lips, he eyed the voluptuous swell of her breasts above her corset and reached out a hand to cup the rounded curve. "Ah, lovely, my dear. Very lovely." He drew back in surprise when tears began to slide down her cheeks. "What is it, my dear?"

Honey's chin quivered as she tried to speak. "It's just . . . I can't . . ." Unable to finish, she lowered her head and began to sob.

"Oh, my dear girl, what is it?" Peters appeared to be the soul of concern, and Honey felt a momentary twinge of guilt.

"I can't do this," she sobbed. "As badly as we need the money, I don't think I can do it." She buried her face in the palms of her hands and continued to cry.

"We? Money? What are you saying? Now, just relax and tell me all about it," he said, putting a fatherly arm around her shoulders.

"My mother is ill and needs an operation. That's why I'm going to St. Louis. The operation is very expensive and I thought I could ... I could get some money by—by ..." Her voice trailed off to a woeful sob.

"By prostituting yourself."

The accusation caused her to wail louder. Peters glanced around nervously. "Hush, my dear, we don't want to attract attention, do we?" He handed her a handkerchief. "Here, use this."

Honey snatched it and brought it to her face. She continued her fake sobbing, and after several more fatherly pats on the shoulder, Peters stood up.

"Now, don't you fret." He withdrew his wallet and extracted a few bills. "Here—take this."

"No, I can't, Mr. Peters."

"Nonsense, of course you can," he protested.

Hesitantly, she reached out and took the money. "Well, thank you, Sheldon." She kissed his cheek. Then she hurriedly buttoned her blouse before he decided to try to extract a partial payment.

The man's gullibility and generosity were beginning to make Honey feel guilty. He was the easiest mark she had ever encountered. Often in the past, she had barely escaped from the clutches of the men she duped. If this one didn't get out of her cabin soon, she'd probably end up giving the stupid man back some of his money. "I'll pay this back to you ... somehow," she sighed, batting her long eyelashes.

"Sooner than you think." He snatched the money from her hand. "You and your partner must think I'm naive."

"What are you talking about?" she gasped.

"I'm not a St. Louis banker, young lady; I'm a detective working for the shipline that owns the *Delta Princess*. In the past year there have been several passengers murdered on the riverboats. We suspect their killer may be one of the gamblers who work the river."

"I know nothing about any murders," she declared.

"Perhaps not. But from the beginning, I've suspected you and Mr. Simmons were cohorts in some kind of crime. I do admit, you surprised me when you insisted I leave the card game when you did. You see, I saw our friend Mr. Simmons's rather shabby deal of the cards."

"If you knew he was cheating, why didn't you arrest him right then and there?"

"Because I expected part of your scheme was for you to bed me. That would have landed you in jail along with him. Frankly, you've disappointed me by spoiling my few moments of anticipated pleasure."

"Pleasure?" she asked, confused. "You mean, believing what you did, you would have arrested me *after* I seduced you?"

"Why not? There aren't too many benefits that go with my job. Pity you accepted the money, my dear. Otherwise, I would have no grounds to arrest you."

"You, sir, are as vile as those you presume to accuse," she said with hauteur. "And I am not guilty of any crime."

His chuckle sent a shiver down her spine. "If you'll excuse me, it's time to inform the captain. Let's hope you can convince him more successfully than you have me." He doffed his hat in mockery. "It's been a pleasure."

As soon as he left her, Honey quickly changed her clothes, grabbed her carpetbag, and slung a canvas-covered guitar over her shoulder. She would get off the boat before he could return with the ship's captain.

She started to step out of the cabin but drew back when she recognized the figures of Peters and Simmons nearby. They were too far away for her to hear what was being said, but she could tell the two men were arguing. Finally, Peters shoved Simmons aside and started to walk away.

A jagged lightning bolt pierced the darkness, and Honey saw a flash of steel in Simmons's hand. She opened her mouth in a silent scream when he grabbed

Peters from behind and slit the old man's throat.

The brutal murder happened so swiftly and unexpectedly that Honey could not have stopped it.

Thunder crashed and rumbled like the boom of a cannon. Terrified, she glanced around the rain-pelted deck, but she saw no one. All the other passengers and crew had sought refuge from the storm inside. Helplessly, she covered her mouth to stifle a sob. Too frightened to run, for fear she would be seen by the murderer, she huddled in the doorway of her cabin and watched Simmons hastily rifle through his victim's pockets. He found the wallet and drew out the wad of bills.

Another brilliant flash streaked the sky, and Honey saw Simmons glance toward her cabin. Then he dragged the dead man across the deck. She watched him struggle to hoist Peters over the railing and drop him into the water. The unresisting body was quickly snatched by the strong current and carried downstream.

Honey found the courage to bolt. She dashed down the deck, but Simmons spun around in time to see her dart away. She ducked into the shadows under the stairway leading to the deck above. Cringing, she held her breath as he came closer, checking the many darkened corners of the boat.

Then his head jerked up, and he swung his glance toward a nearby door that was banging in the wind. He ran toward it and disappeared inside.

Clutching her carpetbag, she willed herself to move from the sanctuary of the shadows. Thick braided ropes stretched from the riverboat to the wharf's pilings, and the vessel bobbed like a cork on the storm-tossed Missouri River. Bracing her slim body against the fury of the tempest, Honey stole down the swaying gangplank. She paused in her flight to hide in the shelter of a warehouse doorway and glance back at the boat. No one followed her.

Peering through the torrent, she saw the humped-back outline of a cluster of wagons. She pulled her sodden cloak around her and ran toward them.

Horses, oxen, and mules shifted nervously in corrals in the center of the forty or more canvas-covered wagons that were grouped in a large square. As she approached, a dog began to bark. Several more took up the chorus. Honey scurried to the nearest wagon, hoping to hide under it and thereby silence the commotion. Suddenly the canvas flaps at the back parted and a young woman peeked out.

"Who are you? What are you doing?" she challenged in a frightened voice.

"Please don't scream," Honey pleaded in a whisper. "I'm running away."

For a brief moment the young woman studied Honey clutching the front of her cloak with one hand, a carpetbag with the other, and what appeared to be a guitar slung over her shoulder. "You better come in here out of the storm."

Gratefully, Honey climbed up onto the back of the wagon.

Once inside, she discovered there was barely enough room for the two of them. The woman sat down on a cot, and Honey hunched down on the floor. "You better get out of those wet clothes." The woman handed her a blanket. "Here, use this."

Honey hurriedly shed her sodden clothing, wrapped herself in the blanket, and then removed her shoes and stockings.

"I'm Abigail Fenton," the young woman said.

"I'm—" Honey halted. Although she was grateful to the woman for offering her shelter from the storm, it would be wiser not to tell this stranger too much about herself. If Peters's body was discovered and traced to the *Delta Princess*, there might be witnesses who would remember seeing her with the victim. Then, not only Simmons, but also the police would be hunting for her. "I'm Mary Jones," she said. She hoped her shivering would cover up her hesitation.

Honey guessed that Abigail couldn't be much older than she was herself. The woman had blond hair, too, although not as light as her own flaxen tresses. Abigail pulled on a pair of thick wire-rimmed glasses that made her look myopic and emphasized the length of her angular nose and sharp chin. In truth, Honey observed, Abigail Fenton wasn't very attractive.

"Who are you running away from, Mary?" Abigail asked.

"My parents," Honey quickly replied. Lying came easily to her; she had lived with lies for the past six years. "They've arranged a marriage for me with a man old enough to be my grandfather. I won't do it. I must get away from here."

"Oh dear!" Abigail responded sympathetically. "I'm almost in the same plight."

With water dripping down her cheeks from her sodden hair, Honey looked askance at Abigail. "You mean you're running away, too?" The coincidence was too much even for Honey's active imagination to digest.

"Not exactly. I'm going to California to marry a man I've never met."

"What? You mean you have an arranged marriage, too?"

Abigail shook her head. "Not exactly. I answered an ad in the *St. Louis Dispatch*."

"An ad?"

"You know, one of those mail-order-bride advertisements."

Honey's mouth gaped in surprise. "You agreed to be a mail-order bride?" Abigail nodded and handed her a towel. "Abigail, why ever in the world would you do that?"

Abigail looked despondent. "I work at the library. I'm twenty-four years old, Mary."

Honey congratulated herself for having guessed the woman's age—another of the skills she had learned in her uncle's medicine show.

"I'm a spinster," Abigail continued, "and not by my own choosing." She smiled gamely. "I didn't want to grow old alone without someone to love or love me. Then I saw the ad of this Mr. MacKenzie in California. He's a widower and wants a wife to help raise his son. I thought that was the answer for me, so I wrote to him. He sent me the money, I purchased the wagon and supplies, and . . . and the wagon train will be leaving at daybreak."

Desperation gleamed in Abigail's eyes as she clutched Honey's arm. "I know now I don't want to go west, Mary. I've completely lost my nerve. I don't want to marry a man I've never met before. I want to go back to the library . . . and my books."

"Well then, just don't go," Honey replied.

"But I've accepted Mr. MacKenzie's money to marry him."

"Then write him and tell him you've changed your mind," Honey said, toweling her hair.

"I can't do that. I've spent most of his money on this wagon and supplies." Abigail's eyes suddenly brightened. "Mary, have you ever thought about going to California?"

"No, I can't say that I have," Honey replied.

"Take my place, Mary," Abigail suddenly blurted.

Honey peered out from under the towel. "What did you say?"

"Take my place, Mary. You said you had to get away from here. It would be a perfect solution for you, and it wouldn't cost you anything."

Honey looked at Abigail in disbelief. "California?"

"Why not, Mary? When you get there, you can explain it all to Mr. MacKenzie. That way he won't think I was dishonest or trying to cheat him. And maybe you'll like him enough to marry him yourself."

Honey had no intention of marrying anyone, although she certainly had no qualms about cheating men. That's how she survived. But California? For a long moment, she thought of Jake Simmons's brutal murder of Sheldon Peters. Because she had witnessed the killing, she knew Simmons would try to kill her, too.

"Won't you take my place, Mary?" Abigail's pleas

jarred Honey out of her reverie. "I just joined this wagon train. No one knows me. You can easily pass yourself off as Abigail Fenton, a librarian from Independence, until you reach California. Will you, Mary, please?"

Desperate, hunted, and fearing for her safety, Honey nodded.

Chapter 1

Sacramento, California
August 1868

"Just like a panther in a passel of alley cats,"
Mordecai Fisher mumbled aloud.

He continued to watch the big man move with a
smooth stride through the milling crowd. The
stranger looked to be a man who spent the better part
of his time on the giving end of trouble. *And headed
straight for me. No doubt about it,* Mordecai reflected
silently.

What worried him the most, the stranger wore a
gun on each hip with the holsters tied down for a fast
draw—he had to be a gunfighter.

The man stopped before him, and Mordecai drew
an easier breath when he saw the partially hidden
badge beneath the stranger's vest.

"You the wagon master of this train?"

Mordecai nodded. "Mordecai Fisher's the name.
What can I do for you, Sheriff?"

"I'm Luke MacKenzie, the sheriff down in Stockton," he said as they shook hands. "I just brought a
prisoner up here and thought I'd stop to inquire if a

15

Miss Abigail Fenton might have come in with your train."

"She sure did. Nice gal, too, Sheriff. She in some kind of trouble?"

"Not that I know of. 'Less you figure marrying me means trouble."

Despite the intended levity of the sheriff's remark, Mordecai observed little humor in the tall man's eyes. He figured smiling didn't come easy to the lawman.

"You don't say! Well, congratulations, Sheriff. You've got yourself a downright pretty bride. Come on, I'll take you to her."

The two men walked through the maze of wagons, mewling animals, and children darting around the men and women who were calling their good-byes to each other. Having reached their destination after the grueling, five-month-long journey, the travelers were preparing to either pull out of the train or settle down for the night.

Mordecai halted, glanced around in confusion, then hurried over to a wagon that was just pulling away from the others. "Hold up there, mister," Mordecai yelled to the driver. "Where are you headed with Miz Fenton's wagon?"

The driver reined up the team of four mules, noticed Luke, and cast a worried glance at the woman seated beside him. "We ain't done nothin' wrong, Sheriff. Bought the wagon and team from the lady. Got a bill of sale right here." He reached into the pocket of his homespun shirt and withdrew a folded paper.

"Where'd she go?" Mordecai asked.

"Cain't say," the homesteader replied. "Told me to leave her belongin's at the freight office and she'd come to fetch 'em later. Then she hurried off, totin' jest a carpetbag and geetar."

"Sure don't make sense to me," Mordecai mumbled.

"May I see that bill of sale?" Luke asked. He unfolded the paper the farmer handed him. The hastily scribbled bill of sale, signed by Abigail Fenton, acknowledged the sale of the wagon and mules in receipt of fifty dollars.

"Sorry to have bothered you folks." Luke handed the paper back to the farmer. "Ma'am," he said politely, tipping his hat to the woman.

As the wagon rolled away, Mordecai took off his hat and scratched his head. "Well, if that sure don't beat all."

"She probably headed for the hotel. I'll check there," Luke said.

"I'll come with you, Sheriff," Mordecai said.

He scrambled to keep up with the lawman's long-legged stride as the sheriff moved hurriedly through the crowded street of this former fort, now the California terminus of the Oregon Trail.

Luke entered the three-story hotel in the center of the small city. The young man behind the desk nodded when the two men entered the hotel and shoved a register and pen at them. "A dollar a day. Bath included. Pay in advance. No Confederate scrip or Union greenbacks."

Luke quickly perused the register. Abigail Fenton was not registered. The last signature on the list was that of a Mrs. B. Sharp. "You haven't seen a young woman come in here, have you?" he asked as he scribbled his own name.

"A yellow-haired, comely little gal with bight blue eyes?" Mordecai quickly added.

The clerk smirked. "Mister, there ain't been no pretty yellow-haired gal come into this place in the two years I've worked here."

"Well, what about this Mrs. B. Sharp?" Luke asked. "Looks like she registered just ahead of me."

The young man glanced in surprise at the book. "Can't say. I just got back from lunch, Sheriff. You'd have to ask Arnie. He was spelling me."

"All right, where can I find this Arnie?" Luke asked.

"Your room's number 7, Sheriff . . ."—he glanced

down at the register—"MacKenzie." His eyes suddenly lit with recognition. "MacKenzie! Say, are you that sheriff who shot it out with those Walden brothers in Stockton?"

"Reckon so," Luke replied tersely.

"Heard tell you gunned down Beau Walden and brought Billy Bob in here to the marshall." A note of awe had crept into the clerk's voice.

"Where can I find Arnie?" Luke asked patiently.

"Folks 'round these parts say Charlie Walden's not gonna be too happy when he hears what happened to his younger brothers."

"Can't worry about that. I'm paid to keep the peace," Luke said.

"Heard tell you arrested Billy Bob 'cause he gunned down a gambler during a poker game. Is that right, Sheriff?"

"The gambler was unarmed. Where can I find Arnie?"

"Why'd you shoot Beau?" the clerk asked.

"He had a mind to stop me." Luke glanced around in disgust, then repeated firmly, "Now, where can I find this Arnie?"

Ignoring the question, the clerk asked, "What're you hunting this gal for, Sheriff?" Then, leaning across the desk, he added in a stage whisper, "Broke the law, did she?"

"Didn't say that." Exasperated, Luke said forcefully, "Arnie?"

The clerk straightened up. Luke could see the young man's nose was out of joint because he missed some fresh gossip to pass around. "In the bar." He nodded toward the door leading to the adjoining barroom.

"Thanks." Luke tossed down a gold dollar and picked up the key the clerk slid across the desk. Followed by Mordecai, Luke headed for the barroom.

Luke MacKenzie never entered a saloon without drawing the attention of everyone in the room. Today was no exception: four poker players at a corner table halted their game to watch the tall man cross the floor; two cowhands leaning against the bar stopped their conversation and shifted down to the far end; and a round-shouldered piano player paused with his hands on the keyboard before resuming a tinny-sounding rendition of "De Camptown Races." Not an occupant in the room had given Mordecai Fisher a second glance.

The man behind the bar looked as if he could wrestle a bear. He placed two shot glasses before them. "Whiskey?"

Nodding, Luke said, "I'm looking for Arnie."

"What's he done?" the bartender asked, filling the glasses.

Luke picked up the glass and swallowed the contents. "Got a couple questions to ask him."

"He's the one playin' the piano."

"Give me a refill, and pour another glass." He waited as the glasses were filled, then picked them up and walked over to the piano. He put a drink down on the piano top.

The piano player glanced up and shifted a toothpick from one side of his mouth to the other. "Howdy, Sheriff. What's your pleasure? You got a special song you want me to play?"

Luke pulled a picture out of his pocket. "I'm trying to find this woman. Her name's Abigail Fenton. Have you seen her today?"

The piano player studied the picture Abigail Fenton had sent to Luke. "Nope. Never seen her today or any other day," he replied.

"You're sure about that? Maybe she wasn't wearing the glasses when you saw her."

"Naw, I ain't never seen her, Sheriff," Arnie said again, more emphatically. He returned the picture to Luke.

"Well, thanks for your trouble."

"Sorry I couldn't be of more help, Sheriff."

"Any luck?" Mordecai asked when Luke returned to the bar.

Luke shook his head. "No. He hasn't seen her."

Arnie picked up his drink and went over to the bar. "Let me see that picture again." After another inspection, he shook his head and handed it back to Luke. "She sure ain't the comeliest gal, is she?"

"Ain't comely?" Mordecai snorted. "You must be blind as a bat or just plumb loco. Let me see that there picture." He snatched the photograph out of Luke's hand. "Well, hell! It's no wonder. This ain't the Abigail Fenton that come in with my train. The gal I'm talking about is real pretty, with hair as yellow as honey and eyes the color of a Texas bluebonnet. Don't recall seeing her wear spectacles either."

"Gal you're describin' sounds more like that widow woman who come into the hotel today," Arnie interjected. "Prettiest thing I've ever seen in these parts."

"What was her name?" Luke asked with renewed interest.

"Name of Sharp." He rolled his eyes. "A real good looker, she was, too."

"Tell me more about this Widow Sharp," Luke said.

"Said she was just travelin' through. Poor gal lost her husband in the war. Brokenhearted little thing could barely speak of it without chokin' up. She come here to live with his folks. I figured she had to have been married to a real damn fool, runnin' off and gettin' himself killed with a woman like her awaitin'."

"Well, thanks for your help, Arnie. You, too, Mordecai. Pleasure meeting both of you." Luke shook hands with the two men, then he tossed a couple of gold dollars on the bar. "Keep 'em coming, bartender, 'til the money runs out."

Luke hurried back to the desk clerk. "Which room is Mrs. Sharp in?"

The clerk checked the register. "In number 6. Right next to yours, Sheriff. End of the hall on the second floor." The clerk's curious stare followed Luke up the stairway.

* * *

Honey leaned her head back on the rim of the tub, closed her eyes, and savored the feel of the hot water. During the nearly five months of bathing in cold-water creeks and even colder mountain streams, she had vowed the first thing she would do when she reached Sacramento would be to take a hot bath.

As she lazed in the water, she thought about the long trip. After having worked in a medicine show as a kid, she'd found that driving a wagon and team had presented no problem to her. However, fearing that someone asking questions about her might follow later, she had avoided long conversations with the others and had stayed close to her wagon in the evenings.

Abigail Fenton's loss had been a godsend for her, Honey reflected. Fearful of attracting attention, Abigail hadn't been able to haul away anything except her clothes, so the tearful librarian had left behind several cartons of books and a box of imitation stones and beads.

Honey had passed the long days and lonely nights on the trail with such traveling companions as *Jane Eyre*, *Alice in Wonderland*, and *Hans Brinker*. And whenever she got tired of reading, she spent her idle hours pasting together colorful brooches and earrings or stringing pearl and beaded necklaces. She was now the proud owner of two pearl necklaces, six sets of rubylike earrings, and four cameo brooches made of imitation jade.

In addition, by the time they reached Sacramento, she had read the first part of *War and Peace* and almost all of the ten volumes of *Chambers Encyclopedia*. She might be a lot more tired than when she left Independence, but she was also a darn sight smarter.

She smiled with satisfaction. Choosing the name of Becky Sharp, the unscrupulous adventuress in *Vanity Fair*, seemed a clever touch on her part. That particular novel had been her favorite among the assortment because the author reflected her sentiments exactly: society was so hypocritical that a person without money or position, such as herself, *had* to violate ethical principles in order to get along.

However, despite her enjoyment of the books, the journey had been tiring and often harrowing. She was relieved it was over. After a night's sleep in a soft bed, she would head out for San Francisco first thing in the morning.

A light tap on the door jarred her out of her languor. "Is time, *señora*," the chambermaid informed her through the closed portal. "I must prepare the bath for next guest."

"All right," Honey said. Reluctantly, she stepped out of the tub and glanced disconcertedly into the mirror. Her hair was still pinned to the top of her head, but the time had passed so swiftly she hadn't had a chance to wash it. Hastily drying herself, she put on her nightgown and robe, then unlocked the bathroom door. Smiling at the young Mexican maid who waited in the hallway, Honey hurried to her room.

She unlocked the door, slipped into the room, then closed the door and relocked it. Turning around, she gasped in alarm.

A man was seated in the corner. His long legs straddled a chair and his forearms rested casually on the top of the chair's back.

Her first thought was that Jake Simmons had tracked her down and sent this man to murder her.

"Who . . . who are you? What do you want?" she asked. Her voice squeaked in a high quiver that sounded unfamiliar to her.

Luke was glad he was sitting down, or his first glance of her might have knocked him off his feet. Mordecai and Arnie hadn't exaggerated about her looks. She was beautiful all right. And taller than they had led him to believe, with more curves than a mountain trail.

Her frilly white robe was made from one of those soft female materials that women liked so much. Cambric or calico or some such name. Anyhow, it sure didn't go far in disguising the curves it was meant to cover.

His glance roved to the rounded swell of her breasts, where a ruffle of lace on the low-cut nightgown peeked out from under the robe. Her body was still damp from the bath, and through the thin fabric of the robe, he could see where the nightgown clung to the curve of her hips and long legs. A fire began to lick at his loins.

His perusal moved up to her face. An abundance of blond hair was swept up and pinned haphazardly to the top of her head. Wispy golden strands were stuck to her cheeks and forehead.

An exotic oval, appealingly blushing at the moment, her face had high cheekbones, a straight nose, and a delicately pointed chin. Her mouth was wide, her lips full and kissable. Damn it! He wasn't a green schoolboy. He forced aside his carnal thoughts to put his mind on his purpose for being there.

His eyes locked with hers. She had regained her composure, and he saw more curiosity than fear in the bright blue eyes that boldly met his stare.

His compelling looks completely captured Honey's attention. If he was a crony of Simmons, he certainly was no gambler. A man didn't maintain a chest that muscular by dealing poker or three-card monte in smoke-filled saloons.

He was wearing a white shirt, buckskin vest, and blue jeans. His shirtsleeves were rolled up nearly to his elbows, and his forearms were bronzed and muscular with a dusting of dark hair. Her gaze continued down to his hands. They were big, with long, tanned fingers. Strange, she thought, how a man's hands could be so appealing.

Despite his casual pose in the chair, his whole attitude generated restrained power and energy. If not the handsomest, he certainly was the most masculine man she had ever seen. Taken individually, his features lacked the symmetry of classic good looks, nor did he have the polish of a sophisticated man in a custom-fitted suit and top hat.

But he didn't need them.

The character and strength reflected in his face made him handsome. Bronzed by sun and wind, the man's profile was rugged and somber with a square jaw that denoted as much stubbornness as confidence. The lines extending from the corners of his eyes and mouth added a dimension of maturity. On another face, his nose might have been considered too long, his mouth too wide; but he was a big man, so the long, straight nose and firm, sensual lips seemed in proportion to the rest of him.

His brows were thick, saved from bushiness by the faint curve of an arch, and a lock of dark hair poked from beneath the worn cavalry hat shoved back on his forehead.

When she met the direct stare of his mesmerizing sapphire eyes, her fear dissipated. Those weren't the eyes of a man who could commit murder.

With a smooth, fluid motion, he stood and walked toward her. "Mrs. Sharp?" Despite the sarcasm in his tone, his voice had a deep timbre that sent a ripple down her spine.

Honey Behr feared she had met her match. And what in hell was he doing in her room?

Chapter 2

As he walked up to her, his compelling gaze held Honey transfixed. Despite his intimidating size, she stood her ground and managed to keep a quaver out of her voice. "Who are you?"

"That's my question to you. And I asked first," he said without humor.

"I don't know what you're talking about. And if you don't get out of here, I'm going to start screaming for the sher—" The word lodged in her throat when she glimpsed the partially hidden badge pinned to his white shirt. She took a longer look at the star, then back at him. His expression hadn't altered.

So the law had caught up with her already, Honey fretted. Well, she would just have to keep her wits about her and talk herself out of the situation. "Oh, I see *you* are the sheriff. Is there something wrong, sir?" she asked with as much wide-eyed innocence as she could muster.

"Only one thing that I know of," he said. "Who the hell are you, lady?"

She widened her eyes in shock. "Why, Sheriff, how indelicate of you to use profanity in the presence of a lady." Feigning indignation, she walked to the door. "My name is Mrs. Becky Sharp, and I am deeply of-

25

fended by your crudeness, sir. Please leave my room at once." With a theatrical flourish, she reached to yank the door open.

Too late, she realized a locked door doesn't budge. "Now look what's happened! I've broken a fingernail," she bemoaned as she tried to regain her composure. "And it's all your fault."

"You're wasting your time, lady. I want the truth."

"I don't know what you're talking about."

His gaze lingered on her mouth as she pursed her lips and began to suck on the tip of her injured finger. "If you were as innocent as you'd like me to think, you'd have started screaming when you walked through that door and found a strange man in your room."

The man was too damned smart for his own good, Honey thought. Seeing that she was getting nowhere with him, she decided to try a different approach. "Why, Sheriff, don't talk about yourself so unkindly," she said flirtatiously. "I don't see anything strange about you at all. As a matter of fact, I've noticed you're a very handsome man."

Luke leaned back against the wall and nonchalantly crossed his arms over his chest. "And I've noticed the same about you, Miss Fenton. It is Miss Fenton, isn't it? Not Mrs. Sharp?" he asked casually.

"Well, yes, it is, Sheriff," she said. "You see I, ah . . . am traveling alone, and I thought it would be safer to register as a married woman."

Reflecting on her words, he nodded slowly. "Yeah, I'd have to say that a pretty lady like you could run into all kinds of trouble traveling alone. What brings you to California, Miss Fenton?"

His friendlier attitude put her at ease. "Well, you see, Sheriff, I've come west to get married." Honey smiled, pausing just long enough for the pleasant expression to have the desired effect on him. "I'm on my way to Stockton to wed a Mr. Luke MacKenzie."

"You don't say?" he said affably. "I know Luke MacKenzie real well. Matter of fact, nobody knows

him as well as I do. 'Pears like he's a very lucky man."
He eyed her from head to foot. "You're a right pretty
woman, Miss Fenton."

The bigger they are, the harder they fall, she
thought confidently. "Why, thank you, Sheriff. That's
most kind of you."

Forsaking any further pretense, Luke straightened
up. "In fact, I'd have to say you're much prettier than
your picture, Miss Fenton." He took a photograph out
of his shirt pocket, walked over, and handed it to her.

For a long moment, she stared in despair at the face
of Abigail Fenton. With a sickly smile, Honey looked
up at Luke. "Well, I declare, wherever did you get
this awful picture of me?"

"It's the one you sent me, Miss Fenton."

"Oh . . . I did, didn't I? I can't imagine why I sent
such an unflattering picture. I remember I wasn't feeling well the day it was taken and I didn't—" She
stopped as his last words penetrated her racing
thoughts. "What do you mean, *sent me* . . . I mean,
sent you, Sheriff?" she said, now clearly flustered.

"My name's Luke MacKenzie."

"You're Luke MacKenzie?" Honey stared in astonishment. "Abigail never told me you were a sheriff!"
She could not believe her bad luck. After all her efforts to avoid the law, she had been caught trying to
hoodwink a sheriff!

"Just who the hell are you, lady?"

Stalling for time, Honey took a deep breath. "Well,
it's a long story, Sheriff. As you may have guessed,
I'm not the real Abigail Fenton."

His expression never changed. "Is that right?" Once
again he crossed his arms and leaned back against the
wall.

She had talked herself out of too many situations
to allow herself to be tripped up by some hick sheriff
so desperate he had to advertise for a wife. As soon
as she got rid of him, she would pack up quick and
get out of town fast.

"You see, Sheriff MacKenzie, my name is Becky

Sharp. Abigail and I were dear friends in St. Louis. We worked together . . . in the library." Pausing, she looked into his enigmatic gaze. This was going to be more difficult than she had thought. Clearing her throat, she continued. "Abigail had grown weary of spinsterhood, so she answered your advertisement for a wife. Her intentions were honorable, Sheriff Mac-Kenzie, but at the last moment, she lost her nerve and asked me to take her place."

"Am I to presume you have come here to marry me in her stead, Miss Sharp?"

"No, that's not what I mean," she answered hastily. "Abigail wanted me to assure you that she did not intend to cheat you, but she lost her nerve about coming to California. I agreed to come and explain the situation to you."

"Most generous of you, Miss Sharp."

Damn the man! His expression hadn't changed one whit since she had begun. "Well, not exactly. You see, Sheriff MacKenzie, I'm running away from an undesirable betrothal."

"Let's cut to the quick, Miss Sharp. If you or Miss Fenton have not come here to marry me, give me the three hundred dollars I sent her and I'll get out of here."

"Abigail spent it on the wagon and supplies."

"Lady, I worked hard for that money. You don't think I'm going to let you pluck it from me like I'm some pigeon, do you? Either you return it to me, or I'm arresting you for taking money under false pretenses."

"I did not take any of your money," she declared. She had more sense than to try to swindle a lawman and would have liked to have told him as much. "If I had any money, I'd gladly give you your three hundred dollars."

"Then I think you were too hasty in selling that wagon and team so cheaply," he scoffed.

"How did you know that?" she asked in further astonishment.

"Now I'm going to tell you what else I'm thinking, Miss Whatever-Your-Name-Is. I don't think there ever was such a person as Abigail Fenton. I think sending a name and a picture is all just a scheme you use to get money out of men."

"If that were true, I wouldn't be dumb enough to come here, now would I?"

"Well, maybe you had no other choice. Maybe you were escaping from something else," he accused.

The man's suspicions were getting too close to the truth. Honey had to get him off this dangerous track. "Sheriff MacKenzie," she cajoled, "I swear, I did not try to swindle you. I just grasped the opportunity to come west and get out of being forced into a marriage I didn't want. I'll give you all the money I have."

"That's for damn sure," he declared. "At least three hundred dollars anyway."

"I don't have three hundred dollars. What I have is in my carpetbag."

"Make sure it's money you draw out of that bag and not a gun," he warned as she began to root through the bag.

She threw him a disgusted look, then pulled out her money pouch. "Here, take it. This is all I have. Apparently you have no qualms about leaving a woman stranded, impoverished and alone. Seems like chivalry went out with the defeat of the Confederacy."

She had a hunch that the Texas twang she detected in his voice might mean he had fought for the South during the war. And if he believed she was sympathetic to that cause, maybe she could shame him into being more lenient. "My papa always warned me that Yankees were obsessed with the love of money. No southern gentleman could ever sleep nights if he took a lady's last dollar and left her stranded without visible means of support."

"Lady, I sleep like a baby at night." He glanced up from counting the money in his hands and measured her with an insolent sweep of his dark blue eyes. "And judging from what's visible in that getup you've wearing, I reckon you won't have trouble supporting yourself."

Broken nail or not, she felt a rising desire to scratch the smirk off his face. But she knew words, not actions, were her best defense for the moment.

"There's only forty-nine dollars here," he said, slipping the pouch into his shirt pocket. "That's a far cry from three hundred."

Honey could see there was no compromise in the man. In desperation, she tried again.

Desolately, she walked back to the carpetbag. She searched until her fingers encountered one of the brooches she had made. Tears glistened in her eyes when she turned back to him.

"All right, take this. It's the only other thing of value I possess. My grandmother gave it to me right before she died."

"What am I supposed to do with a brooch?" he questioned.

What she wanted him to do with it could not be said aloud. Instead, she answered sorrowfully, "You could easily sell it. The brooch is made of real jade, and it's very valuable."

He slipped the cameo into his pocket. With relief, she watched him walk to the door. Then to her distress, he pocketed the key that was in the lock.

"What are you doing?" she cried in alarm. He turned around, his dark eyes hooded. He looked sexy and dangerous. She put up a hand and backed away. "Don't you dare come near me," she warned, "or I'll start screaming at the top of my voice."

He moved to the door that connected her room to the next room. Her fear turned to shock when it opened at his touch. The door had been locked when she left the room to take her bath.

In answer to her puzzled look, he took a key out of his pocket. "When I discovered our rooms connected, I went down and got the key from the desk clerk. You're not getting out of here until I wire Independence to check out that story of yours."

"You can't keep me locked up in this room," she declared.

"It's either here or a cell in the county jail. Bed's much softer here. Which do you prefer?"

Putting her hands on her hips, she glared at him. "And just what am I supposed to do while I'm locked up like a prisoner?"

His expression changed to an insulting smirk. "I suppose I could find someone in the bar to come up here and keep you company."

His meaning was clear, and the insolence in his dark eyes met the fury in hers. "Is procuring one of your duties, Sheriff?"

"Matter of fact, I've got a hankering right now that's scratching at my loins like a hound dog at a neckful of fleas. There's a gold eagle in it for you if you want to cure the itch."

Drawing herself up to the full height of her sixty-six inches, she lashed out with loathing. "I'd curl up with a snake before I'd ever go to bed with you!"

"Doggone it!" he exclaimed, feigning chagrin. "My brother Flint always bragged that approach worked for him." His chuckle caused the hair on her arms to rise; she realized he had been mocking her. "Have a pleasant evening." He touched a finger to his hat brim and disappeared through the connecting door. She heard the key click in the lock.

Furious, she stalked over to the door, yanked at it a few times, then kicked it for good measure. She limped over to the open window on her now aching foot. There was no escape from the room unless she could fly. Frustrated, she crossed her arms over her chest and began to pace the floor. Her greatest fear was that by now, somehow, someone had connected her with the murder of Sheldon Peters and that that busybody sheriff would discover it.

Dusk had descended on the city by the time she dropped with exhaustion onto the bed.

* * *

A short time later, Luke unlocked the door and paused in the doorway between the two rooms. By the light cast from his bedside lamp, he saw her sleeping figure on the bed.

He stepped into the room and put a dinner tray on the table. For a long moment, he stood silently looking at her. In sleep, she was even more beautiful. Serene. Innocent. What would cause a woman with the face of an angel to choose the path she was traveling? Surely, she must have had some other choice. She seemed to be as smart as a whip.

In his heart, he hoped at least part of her story was true. But his instincts told him it was not all true. He had read the guilt in her eyes. She must be running away from something a lot more serious than an unwanted marriage. No doubt about that!

Nevertheless, his plans had suffered a setback. Now it would probably be another year before he could find a suitable bride, unless he was lucky enough to encounter a woman nearer to home. Up to now, he sure hadn't had any luck. There just weren't any respectable women available: the decent single women who came west were snatched up as soon as they arrived, and widows remarried practically before their husbands were cold in the grave.

Poor Josh, Luke thought regretfully, recalling the sad face of his six-year-old son. The boy needed a mother so badly. That was the only reason he had advertised for a wife. Josh seemed to be withdrawing more and more every day. He refused to speak and had forgotten how to smile, let alone laugh. Of course, seeing his mother and grandmother killed by . . .

Luke tried to shake off the painful recollection of how Sarah and his own mother had died. But the thought never faded easily. After Josh was born, he shouldn't have left them to go off to war, especially since Flint and Cleve had gone ahead of him. He should have stayed home to protect the women. Now he was driven by guilt—and the need to avenge their deaths. Once he remarried and could leave Josh in caring hands, he would track down every last one of the murdering bastards who had raided the ranch and killed his womenfolk.

He suddenly sensed the woman on the bed watching him. His gaze locked on hers, and for a long moment they stared at each other. In the pale shaft of light from the next room, he saw neither the guile nor the loathing in her eyes that had been there earlier. Her eyes looked like Sarah's—blue and trusting.

Lord, how he ached to lie down beside her and lose himself in her lush curves. He clenched his hands into fists, then pivoted and hurried back to his room. His hand was shaking as he turned the key in the lock.

Once again the room was pitched into darkness. Honey lay still, thinking about the past few moments. When she had awakened to see him standing above her, she had not been frightened. For a few seconds, the look of anguish on his face had made her heart swell with sympathy. *Why?* she asked herself, rising from the bed. *Why should I have any feeling for this browbeating sheriff?*

She lit the lamp and noticed the tray of food on the table. Eagerly reaching for the contents, she poured herself a cup of coffee and began to pace the floor, alternating sips of coffee with nibbles on a chicken leg.

So Luke MacKenzie had an Achilles' heel! Under that stubborn jaw and tanned, muscled hide, he just might be vulnerable. Remembering the look of torment on his face, she stopped pacing. What secrets were hidden behind that brooding stare?

With a calculating smile, she took another bite of the chicken leg.

Chapter 3

The next morning, Honey awoke to see bright sunlight streaming into the room. She hurried to the window and saw that the street below was alive with action. Obviously the hour was late, but without a clock, she had no idea of the time. After Luke MacKenzie's visit last night, she had been unable to fall asleep and had sat up re-reading *Vanity Fair* until almost dawn.

She wondered what the sheriff was up to, but she had no intention of rapping on the door to inquire. As she washed her face and hands in cold water, she thought of the hot water available at the end of the hall. Then, damning Luke MacKenzie for keeping her locked up in the room, she began to dress.

She had finished putting her corset on over her camisole and pantalets when she heard the key rattle in the lock. Honey made a quick grab for her robe and succeeded in slipping her arms into it just as Luke opened the door between the rooms.

"Can't you knock?" she demanded angrily. "Furthermore, if you don't release me from this room, I am going to start screaming for help." To verify the threat, she walked over to the window and leaned out.

"Lady, with what's sticking out from those fancy trappings you've got on, you won't have to scream. You'll get a whole stampede up here."

Honey glanced down and saw the generous and very exposed cleavage of her breasts. Swept with a heated flush, she quickly jerked back inside, closed the robe, and belted it. "I demand you release me from this room, Sheriff MacKenzie."

"Just got a return wire from Independence. Your story checks out; there *is* an Abigail Fenton and she confirmed what you told me, Miss Sharp."

Honey said a quick prayer of thanks to all the saints she could think of. "Well, since you've checked out my story, I hope you will release me from this unwarranted incarceration."

"Yeah, everything checks out except for one thing."

"Which is?" she asked warily.

"Abigail Fenton said that a Mary Jones took her place. Now, if you're Becky Sharp, then what happened to Mary Jones?"

"Oh, good Lord, Sheriff! *I'm* Mary Jones. I just took the name of Becky Sharp as a lark. It's the name of my favorite heroine." She snatched the book from the table and handed it to him. "Here, read it for yourself."

After a quick perusal of one page, he glanced up slowly. "It made sense to me why you called yourself Abigail Fenton, but it doesn't make any sense at all why you would use the name of the gal in this novel instead of your real name. Unless—"

"Unless what, Sheriff MacKenzie?" she asked impatiently.

"Unless you're running from something and don't want your real name known."

"Of course I'm running from something. An unwanted marriage. I told you as much yesterday."

"Yes, you did. At the same time, you told me your name was Becky Sharp and then Abigail Fenton." A faint smile cracked his somber face as she stared in exasperation. "If neither is true, why should I believe your reason for running away? So I've sent a wire to Independence to check out a Mary Jones."

She threw up her hands in frustration. "That's it, Sheriff. I've had enough." She stomped over to the open window. "I demand you release me now, or I start screaming."

"Go ahead, but it's not going to get you anything except a visit from the United States marshal. He'll probably be very interested in hearing this whole story."

Attracting the attention of a U.S. marshal was the last thing she wanted. "I just can't believe it! After enduring a hellish trip across prairies and plains swarming with insects and hostile Indians, after driving a wagon and team of mules through impassable mountains, I am now at the mercy of a provincial sheriff suffering from . . . paranoia." Honey was quite proud that she had gotten past the P section of the encyclopedia.

Luke appeared perplexed by her outburst. "I stayed with you until the part about paranoia. 'Fraid you lost me there, ma'am. Never heard the word before."

"Of course! It's common not to recognize your own sickness when you're mentally ill."

"Mentally ill?" He calmly shook his head. "It appears to me, ma'am, that you're the one who's . . . Oh, never mind. Anyway, I should be getting an answer back before nightfall."

"I'm surprised you didn't check out the background of Becky Sharp, too," she taunted angrily.

"What makes you think I didn't?" Walking to the connecting door, he laid her key on the dresser. "You stay in town until I say you can leave," he said.

"And I say, you can lock this door between our rooms and return that key to the desk clerk," she declared, slamming the door in his face. She heard the key turn in the lock.

Honey continued to fume as she pulled a pink calico dress over her head. With her luck, there would be a Mary Jones who's an ax murderess and a Becky

Sharp wanted for treason by the U.S. government. "Or vice versa," she mumbled aloud.

Leaving her room, she went downstairs to the lobby. She stopped at the desk and smiled at the desk clerk. The man stood with his mouth agape and eyed her with curiosity.

"How do you do, sir?" she said demurely.

"Ma'am," he said, his Adam's apple bobbing.

"Could you tell me if Sheriff MacKenzie has returned the key to the connecting door between rooms 6 and 7?"

"Yes, ma'am, not more than five minutes ago," he said, clearing his throat.

She batted her eyes outrageously. "Thank you, sir, that's all I wanted to know." Flashing a smile over her shoulder, she left him standing there with his mouth gaping.

Honey stepped out onto the street and looked around. She didn't have any money; that insufferable sheriff had taken her last dollar. And she didn't dare work any of her scams, with him minding her business so closely.

She would have to find an honest job for the day to earn enough to get on the first stage leaving in the morning for San Francisco.

It was late afternoon by the time Luke returned to the hotel. He stopped and knocked on her door but received no answer. As he entered his own room, he felt uneasy. His conscience bothered him. Had he really taken her last dollar, or had she managed to hold on to a few for herself? He had spent most of the afternoon looking for her but had failed to find her. She hadn't left town, though, because the desk clerk told him she had not checked out or taken her bag when she left.

God, he felt like a cad. He'd never treated a woman so badly. But he knew she must be lying about something; the question was, did it concern the law?

He grinned despite his apprehension. She was a

tough little scrapper. Maybe too tough. What secrets
did she keep hidden behind those big blue eyes of
hers? Well, whatever they were, if the wire from Independence cleared her, he would give back her
money. He must return to Stockton anyway. He had
been away from Josh for too long.

For a moment, he studied the picture of Abigail
Fenton and then picked up the brooch lying next to
the photograph. He'd find her and give it back to her.
Good Lord! He didn't want her keepsake.

The brooch slipped through his fingers and fell to
the floor. Dismayed, he bent down and picked up a
piece of jade that had broken off. He could see it was
not a hard genuine stone. He squeezed the small piece
between his fingers until it crumbled like powder. He
checked out more of the stone, and it appeared to be
nothing more than painted paste. He shook his head
in disgust. She had hoodwinked him. The lying little
bitch had hoodwinked him!

Scooping up the remains of the "valuable brooch,"
Luke stormed out of the room. His first stop would
be the telegraph office. Then he would find her—if he
had to scour every inch of town!

Honey had never before attempted to perform in
public, but after a day of searching the city, the only
job she could find was singing at the Golden Palace
saloon. Ben Rivers, the owner of the bar, had offered
her twenty dollars to spend the night with him. She
had received many such offers that day along with an
abundance of marriage proposals. When she declined
Ben's lewd proposition, he suggested she might want
to work one of the upstairs rooms.

"Why, Mr. Rivahs!" she'd said as she fluttered her
eyelashes. "Whoring is simply not a consideration for
a southern belle."

"Why, I didn't realize you were from the South,
sweetheart." Ben laughed and shook his head. "Well
then, would a southern belle consider singing a few
songs, and just moving around enough to titillate the

men and get them thinking about them upstairs
rooms?"

Honey figured she could do that. What she had not
figured on was the outfit Ben expected her to wear.

Red and black lace, stitched to flesh-colored cloth,
hugged her like a corset from her breasts—which
were barely covered—to the top of her thighs. Black
tights, glittering with jet, sheathed her legs. Although
long, red opera gloves reached far above her elbows,
her shoulders were bare.

Unaccustomed to makeup, she applied the grease
paint Ben had given her as best she could and then
tucked the black plume amid her upswept curls.

When she stepped out on the stage, the room
erupted with the clamor of whistles, hoots, and hol-
lers. A stagehand lifted her up on a swing suspended
from the ceiling. She gripped the ropes of the swing,
crossed her legs, and tried to relax on the unsteady
perch.

Honey managed to stop trembling, released her
grip on the ropes, and hooked her arms around them
instead. Drawing a deep breath, she took her guitar
from the stagehand. He began to gently push the
swing. She swung back and forth over the audience
as the piano player began the opening chords of
"Shenandoah."

"Come on, Belle." She heard Ben's voice coming
from the left. "Let's see you shake 'em up."

Steeling herself, she shut her mind to her surroundings and began to sing.

Attracted to the sounds coming from the Golden
Palace, Luke stepped into the crowded room. The
men in the rear stood six deep, cheering the performer
on the stage. As he got a good look at the goings-on,
his stomach twisted into a knot. It was her! He forgot
his anger and stared mesmerized at the woman
perched on the swing. Her tight, low-cut costume ex-
cited the imagination, and her long legs seemed to
stretch on forever.

The piano player struck a chord, the room quieted, and she began to sing in a husky, mellow voice. Everyone stared, spellbound. The poignant lyrics of the ballad awakened memories that these hardened muleteers, mountain men, and drifters had held buried within them. In these hushed moments, she became the lover, the wife, the mother of their past— the one woman each man had shoved into the back of his mind, the one whose visage each had forgotten or had tried to forget.

For a long moment after her performance ended, silence prevailed. Then the spell was broken by loud applause, the clinking of tossed coins, and cries for more.

She was good, Luke thought. Damn good. She could stoke a fire in any man. Moved by her performance more deeply than he cared to admit, he sought the solace of anger. The little tart didn't miss a trick. She had no right to tear up the insides of a man just to work one of her cons. Disgusted, he left the room.

Honey sang several more songs, then scooped up the money from the stage and hurried back to the dressing room. With a sigh of relief, she closed the door behind her and took a deep breath. She'd never climb on that damn perch again. It was a blessing she hadn't fallen off and broken her neck!

Then she saw him in the corner, straddling a chair. "Lady, whoever told you that you could sing?"

With flashing eyes, she glared at him. She didn't think she'd been that bad! "Well, since a certain cad took all my money, I thought I'd give it a try. I have to support myself somehow, and this job sounded better than the other offers Ben made me." She laid her guitar down on the table.

"It's a good thing those legs of yours are distracting enough to take a man's mind off of other matters, or you'd have been hooted out of the place."

He swung his sapphire gaze to her legs. Disgusted, she snatched a robe from a wall hook and quickly donned it. "Before you get too distracted, Sheriff, what are you doing here?" She sat down at the dressing table and began to wipe off her makeup. The man had a disturbing effect on her, and the sooner he left, the sooner her nerves would settle down.

"I got a wire from Independence. You'll have to refresh my memory. I seem to have forgotten. Did you say your name was Mary Jones or Becky Sharp?"

"I told you, my real name is Mary Jones."

"That's good to hear, because the police are looking for a Becky Sharp. Seems she shot her husband and took off. That wouldn't be why you were so anxious to get out of Missouri, would it?"

"Sheriff, I took the name out of a book. I never heard of Becky Sharp until I read the book on my way here. I swear, I'm telling you the truth."

Luke walked over to her and tossed the broken pieces of the imitation cameo onto the tabletop. "Telling me the truth like you did about this? Shame about your dead granny's brooch."

As she stared forlornly at the scattered pieces of paste jewelry, he walked back and straddled the chair.

Honey cradled her head in her hands. Luke MacKenzie was her nemesis. What was the use of lying to him any longer? If she'd only had a few more hours, she would have been gone in the morning and would never have had to see him again.

Sighing, she lifted her head and met the reflection of his steady gaze in the mirror. "Well, I was desperate. What did you expect me to do?" she asked.

"Did you ever think of telling the truth, lady?" Angrily, he got up, shoving aside the chair.

Honey flinched as the chair skidded across the wooden floor and crashed into the wall. "And what difference would the truth have made to you, Sheriff MacKenzie? Your mind was made up about me from the first moment you saw me."

"Let's go," he ordered. The cold, obdurate command allowed no further argument.

"May I change my clothes?"

He nodded. "I'll be right outside." He opened the door, then glanced back. His voice was as hard as his steely glare. "And, lady, for God's sake, do Him and yourself a favor by not trying any more of your damn foolish stunts."

A short time later, properly clothed and her face washed of the garish makeup, she emerged from the dressing room. Despite her above-average height, she felt dwarfed by Luke as he took her arm to lead her away.

When they stepped outside, Honey took a deep breath of the night air. After an evening in the smoke-filled saloon, the fresh air felt heaven-sent. She cast a covert glance at Luke MacKenzie. He walked silently beside her, matching his steps to her shorter ones. They could have been a young couple out for an evening stroll; instead, she was his prisoner and she suspected he had lost patience with her and was toting her off to the jailhouse.

Honey was surprised when he stopped in front of the hotel and led her through the lobby door. His hand remained firm on her arm as they climbed the stairway. Since he said nothing, she kept silent as well.

Finally, stopping before her room, he held out his hand. "The key." She opened her drawstring bag, retrieved the room key, and handed it to him.

"I don't understand. I thought you were taking me to jail," she finally said after they entered the room.

He struck a match and lit the lamp. "I'm taking you back to Stockton with me," he said, closing the door.

Desolately, she tossed her bag on the table and put aside her guitar. "I suppose one jail is as good as another."

"I'm sure you would know that better than me."

"On the contrary, Sheriff, I have never been in a jail before."

"Always wiggled out of it, huh?" His dark gaze swept insolently down her body.

Honey smiled despite the intended innuendo in the

remark. Did she dare attempt to seduce him? she wondered. And once begun, how would she end it before it went too far? He was suspicious of everything she did, but she suspected one thing about *him* that might work to her advantage. Perhaps this was the time to find out if Luke MacKenzie really did have an Achilles' heel. Anyway, the situation was desperate, and if he didn't fall for her routine, she couldn't be any worse off than she was now.

Her eyes brightened with devilment. "Oh, I can see what's on your mind right now, Sheriff," she said with a teasing smile. "A handsome, hot-blooded man like yourself must get weary of having to maintain law and order all the time. You're thinking about having a little pleasure, too, aren't you?" Smiling seductively, she stepped closer and put her hands on his chest. "Or don't you ever take off that star and gunbelt, Sheriff . . ."—she lifted his hat and tossed it aside—"or kick off your boots and just forget you're a lawman?" she asked in a husky whisper.

"I've been known to do that a time or two," he responded. He shifted his glance to her luscious lips, parted in invitation.

She saw lust glimmer beneath the skepticism in his eyes as his hands spanned her waist and drew her against the long, muscled length of him. She gasped at the unexpected jolt of pleasure from the contact— a sensation that drove her on to more daring recklessness. Slipping her arms around his neck, she molded herself even closer against him. She felt a heady excitement from the power and strength that lay beneath the hard contours of his body. The sensation escalated when he slid his hands down her hips and filled his warm palms with her derriere, pressing her tighter against his hot arousal.

Then he kissed her. She was unprepared for the thrill from the warm, firm lips that covered hers and took possession of her mouth as easily as his arms controlled her body. Shivers raced along her spine as the kiss deepened. Shocked by the intensity of her own response but helpless to stop it, she welcomed the slide of his tongue between her parted lips, her body tingling with erotic delight.

After they broke apart, she reveled in the afterglow of the kiss for a long moment, with her eyes closed, listening to the husky murmur of his voice at her ear. "Yeah, lady, you guessed it, all right. My mind's been thinking of nothing else but that body of yours . . . wearing that fancy white nightgown . . . on that bed over there . . . writhing and wiggling with a big squirming snake wrapped around you."

Stunned, she opened her eyes to his mocking stare. "What did you say?"

"That's what you said, remember? You'd much rather curl up with a snake than go to bed with me."

He walked over, picked up his hat, and plopped it on his head. "The stage for Stockton leaves at eight tomorrow morning. Be ready at seven, Miss . . . Just what in hell *is* your real name anyway?"

"If you must know, it's Honey Behr," she murmured softly, still reeling from the kiss.

"Lady, I've been more than patient with you. I want some straight answers now."

This time his declaration didn't bring a denial; she just continued to stare at him. In amazement, he realized she was telling the truth. Shoving his hat off his forehead, he began to laugh. "Honey Bear!" he exclaimed.

"Now you know why I don't use it," she said. "I hate the name, and before you get any smart ideas, I've heard all the jokes I ever want to hear: what a real honey I am or that I'm as sweet as honey."

"No need to worry about me. Sweet is the last thing I'd ever accuse you of being." He crossed his arms over his chest. "Fact is, on occasion I've found you downright un*bear*able." He chuckled warmly.

"The name is spelled B-E-H-R." Honey articulated every letter precisely. "Not the furry animal that growls, MacKenzie."

"Is that so? Well now, you couldn't prove it by me

. . . judging from those bear hugs I just got."

Despite the captivating smile that carried to his sapphire eyes, she had no sense of humor where her name was concerned. She picked up her hairbrush and threw it at him. It bounced off the door, and he laughed.

She walked to the door and opened it. "Before you laugh yourself senseless, would you mind getting out of my room? I'm tired and would like to go to bed."

"Now, you wouldn't be riled because of a little kiss, would you?"

"Don't flatter yourself, MacKenzie. In my business, you win some and you lose some. Now, will you please get out of here?"

He brought a finger to the tip of his hat. "My pleasure, Miz Honey."

Her lips curled in a meaningful smile. "It could have been, Sheriff MacKenzie."

For a quick moment, admiration flashed in his eyes: she had managed to have the last word. He acknowledged the gibe with a good-natured grin and departed, this time through the hallway door.

But she heard the familiar click of the key in the lock.

Chapter 4

Bright and early the next morning, Honey pounded on the door between the two rooms. "Sheriff MacKenzie," she shouted.

"What's wrong?" Luke asked sleepily, sitting up in bed.

"I want out of this room. If I'm going to be locked up in a stinking jail, I intend to take a bath before I leave here."

Luke picked up his pocket watch from the bedside table. It was only six o'clock. The stage was scheduled to depart at eight.

"Sheriff MacKenzie, do you hear me?" Honey called out impatiently.

"Yes, I hear you," Luke grumbled, getting to his feet. "And no doubt, everyone else in the hotel does, too."

He pulled on his jeans and grabbed her door key from the table. Padding barefoot across the floor, he unlocked his own door and went out into the hallway.

As soon as he turned the key in the lock, Honey yanked the door open. The scathing comment she intended to unleash lodged in her throat, and she drew back at the sight of him. His massive, broad shoulders filled the doorway. She gawked openly, mesmerized.

46

He looked rumpled, sleepy-eyed—and hairy!

His dark head was tousled, his face shadowed with whiskers, and his powerful, well-muscled chest generously matted with crisp dark hair that narrowed into a slim line, trailed down his lean, flat stomach, and disappeared beneath the faded jeans that rode loosely on his hips.

She swallowed hard, then raised her glance to his sapphire eyes. Passion burned through his sleepy glaze like sunshine through hazy clouds.

"Good morning," he greeted in a sleepy, desirous voice that conveyed the impression they had spent the night together.

With a flaming blush, she remembered her thin nightgown and peignoir. And judging from the gleam in his eyes, she knew he was well aware of her scanty attire.

Nervously, she raised a hand to her breast. "Good—good morning."

She wanted to kick herself for stammering. Meanwhile, the arrogant so-and-so seemed to enjoy her embarrassment. Just as he had done last night, he was like a big black cat playing with a trapped little mouse.

Recalling the thrill of his kiss, Honey fumed silently. *Damn him anyway! The man wants to put me in jail, and I hate him. So why does he have this effect on me? I'm not a dewy-eyed schoolgirl. He can take that animal sexuality of his and climb right back into bed—alone!*

"If you'll please step aside, Sheriff, I would like to use the bathroom."

Luke shifted enough for her to slip by sideways. As she attempted to pass him, he put his palms on the door frame, trapping her in the circle between his outstretched arms. "You have exactly half an hour to get ready, Miss Honey Behr." Moving closer, he taunted, "It is still Honey Behr this morning, isn't it, or did you dream up a new name overnight?"

Once again she felt the heady excitement from his

nearness. Well, this time she was determined to maintain a strong grasp on her composure.

"Now, how could I do that, Sheriff, when all my dreams were about you?" Smiling up into his eyes, she reached down and yanked the waistband of his jeans so hard that the pants started to slide off his hips. He grabbed for them with both hands, and Honey stepped quickly past him.

Without a backward glance, she continued down the hall to the bathroom. "I suggest you put some clothes on, Sheriff MacKenzie, or the U.S. marshal may have to arrest you for indecent exposure."

When she left the bathroom thirty minutes later, she found Luke lounging casually against the wall outside her room. Fully clothed and freshly shaved, he looked great, she thought grudgingly. He wore a blue shirt that made his sapphire eyes appear even bluer. His saddlebags lay on the floor. She walked past him without acknowledging his presence and closed the door.

Honey took her time dressing and packing. She emerged from the room forty-five minutes later wearing a green-striped, ankle-length poplin gown. A tiny leghorn bonnet with turned-up sides, trimmed with green ribbon and a tuft of white feathers, nestled at a jaunty angle atop her honey-colored curls.

Luke didn't appear to have moved a muscle. With an impatient glance, he unfolded his long length, picked up his saddlebags, and slung them over his shoulder. He took the carpetbag out of her hand but left the guitar for her to carry.

She followed him down the stairway. Upon reaching the lobby, Honey smiled at the gaping clerk as they passed the desk. "Thank you, sir. I have enjoyed the accommodations."

"Good-bye, ma'am," he said, still pop-eyed.

Once outside, Luke took her arm and led her directly to a stagecoach parked in front of the Wells Fargo office. A bearded driver was lashing several crates to the roof. Honey recognized them as the ones she had left at the freight office. She glanced askance at Luke. How had he known about the boxes? He didn't seem to miss anything. *But after all, he is a lawman,* she reasoned. Following through with an investigation was part of his job. And he certainly had spent enough time investigating her!

"Those are Abigail's books. I intended to send them back to her."

"I'm sure you did," he said sarcastically.

"You headed back to Stockton, Luke?" the stage driver asked before she could offer a retort.

"Yeah," Luke replied. He tossed her carpetbag and his saddlebags to the man.

"Be careful with this," she warned, handing Luke the guitar. She gritted her teeth as he casually tossed it up to the driver.

"Is there time for breakfast before you pull out?" Luke asked. The disgruntled glance he cast at Honey left no doubt where the guilt would lay if there wasn't enough time.

"Reckon so, if you hurry," the driver said. He looked at Honey. "Howdy, ma'am. Name's Will Hutchins. Whatta you got in these crates anyway?" He grunted, shifting one of the boxes.

"Only books, Mr. Hutchins," she said lightly.

He shook his head. "Feels like rocks."

"We'll be back, Will." Luke put a firm hand on her elbow.

She tried unsuccessfully to jerk free. "Will you stop leading me around as if I'm about to bolt," she snapped. With his usual officiousness, he tightened his grasp as he led her across the street to a diner.

After they sat down and ordered their meal, Luke stared silently out of the window until they were served. "Is that all you're going to eat?" he asked after a casual glance at the plate of toast the waiter had set before her.

"I don't usually eat much for breakfast," she replied, taking a bite of the toast. "But *you* seem to enjoy breakfast, Sheriff," she commented as she sipped her coffee and watched him devour a large plate of eggs, ham, and beans.

"I enjoy someone else's cooking much more than my own," he said.

Honey had forgotten that he was a widower. "Don't you have a housekeeper or cook at home?" she asked. Mouthing a forkful of food, he shook his head. "Had a Mexican housekeeper for a time, but she went back to Mexico to take care of her grandchildren."

"Abigail said you have a son. What's his name?"

His dark glance swung up to her. "Joshua."

"How old is he?"

"Six years old," Luke said, returning his attention to his meal.

"And how long has your wife been . . . gone?"

For several seconds, the fork in his hand remained suspended in midair. "Four years," he said, then continued eating.

"I'm sorry." Honey could see he did not want to talk about his personal life, but by now she had become too curious about him to stop. For as bizarre as it seemed, when she wasn't loathing him, he fascinated her. "Had she been ill for a long time?"

He stared at her, his eyes filled with bitterness. "She and my mother were. raped and murdered in Texas by a band of Comancheros. You want the full story, with all the details of what they did to them?"

She gasped in shock, staring for a long moment into his fury-filled eyes. Finally, she found her voice. "I'm sincerely sorry, Sheriff MacKenzie."

They finished their breakfast in silence.

It was a silence that continued on the stagecoach ride to Stockton. They were the only passengers. Luke covered his face with his hat and immediately fell asleep. Honey gazed out the window. The fifty-mile ride led them through spectacular, thickly wooded hills, but following on the heels of her five-month journey west, she paid little attention to the countryside. Her thoughts dwelled on what lay ahead, how long she would have to be incarcerated, and the conflicting emotions she felt toward Luke MacKenzie. She studied his sleeping figure on the opposite seat, for now a new sentiment had been added to the puzzlement. She had begun to feel sympathy for her jailer. At breakfast that morning, she had seen a glimpse of the pain he carried within him.

Honey peered out the window and glanced around as the stage rumbled down Stockton's unpaved main street. Nothing appeared to distinguish the community from most of the small towns she had often traveled through in the Midwest.

Each side of the dusty street was lined with side-by-side wooden buildings, the only exception being a brick building bearing a sign that said Cattlemen's Bank. She glimpsed a church steeple at the far end of the street. The stage stopped in front of a two-story hotel in the center of town.

As Honey stepped out of the coach, the inviting aroma of baked ham emanated from a diner next to the hotel. She wished now she had eaten more for breakfast and hoped that the sheriff would feed her soon.

While Luke retrieved their luggage, Honey glanced across the street to where the tinkle of a piano carried through the open doors of a saloon. A tall, dark-haired woman stood in the doorway. She waved at Luke, then tossed away a cigarillo and disappeared inside.

"You can drop off those cartons at the jail," Luke told the driver and handed Honey her guitar. "Let's go, Miz Honey." This time, he did not take her by the arm but rather matched his steps to hers and strolled casually toward the jail.

Several townsfolk called out greetings to him and waved. Luke returned their comments but made no effort to halt and speak to anyone. Honey could feel their curious stares as she passed, but she looked neither to her right nor left.

The jailhouse was located at the opposite end of the town from the church. Honey saw an amusing irony in this obvious separation of saint from sinner.

Upon entering the small building, she saw there were only two rooms: an office and an inner room containing two cells. Luke led her to one of the small but tidy cells. "How long do you intend to keep me locked up here?" she demanded. "And aren't I entitled to some kind of a trial? And a meal."

"As soon as you pay me the money you owe me, you're free to leave, Miz Honey." He closed the steel door and locked it.

"And how do you expect me to pay you when I'm locked up here and unable to earn the money?"

He arched a brow. "Did you say *earn*? I must have misunderstood you."

"I do not find you amusing, Sheriff MacKenzie." She folded her arms across her chest and began to pace the floor of the narrow cell.

"I thought maybe you did, since you volunteered to come here," he said.

Disgusted, she pivoted and glared at him. "Volunteered, indeed! If you hadn't arrested me in Sacramento, I'd be halfway to San Francisco by now."

"I didn't arrest you in Sacramento. I have no authority there to do so."

Her body grew taut with astonishment. "Are you telling me you actually had no legal right to arrest me in Sacramento?"

"That's right, Miss Honey Behr. Sacramento is out of my jurisdiction. It was very obliging of you, though, to accompany me here to San Joaquin County." Raising his arm, he used his shirtsleeve to polish the star pinned on his chest. "This *is* my county."

She clenched her hands into fists as she felt a rising tide of outrage. "Oh, you are the most loathsome creature I have ever met! Of all the sneaky, scheming, underhanded, lowdown tricks, this is the worst! You told me in Sacramento that you were arresting me."

"I never once said that," he declared. "I said I was taking you back to Stockton."

She stamped her foot in frustration. "That's the same as saying you were arresting me."

"I didn't actually say you *had* to come."

"Oh, don't split hairs now that you've illegally lured me into this cell." She gritted her teeth, trembling with rage. "How I would like to punch you right in the middle of your smirking face."

" 'Fraid that's against the law, ma'am. Town ordinance against street fighting on Saturday nights. Now if you give me the two hundred and fifty-one dollars you still owe me, I'll let you out of here."

She glared at him through the bars, her blue eyes flashing with anger. "You know I don't have two hundred and fifty-one dollars!" she shouted. "I can give you the twenty-six dollars I made last night."

" 'Fraid that's not enough, Miz Honey Behr." He did a quick calculation. " 'Pears like you've got about two hundred and twenty-five dollars to go."

"I don't have any more!" she screamed.

"Well then, I have a proposition."

Her anger changed to scorn. "Save your breath, MacKenzie. I've turned down better and richer men than you."

"Rein up there, lady. Best not to go running through a fence till the gate's open." He grinned, but before she could respond, he added, "Come on now, Miz Honey Behr, can't I interest you in a legitimate offer for an honest dollar?"

She eyed him with suspicion. "Go on. And do not call me Honey Behr."

"I propose you work off the debt by, ah, being a nursemaid to my son."

"What?" She was dumbfounded.

"You know, teach him, be with him, and live in my house. Joshua needs a woman's touch."

"And, of course, Joshua's father does, too," she scoffed.

"What you have to offer me, lady, I can get a lot cheaper than for two hundred and twenty-five dollars."

"I'm not offering you anything, MacKenzie. I'd rot in this cell first. So get out of here and leave me alone."

Luke returned to the office and sat down at a battered oak desk. He buried his head in his hands. She had been his only hope. He had thought he could coerce her into helping him, but he had failed. Now he would have to release her. Her story had checked out, so he had no reason to hold her.

Luke stood up and walked to the window. He had been desperate enough to advertise for a wife. Now that plan had fallen through, and it might take another year before he could find a woman willing to marry him. Josh needed help now. The kind of help he himself couldn't give the boy. He doubted if his son even liked him.

"Sheriff MacKenzie."

Her voice calling to him snapped him out of his reflections. He grabbed the keys and stepped into the next room.

Honey eyed him warily through the bars. "Tell me more about this proposition of yours. You say there will be nothing personal in it?"

She saw the gleam of renewed hope in his eyes. "I swear. I'm doing this for my son's sake. Ever since his mother died, Josh has kept too much to himself. He doesn't speak or respond to people. He needs a mother. That's why I wrote for a wife. And you're what showed up."

"Are you suggesting we get married?" she asked, disturbed.

"Hell no! I need to find a *fit* woman as a mother for Josh."

The words were like a slap in the face. Only a slight wavering of her eyes betrayed her hurt.

"I'll place another ad, but that will take time," he said. "I thought you could stay with Josh temporarily."

"Aren't you afraid I might corrupt him? Even temporarily," she said sarcastically. He responded to the gibe with an impassive stare. "How will it look if we're not married and I'm living in your house? Don't you think people will talk?"

Luke knew she was unfit to be a good mother, much less a wife, but desperate times called for desperate measures. "If that's what you want, I'll marry you," he said.

"Marry? Not on your life, MacKenzie. If I'm ever stupid enough to get married, it'll be to a man who has more money than I can spend. It's for certain it won't be to a two-bit sheriff looking for a mother for his kid."

"Look, lady, I don't like this arrangement any more than you do."

"Well, if I agree to this plan of yours, and mind you, I said *if*, one thing is for sure: I'm not sleeping in the same house with you."

"I can't afford to put you up in the hotel. But since my house is right next door, I'll sleep here in the jail at night if that'll put your mind at ease."

"There's a couple more things I insist upon," she declared.

"What are they?"

"Saturday nights are my own to do with as I please."

"Saturday is my busiest night of the week. We're more likely to get strangers in town, and the saloon's always full of rowdy cowboys."

"That's why I want Saturdays free."

He stared grimly at her. "I suppose I can work something out with my deputy. But it's too late to do anything about tonight. What else do you have in mind?"

"Ninety days. That's it. Then, no matter what, I get on that stage and head out."

"How do you expect me to find a wife in ninety days?"

"The same way you expected me to earn two hundred and twenty-five dollars locked up in this cell."

For a long moment she met his steady gaze. "I'll live up to my part of the bargain," she said, "but remember, if you don't, the deal's off and I'm free to climb on a stage out of here. Agreed or not?"

A muscle jumped in his cheek. "'Pears like you're holding the winning hand, lady. For Josh's sake, I'm desperate enough to try anything."

As she glanced around at the small cell, Honey knew she was desperate enough to try it, too.

"Then okay, MacKenzie," she said with a nod of her head, "you've just hired yourself a nursemaid."

Chapter 5

Honey walked out of the cell and looked back as the door slammed behind her. She hoped she was seeing the tiny cubicle for the last time, for she knew she could not endure being locked up anywhere, much less behind bars.

It would be "un*bearable*."

"What did you say?" Luke asked as they stepped into the office.

Honey realized she had spoken the word aloud. "Oh, nothing," she answered hastily. "I was just reminding myself of something you once said."

She spied a cot in the corner and thought that it must be about half the length and width of him. "Are you sure you'll be able to sleep on that cot? It looks too small for you."

"I've slept on it before. Besides, I can sleep anywhere if I have to. Habit I picked up in the army."

He wouldn't get an argument from her on that subject, she thought, recalling his ability to sleep while being bounced around in a creaky, rocking stagecoach.

Luke picked up her carpetbag and guitar, and they left the jailhouse, stopping in front of a small, gray clapboard house right next door. The house had three steps leading up to a porch. Luke opened the front door and stepped aside for her to enter.

The small home consisted of a parlor and kitchen, separated by a table and four chairs, and two bedrooms. The rooms were tiny and although spartan in furnishings, the house appeared to be well kept. Certainly not what she had expected in a bachelor's home.

"Where is your son?" she asked, surprised to discover the house was deserted.

"At the Nelsons. The doctor and his wife were nice enough to take Josh while I went to Sacramento."

"Why didn't you take him with you? I'm sure he would have enjoyed the trip."

"I was on official business, transporting a dangerous prisoner. I don't take risks with my son's life, Miss Behr."

Honey felt as if she had been put in her place.

He walked past her into one of the bedrooms. "I'll move my things into Josh's room, and then we'll go and get him." He pulled clothes out of a battered chest of drawers and carried them into the other room.

"Don't you think you should go without me? After all, you've been separated from your son for a couple days. Josh might want some time alone with you."

She saw the downward shift of his eyes. "Once you meet Josh, you'll think differently." For a brief moment she once again glimpsed that crimp in his armor that made him vulnerable. Then his imperious manner returned. "Besides, he has to get used to you being around. The sooner he accepts you, the sooner you might be able to break through to him."

"Oh, I'll get through to him, MacKenzie. I've never yet met a male who could remain immune to my charms for long," she said coquettishly.

"I hope you're not depending on your obvious physical endowments to hold the attention of a six-year-old," he said mockingly and walked out the front door. For several seconds Honey wondered how she could have ever felt compassion for the arrogant bastard. Then she hastened to follow him.

They walked down to the next street, where the houses were more scattered and impressive. White picket fences or wrought iron grids enclosed well-kept lawns, lush with blooming flowers and trimmed hedges. Several of the houses were two stories high, with domed roofs and gabled windows.

Having spent her youth living in a carnival wagon, then later in cheap boarding houses, Honey couldn't imagine what it would be like to live in such luxury.

Luke stopped before one of the more modest homes and opened the picket gate. A thin, almost frail young boy sat alone on the porch stoop and watched their approach but made no move to get up and greet them. Honey did not have to be told that the youngster was Joshua MacKenzie. He was a dead ringer for Luke: the same high cheekbones, square jaw, and dark hair. The boy stared at them through sad, round eyes that were as blue as his father's.

"He sure looks happy to see you, MacKenzie," she said in a wry aside to Luke.

"I warned you he doesn't cotton to people too easily."

"I didn't think you meant including his own father."

Luke bent down, resting on his haunches before the boy. "Hi, Josh. How have you been?" The youngster did not reply. "Josh, this is Miss Behr. She's going to stay with us for a little while." Josh didn't even glance in Honey's direction.

Good Lord! They act like strangers with each other, Honey observed.

She hurried past Luke and sat down next to Josh. "Hi, Josh. I'm happy to meet you." When he did not answer, she tried again to make him feel at ease. "Josh, will you please call me Honey? I know it's a strange name, but like it or not, I'm stuck with it." He stared at her—bewildered, sullen, and unresponsive.

The screen door creaked open, and an attractive,

dark-haired woman stepped outside. Her gown and apron did not conceal her advanced pregnancy. "Welcome back, Luke."

Luke smiled warmly. "Hi, Cynthia. Hope Josh hasn't been too much trouble for you."

She placed a hand on top of the boy's head. "Trouble? Heaven's no!" She shook her head sorrowfully. "I just wish the little darling *would* be a little troublesome." She cast a curious glance at Honey. "How do you do? I'm Cynthia Nelson."

"Oh, I'm sorry, Cynthia," Luke hastened to say. "I'd like you to meet Miss Behr. She's come here to take care of Josh."

Cynthia Nelson smiled warmly. "Welcome to Stockton, Miss Behr. We're certainly in need of another schoolmarm in this town."

"I'm afraid I'm not a schoolmarm, Mrs. Nelson."

When Honey did not offer a further explanation, Cynthia looked confused but did not pursue her questioning. "Have you heard from your future bride, Luke?"

"Indirectly. Miss Fenton changed her mind about coming west. I guess I'll have to start my search all over again."

Cynthia's brown eyes warmed with sympathy. "Oh, I'm sorry, Luke. I know how much you were looking forward to her arrival." She turned to Honey. "I can't understand why a handsome man like our sheriff cannot find himself a wife, can you?"

"I can't imagine," Honey said with a forced smile. "Must be his line of work."

"Well, I think we ladies will have to take the matter into our own hands," Cynthia declared. She eyed Honey hopefully. "Are you here temporarily, or do you intend to make your home in Stockton, Miss Behr?"

Honey figured if this woman had any thoughts of including her in any marriage plans for Luke Mac-Kenzie, she'd better set her straight. "No, I intend to make my stay here a short one."

"That's too bad. Will you be living at the hotel?"

"No, at Sheriff MacKenzie's house," Honey replied boldly, hoping to embarrass Luke.

"Well, thanks again for taking care of Josh, Cynthia," he quickly interjected. He reached a hand out to his son. "Let's go, Josh."

If the conversation had held any interest to the boy, it did not show in the youngster's eyes. Obediently, he slipped his hand into Luke's and they walked away.

Honey knew that her reply had had a different effect on the doctor's wife, but Cynthia Nelson concealed her shock behind a gracious smile. "It's been a pleasure meeting you, Miss . . . Did I hear you tell Josh that your name was Honey?"

"Yes, it is, unfortunately."

"Well, please call me Cynthia," she said. "I do hope you can help Josh. He's so solemn. It breaks my heart to see the young lad so sad."

She took Honey's hand in a warm grasp, her eyes brimming with interest as she raised her brows meaningfully. "In the meantime, we'll have to talk again, Honey."

"Yes, I'd enjoy that."

Smiling, Honey hurried after Luke and Josh. She made a habit of avoiding women; she was often on the receiving end of their stuck-up noses. But this Cynthia Nelson seemed different, Honey thought. She liked her. Maybe because it looked like that arrogant sheriff wasn't going to slip too much past the doctor's young wife.

"Can you cook?" Luke asked as soon as they got back to the house.

Hands on hips, Honey pivoted to face him. "Am I expected to do the cooking, too?"

"Yes or no?" he grumbled, waiting for a reply.

"Well, as a matter of fact, I can cook," she responded with defiance.

"I hope it's better than your singing."

"I've been doing the cooking since I was twelve

years old. My mother taught me how before she died." Honey picked up her carpetbag and carried it into his bedroom. "Is this where I sleep?"

"That's right. You'll find clean sheets in the hutch. I've got to get back to work. You can go to the general store and get what you need for supper tonight. Tell Jeb Grange to charge it to my account."

"Oh, I guess that means I'm doing the cooking tonight?"

He plopped his hat on his head and started for the door. "We'll trade off."

Joshua was sitting on the steps when Luke stepped outside. He hunched down so they were face-to-face. "Son, I'm going to work now," he said gently. "You do whatever Miss Honey says. I'll be back home for supper. Tomorrow's Sunday. After church, maybe we can go down to the river and try to catch us a fish." He hugged the boy and left.

Honey stood inside, listening. No matter how she felt about Luke, the sad little boy tugged at her heartstrings. She waited until Luke left, then she went outside and sat down next to Joshua. Honey slipped an arm around his shoulders and felt his little body stiffen.

"Well, Josh, I bet you must be feeling kind of scared and alone. I know I would be if I were you. And even though I'm a stranger to you, I want to be your friend. And I hope you'll be my friend, too." The boy remained impassive. "Believe me, I'm just as scared as you are. I've never been in this town before. Or even this far west. Everything here is strange and different to me. So I'm going to depend on you to explain to me what I don't know. Will you do that, Josh?"

When he still didn't reply, she gave him a quick squeeze and in a lighter tone asked, "Now what would you like for supper? I'll be glad to make it for you if I can." He shrugged off her arm and shifted away. "Okay, if you won't tell me, I'll make my favorite meal instead." Standing up, she took his hand and pulled him to his feet. "C'mon, Josh, let's you and me go to the general store and run up your daddy's bill."

She ignored his wary glare.

Returning home at dusk, Luke paused in the doorway. The aroma of cooking food permeated the house. Gaping, he stared speechless at the sight before him. The sinkboard was piled high with soiled dishes.

Joshua stood on a stool at the kitchen table rolling out a chunk of dough. His hands and face were covered with flour. Luke could see signs of the fine powder even in the boy's hair.

With a white towel wrapped around her midsection, Honey was leaning over Josh. "That's thin enough, love," she said. "Now you take this glass and press it into the dough." She demonstrated by cutting out a round circle of the rolled dough using the mouth of the glass. "And there's your biscuit. Then you carefully pick it up and put the biscuit on top of this pan of hot chicken stew," she instructed. "See how easy it is? Now you do it," she said, handing him the glass.

Luke continued to watch as Josh took the glass. His expression looked more serious than ever as he tried to cut a biscuit out of the rolled dough. He looked sorrowfully at Honey when the piece of dough remained stuck to the mouth of the glass.

"Aha, what you have to do, love, is put a little more force into it." She took the glass, pressed it into the dough, then swiveled her hips as she twisted the glass. "See what I mean?" she said with a smile of satisfaction. "It's all in the way you move your hips."

Luke grinned when Joshua tried to roll his little hips in an imitation of Honey. He continued to watch for another long moment, then, erasing any sign of amusement from his face, he stepped into the room.

Hearing the screen door slam, both turned their heads toward him. "What's going on here? Room looks like it's been hit by a tornado."

Startled, Joshua jumped down from the stool and

raced out the door, leaving a trail of flour behind him.

"Good job, MacKenzie," Honey snapped sarcastically. Distracted, she grabbed the hot handle of the door of the wood-burning stove. "Ouch," she cried out in pain and began to suck on her injured fingers.

Luke hurried over to her. "How bad did you burn yourself?"

"Don't worry about it," she said bitterly. Using her skirt to keep from burning her hand again, she opened the oven door and popped the pan inside. Then she slammed it shut.

"For God's sake, Miss Behr, let me see it." He grabbed her hand and examined her fingers. "That was a fool thing to do." Despite his censure, his touch was surprisingly gentle as he slathered lard on her fingers. "Next time be more careful."

"It wasn't any more foolish than you barging in here and scaring Josh half to death."

"I didn't mean to scare him away."

"A frightened little boy who doesn't trust people shouldn't be surprised like that." She snatched her hand out of his grasp.

Luke hung his hat on a wall peg. "What do you expect me to do, lady, stamp my feet or rap on the door before I enter my own house?"

"It's not what *I* expect you to do. By now, you should know better. Did you ever think to put yourself in Josh's place and figure out what he'd want you to do?" She lowered her head and started to wash the flour off the table. "And speaking of the way you barge in here unannounced, where is the door key?"

"There wasn't any when I moved into the house."

"I hope you don't expect me to go to bed at night with an unlocked door."

"Most of the people in this town go to bed with unlocked doors. Besides, you'll be perfectly safe. I'll be right next door."

"Did you ever think that's what I mean?"

"You can put that worry out of your mind." He

laughed contemptuously. "Or maybe you're hoping I won't keep my word."

"If I thought that, I wouldn't worry about a key, would I, Sheriff MacKenzie?"

Irritated by her insinuations, he plopped several of the soiled dishes into the pan of dishwater in the sink. "What in hell did you do, dirty every kettle you could find?"

"Next time, you can cook the damn meal!" Water splashed in all directions as she flung the dishcloth into the water. "Dinner's in fifteen minutes. You better go and find Josh."

Luke grabbed his hat and stomped out of the house.

What a pair, she thought with a disgusted shake of her head. *One is angry all the time, the other frightened — and neither one of them trusts me.*

Ten minutes later Luke reentered the house with Josh at his side. They had washed up outside at the rain barrel, and their identical dark heads were slicked back with water.

"Sit down; dinner's ready," Honey said.

"Better let me do that," Luke said when Honey opened the oven door. He grabbed a towel, nudged her aside, and lifted the hot kettle out of the oven. After putting the hot pan on the table, he sat down. "If a body takes time to do it right, there's less chance of getting burned."

Glancing at Josh, Honey withheld her retort. It would not do the boy any good to hear her and his father quarreling at the dinner table. She recalled how often as a child she had listened to her father and mother fighting.

"Uhmmm, this looks as good as it smells, doesn't it, Josh?" Luke said as he ladled a helping of the hot chicken dish onto a plate and handed it to Honey. Luke filled a plate for Josh and finally served himself.

"Josh, these biscuits are delicious," she said, cutting into a biscuit that had been baked on top of the bubbling sauce brimming with pieces of chicken, carrots, fresh peas, and small round onions.

"You mean you helped make these, Josh?"

When the boy didn't answer Luke, Honey quickly added, "He shelled the peas, too."

"Hey, I think you can take over my cooking duties, buddy," Luke said.

Honey watched Josh's reaction to his father's teasing, but the boy's expression remained impassive. He continued his silence throughout the meal, barely touching his food.

After they finished eating, Luke and Josh went outside to get wood to restock the wood box. Honey tried to do the dishes, but the soapy water stung her burned fingers, so she set the dishes aside to finish the next morning.

While Luke got Josh ready for bed, she stepped outside for some fresh air. The strain of the day had exhausted her. Just that morning she had still been in Sacramento, arguing with Luke. It seemed like days ago. And working with Josh had made her tired.

Maybe she was trying too hard. The boy seemed unreachable. He obeyed her, but he never spoke to her. For that matter, he didn't even respond to his own father! Her heart ached for the frightened youngster, for she remembered how she once had been just as frightened.

Despite an effort not to cry, her eyes were soon overflowing with tears. Josh's condition had resurrected painful memories—memories best forgotten.

"I never said it would be easy."

She stiffened in surprise at the sound of Luke's voice. She had not heard his approach. Quickly wiping away her tears, she turned to face him. "My heart aches for him. He's so young."

"Yes, and, unfortunately, too young to remember his mother."

"Maybe it's easier for him that way. Please don't misunderstand what I'm saying, Luke, because I'm not trying to lessen the tragedy of your wife's death. But since Josh was too young to remember his mother, at least he doesn't have to suffer the grief of missing her. My mother died when I was twelve years old. It still hurts to think of her . . ."

She raised her head, and he saw the glint of tears in her eyes. Suddenly he wanted to reach out and take her in his arms. But he quickly reminded himself who she was and why she was there. He would gain nothing by surrendering to passion in a moment of weakness.

Feeling awkward, he cleared his throat, breaking the breathless tension between them. "Guess I better get back to my job. Saturday night always brings a lot of strangers into town." He started to leave, then stopped and turned back to her. "Ah, about a key. If you'd feel more comfortable, I'll have one made."

"No, I guess it doesn't matter. I won't be here that long anyway."

For a long moment after he departed, Honey stood wrestling with the mixed emotions that had plagued her since she'd first met him. She cursed the circumstances that had brought her to Stockton. Unlike the narrow escapes from many of her other predicaments, she sensed this was one situation that she would not walk away from unscathed.

Chapter 6

━━━━━━━ ⚬〜◯◯〜⚬ ━━━━━━━

The next morning, Honey sat on a hard wooden pew. *What am I doing here?* She tried to remember the last time she had been in a church. Even when her mother died, there had not been a church service.

In painful reminiscence, Honey recalled standing in the bleak cemetery and listening to her father sob as her uncle and the undertaker lowered the wooden box that contained her mother's body.

The sudden sound of a gun blast rent the tranquility of the Sunday morning, jolting her out of her memory. She felt Joshua press against her. Slipping an arm around the trembling boy, she hugged him to her side.

The pastor paused in his sermon, and the church members began to whisper. Dipping his head toward Joshua, Luke exchanged a meaningful glance with her. Honey nodded in understanding, then Luke silently got up and left the church. The pastor continued the sermon, but many of the men nervously shuffled their feet.

When the gunfire resumed, a murmur swept the small wooden building. Joshua's little head slumped forward, his chin on his chest. Preoccupied with her concern for Luke, Honey reflexively hugged the frightened boy even tighter.

Suddenly, she felt a drop of moisture on her hand and saw that Joshua was silently shedding tears; the young boy was in torment. Overwhelmed with compassion, she gathered him on her lap and rocked him in her arms.

Pastor Wright abruptly offered a benediction and hastily announced, "Friends, I want you all to wait here in the church. Since none of you men are wearing gunbelts, it will be wiser to remain with your families until we find out what's happening."

Once again gunfire erupted, and he left the pulpit to hurry up the aisle. Honey watched in shocked silence as several male members of the congregation trailed after him.

Honey was tempted to follow; waiting patiently was not her forte. But Joshua continued to cling to her, his dark head buried against her chest. She could not thrust the frightened child into someone else's arms, so despite her anxiety over Luke, she continued to hold Josh on her lap, rocking him back and forth.

After what seemed like hours but was actually only five minutes, the onslaught of gunfire ended. Along with the others, Honey hurried outside. The small congregation gathered at the front of the church.

Cynthia Nelson came over to where Honey stood, holding Joshua. The boy still had his face buried against her, his arms hugging her neck, and his legs wrapped around her waist.

"Do you have any idea what's happening, Cynthia?" Honey asked. "All that shooting has frightened Joshua."

Cynthia stroked the back of the boy's head. "The poor little darling. The only thing I can think of is that some more of that Walden gang rode into town."

"Walden gang? Who are they?" Honey asked.

"Oh, it's a gang that's been raising trouble with some of the ranchers—stealing cattle and such. Last week a couple of them rode into Stockton, and one of them killed a gambler in the bar. Luke shot it out with them, killed Beau Walden, and arrested the other one."

"Was this Beau the leader?"

"No. The gang's leader is Charlie Walden. Beau was Charlie's younger brother, and I guess the man Luke arrested was his other brother. Rumor has it that Charlie once rode with Quantrill."

Honey gasped in shock at the mention of the infamous Confederate guerrilla commander. Even she had heard of the murderous raids conducted by the notorious leader in Kansas and Missouri.

"Doug told me Charlie's got a reputation for being vicious and spiteful, and someway he'll get even with Luke for what he's done to his brothers."

"You mean he may try to . . ." Honey glanced worriedly at Josh burrowed in her arms. Cynthia rolled her eyes and shrugged.

"Oh, here comes Pastor Wright now," Cynthia said as they saw the clergyman hurrying back to them.

Asking a multitude of questions, the throng swarmed around him. The pastor raised his hands for silence. "It's safe now to go back to your homes," he announced.

"What was all the shooting about, Pastor Wright?" Cynthia asked.

"It seems that some of the Walden gang came back for a showdown with the sheriff."

Honey felt the quick rush of blood to her head and heard the sound of her heartbeat pound in her ears. "And Sheriff MacKenzie?" she asked.

"He's fine, ma'am." She felt Cynthia's comforting hand on her shoulder. "Deputy's been shot in the arm, but Doctor Nelson said the wound's not serious. Three of the gang are dead, so all of you stay clear of the jail until the sheriff and Del Quinn can cart away the bodies."

People started to mumble among themselves, and the pastor raised his hands again. "Let us offer a prayer of thanks to our precious Lord for once again delivering our town and shepherding Deputy Brennan and Sheriff MacKenzie safely through the perilous valley."

The men removed their hats, and all bowed their heads, but Honey's thoughts were not on the minister's words. She glanced fretfully toward the end of the street, hoping for a glimpse of Luke MacKenzie's tall figure.

With the crisis past, Honey carried Joshua back to the house. She thought she had regained her composure until she caught sight of Luke in front of the jail. She felt a fluttering in her heart. Tall and just as officious as ever, he was directing the undertaker in the disposal of the bodies.

"Bury them on Boot Hill and make out the bill to the county," he ordered. "I'll sign a voucher."

"Yeah, Sheriff, I know," replied the town's mortician. "The way you've been shooting up this gang lately, I'll soon be able to retire a rich man."

"None of your twenty-five-dollar burials, Del. As far as I'm concerned, you can dump the lot of them into a hole and feed 'em to the worms. If Pastor Wright wants to speak over them, that's up to him," Luke ordered.

Shaking his head in disgust, Luke turned away, only to see Honey holding Josh. His expression changed at once to one of grave concern. "What's wrong with Josh?" he asked, hurrying over to them.

When Luke tried to take him out of her arms, Josh clung tighter to her. "He's just scared," she assured Luke when she saw the pain in his eyes. Trying to ease the awkwardness of the moment, she added lightly, "Well, Sheriff MacKenzie, I see you dodged the bullet again."

He countered the ache of his son's rejection with a cold glare at her. "It must be comforting to you, Miss Behr, to know that someone would like to see me dead as much as you do."

The absurd accusation astounded her. "Luke, I

don't ..." But he had already pivoted and walked away.

With his deputy recuperating from a bullet wound, Luke had to call off his promised fishing trip with Josh that day. "Not that it much matters to the kid," he said churlishly between bites of the cheese sandwich Honey had made for him. He returned his glance toward the open door where he had been watching Josh sitting on the front stoop.

"Of course it matters to him," Honey said. She wondered how many other times Luke had disappointed his son. "I don't see where you spend much time with him."

"And I don't see where that's any of your business, Miss Behr."

"Maybe you've also forgotten this is your day to do the cooking."

"We'll go to the diner for supper tonight. The food there will taste better than my cooking anyway."

"No, I'll fix a meal. I really don't mind," she offered.

"I pride myself on my fairness, Miss Behr. I never break a promise unless I can't help it."

"Try explaining that to Josh instead of me. You're acting testy just because a scared little boy couldn't let go of someone he was holding on to for dear life."

"You're the stranger to him," he snapped, "not me." He finished the sandwich and shoved aside the plate as he resumed his brooding stare at Josh's back.

"That's a big load for his little shoulders to have to carry around," Honey commented.

"What load?"

"The weight of that heavy, black look you're heaping on him," she said, slicing another piece of bread.

"Maybe if he was your son, you wouldn't think it's so funny." Angrily, he stood up and carried his plate to the sink. He slammed it down next to the dishes still piled there from last night. "Goddammit! How much longer do these dirty dishes have to set here?"

"Until I get good and ready to wash them."

Disgusted, Luke grabbed his hat. He stopped on the porch to say good-bye to Josh. Honey listened to the one-sided exchange. *One's as withdrawn as the other*, she thought with dismay. *Only the bigger one is too blind to see it.*

After Luke returned to duty, Honey put her mind to how she would entertain Josh. She drew the line at carrying through with Luke's fishing promise. After all, certain tasks were best left to a father—and skewering a squirming worm on the end of a hook was one of them.

Throughout the afternoon, Luke couldn't shake his ornery mood. He intentionally stayed in his office to avoid people. He was in no frame of mind to discuss the shooting that morning, which was all anyone wanted to talk about anyway.

Shortly before dinner, Delmer Quinn came in and tossed down the few things that had belonged to the three dead men.

"Any clue as to their identities?" Luke asked.

"Nope. Just the usual. Makings for cigarettes, a few coins, a couple rings. These guys sure didn't live high on the hog, did they? Makes no sense to me why anyone chooses a life of crime. All it ever gets them is a early trip to Boot Hill."

Luke immediately thought of Honey's lies and confidence games. "Guess some people prefer that to an honest day's labor."

As he rifled through the few personal belongings, Luke half listened to the undertaker. Then he swept everything into the bottom drawer of his desk—except for the coins, which he gathered up and handed to Quinn. "Here, give these to the church fund as usual," he said.

"Sure thing, Sheriff. Well, I best get home. As it is, wife's madder than a hoot owl at me for working on a Sunday. More than likely you can bury me tomorrow along with them outlaws." He left hurriedly.

When Luke got home, he discovered that Honey had ignored his earlier decision and made dinner anyway. Not used to having his wishes opposed, he was even more unpleasant at the supper table than he had been at lunch. He left immediately after eating without so much as a thank you to Honey or a good-night to Josh.

Good Lord, what's gotten into me lately? he lamented, back in his office. No matter what he tried to concentrate on, his thoughts strayed continually back to Josh and Honey. His son's rejection of him that morning had felt like a punch to the gut. It hurt like hell. He knew he didn't understand Josh like he should, but that damned Honey Behr telling him what he was doing wrong hadn't helped.

When the point of his pencil broke, he threw it aside with a mild curse and rubbed his throbbing temples. Damn her! Lord, she tested a man's fortitude. She was all woman, from the blond curls on top of her head to the end of those long legs.

Try as he might, he couldn't get out of his head the image of her perched on that saloon swing, those incredible legs dangling in front of her. He allowed his thoughts to follow a dangerous trail and imagined how it would feel to have her legs wrapped around his hips.

Then to lessen the torment, he envisioned how she had looked the previous evening—gazing up at him with moonlight glistening on her tears.

"Dammit, MacKenzie, what are you doing to yourself?" He shoved back his chair and stood up. Grabbing his hat, he slammed it on his head and went out to make his nightly rounds of the town.

It was almost midnight by the time he returned to the office. He hung up his gunbelt, turned off the oil lamp, and stripped down to his drawers. Then he laid down on the cot.

An hour later, he was still awake. He just couldn't fall asleep. Disgusted, he realized he had suffered several sleepless nights since Miss Honey Behr had entered his life. He shifted restlessly, trying to get comfortable on the small cot, all to no avail. He got up and opened the door to catch the evening breeze. It didn't help.

Finally, he decided to get something to eat. A full stomach always made him sleepy. After pulling on his jeans and a shirt, he padded barefoot to the house next door. He was surprised to see a light gleaming in the parlor window.

Luke opened the front door and saw Honey sitting in a chair with Josh curled up on her lap. They were both sound asleep. The book she had been reading to him had slipped out of her hands and dropped to the floor.

For a long moment he stood in the doorway, savoring the sight: Honey's blond hair combed out and covering her shoulders like a shawl woven in silver and gold, Josh's dark head nestled against her chest, the bare toe that peeked out from under her white robe.

Finally, he moved quietly to the chair, picked up the book, and put it on the table. He gently eased Josh out of her arms. He carried the boy to his bedroom, and after tucking him in, he let his yearning gaze rest on the face of the sleeping child.

Why, son? Why do you shut me out? I wish I knew a way to convince you of how much I love you. A trace of moisture glistened in his eyes as he leaned over and kissed the youngster's forehead.

Returning to the parlor, he slipped his arms under Honey's body and gently lifted her. She stirred slightly, then settled comfortably against him.

She felt light. She felt warm, soft, sensuous. She felt good.

He carried her into his bedroom—to his bed.

As he looked down at her silver gold hair covering his pillow and the curve of her pink lips parted in slumber, a tide of hot blood engulfed his body, battering his reason.

He must avoid touching her, breathing in the soft

scent of her, looking into her round blue eyes. He had to remember who she was, what she was, and why she now lay in his bed.

He cursed himself for being ten times a fool. The arrangement was stupid, senseless—and of his own making. What had he expected? He had desired her in Sacramento. How could he have thought she'd be less desirable under his own roof?

Lest he completely surrender to his carnal desire, he spun on his heel and hurried from the room. He paused and glanced into the kitchen. The dishes were still piled on the sink. That kind of laxity was beyond his comprehension. If she had time to read a book, why hadn't she had time to do the dishes?

He lit the stove and put water on to boil.

An hour later, after the last dish was washed, the final pot scoured, Luke turned off the lamp and returned to the jailhouse.

Chapter 7

⌒〜⌒oo⌒〜⌒

Honey couldn't believe how Jeb Grange got away with gypping his customers. Since her arrival in Stockton a week earlier, she had made several trips to the general store and observed that the merchant overcharged for everything he sold. It seemed to her that the town's straitlaced sheriff spent his time beleaguering innocent people like herself when he should be worrying about the lawbreakers right under his own nose.

"I'd be obliged, Mr. Grange, if you'd keep your hand off the scale when you weigh those coffee beans," she declared to the shopkeeper.

The admonition drew an outburst of clapping from another customer in the store, a man who appeared to Honey's sharp eyes to be in his midsixties. Despite a full shock of white hair and a beard to match, his friendly, chubby face reminded her of an overgrown cherub with twinkling blue eyes.

"Bravo, my dear lady, a most astute observation," the man said. "Daniel Webster O'Leary at your service." After doffing a battered stovepipe hat, he attempted a sweeping bow, which threw him slightly off balance, and he nearly staggered into her.

Honey returned his wide Irish grin with a warm

smile of her own. "How do you do, Mr. O'Leary?"

"Will you be callin' me Pop? 'Tis what others do."
Besides a thick Irish brogue, she detected the whiff of
whiskey on his breath.

"My name is Honey Behr."

"Honey indeed. For 'tis a sweet name for one so
sweet, Miss Honey."

Rudely clearing his throat, Jeb Grange interrupted
the conversation. "What do you want, Pop?"

"A simple spool of black thread, good merchant."

O'Leary turned to Honey. "A wee break in me coat
seam requires some attention." Eying his black suit,
Honey decided it must have seen better times. "But
do finish with servin' the needs of the lady, Mr.
Grange."

"No, go ahead. I have to pick out something else.
It's been a pleasure to meet you, Mr. O'Leary."

Honey took Josh by the hand and went to a table
containing boys' trousers. Luke had informed her at
breakfast that Josh would be starting school on Monday morning, and after much persuasion, she had finally convinced Luke that the boy needed new
clothes. She selected a pair of trousers and a shirt and
added a tin lunch box to the purchases.

A bolt of red-and-white-checkered gingham caught
her eye. The cloth would make colorful window curtains to brighten the stark house. She picked up the
bolt and several spools of thread.

She saw Josh wander over to a shelf of toys. Curious, she followed him to see what had caught his attention. The youngster seemed mesmerized as he
stared at a rocking horse. Painted the same dull
brown as Alamo, the dun gelding Luke rode, the
wooden horse stood about twelve inches high. It had
black marble eyes and a flowing mane and tail made
of real horse hair.

"Do you like it, sweetheart?" she asked. Josh
blushed and lowered his eyes.

O'Leary quietly joined them. "Aye, lad. And 'tis a

noble steed, indeed, Josh, me boy," he exclaimed with a pat to Josh's head.

"Mr. Grange, how much is this rocking horse?" Honey called out.

"Six dollars," the shopkeeper said.

"Six dollars!" Honey gritted her teeth as she turned back to O'Leary. "The man is an out-and-out crook."

"That he is, Miss Honey," O'Leary agreed.

Honey handed the rocking horse to Josh. "Here, sweetheart. You can go outside and play with it." Josh hurried off with the toy clasped in his hands. She knew Luke would probably raise the roof when he discovered the cost of the horse, but she would worry about that when the time came. She put her selections on the counter and said, "Add the horse to the bill, Mr. Grange."

As the shopkeeper began to total her purchases, Honey's glance fell on a jar of peppermint sticks. She would show that tight-fisted old crook! With a wink at O'Leary, she sidled over to the jar. After a quick glance at Mr. Grange, who was putting her purchases into a bag, Honey took a peppermint stick and slipped her hand into the pocket of her skirt. With tongue in cheek, she glanced at O'Leary.

Pop O'Leary stifled his grin, cast his twinkling blue eyes heavenward, and began to whistle "Oh! Susanna!"

"So including the rocking horse and the peppermint stick, the total is twelve dollars and fifty-nine cents," Jeb Grange said.

"Peppermint stick?" Honey asked with wide-eyed innocence.

"The one you put in your pocket." The shopkeeper's mouth was curled into a grimace of disdain.

"Why ever would you think that, sir?" Feigning shock, Honey turned her pocket inside out.

Befuddled, Grange stared in amazement at the empty pocket. "Well, I swear I saw ..." He stammered. "Guess that'll be twelve dollars fifty-*four* cents."

"Yes, I should say so," Honey said smugly. "And considering you overcharged for the rocking horse, you should have the decency to *offer* the boy a stick of candy." She snatched up her bag of purchases and walked out.

Pop O'Leary followed her outside. "Ah, well done, me dear. I'm suspectin' the good merchant has met his match."

"You can bet he has," Honey said as she retrieved the candy stick from the cuff of her long-sleeved dress. "Anyway, he deserved exactly what he got," Honey declared. "A candy stick is a small cost to pay for his thievery."

"And may I carry that parcel for you, Miss Honey?"

"That's most kind of you, Mr. O'Leary."

"Pop," he admonished with a grin.

Upon reaching the house, Honey said cheerfully, "Would you like to come in for a refreshing drink?" His face beamed with anticipation until she added, "There's always a pot of coffee setting on the stove."

"C-coffee?" he stammered as his eyes seemed to round with chagrin. He quickly handed her the bag. "Perhaps another time, darlin'." He tipped his hat. "'Tis been me pleasure, dear lady. You're a revivifyin' breeze to the likes of a valley that has lain stagnant for too long."

Honey watched Pop O'Leary walk away with his slightly unsteady step. He's a drunkard just like Pa was, she thought sorrowfully. But other than Cynthia Nelson, the old man was the only one in town who had given her a kind word.

For a long moment, she watched him work his way up the street. While he offered a friendly nod to those he passed, he received only disgruntled glances or haughty snubs for his effort.

"We're kindred spirits, Pop," Honey said sadly, then entered the house.

* * *

Luke posted his letter to the *Sacramento Chronicle* and headed home for lunch. The letter, containing his ad for a housekeeper, would leave on the noon stage. He hoped it would get results. He was hot, edgy, and in a foul mood. The talk he'd had with Jeb Grange had added to his irritation.

Luke stopped when he saw Josh on the porch steps. "Hi, son." He sat down beside Josh and watched him rock a toy horse back and forth. "That horse you've got there looks like Alamo, Josh. Tell you what, as soon as I'm through working, we'll go for a ride on Alamo. Would you like that?"

When Josh failed to respond, just continuing to play apathetically with the toy, Luke got to his feet and went inside. There was no sign of lunch. Instead, Honey was measuring red and white material that she'd spread all over the kitchen table.

She offered him a quick glance. "Oh, are you home already?"

"It's time for lunch."

"Oh my, I seem to have lost track of time," she said and began to cut the material.

He walked over to the table. "What are you doing?"

"I'm making curtains for the kitchen and bedrooms."

"Curtains? If I wanted curtains, I would have had them by now. Where did you get the material?"

"At the general store," she said offhandedly.

"What did you use for money?"

Jauntily, she cocked her head and looked at him. "I put it on your account."

"And how do you propose to hang those curtains? There are no rods."

"Can't you make rods?"

"Whether I can or not is beside the point, Miss Behr. The question is, can *you*? And I suppose you put that rocking horse on my account, too?"

She straightened up and glared at him. "Matter of

fact, I did. Josh seemed taken by it, so I thought he should have it."

"Dammit! Do you think I'm made of money like those other men you fleece?"

"Why must you bring up my past? What has that got to do with this?"

"Plenty. Jeb Grange claims you stole a candy stick from him."

Defiantly, she thrust up her chin. "I did."

"You stole a five-cent candy stick!"

"The old reprobate overcharges for everything he sells. I thought he deserved it."

"You thought! Of course that's what you would think. Lying, stealing, and cheating are a way of life with you. Well, they are not accepted here in Stockton." He dug a coin out of his pocket and slammed it down on the table. "You can just go back now and pay him the five cents."

"You can go to hell, MacKenzie. And not too soon for my comfort." Without a backward glance, she flounced into the other room.

Honey remained in her bedroom while Luke made lunch. She felt a sense of relief when he tapped on the door and told her he was leaving. She was content to put off the dreaded moment of confronting him again for as long as possible.

Supper was on the stove when Luke returned that evening. Hearing him enter, Honey came out of the bedroom wearing a skin-tight black dress with only narrow straps for shoulders.

"There's stew on the stove, and after you finish supper, Joshua needs a bath," she said.

"Where in hell do you think you're going?" he asked, astonished.

"Saturday night, remember? My night out, Sheriff MacKenzie."

"But—"

She stopped at the door and pivoted to face him. "You breaking our agreement, Sheriff?"

She saw a muscle jump in his cheek, and his sapphire eyes turned dark with anger. "No, of course not. What time will you be back?"

She slipped a black lace shaw around her shoulders. "I guess that would depend on whom I might encounter, MacKenzie," she replied with a brazen toss of her head.

As she strolled up the street to the Long Branch, Honey purposely ignored the curious and disapproving glances she received. She pushed open the swinging doors of the saloon and stood in the doorway to assess the room.

The tavern didn't differ from most of the others she had seen. At several of the dozen round tables in the smoke-filled room men played cards, while a piano player pounded out a time-worn tune on the yellowing keys of an old Chickering upright that occupied a corner.

Honey shifted her glance to a tall woman who stood at the end of the long black mahogany bar that ran the length of the opposite wall. Honey recognized her as the woman she had seen on the day of her arrival in Stockton.

Then she recognized another familiar face at one of the tables. She walked over to the man. "Hi, Pop."

He smiled broadly. "Ah, Miss Honey, sit down and join me." He waved to the woman at the bar. "Lily, come here." She sauntered over to them. "Lily, meet my good friend, Miss Honey Behr."

The brown-eyed brunette eyed her with curiosity. "Lily LaRue," she said. She sat down next to Pop. "You plan on working the tables or upstairs, sugar?"

"The upstairs is all yours, Lily. I wouldn't mind sitting in at one of those tables though."

"You better clear it with Sam Brazner first," Lily warned.

"Is Sam the bartender or the owner?"

"Both."

Honey glanced up to see him headed their way, carrying a bottle of whiskey in one hand and several shot glasses in the other. After setting them on the table, he plopped down in the remaining chair.

"What's your name, honey?"

"You just said it," Honey remarked.

"Sam, me good man, allow me to be introducin' you to Miss Honey," Pop put in.

"That really your name?" Sam asked.

"Why would I lie about a name like that?"

" 'Cause it sounds good. Get it?" Sam snorted. He pulled the cork out of the bottle and poured a drink for each of them. Pop O'Leary grabbed his greedily and gulped it down at once.

"You're wise to me, Sam," Honey replied. "My real name is Mary Jones."

"That makes more sense. Now I can see why you'd wanna call yourself Honey. Ain't you the sheriff's gal?"

"Good heavens, no!" Honey exclaimed. "Absolutely not! I'm working out a debt, that's all."

"Oh, yeah? What kind of debt?"

"Claims I owe him some money. I say I don't, but I agreed to take care of his son for ninety days. Saturday is my night off, so I figured if I earn some money here, I can pay him off sooner."

"You're sure there's nothing between the two of you? I don't wanna get the sheriff mad at me."

"Sam, trust me. The sheriff and I don't even like each other."

"Well, what have you got in mind?"

"I'd like to deal one of the tables." Then remembering the money she made at the Golden Palace in Sacramento, Honey added, "And I can sing a little, too."

"We run a clean game here, sister. And the house gets half of what you win."

"Sam, I don't have to cheat at cards to win. But you'll have to stake me to get started."

"We'll see." He motioned to the piano player. "Talk it over with Fingers and let's hear what you sound like. If it's half as good as you look, you're hired."

" 'Tis a drink we be needin' to seal the bargain,"

Pop O'Leary said. Picking up the bottle, he moved from Honey to Lily and finally to Sam. None of them had touched the drink Sam had previously poured. With a broad wink at Honey, Pop refilled his own glass.

After a quick introduction to the piano player, Sam returned to his usual place behind the bar.

"Good luck, Honey," Lily said.

"Thanks." Honey followed Fingers to the piano, and they shuffled through some music. Finally, Honey found a song her mother used to sing.

With a nod to Sam, Honey began the sentimental ballad "Annie Laurie."

The gamblers at the tables halted their play. Lily LaRue and Pop O'Leary sat in deep concentration. Chomping on the end of his cigar, Sam Brazner watched and listened, his curious glance sweeping the room.

When Honey finished the song, she looked at Sam. He nodded his approval.

Smiling, she hurried over to Pop and Lily. "How did I sound?"

Lily stood up. "You're gonna have them crying in their beer, Honey gal." Then she patted Honey on the shoulder and walked back to the end of the bar.

Honey sat down with Pop. "How did I sound to you, Pop?"

Teary eyed, the old man blew his nose. "Like an Irish nightingale, darlin'."

It was past midnight when Honey returned home. Luke put down the newspaper he had been attempting to read for most of the evening.

Lightly swinging her purse by the strings, Honey leaned back against the door. "Oh, are you still awake?"

"It's about time you got home," Luke said gruffly.

She pulled open her purse. "Here's the money for the curtains and the rocking horse." She tossed several gold eagles on the table as she sauntered past him.

"Do you think I'd touch a penny of any money you made that way?" he said with contempt.

Honey paused in the bedroom doorway and turned to look at him. Her lips were pursed in a pout and her eyes rounded in innocence. "What way is that, Sheriff MacKenzie?"

With taunting laughter, she closed the door.

Chapter 8

⌒⟨♡⟩⌒

Near dawn, Honey awoke, smiled, and stretched. Despite having had only a few hours of sleep, she felt refreshed and contented. Closing her eyes, she focused her thoughts on the reason for this unfamiliar feeling of peacefulness.

Certainly, there was little cause for it. She had been in Stockton for a week, and jail cell or not, she was literally a prisoner of Luke MacKenzie. But to her utter astonishment, she was enjoying it.

She liked waking up each morning without having to worry about finding a gull to dupe for her next meal, without having to suffer the fondling and kisses of some man cheating on his wife. She liked sitting at the dinner table and sharing meals with Luke and Josh. She even liked cooking those meals.

And she loved Josh. Every day she saw a slight improvement in him. His glances at her were more frequent, his interest in life more apparent. She had foolishly tied her heartstrings to the frightened and sorrowful little boy, and she dreaded the day when she would have to leave him.

And then there was Luke.

Tucking her hands under her head, she lay in the dim light, thinking about Luke MacKenzie. He was unlike any man she had ever known. Her father had been a weak man, a drunkard. Her uncle . . . She shuddered in revulsion remembering why she had fled the medicine show. And Robert Warren—for a moment her eyes glazed with pain. Robert had been the weakest of the lot.

But Luke MacKenzie—he was nothing like any of them.

Luke had strength, integrity. Luke was the kind who would cherish and protect the woman he loved.

Luke had a penetrating dark gaze that set her pulses to throbbing; a heated touch that sent warm, sensuous shivers throughout her; an inflaming kiss that ignited the fire of her passion.

Her body tingled under a heated flush of desire. It was pointless to deny the attraction. Every time she saw him, the feeling grew more forceful, drawing her inexorably toward him.

Oh, if only she were the whore Luke thought her to be, then she could ease the ache within her just by luring him into bed, where emotions other than pure pleasure were not necessary.

Then the fact that he didn't love her would not matter.

Next door, Luke struggled with his own tortured thoughts as he spent another restless night tossing and turning on the small office cot. He was a damn fool. Earlier, he had made arrangements to spend the night with Lily in her room at the Long Branch. She would have taken him to bed and with her hands and mouth relieved the ache that had kept him tied in knots ever since he'd met Honey. Why had he backed out?

Because he knew being with Lily wouldn't help. He wanted Honey. God, how he throbbed for the feel of her hands and mouth on him. Even more, he yearned to put his hands and mouth on her, to ease his body's carnal demands in her luscious curves.

Since Sarah's death, he had not hesitated to seek

sexual satisfaction in the beds of whores—an expedient procedure that required no commitment other than the coins in his pocket.

But then Honey Behr had entered his life.

For hours he watched the silver threads of gleaming moonlight brighten the darkness until they were replaced by the golden streaks of a rising sun. Then he abandoned any further attempt to sleep.

Luke sat up. For several moments he remained sitting on the edge of the cot, his head cradled in his hands. Finally, he got to his feet. He needed a cup of coffee.

He took a painted coffee tin from a shelf over the stove. After removing the lid, he discovered the tin was empty. Grunting with disgust, he slammed it shut. He needed a cup of coffee *now.*

Luke dressed hurriedly. Then, grabbing the empty coffee tin, he headed next door.

The sun had just topped the tree line when Honey rose from bed. She would put a pot of coffee on to brew, then get dressed. Fearful of waking Josh so early, she carefully closed his bedroom door, then padded barefoot across the wooden floor. She drew up startled when she saw Luke at the sink. Her heartbeat quickened when he turned his dark head at the sound of her muffled gasp. "Oh, you scared me," she said. "I didn't expect you so early."

"I didn't think you'd be"—his gaze shifted from her face and swept slowly down the length of her body—"up so early."

She felt her nipples harden under the intensity of his dark-eyed gaze and realized her thin nightgown did little to disguise her nudity.

Suddenly the air felt suffocating, and in an effort to ward off dizziness, she drew in a deep breath. His hooded stare followed the rise and fall of her chest.

"I'll, ah, go and get dressed."

Pivoting to leave, she was halted by an iron grip on her wrist. She inhaled sharply; the shock of his touch was like a firebrand. She turned to him, separated only by the length of her outstretched arm. Instantly mesmerized by his sapphire eyes, which were ablaze with arousal, she felt desire surge through her in an instinctive response. Their gazes remained locked until, impelled by escalating passion, she moved toward him and was drawn into his embrace by the slow slide of his hand up her arm.

In a single blink, his control shattered, and his dark eyes became flooded with raw lust. He pulled her roughly against him, crushing her breasts against the hard wall of his chest. His mouth swooped down to capture her quivering lips.

Rather than recoiling, she welcomed the forcefulness of the move. Matching his urgency with her own hungry need, she threw her arms around his neck, curving her heated body against the long hardness of his. He shoved up her gown, and the feel of his roving hands on her hips and spine fueled the fire raging through her.

The kiss consumed her—as hot and relentless as the hands that explored her flesh. Each thrust of his tongue sent erotic shocks spiraling to the core of her feminine chamber. Her head reeled and blood pounded at her temples, but his mouth continued to possess hers with a divine mastery.

When he finally freed her lips, her quivering legs could barely support her and she slumped against him. For endless seconds his lips plundered the hollow of her throat and neck, then trailed to the swell of her breasts. The thin fabric of her gown did little to dispel the heated moistness of his mouth on her breast as his teeth tugged at a hardened peak.

Aching for the return of his mouth and tongue on hers, she pulled his head up and pressed her lips to his. Her passion was out of control, and she kissed him with savage intensity.

Her trembling legs began to buckle, and he lifted her onto the edge of the table. Recapturing her lips, he slid his heated palms along her thighs until the bunched-up gown impeded his progress. With an impatient growl, he released her and started to pull the gown over her head.

"Sheriff MacKenzie!" His body stiffened, and frozen in motion, he stood alert, listening.

"Sheriff MacKenzie!" The shout was accompanied by a repeated pounding on the front door. "You in there, Sheriff? It's Delmer Quinn."

Honey shifted her startled glance to his and saw that his face was set in grim lines. A muscle jumped in his cheek, and in a voice hoarse with bitterness, he threw back at her the flippant remark she'd made to him the previous Sunday when the Walden gang had attacked Stockton. "Well, Miz Honey Behr, 'pears like you dodged the bullet again, didn't you?"

Then he released her arm. Honey dashed into the bedroom and closed the door behind her.

After a backward glance to make certain Honey was safely hidden behind the closed bedroom door, Luke opened the front door.

"Why the hell are you making all that noise, Del? You're gonna wake up everybody in the house," he grumbled.

"Thought you were spending your nights at the jail, Sheriff," Quinn said with a smirk.

"You thought right. Just what in hell do you want at this time of the morning?" With his groin still aching, he was too irritated to give a good goddamn whether the undertaker believed him or not.

"Don't get huffy, Sheriff. You know old Grandpa Williams died in his sleep yesterday, and since he ain't got no kin, I want to get it over with."

"He died of natural causes, so what do you want with me?"

"I need your help burying him; he's too damn heavy for me to lift by myself."

"Why don't you get yourself an assistant?" Luke mumbled in exasperation.

Quinn's face curved into a wide, toothy grin.

"Cheaper using you, Sheriff. You're on the county payroll."

"Can't it wait until after church?"

"No. Myrtlelee's made plans to visit her sister in Sacramento and wants to leave on the morning stage. I promised her I'd be back home in plenty of time."

"All right then, let's go." With a backward glance at the bedroom door, Luke grabbed his hat.

After the two men left, a silence once again descended over the house. Honey stood motionless and tried to calm the tide of emotions sweeping through her. A blush of mortification stained her cheeks as she reproached herself for her unhesitant surrender to him.

And he clearly loathes me, she lamented. The bitterness in his parting remark proved that.

She chastised herself for being a fool—such an easy mark! He had worked a better con than she ever had. He had almost seduced her into surrendering to his damn animal magnetism. Had she fallen into his arms and succumbed to his debauchery so easily, it would have thoroughly convinced him that she was absolutely unfit!

She would have to face him again. See the contempt in his eyes. The smugness on his face.

"I hate you, Luke MacKenzie!" She grabbed her clothing and tossed it on the bed. Then she slumped down on top of the pile and pressed her face into the pillow. "Oh, how I hate you, Luke," she sobbed pitifully.

By the time Luke returned, she had Josh fed and dressed for church. She did not accompany them. For the rest of the day, she and Luke spoke to each other only when necessary.

Chapter 9

On Monday morning, as she dressed Josh for his first day of school, Honey could tell by his downcast expression that he didn't want to go. "You'll like it, sweetheart. There will be boys and girls your own age to play with, and you're sure to find a good friend among them."

After slicking down his hair with water, she stepped back to admire the result. "My, don't you look handsome! You're going to set all those little girls' hearts to fluttering." She hugged and kissed him. "Oh, how I wish I could be there, sweetheart."

Outside, the sound of Honey's voice carried to Luke's ears. Since the incident the previous morning, she wouldn't even look at him, much less talk to him. Damn the woman anyway! What in hell was her problem? Sure he had made the first move, but she sure hadn't tried to stop him. She was acting like a blushing virgin instead of the scheming little tart he knew her to be. Look how she flaunted her indiscretions Saturday night by tossing that money down in front of him! What con was she working on him now? If she wasn't so damn good with Josh, he'd kick that tempting little rear end of hers out of town!

He entered the house and continued to listen to

Honey's chatter. Luke shook his head. He had to give the devil his due—or the devil's disciple, he thought wryly. The woman seemed to approach every new experience with exuberance and, if he hadn't known her better, innocence. He hoped some of her enthusiasm would rub off on Josh—but after one glimpse at his son's sad face, Luke knew her efforts had gone for naught. Josh just didn't know how to smile. *Like father, like son,* he thought regretfully. If only he had the same zest for life that Honey did, he might be able to reach his son.

"All set, Josh?" he asked after Honey finished. As Luke took his son by the hand, he felt the boy trembling. Luke glanced at Honey. "I think he believes he's being punished. Wish I could pick him up and hug him to convince him otherwise."

"Go ahead. What's stopping you?" she challenged.

"Gotta start thinking about making a man out of him. He's getting too big for babying."

"I never yet met a male who didn't like a little babying of one kind or another, MacKenzie."

The remark conjured up the image again of the gold eagles she had tossed down on Saturday night and how she had no doubt earned them. He said sarcastically, "He's a bit young for *that* kind of babying, Miss Behr."

Cursing Luke under her breath, she followed them outside to the hitching post. She yearned to be the one to take Josh to school. The schoolhouse was only a mile away, but Luke had told her he would take Josh there on horseback.

After settling Josh on the saddle with him, Luke said to her, "After I drop Josh off, I'll be riding out to the Fletcher spread, so I don't figure I'll make it back for dinner."

"I'll try to get through the day without you looking over my shoulder, Sheriff."

Shielding her eyes from the sun's glare, Honey watched them ride off. Josh looked so forlorn that she wanted to cry. The child was obviously scared and

confused. Luke was right; Josh didn't understand
what was happening to him.

She spent the next thirty minutes fretting over how
he was doing. Finally, she decided to make use of the
sunny day by doing the laundry. After setting several
large kettles of water on the stove, she gathered up
all the dirty clothes and bed sheets and divided them
into several piles on the floor in front of the fireplace.
Then she went out to the shed, found the wooden
laundry tub and washboard, and brought them inside. She had no desire to stay outside in the blazing
sun.

But once the tub was filled with hot water, Honey
stood looking down at it with her hands on her hips.
"Doggone it," she exclaimed. "It sure seems a shame
to waste a whole tub of hot water on just dirty
clothes." A hot bath was a luxury that was rarely convenient or affordable to her. With Josh in school and
Luke gone for the day, she couldn't think of a better
opportunity to take one.

She sprinkled the last of her lavender bath salts into
the water, shed her clothes, and climbed in. The tub
was snug—she had to sit with her knees practically
up to her chin—but the water was hot. Thoughts of
Luke and Josh were momentarily forgotten as she
closed her eyes and yielded to the pure pleasure of
the moment.

When the water turned tepid, she regretfully
climbed out of the tub and quickly toweled dry. Since
her robe was somewhere in a wash pile, she wrapped
a towel around herself and hurried over to the sink
to refill a kettle.

Without warning, the front door slammed. Startled,
she dropped the kettle and turned to see Luke frozen
in the doorway. "What—what are you doing back
here?" she asked.

For what seemed the longest moment of her life,
she stood stiffly as he slowly swept his gaze from her
head to her toes. She felt her cheeks flush under the
heat of the intense perusal, and her skin tingled as if

his hands, not his eyes, caressed her. Then he folded his arms across his chest and leaned back against the wall. Quirking a dark brow, he asked mockingly, "You expecting company, Miz Honey, or were you hoping to finish what we started yesterday?"

As long as the moment had arrived to face off with him, she wasn't going to give him the satisfaction of taunting her. Defiantly, she raised her head. "We, MacKenzie?"

"Who are you trying to fool? I'm not one of your pigeons, lady. You trying to say you're not as much to blame as I am for what happened yesterday morning?"

"I'm saying we have an agreement, Sheriff. The conditions are that I'm here to help your son and you are to keep your distance. I've been living up to my end of the bargain."

"I don't remember any of those conditions give you call to parade around half naked in front of me," he retorted.

"Perhaps not, but as long as you're holding me a prisoner in this house, I'm holding you to the conditions of the agreement, Sheriff. So if you touch me again, it's off. Do you understand?"

"I think you're the one who doesn't understand, lady. Yesterday, you wanted it as much as I did. But you've lied so often, you can't even be honest with yourself." Her fingers itched to scratch the smirk off his face as he continued. "Well, it appears like you're dealing the cards, so it's your call, lady. But I've played enough poker to know that we're both betting on a bluff." His brow arched in amusement. "So the hand's not finished yet. We'll see which of us folds first, Miz Honey."

"It's finished as far as I'm concerned," Honey said haughtily. She walked with as much dignity as she could toward her bedroom. With every step she took, she could feel his fixed stare following her.

Once in the privacy of the room, she closed her eyes and leaned back against the door. Her body was shaking, her heart racing. So he thought she was running a bluff, did he? It was time she taught that arrogant sheriff the real meaning of the phrase.

She dressed quickly, fastening the buttons of her bodice with trembling fingers. When she finished, she drew a deep breath, squared her shoulders, and opened the door.

He had moved across the floor and now stood gazing down at the tub of water. "I was just getting ready to do the washing. If you want something washed, you can bring it over," she said, offering a friendly smile.

"It might smell great on you, but I don't think it would ride well on me," he said sarcastically. Confused, she glanced at him. "Lavender," he explained.

"Oh, I forgot," she said sweetly. She turned away and went into the kitchen to refill the kettle. "I didn't expect you back so soon. Then you will be home for dinner."

"No. My horse threw a shoe, so I had to turn back. I'll be going now."

She detected enough of an undertone of suspicion in his voice to cause her to smile secretly. She knew he had expected her to come out of the bedroom primed for bear. Her sweetness had confused him.

"Sorry I interrupted your . . . laundering," he said. She heard him cross the room to the door, but she didn't turn around. "Reckon you're right, Miss Behr. Might be wise to have a key for this front door."

Glancing out the window, she watched him ride away. "I just raised the pot, Sheriff MacKenzie. You gonna see it, call it . . . or fold?" With a wide smile of satisfaction, she set the kettle on the stove.

Honey finished hanging the last sheet on the line, then climbed the porch steps and sat down. Since there was no more clothesline, she saw no reason to wash the rest of the clothes until the sheets dried. She began to fan herself with a folded newspaper. She sure had wasted the effects of a good bath, because she now was hot and sweaty from being in the sun.

As she glanced down the road, she saw a small figure in the distance. There was something familiar about his walk and the slump of his shoulders. She stood up for a better look. Good Lord, it was Josh! His lunch pail was clutched in his hand.

Honey jumped down from the porch and raced down the road. Had she misunderstood the instructions? It was only noon, and school was not over until four o'clock. She certainly had intended to go and get him at that time. Josh was too young to be on his own.

Honey was breathless when she reached him. "Josh, what are you doing home so early?" She had learned to understand most of his gestures and facial expressions, and now the set of his head and downcast eyes made her suspicious. She got down on her knees and grasped his shoulders.

"Josh, you didn't run away from school, did you?" He looked up at her, and she drew in a sharp breath when she saw his blue eyes shrouded with pain. "Oh, sweetheart, what happened?" For several moments she held him in an embrace, then she stood up.

She had to get to the bottom of whatever was troubling him, and the only way to do it would be to ask the teacher. "If you won't tell me, we'll have to go back to school so I can find out what happened." Taking him by the hand, they walked the mile back to the schoolhouse.

Honey asked Josh to wait outside and entered the classroom. The schoolmarm glanced up over the pair of glasses set on the bridge of her long, pointed nose. She was not a young woman; her face was heavily lined and her hair streaked with gray. However, her pencil-thin body bore no middle-age bulges. Despite the unpleasant heat of the day, the high bodice of her brown serge gown remained buttoned to the neck.

"May I help you?" she asked in a stringent tone. Cynthia Nelson had told Honey that the schoolmarm was the wife of Hiram Webster, the town's mayor. At the moment, neither the woman's manner nor position in the community could intimidate Honey.

"If you don't mind, Mrs. Webster, I would like to speak to you for a few moments."

The schoolmarm stood up. "Children, you may go outside and eat your lunch. Remain in the school yard and remember, I will not abide any rowdiness or cussing." She turned a severe glare on one of the older students. "Is that clear James Cabot?"

The children grabbed their lunch pails and ran outside.

"Now how may I help you, Miss . . . ?"

"Behr," Honey said. "I'm Josh's nanny."

"Oh, yes. I've heard of you." Her voice was rife with disapproval.

"I came to find out why Joshua came home so early today."

"I would prefer to discuss the matter with Sheriff MacKenzie, Miss Behr."

"Since I'm responsible for Josh during the day, I prefer that you discuss it with me, Mrs. Webster."

"Very well, Miss Behr. I sent Joshua home because he is a disturbance in the classroom."

"Disturbance! He doesn't make a sound."

"Exactly. His refusal to respond to my questions is an intentional disobedience to my authority."

"But Josh doesn't respond to anyone, Mrs. Webster. Surely, you were aware of that."

"I won't tolerate such conduct in my classroom. And I advise you and Sheriff MacKenzie not to tolerate it any longer either."

"But he's a very bright boy, Mrs. Webster. And even if he doesn't speak, Josh will follow instructions."

"I cannot permit his attitude, Miss Behr. I have a responsibility to my other students. Before I know it, the rest of the children will attempt the same trick. One bad apple spoils the barrel."

Honey saw red: a hot, crimson wave of anger that flooded her senses, sweeping away her control.

"Why you pompous, overbearing, old . . . old Pecksniff," Honey sputtered, unable to think of anything except the name of the hypocritical Dickens character. "And you call yourself a teacher!" She stormed up the aisle. "I'll teach him myself before I'd trust him to a prune face like you."

"Well! I've never heard anything so rude. I intend to speak to Sheriff MacKenzie about your insolence, Miss Behr. I am certain the boy's father will not approve."

"And when you do, Mrs. Fuss and Feathers, be sure and tell Sheriff MacKenzie how you turned away his six-year-old son and left him to find his way home alone. I don't think the boy's father will approve of that either."

The schoolmarm jumped back in alarm when Honey raised an arm and shook a fist at her. "And if I hear of you calling Josh a bad apple again, I'll punch you right in your big, ugly nose."

By the time Luke returned to Stockton, twilight had lengthened the shadows into deep patches of indigo filled with the trill of chirping crickets. Stirred by the rise of an evening breeze sweeping in from the north, the white sheets on the clotheslines fluttered like ghostly specters.

Luke walked over and began to remove them. Disgusted with Honey's failure to bring in the wash before nightfall, he angrily tossed the clothespins into a nearby bucket. As he did, he heard the sound of her singing coming from the open window. He went over to tell her to come out and finish what she had started, but the words stuck in his throat.

Honey sat in the center of the parlor, strumming her guitar to the tune of "Blue-Tailed Fly." Josh sat cross-legged on the floor before her, his gaze riveted on her face. When she reached the chorus, she cried out to him, "Okay, sweetheart, this is your part."

To Luke's amazement, Josh started to clap to the music as Honey sang, "Jimmy crack corn, and I don't care. Jimmy crack corn, and I don't care. Jimmy crack corn, and I don't care . . ." She strummed a slow chord, and then, leaning her forehead against his, she sang out, "My master's gone away."

Giggling gaily, she put down the guitar, and taking him by the hands, she stood up and pulled him to his feet. Swinging their grasped hands, they hopped lightly around the room as she repeated the chorus.

Josh wasn't smiling, but his face was flushed with an animation Luke had never seen before. He swung his gaze to Honey. Her blue eyes gleamed with gaiety, and her mass of golden hair bounced on her shoulders as she danced. When she completed the song, she stopped and hugged Josh.

Luke turned slowly away.

He went back to finish removing the sheets. The faint aroma of lavender teased his senses, and he drew one of the flapping sheets to his nose. For a long moment, he breathed in the sweet scent.

Chapter 10

Luke was quiet throughout breakfast. He constantly shifted his brooding stare to the little dark head bent over a plate of untouched scrambled egg.

"Sweetheart, would you like something else to eat instead?" Honey asked Josh.

"Why do you keep pampering him about food? You know he won't eat," Luke grumbled.

"He eats more of my cooking than he does yours."

"So do I. So what does that prove other than you're a better cook?"

"I thought it might mean you never give him an opportunity to make a comparison. You've cooked oatmeal one time since I've been here—which, I should add, was on the salty side."

"Who do you think did the cooking before you arrived?" he said. "I'm willing to do it again, but I've given up asking you to wait until I'm off duty. You won't listen to me."

"Can you blame me after that salty oatmeal?" she teased. "And, besides cooking, I'm better than you are at a lot of other things." She turned back to the stove. "Poker, for one."

"And cheating people out of their money for another."

Honey gritted her teeth. "That, too," she said lightly. She would not let his foul mood provoke her into an argument, especially not in front of Josh. "I'm also better with children. For instance, I have more sense than to argue in front of youngsters. They take every word too seriously."

She turned her head and smiled sweetly at him. "Would you like another egg?"

Luke shook his head. "I'll eat his. No sense in wasting it."

"But that one's cold now. I'll fix you a fresh one."

"I said I'd eat his. Eggs cost money." He reached for Josh's plate. "You finished with this, son?"

Josh got up and ran outside.

"Looks like you're making headway there, MacKenzie. He used to run away crying."

"Guess I don't have your soft touch, Miss Behr." He began to fork the cold egg into his mouth.

After a lengthy silence, she finally asked, "Another cup of coffee?"

"I can get it if I want one," he replied.

She had had enough of his ill temper. "You do that," she agreed and walked into the bedroom, slamming the door.

For a long moment Luke sat woodenly, staring at the closed door. God, he was a bastard! Then he got up and left.

When Luke returned fifteen minutes later to take Josh to school, he received a surprise.

"Josh isn't going to school," Honey informed him. "I can teach him reading and ciphering right here at home."

"Isn't he feeling well?"

"He's feeling fine. Better than he did yesterday. Must be that children have better instincts than their parents."

"What are you talking about?"

Honey spoke to Josh. "Sweetheart, I have to talk to

your father. Please go outside until I'm through, then I'll come out and play with you."

"What's this all about, Honey?" Luke asked as soon as Josh disappeared through the door.

"That wicked schoolmarm bitch threw him out of school yesterday." She mumbled an epithet under her breath.

"For God's sake, watch your language around Josh," Luke demanded.

"That's certainly the pot calling the kettle black," she retorted.

"Good Lord! Why can't you ever answer a question with a direct answer? I'll have to find out for myself." He marched out of the house, mounted Alamo, and galloped away.

Honey had just finished the breakfast dishes when Luke returned. As he strode into the house with long, purposeful strides, she saw that his mouth was tight and grim, his jaw set in a stubborn line, and his dark eyes were stormy under furrowed brows. It was enough to set a timid person to quaking.

Honey Ann Behr was not such a person and she stood her ground.

"What the hell are you trying to do to me in this town?" he demanded. "So far you've cheated Jeb Grange and threatened to punch the mayor's wife; then there's your illicit conduct at the Long Branch on Saturday night to consider. Is it your intent to alienate all the good citizens of this town?"

"Good citizens?" she fumed. "If that cheating shop owner and overbearing schoolmarm are what you consider good citizens, then thank God you deem me unfit."

"Unfit is right. You're not qualified to pass judgment, lady."

"Maybe not, Sheriff MacKenzie, but as bad as I am, I wouldn't cheat a child out of his pennies or turn away a frightened and confused six-year-old. Lord knows what might have happened to Josh walking home from school all alone."

"What are you talking about?' "

"Oh, didn't that good citizen tell you that Josh was such a *disruptive force* in the classroom that she couldn't even wait for the day to end before she sent him home?"

"No, she didn't tell me that," he replied.

"Well, she did, Sheriff MacKenzie. And I'm not sorry I called her a prune face."

"You called her a prune face?"

"She's lucky I didn't carry through with my threat to punch her in her ugly nose. If she's a lady, I don't want to be one."

"You couldn't be a lady if you tried."

"And as for that money-hungry old shopkeeper, I'm sure he didn't tell you that the wooden horse he sold to Josh for six dollars probably cost him less than six dollars for a dozen of them. And don't try to tell me I don't know what I'm talking about. I've seen that cheap toy used in carnivals."

"That doesn't justify theft."

"Yeah, you're right, Sheriff. So do your duty and lock him up."

"There's no crime in running an honest business."

"No, there isn't. Sam Brazner, for example, doesn't allow a crooked deal in his saloon. Must be because he's also not considered one of the town's *good citizens*."

"There's no reasoning with you, lady. For Josh's sake, I thought you would try to cooperate, but all you're interested in is embarrassing me in the eyes of the town. I can't afford to lose this job, Miss Behr, and I wish you'd try to show a little restraint." He left her standing there, fuming.

Luke continued to brood all morning. He didn't know what to do about Honey or Josh. Why was she able to get through to the boy when no one else could? And with Josh not permitted in school, he needed her more than ever. She had him between a rock and a hard place. And she knew it!

When he returned to the house, he stopped in the doorway. Honey and Josh were seated at the kitchen table.

"Now, you deal out five cards," Honey said. She counted aloud as she dealt. "That's one, two, three, four, five. Five for you and five for me."

"What in hell are you doing?" he shouted, enraged. He strode across the room and brushed the cards off the table.

Josh's eyes were round with fright. "Sweetheart, why don't you go outside and play with your horse," Honey suggested calmly. "We'll do this later."

As soon as the door closed behind the child, she turned to Luke. Her initial shock had yielded to anger. "Well, congratulations, MacKenzie, you've succeeded in scaring him again."

"Everything I do scares him. The boy dislikes me."

"Hard to understand," she snapped, bending down to pick up the cards.

"Whether he likes me or not, I'm responsible for him, and I don't want you teaching him any of your damn cheating card tricks."

She glared at him with mounting anger. "What are you talking about?"

"You said you'd teach him reading and ciphering."

"That's what I'm doing."

"With card tricks? Some lesson!" he snorted.

"That's how I learned, MacKenzie. Adding up the spots on the cards or counting the number in the deal."

Her candid response momentarily caught him by surprise. "I noticed last week you were showing him how to paste together your fake jewelry. What was the lesson in that?"

Honey hadn't realized Luke had seen them. She had only done it to give Josh something different to do. But she was sick and tired of defending her actions to him. "Boy, I just can't slip anything past you, can I?" she said with mockery. "I was giving him an art lesson."

"Next you'll have him out peddling that junk."

"You're wrong, Sheriff. I know I can get a better price if I peddle it myself. But fear not, MacKenzie, I promised Josh half of whatever I get for it. That was his business lesson for the day."

Exasperated, she turned away from the accusing glare she always saw whenever he let his suspicions run riot. "You brought me here; you wanted my help. Why don't you just admit it won't work? If I can't be trusted, why leave your son with me?" She spun back to face him. "Isn't he worth more to you than two hundred and twenty-five dollars?"

Luke felt the sharp stab of guilt attached to the reproach. He trusted her with Josh. Lord, he knew she was doing a great job with the boy. He had told himself as much dozens of times in the last week. Why couldn't he tell her?

An apology hovered on the tip of his tongue. Intending to put a hand on her shoulder, he reached out, then swiftly drew it back when she turned to him with a piercing, blue-eyed glare.

"I'll tell you what's bothering you, Sheriff MacKenzie. You're jealous. In your overbearing arrogance, you can't accept the idea that your son would prefer me to you. Well, I can tell you, MacKenzie, it's easy, even for a six-year-old."

His feelings remained concealed behind an inscrutable mask. He cleared his throat. "I apologize for my outburst. And I admit you've done a remarkable job with Josh." He hesitated in the doorway. "I guess I just can't do anything right when it comes to my son. I try. Maybe you don't think so, but I do. I want him to love me like I love him. I guess I've been putting my own interests ahead of his. Letting this quarrel between us get in the way."

In the face of Luke's confession, Honey momentarily forgot her past grievances. "It was a bad bargain, Luke," she said gently. "It's always been a bad bargain between us."

"But you've tried to make it work much harder than I have, Honey, haven't you?"

As she watched him walk away, she felt as guilty as he did.

Later that afternoon, Cynthia Nelson came by and asked Honey to join her on the walk her husband insisted she take daily.

In the time Honey had been in Stockton, other than Lily at the Long Branch, Cynthia was the only woman who had been friendly toward her. Of course, listening to Cynthia's glowing account of the merits of marriage, Honey suspected the congenial woman had an ulterior motive in mind: finding the sheriff a wife. Her blatant attempts at matchmaking were a source of embarrassment to Honey.

"Are you sure you want to be seen in my presence, Cynthia? You know I'm the talk of the town."

"Let them talk, Honey. I know you're not any of the things they say."

"That's not true. I am scandalous. I did take the candy stick and threaten to punch the mayor's wife in the nose."

Cynthia put a hand to her mouth to stifle her giggle. "Did you really call Clarabelle Webster a prune face?"

"I certainly did."

"Oh, I've wanted to do that for years."

In a further effort to be honest, Honey confessed to her new friend the truth as to why she had come to Stockton, Luke's dislike of her, and her personal aversion to the man. To Honey's dismay, the explanation enthralled the persistent romantic, and Cynthia became more determined than ever to get her married to Luke.

As they strolled along with Josh between them, Cynthia was once again relentlessly pursuing that very subject when they passed two cowboys lounging against the front of the saloon.

One of the men staggered forward into their path and doffed his hat. With a theatrical flourish, he bowed. "Good afternoon, ladies." The young man, who didn't look to Honey more than twenty years old, was obviously intoxicated.

"Good afternoon, Mr. Calhoun," Cynthia responded and moved on. Honey glanced back and saw the two men enter the saloon.

"Looks to me like that young man has already had enough to drink," she remarked.

Cynthia nodded. "Yes, I'd say so, too. That's Jess Calhoun and his brother, Randy. Their father owns a big ranch nearby. Randy's nice enough, but Jess is a hot-headed troublemaker. He plays too fast and loose with that Colt he wears. Doug says Jess was born for a bullet."

They continued their walk, and Cynthia picked up the conversation exactly where she had left off, praising the virtues of Luke MacKenzie. Honey wondered what Cynthia would say if she told her friend about their bitter quarrel that morning.

Luke came outside and sat down on a chair on the stoop. His sweeping glance fell on Honey and Cynthia as they strolled down the opposite side of the street. His gaze remained riveted on Honey's animated face. She sure was one beautiful woman, he thought grudgingly. But an impossible one as well.

He had wanted her from the moment he first saw her. And the lying little harpy knew it, too. She didn't miss an opportunity to bait him—either with her tempting body or her luscious mouth. A mouth meant for kissing, not spewing out lies.

Still, she didn't deserve what he had said to her. She wouldn't even be in Stockton if it hadn't been for him. He still felt he had been right about bringing her here; she was so great with Josh. Every day he saw an improvement in his son—but not in his son's attitude toward him.

Luke blew a long sigh through compressed lips. She was right; he *was* jealous that Josh preferred her company to his. And he resented her refusal to live by the rules. That's why he wore a badge: there were too many people who thought they were above the law.

Yep. Somehow, he'd have to swallow his pride and tell her he was sorry for his earlier words. As long as she was in Stockton, they had to stop their spatting and try to get along.

"Sheriff, you best get up to the Long Branch. Jess Calhoun's in town and he's as drunk as a skunk."

Startled, Luke looked up at Matt Brennan. Deep in thought, he had not heard his deputy approach. "I'll check it out," Luke said, rising to his feet.

They started the hike up the street toward the Long Branch just as the Calhoun brothers emerged from the saloon. A whiskey bottle dangled from Jess's hand. He took a deep swig from the bottle and polished off the contents. With a wild whoop, he tossed the empty bottle in the air, drew his Colt, and fired twice, shattering the bottle.

Next to the saloon, the local banker was just stepping down from his carriage. The sudden explosion of gunshots spooked the team of horses, and when the animals bolted, the banker tumbled to the ground. Amidst a clamor of shouts and screams, people scrambled to avoid the path of the runaway horses and careening carriage.

The carriage crashed against a hitching post and flopped over. The accident slowed the horses but did not stop them. As the flight of the frightened team continued, the tipped carriage swept the dusty road like a broom, raising a black cloud in its wake.

Luke jumped into the saddle of a horse tethered at a nearby hitching post and galloped in pursuit. Once abreast of the runaway team, he leaned over and grabbed the bridle of one of the horses. By the time Matt thundered up behind him, Luke had managed to halt the team.

"Take care of the horses, Matt," Luke shouted. When Matt climbed down and began to calm the skittish animals, Luke wheeled his mount and rode back to the banker. "You okay, Wes?" Luke asked.

The banker nodded. "How's my team?"

"Just winded some. Your carriage'll need some repairs though."

"Well, that young scalawag ought to pay for them," Wes Douglas said bitterly, pointing a shaking finger at Jess Calhoun.

"You fire those shots, Jess?" Luke asked.

"Ain't my fault the man can't handle a team," Jess snorted.

"Our pa will cover the damages, Sheriff," Randy Calhoun quickly interjected.

"All right. Mount up and ride out of here."

Jess Calhoun's eyes were dark with resentment. "Supposing I ain't ready to go, Sheriff?"

"Then you can sober up in a cell. Choice is yours, Jess," Luke replied. His gaze remained unrelenting.

"You ain't puttin' me in any cell, Sheriff,"

"Shut your mouth, Jess, and let's get going," Randy said.

"I'll lock you up if I have to, Jess. We don't like drunken cowboys shooting up our town, so get on your horse and ride out of here. If I see you drunk in Stockton again, you'll stay in that cell for a month."

"You know who you're talking to, Sheriff?"

Luke had lost his patience with the argument and particularly with Jess Calhoun's irresponsible actions. "Yeah, a drunken, big-mouth rowdy who almost got one of the residents of this county killed."

"You wanna eat those words, Sheriff? Or maybe you'd rather eat that dust at your feet."

Luke continued to stare at him. "You heard me, Jess. Start riding."

"And if I don't?"

"I'm paid to keep the law here," Luke said in warning.

"Well, I ain't goin' till I'm ready to," Jess said like a petulant child.

"I don't want to hurt you, sonny. Maybe I should just put you over my knee and paddle your butt instead."

Calhoun snorted derisively. "Getting cold feet, Sheriff? I figure I can take you."

"You figure it's worth dying for you to find out?" Luke asked calmly.

He realized his pent-up frustration had pushed him into a showdown with a drunken braggart who only needed cooling off in a cell for a couple of hours. Now he might have to kill the young man.

Randy Calhoun was just as concerned for his younger brother's welfare. He tugged at Jess's arm. "Ah, come on, Jess, let's go. Sheriff's only doing his job. Besides, you gun down a sheriff and you'll have a U.S. marshal on your trail."

"Let me alone," Jess snarled, shoving Randy away. "Time I shut you up, Sheriff."

"Sheriff MacKenzie, he's drunk. He don't know what he's saying," Randy pleaded.

"Do I have to take on both of you, Randy?" Luke asked, shifting his glance to the other cowboy.

Randy Calhoun looked desperate. "He's my brother, Sheriff. What do you expect me to do? I can't just stand here and watch you gun him down."

"I don't need no back up," Jess snarled. He started to draw, but before his gun could clear the holster, Luke's hand shot to the pistol at his own hip. Shocked, the cowboy sobered, paling at the feel of the drawn Colt pressed against his stomach.

"Now slide that iron back into its leather, real easy like, Jess," Luke ordered. "And, Randy, you just keep your hands where they belong," he added in a warning. "No sense in you having to pay for your brother's mistakes."

For several breathless seconds, Luke saw Jess's inner struggle as the young cowboy's youthful pride and recklessness dueled with the instinct to survive.

"I said leather it, Jess."

Jess slid the gun back in the holster.

"Let's go, Jessie," Randy said softly, slapping his brother on the shoulder. Wordlessly, Jess walked to their tethered horses at the hitching post.

"Thanks, Sheriff MacKenzie." Randy made no effort to hide his gratitude.

"Keep him out of Stockton when he's drinking, Randy. I'll have a talk with him the next time he's in town."

Luke sheathed his Colt and never budged from where he stood until the two men rode out of town.

Still clasping the hand of Josh, Honey had watched breathlessly along with the other citizens. She feared for Luke, and all of her earlier thoughts and resentments concerning him had dissipated. In those few tense moments, Luke could easily have killed Jess Calhoun, but he was a just man who chose not to. Was this the same man who bullied and condemned her so unjustly? Had she totally misjudged Luke MacKenzie?

Her chest ached so badly it hurt to breathe. She felt as if her pounding heart had bludgeoned the cavity. For a long moment she closed her eyes and drew slow steadying breaths. When she ceased trembling, she discovered Cynthia was still beside her, but Joshua was gone. Nervously looking around, she finally spied him sitting on the street nearby. A dog lay on the road, its head cradled in Josh's lap.

"Oh, dear God," Honey cried softly. The two women hurried over to him.

"Dog got trampled when those horses bolted," Delmer Quinn said, kneeling down beside Josh.

In despair, Honey looked at the gray and black mongrel hound. Its hazel eyes were watery and glazed with pain. A muscle leaped spasmodically in its long, lean body.

"Oh, how awful," Cynthia said sadly.

"Whose dog is it?" Honey asked, kneeling down next to Josh.

"Nobody's," Quinn said. "Just a stray mutt that's been hanging around town for the past couple weeks." Honey saw Joshua's round blue eyes well with tears as he stared at the wounded animal.

"Here comes the sheriff. He can put the hound out

of its misery. I best get out of here or he'll give me the job." Delmer hurried away.

As Luke approached, he took in the mournful sight with a quick glance. "What happened here?"

Honey ceased stroking the dog and stood up. "I guess the poor thing got trampled by those runaway horses."

When Luke knelt down, she watched, fascinated by the movement of his hands as he gently ran his long fingers over the wounded animal. The dog whimpered a few times and tried to raise its head.

"I think you better take Josh away," Luke said to Honey. "I'll put it out of its misery." He drew his pistol.

"No-o-o!"

Everyone turned their heads in amazement. The horrified wail had come from Joshua.

Chapter 11

Tears streaked Josh's cheeks as he looked up at them, pleading. It was the first sound Honey had heard the youngster speak since she had arrived. And the pitiful cry sounded as if Josh himself was in excruciating pain.

"No," he repeated.

Sheathing his Colt, Luke grasped the boy's shoulders. "Son, the dog is suffering," he said gently.

"Please don't kill the dog, Daddy," Joshua pleaded.

Shocked at his predicament, Luke looked at Honey.

She glanced worriedly at Josh. The little boy's dark head remained bent over the dog. "Luke, can we take the dog to the doctor? Maybe something can be done for it."

"I think it's a waste of time, but we've got nothing to lose by having Doc Nelson take a look at it," Luke said.

"The dog has if we don't," she countered cryptically.

Cynthia nodded in agreement. "That's for certain. Besides," she said with wifely pride, "Doug will know what to do."

The dog whimpered pitifully as Luke gently picked

it up. Honey lifted Josh into her arms, then she and Cynthia followed him.

The adults were asked to wait outside the doctor's office while he examined the suffering animal. However, sensitive to the situation, Doug Nelson allowed Josh to remain with the dog.

After what seemed an interminable length of time, Doug came outside carrying the poor creature swathed in gauze bandages, with only its eyes and snout uncovered. Josh followed closely on Doug's heels.

"Josh, you keep an eye on our friend here while I talk to your daddy," Doug told him. Josh quickly sat down on the stoop and cradled the dog's head in his lap.

When Cynthia started to follow Honey and Luke into the office, her husband stopped her. "Are you in labor, sweetheart?"

Cynthia's brown eyes were widened in surprise. "Of course not, Doug. You told me the baby's not due for at least two more weeks."

"Do you have a pain of any kind?"

"No."

"A shortness of breath? Or light-headedness?"

Totally confused, Cynthia raised her brows and glanced at Honey. Honey shrugged in return, just as mystified as Cynthia. "No, Doug, I feel better today than I have for a week."

"That's fine. Then come back later; I'm with a patient now. Your appointment's at two o'clock on Monday, Mrs. Nelson." With that he gave her a quick peck on the lips and closed the door in her face.

"She's going to be livid," he remarked, grinning broadly at Honey. "It's a pleasure to finally meet you. Cynthia's told me all about you."

"Thank you, Dr. Nelson."

"I prefer Doug. I don't stand on much formality." He took her arm and assisted her to a chair. "You're as beautiful as Cynthia said you are, Honey."

"Your wife is very kind, Doctor, ah, Doug. In more ways than one."

"So I understand you're planning just a short stay in Stockton with us," Doug said cordially.

Honey cast a disgruntled look at Luke. "Ninety days to be exact."

Doug chuckled. "You make it sound like a jail sentence, Honey."

"Oh, really! I hadn't realized."

Luke leaned against the wall. As he watched and listened to them, he couldn't help but notice how they chatted together like long-time friends. Why did he have such a problem talking to Honey? Getting along with her? Of course, Luke thought resentfully, she might not be so well received with Doug and Cynthia if they knew what he knew about her.

"From the looks of that dog, 'pears like you've been practicing bandaging, Doc," Luke commented, deliberately interrupting their little tête-à-tête.

Doug looked up, as if just then remembering Luke's presence. "Yeah, I charge by the yard, not the visit," he said good-naturedly as he walked around the end of his desk and sat down.

Honey tittered in response, which further irritated Luke. "What about the dog?" he asked.

"Actually, I only swathed him in those bandages as a show to Josh. Thought it might ease his mind a little to see I did something for the animal. In truth, I can't make any promises, Luke. The dog has one broken hind leg, so I put a splint on it, but I have no way of knowing how badly he's busted up internally. His heartbeat is fast but steady. Of course, I'm not a veterinarian, so I don't know what a dog's heartbeat should be."

"What's your gut instinct, Doc?"

Doug shrugged. "Dog urinated, and I didn't see any blood. That's a good sign. Maybe there's no internal bleeding. I hope the dog can pull through for Josh's sake. The boy seems to have formed an attachment to it. I think you should take it home with you."

"Not a chance! Look, Doc, if I wanted a dog around the house, I would have one."

"But it needs constant care," Doug protested.

"Exactly. And that's why it should stay here with you."

"I'm not a veterinarian, remember? The dog should be watched closely. There's a little boy outside who's able and willing to do just that. So the logical thing would be for you to take the dog home with you."

Luke definitely did not intend to take the dog home. He had his hands full already coping with Honey and Josh. "He's your patient, *Doctor* Nelson."

"I recall you carrying him in here, *Sheriff* MacKenzie."

"Only in a legal capacity. Line of duty, you know."

As the two men continued to argue, Honey was able to take a long look at the young doctor. Despite the glasses that covered his warm brown eyes and the slightly receding line of blond hair at his temple, Doug Nelson was a handsome man. Although not as tall as Luke, he had a lithe, muscular build that reflected the years he had worked as a lumberjack for Cynthia's father in Oregon, where, according to his wife who worshipped him, the two had fallen hopelessly in love. As soon as he had finished his medical studies, they had married and moved to Stockton.

"I'll make a deal with you, Luke. You take the dog with you, and I won't charge you for the better-than-average medical attention it received," Doug said, grinning.

"Not to mention all those yards of gauze," Honey interjected hopefully.

"Should have shot him when I had the chance," Luke grumbled. Then all humor left his eyes. "Seriously, Doug, if the dog dies, how hard do you think Josh will take it? You should have seen his reaction when I tried to put the animal out of its misery."

"He even spoke," Honey quickly added.

Doug's features sobered. "Josh spoke?" He resumed the mien of a doctor as he earnestly pursued the discussion. "That's certainly a good sign. Some children just don't talk as early as others and if Josh said a few words, then he's sure to say more."

"Then maybe he won't be so withdrawn after all," Luke said hopefully.

"I don't know, Luke. I'd like to think so, but it may not be so simple."

When Doug appeared hesitant to continue, Luke said solemnly, "Tell us what you think, Doug."

"Well, I can't help wondering why Josh doesn't respond to people emotionally."

"Emotionally?" Honey said, exchanging glances with Luke.

"Yes. He certainly understands as much English as any typical six-year-old, because he does do what you tell him to do."

"Then why doesn't he talk?" Luke asked, bewildered.

"Don't rightly know. He's not responding to his environment the way a child normally does."

Luke asked the question that was closest to his heart. "Why does he shut out even his own father?"

Doug shrugged. "I can only guess."

"Well, what's your guess then?"

"My guess?" Doug stopped, trying to phrase his theory, then continued. "You've told me Josh was only two years old when your wife and mother were killed. Then a ranch hand—"

"Juan Morales."

"This Morales took Josh to Mexico, where he lived for a couple more years."

"That's right, until he was four," Luke agreed impatiently.

"By that time the youngster must have had at least a limited vocabulary, or Morales certainly would have told you that Josh had never spoken. Then you came, you spoke a different language, and you snatched him away from the only home he knew. Most likely the frightened little guy only understood Mexican," Doug said compassionately. "I think it boils down to that he simply doesn't trust you."

Honey thought that most of what Doug said made sense. But she still had a few doubts. "That would explain shutting out his father. But why everyone else?"

Doug shrugged matter-of-factly. "So now he won't trust anyone."

"That's for damn sure. I don't need a doctor to tell me that." Luke snorted.

Honey glanced at Luke. She sensed how deeply Doug's theory was affecting the proud man.

"Hey, you two, it's just a guess," Doug said. "I'm a medical doctor. You want a cough cured or a bone set, you came to the right man. I'm not a veterinarian, yet you bring me a busted animal to patch up. And I'm not what is called a psychologist either; those studies are done in Europe. I got my degree in California, not Paris or Vienna."

Perplexed, Luke asked, "What's a psychologist?"

"Psychology's got something to do with the study of behavior patterns. I don't know too much about the subject myself other than what I read in the medical journals I receive. There's some French neurologist who has even started a clinic where they treat hysteria and such symptoms. They've even been successful using hypnosis. And I know Dr. Josef Breuer in Vienna has delved into the subject as well. He refers to it as psychoanalysis."

Doug started to root through a pile of periodicals on the table behind his desk. "I read an interesting article on it not too long ago. Ah, here it is." He glanced at the journal. "The French doctor is Jean Charcot; he's a professor of pathology anatomy in Paris."

"Doug, this is all Greek to me," Luke replied, exasperated.

Doug handed Honey the periodical. "Take this with you. I want both of you to read it. It might help you understand what I'm trying to say."

He pondered the matter for a moment. "But think about this. If you were Josh, would you trust people? Remember, this is a six-year-old. All he knows is that his mother and grandmother left him, then he lost this Morales fellow, to whom he had probably switched his affection. And I'm sure he's aware that Honey is going to leave him, too." Doug paused to cast a disapproving glance at Luke before saying, "You have already informed him of that."

Then he continued. "So there's no doubt in his young mind his father is sure to leave him, too. He may be afraid to become attached to anyone because everyone he has ever cared for has left him"—this time Doug's pointed glance fell on Honey—"or intends to leave soon." Honey guessed that Cynthia must had been discussing that dreaded subject with her husband.

Doug put his feet on the desk, leaned back with his hands behind his head, and glanced up at the ceiling. "Say, I'm getting better at this. Maybe I should hang up another shingle."

Luke groaned and began pacing the floor. Honey sat deep in thought. Finally she cast a worried glance at Doug.

"What do you think we should do, Doug?"

Luke stopped pacing to fix an angry glare on her. He resented her familiarity with the man, more than the question. "Yeah, Dr. Nelson, what do you advise?" Luke asked, clearing his throat authoritatively.

"I say, give him a lot of love and understanding, and keep right on with what you're doing. Josh has to learn how to trust again. That shell of his has begun to crack. The incident with this dog has proven that he's willing to respond to someone, even if it's just a dog."

"And what if the dog dies?" Luke asked.

Doug's confidence deflated like air out of a balloon. "Then we've got a problem."

With a deep frown, Luke crossed his arms over his chest. "So what do you feed a dying dog?"

Chapter 12

⌒◯◯⌒

"**D**o you think he has a chance?" Honey asked softly.

More than twenty-four hours had passed since they had brought the dog home. Luke stood at her side in the kitchen, working the pump handle for her as she filled a kettle to heat for dishwater.

He swung his glance to Josh. The youngster sat on his bedroom floor next to the dog, who was lying in a box. "I hope so," he said grimly as he lifted the heavy kettle and carried it over to the stove.

"Luke, I've been reading that journal Doug gave us, and it made me remember something else about Josh. He's terrified when he hears gunfire."

"Yeah, he gets scared all right."

"I recall that incident in church. He was actually shaking with fright. I think it's more than just being scared."

"What are you getting at?"

"Maybe it's got something to do with the attack on the ranch. Even though he may have been too young to remember the actual attack, the fear he experienced could stay with him a long time."

"I think he was too young," Luke said skeptically.

"Well, what if he doesn't remember why that sound

122

frightens him, but he still reacts to it? And maybe he connects gunfire with a great loss. In this case, his mother and grandmother, even though he might not remember them."

"I still don't see why that would make him want to shut me out," Luke said.

"You walk around with the very instrument of his terror strapped on your hips," Honey replied.

"You think that's why he's afraid of me?"

Honey shook her head. "Afraid of *losing* you maybe. If he associates that sound with a sense of loss, then"—Honey spread her hands open—"why not?"

"I think Doug's filling your head with too much of that psychologist hogwash."

Honey yawned. "Maybe you're right." For a moment she leaned against the sink and closed her eyes.

"You tired?"

She opened her eyes and discovered Luke's dark gaze on her. "Oh, a little," she confessed. "Josh and I were up most of last night. I guess he was afraid to go to sleep for fear the dog would die while he slept."

"Go to bed, Honey. Get some sleep," Luke said gently. "I'll stick around."

Luke's gentleness unnerved her. She could withstand the fury of his anger, but she crumbled under the assault of his concern. "Are you sure you don't mind?" She shifted her gaze to him and saw sympathy in his eyes. "What about these supper dishes and getting Josh ready for bed?"

"I can do it. Remember?" There was no tone of sarcasm, just his engaging grin.

Honey eyed him suspiciously. "Are you feeling okay?"

To her astonishment, he started to chuckle. The sight and sound were devastating. She felt her heartbeat quicken to it and smiled back.

"I'm fine. I guess I feel more hopeful than I have for years. If what Doug says is true, Josh should be coming around soon."

Instinctively, she reached out a hand and put it on

his arm. "Let's just hope that dog doesn't die, Luke."

He shifted his glance back to Josh's open bedroom door. "Yeah. Let's hope."

Honey walked to her bedroom, but before closing the door, she paused. "Well, I'll just take a short nap. You'll wake me if . . ."

"Yeah, I'll wake you," he said solemnly.

From the moment she climbed into bed, Honey didn't remember a conscious thought until she awoke to sunlight streaming in the window. Then, horrified, she realized that she had slept through the night.

Grabbing her robe, she bolted out of the room. Luke and Josh were asleep, stretched out on the floor alongside the dog. With unblinking eyes, the dog lay awake but motionless except for a slightly twitching tail that extended from its gauze-swaddled body. As she approached on tiptoe, putting a finger to her mouth, she cautioned the dog to remain silent, then she tiptoed out of the room and closed the door.

Grinning, Honey crossed the floor to the kitchen. She felt good. *My, what a full night's sleep could do for a person*, she thought. Then her grin widened. Her spirits now seemed brighter than the morning sunlight. It wasn't only the sleep, it was everything. She felt certain the dog would survive; she felt certain that Josh was on the road to recovery; and she felt that maybe, just maybe, Luke MacKenzie didn't dislike her as much as he made out. They hadn't said a cross word to each other in over twenty-four hours!

She stopped suddenly and put her hands on her hips. "Honey Ann Behr, just what difference should Luke MacKenzie's opinion make to you? You're just setting yourself up for a lot more heartache." Nevertheless, her smile remained as she began to prepare breakfast.

A short while later, when Luke emerged from Joshua's bedroom, Honey was seated at the table with a cup of coffee in front of her. Biscuits were baking in the oven, and a kettle of oatmeal bubbled on the stove.

"Oh, God," he moaned. He stretched to get the ache out of his back. "I feel like I've been kicked by a horse."

She glanced up at him, her eye gleaming with mirth. "Sure you're not confusing yourself with the dog? Remember, he was the one kicked by a horse. But if you think it will help you feel better, maybe you ought to pay a visit to Doug. He might still have some gauze and tape left."

"Very funny, but coffee will do for me." He poured himself a cup and set the pot on the table.

"Maybe I should give the dog some of that to drink instead of water." At his puzzled look, she teased, "Well, the dog claims to have been run over by a herd of horses, too."

Luke plopped down on the chair and began to sip the hot brew. "Are you always as chipper as a jaybird in the morning?"

"Just be careful what you say, or I might start singing. I know how much you'd appreciate that."

He cradled his head in his hand and fixed his gaze on her. "You remind me of my kid brother, Cleve. My other brother, Flint, and I used to take turns threatening to beat him up if he didn't wipe the grin off his face in the mornings."

Honey glanced askance at him. "I see what I missed by not having any brothers." Feeling nervous under the scrutiny of his steady stare, she quickly changed the subject. "There are hot biscuits and oatmeal. You ready for some?"

Luke shook his head. "No, I'll settle for another cup of this coffee for now. It's pretty good." He refilled both of their cups.

"Well, you must be feeling better than you claim. I think that's the first compliment you've ever paid me," she said with a very feminine smile of pleasure.

"Brother Flint used to warn us that the prettier the gal, the worse the coffee."

"I might have known the compliment was too good to be true. And it's always a pleasure to hear another one of your brother's gems of wisdom. I recall the one you quoted to me in Sacramento. Brother Flint sure understands women," she intoned drolly. "Do you have any other brothers or sisters?"

"Just Flint and Cleve. I'm the eldest; Cleve's the youngest."

She wondered if Luke's brothers were as handsome as he was. Judging from Luke's earlier remark, Cleve seemed to be friendly and good-humored, but Flint sounded contentious and arrogant—a man who could put Jane Austen's Mr. Darcy to shame. "And where are your brothers now?"

"Can't say for sure. They left home in '62 to join the Confederacy. Haven't heard from either of then since."

"You haven't heard from either one in six years?" Honey shook her head in amazement. The possibility that they had survived the war seemed remote to her.

"I know what you're thinking, but you're wrong. My brothers can take care of themselves. Flint's too shrewd to fall into any Yankee trap, and Cleve can talk his way out of any situation." He laughed derisively. "Naw, they're alive all right. There's never been a Yankee born who could outwit, outride, or out-shoot either of 'em."

Seeing the pride in his eyes, she said softly, "How will they know where to find you?"

"Our trails will cross again. Knowing my brothers, whether they're together or not, it's for damn sure they're out sniffing the trail of the gang that raided the ranch."

He smiled and added, "Flint could follow an ant's trail in a sand storm, and Cleve can shoot the eye out of a gnat at three-hundred yards." Then his grin faded, and he stared far off into the distance.

"And you'd be on that trail with them if it weren't for Josh," she guessed.

"It's my fight more than anyone's." For a brief moment, they exchanged a long look, and then he told her. "When I got back to the ranch, I had to track down Juan Morales across the border to find Josh. And then I discovered Josh wouldn't talk. I knew Sarah would want me to do what's right for our son, so I couldn't just leave him there. I came here to California."

"Why here? Why didn't you go back to the ranch?"

"I did go back, hoping to chance upon my brothers. Heard from one of the rangers that Flint had come and gone."

"Why didn't you stay there?"

"Texas was dirt poor after the war. Loaded with beef with no one to sell it to. Rebuilding and stocking the ranch again would have taken a lot of time and money. I had a four year old to look out for and no money. The ranger told me Flint was following a lead to California, so I headed west and ended up here in Stockton. But as soon as I can, I'll be on the trail, too."

"Then Doug was right. Just when Josh starts to trust again, he'll lose you."

Seeking to buoy her slumping spirits, he grinned broadly and said, "Not for long. Just until this unfinished business is settled. Then we'll go back to Texas. I sure hope I don't miss Flint catching up with those outlaws though; when he gets riled, he's as dangerous as a greased rattler."

"I thought you were dedicated to law and order, Sheriff MacKenzie."

"I am. And finding the men who killed my wife and mother is part of that dedication."

"Then you intend to arrest these murderers and bring them to trial?"

"When I go after them, I won't be wearing a badge." He stood up. "Well, I best spell my deputy now. Call me if I'm needed." He stopped at the door and lifted his hat off a hook. Pausing, he turned back with a grin. "Ah, you brew a right good pot of coffee, Jaybird."

After he departed, Honey remained seated at the table. Funny how one incident could change people's lives, she reflected. Just yesterday, she and Luke had been arguing and tense toward each other. Then run-away horses and a dog had led to the revelation about Josh. Now, they were talking together like old friends.

She shoved back her chair and stood up. Picking up the cups, she carried them to the sink. "But nothing has *really* changed," she cautioned herself.

After cleaning off the table, she went to check on Josh. She found him sitting on the floor with the dog's head in his lap. She sat down beside him.

"How's our friend doing this morning? Oh my, he looks a bit livelier to me," she said cheerfully. Without acknowledging her presence, Josh continued to stroke the dog's head.

"What do you think we should call him?" she asked. When he didn't reply, she said firmly, "Now you listen to me, young man. I know very well you understand me, so I don't want any more of your silence. So we'll make a deal, Joshua MacKenzie. If you want to keep this dog, you give it a name—so he'll know he belongs to you."

Josh lifted his head, and the troubled look in his round blue eyes clutched at her heartstrings. In a trembling little voice, he said, "Amigo."

"Amigo? Oh, that's Spanish for friend, isn't it?" Tears glinted in her eyes, and her lips quivered in a smile. "Friend. That's a wonderful name for a dog, Joshua." She slipped her arm around his shoulders. "Look, Josh," she cried joyously, pointing to the dog's wagging tail, "Amigo likes the name, too."

Then she tipped up Josh's chin to look at him. "Now I think it's time you and I had a long talk. There's going to be changes made here. From now on, when I ask a question, I want an answer from you."

When Luke returned home later that day, he stopped outside to listen as Honey's voice carried through the open door. "Now, this card is called the Empress."

To Luke's amazement, he heard Josh say, "Honey."

"Well, yes, I guess you could say there's a resemblance to me. She is blond like I am, and she represents initiative and creativity and, ah, fruitfulness." After a slight pause, she asked, "You don't understand, do you?"

Soundlessly, Luke stepped into the doorway in time to see Josh shake his head. He was sitting across the kitchen table from Honey, with the dog lying on the floor at his feet.

Deep in thought, Honey tapped at her chin with a slender finger. "Well, let's see . . . How can I explain this clearer? The Empress can also represent light and truth."

Truth! And Josh thought Honey resembled her! Luke almost choked on the naïveté of youth. Blond hair was where the resemblance ended. Grinning, he remained silent.

"Well, let's continue," Honey declared, turning over the next card. "Now this is the King of Wands," she explained. "This is a very good sign, Josh. He represents a dark man in your life—honest and conscientious." She made a long face and deepened her voice. "But he can also be very stern and dominating." She leaned toward him, grinning. "Well, we both know who that is, don't we?"

Josh thought for a second. "My daddy." When Honey rolled her eyes and nodded, the youngster giggled in delight.

Luke's grin slid into a poignant smile. It was the first time he had ever heard his son's laughter.

It was a beautiful sound.

Chapter 13

By the week's end, Amigo's bandages had been replaced with a simple splint on his hind leg. Hobbling around after Josh, the dog looked like the boy's shadow. In turn, Josh seemed to follow Honey everywhere.

And Luke's silent gaze followed all three.

Having come out to escape the heat inside the jailhouse, Luke once again found himself watching the threesome as they accompanied Cynthia on her daily walk.

For the past two years, he had felt the weight of the world on his shoulders. But since Honey had arrived, his life seemed to have turned around—Josh appeared to be recovering at the same speed as the damn dog. And even though both Josh and the dog still viewed him with leery regard, the breakthrough had been made.

Honey was foremost on his mind now, and he allowed his eyes to rest on her alone. She was wearing the green-striped gown he had seen on her often, and that ridiculous little hat perched on top of her head. From where he stood, he could see the amusement on her face as she listened to Cynthia Nelson.

Often, during the past week, he had noticed that in

his and Honey's shared joy over the improvement in Josh, they had put aside their past grievances. Like proud parents, they sought each other's gaze whenever Josh said or did something that touched their hearts.

Looking at her now, Luke felt a wave of heat sweep through him. The damn woman had begun to monopolize his waking thoughts. Despite all their arguments, he still desired her. Lord, how his body ached for her! But he had made a promise to live up to his end of their agreement. And like a damn fool, he had even tossed a gauntlet in her face! He'd better receive an answer to that ad soon, because he sure couldn't put up with the ache in his groin for ninety days!

"Good morning, Sheriff."

Luke grimaced at Cynthia Nelson's greeting. Realizing he could not escape the encounter, he wiped the scowl off his face and ambled across the street.

"Morning," he said. He took off his hat and wiped his brow on his sleeve. "Hot enough for you ladies?" As he settled the hat back on his head, he cast a disgruntled glance at Amigo, who had limped over to him and was sniffing his boots as if Luke were a stranger. He lightly nudged the dog away with the side of his foot.

"Yes indeed, Sheriff," Cynthia said warmly. "Shame you have to work."

"I'm through in an hour." Luke bent down to Josh. "What say the two of us go fishing, son?"

Luke saw the glow in the youngster's eyes that betrayed the excitement behind his shy smile. "Honey, too?" Josh asked.

Luke stood up slowly and glanced at Honey. "Well, maybe she'd rather stay home."

Honey could see that he preferred she not accompany them. "That's right, Josh. I've got some things to do, but I'll pack you a picnic lunch."

"Did you hear that, Amigo, we're going fishing," Josh said. He ran on ahead of her to the house.

"Well, I better be going, too," Cynthia said. "Doug will soon be home for lunch."

For a long moment after she left, Honey and Luke stood in silence. Finally, he spoke. "If you want to, you're welcome to come along."

"No. I know you would rather spend the afternoon alone with Josh. Besides, putting a squirming worm on the end of a hook is not my idea of a good time." Feeling uncomfortable under his scrutiny, she smiled nervously. "I guess I'll get that lunch packed." She hastened away.

As Luke watched her slim figure disappear, he realized he should have been honest and admitted how close she had come to the truth: he *did* want to go with Josh alone, but not for the reason she thought.

Lately, more and more frequently, they had begun to slip into the pattern of a family circle—even that damn lame dog had become a part of it. And certainly the time was swiftly approaching when the circle would be broken. He knew that once the ninety days was up, nothing would keep her in Stockton. Josh's condition had been a challenge to her in the beginning, and it was obvious to him that she thrived on challenges. But with Josh well on the road to recovery, life in Stockton must seem monotonous to her. It would be a matter of time before she packed up the tarot cards, paste jewelry, and that damn white nightgown of hers and climbed on the stage to San Francisco.

And not a day too soon as far as he was concerned.

By the time Luke appeared, Honey had packed cheese sandwiches, a jug of lemonade, and the remaining half of a chocolate cake.

"Josh, get a blanket from your room while I get the poles down from the loft," Luke said.

Honey followed Josh into his bedroom and stopped him before he could pull the blanket off the bed. "I saw an extra blanket in the chest. You can take that one." She hurried over to the bureau, knelt on the floor, and pulled out a threadbare blanket from the bottom drawer.

"Put that away!"

The shouted command startled Honey, and she dropped the blanket to the floor. Luke put down the fishing rods in his hands and strode over to her. "I don't want this touched," he said angrily and picked up the blanket. "We don't need a blanket anyway. Let's go, Josh."

Luke's burst of temper had frightened Josh. His face stricken, he sped from the room as Luke refolded the blanket and returned it to the chest.

Honey's temper flared. "You've scared Josh half to death. And now you say, 'Let's go'?"

"I'm sorry I don't have your expertise at raising children," he snapped. Angry with himself, Luke stormed into the kitchen and, in frustration, slammed his fist down on the sink board. He knew he was wrong. His outburst had been unwarranted. Josh was still too shy and unsure of himself to witness such a tantrum from a father he was still frightened of.

Honey had had enough of his moody tantrums. She strode toward the front door with the intention of offering comfort to Josh. "Where are you going?" Luke asked.

"Away from you. I think you can forget about any fishing trip with your son today." She turned to leave.

"No, wait. Please, Jaybird."

The plea in his voice stopped her. Looking at him, she saw the remorse in his eyes.

"I'm sorry. Let me talk to Josh for a moment." When she nodded, he walked past her and paused at the door.

Josh sat on the stoop with his chin drooping. Amigo lay with his head in Josh's lap. Luke took a deep breath, then walked outside and sat down beside him. Amigo raised his head and eyed him warily, then settled back down again.

"Son, I'm sorry I shouted," Luke said gently.

"You scared me," Josh said timidly.

"I know, and I'm sorry about that."

"Are you mad at Honey?"

"No, I'm not mad."

"Then why'd you shout at her? You scared her, same as me."

"Sometimes people shout when they're surprised or just happy, too, don't they?"

When Josh nodded and looked up at him, Luke slipped an arm around the boy's shoulders. "When I shouted, I really wasn't mad at anyone, Josh; I was just surprised. You see, that blanket . . . Well, your mother gave me that blanket the day I left her in Texas. I used it all through the war, and it's the only thing I have left of hers—except you, son. That's what makes you extra special to me."

"More special than the blanket?"

He chuckled warmly. "Much more special than the blanket. There's nothing in this world as important to me as you are, Josh. I love you, son. I'll always love you."

"Was my mother like Honey?" Josh asked.

"No, nothing like her," Luke said quickly. "Your mother had dark hair and blue eyes."

"No, I mean was she fun like Honey?"

For a long moment Luke thought about Sarah, then he said softly, "She was gentle and soft-spoken. And shy like you, Josh."

"Why did she go away? Didn't she love us anymore?"

Luke hugged Josh to his side. "Oh, she loved us both, son. And I know she didn't want to leave us. But she had been . . . hurt. Do you understand what death means, Josh?"

"Amigo almost died." He started to stroke the dog's head.

"That's right, son. But Amigo was luckier than your mother, and he got better."

Luke drew Josh closer to him, and they sat quietly for several more moments. Finally Luke said, "Still want to go fishing, Josh?" The boy looked up and nodded. "Well, what are we waiting for?" He swung Josh up on his shoulders. With Amigo barking excitedly at his heels, Luke carried Josh to the buckboard he had rented. Luke glanced down to see Amigo looking up at him, the dog's tail wagging furiously. With a tolerant sigh, he lifted up Amigo. To Luke's disgust, he was rewarded with several grateful swipes of a tongue as he put the dog in the back of the wagon.

"Make sure this dog doesn't pee back there," he grumbled.

Honey had been standing near the door, listening to the conversation. At the mention of the blanket, her sorrowful glance had swung to the chest. *He's still mourning her,* she thought sadly.

She was staring at the chest when Luke returned to the house. He collected the fishing poles from the foot of the loft ladder. "Last chance. You're welcome to come with us."

"You know, MacKenzie, sometimes all it takes is a simple explanation to avoid lots of anger and hurt feelings."

"Dammit, I said I was sorry!"

She held out the picnic basket to him. "Take Josh fishing just as you planned. You don't need me along. Anyway," she added with a defiant smile, "I've got plans for later. This is Saturday, Sheriff MacKenzie."

For a brief moment, his eyes burned with anger and reproach, then he grabbed the basket and walked out the door.

She stood in the doorway and watched until the wagon disappeared around a bend in the road. It was better that she hadn't gone with them. Luke and Josh needed more time alone together—to learn to feel comfortable with each other. Besides, when the day of her departure arrived, the memory of shared picnics and fishing trips would only make the ultimate separation harder on Josh . . . and herself.

Most of the tables were already filled when Honey entered the Long Branch that evening. The barroom reverberated with the drone of voices and raucous laughter from the ranch hands who were lined up at the bar for a Saturday night on the town. Honey strolled over to the lone figure sitting at a corner table. "Hi, Pop."

"Evenin', darlin'." Pop O'Leary's wide grin and round eyes were as warm as ever. She had come to recognize the state of inebriation behind his happy-go-lucky facade.

Sam Brazner approached, carrying a bottle. "Howdy, Honey. You want a drink?"

She shook her head. "No, but pour Pop one. And leave the bottle."

"Who's paying for it?" Sam asked belligerently.

"Put it on my tote," Honey said.

As he filled Pop's glass, Sam eyed her cautiously. "Don't suppose you're willing to work one of the rooms tonight. Lily's got her hands full."

"We had an agreement, Sam. I'm not whoring."

"Okay, okay," Sam grumbled. He put down the bottle and walked away shaking his head.

Pop lifted his glass in a salute. "I'm beholden to you, darlin'. The good Lord has blessed me for just the knowin' of you."

"I'm not doing you any favors, Pop. That whiskey'll kill you one day."

"Then I'll be getting the best of the trade."

Honey covered his hand with her own. "I don't think so." She smiled at him tenderly. "Where's your home, Pop?"

"I've set up me residence at the bottom of this bottle here, darlin'."

"You weren't born at the bottom of that bottle, Pop. What happened?"

"What happened?" With puckish rascality, he cocked a brow. "'That way madness lies.'" He followed up his confusing answer with a wink. "Shakespeare, darlin'. The great Bard himself."

"Sounds like you were an actor, Pop."

With a theatrical flourish he doffed his hat and

bowed. " 'All the world's a stage, and all the men and women simply players.' "

"So you were in the theater."

His grin narrowed. "You might say that, darlin', for if ye can stretch your believin' a mite, I'll confess I was once a barrister. A noble knight and defender of truth and justice."

"A barrister?" she asked, surprised. "And what happened to make you give it up?"

" 'Tis a long story and not to your likin', I'm thinkin.' "

"And I've been around you enough to notice that Irish brogue is a little thicker at times than others. In fact, Dan'l Webster O'Leary, I'm thinkin' there's more learnin' under that County Kerry lilt than you'd be likin' us to believe."

He chuckled in delight. "Ah, you're a shrewd colleen, darlin'. 'Tis no wonder I'm so fond of you."

"Well, I've spent most of my life pretending to be someone I'm not, so it's not hard to recognize someone else who's doing the same." Her smile disappeared. "So what are you hiding behind that grin, Pop?"

Pop's face settled into somberness. "Have you ever heard of James Worthington Huntington III?"

"No, but with a name as impressive as that, I suppose I should have," she said lightly.

"Yes, Mr. Huntington III was as impressive as his name, for he came from money that was as thick as his blue grass roots."

"You mean Kentucky blue grass, Pop?"

He nodded. "Could afford the best attorneys, he could, and ten years ago, Daniel Webster O'Leary was the best of 'em." He paused to pour himself another drink. "Huntington married a young girl named Francis Mary McDonnell, a lovely young thing with hair as golden as sunshine and eyes as blue as an Irish sky. Her daddy, a horse trainer, raised thoroughbreds on the plantation of Mr. Huntington II. When Francis Mary McDonnell found herself with child, the Huntingtons couldn't buy her off, so she and James Worthington Huntington III were wed. By the time I met them, they had two children: a three-year-old boy and a two-year-old girl with big, round blue eyes and long curls hanging to her shoulders. The spittin' image of her mother, she was."

"So what did he need a lawyer for, Pop?"

"Huntington's wife asked for a legal separation with full custody of the children. She said he had abused all of them, and she claimed he was insane and dangerous. She pleaded to the court to have him committed to a mental institution for examination. For years there had been other rumors about Huntington's wildness, which his family had paid well to quash, and I closed me ears to them; me duty was to me client. In defense of Huntington, I reminded the judge of the woman's impoverished background, implied that she had married Huntington for his money, and I accused her of attemptin' to get control of his wealth. Me argument was so eloquent and impressive, the judge dismissed the case. Threw it out of court, he did, without so much as a day's thought on it. I collected me big fee and went me way."

"And what happened to the Huntingtons?" Honey asked.

"That same night James Worthington Huntington III hung himself from the Waterford chandelier in his bedroom . . . but not before he dismembered the bodies of his wife and two children."

Honey gasped and reached out and covered his hand. "Oh, Pop, how tragic."

"I left Lexington and have never stepped me foot in a courtroom again."

"But it wasn't your fault. The judge made the decision, Pop, not you. Why are you blaming yourself?"

His eyes were glazed with moisture. "Aye, darlin', why? For 'that way madness lies.' "

"Hey, Honey, thought you were here to make money," Sam called out to her. "You ready to sing, or you gonna listen to that drunk all night? Let's have some music." Others in the room picked up the chant.

"Your audience is awaitin', darlin'," Pop said. He raised the bottle and poured himself another drink.

Later, as she played cards, Honey glanced frequently at the lone figure sitting at the corner table. When the bottle was empty, his head slumped to the table, and he fell asleep.

Luke was awake when she returned to the house that night. Wordlessly, he stood up and walked past her to the door.

"You catch yourself a fish, Sheriff?"

Luke paused with his hand on the doorway. His face was like a stone mask.

"Yeah. And what about you, Miz Honey Behr?" he asked in a voice sharpened with rancor.

A week ago she would have welcomed such an innuendo and flung a nastier one right back at him. Now, she didn't want these bad feelings between them. In the past few days, baiting each other had been forgotten in their shared joy and pride over Josh's recovery. Today they had begun to slip back into that familiar pattern.

"Luke," she called out.

His hand remained suspended on the door. "What?"

"Luke, I'm not whoring," she said softly.

He stood stiffly and did not turn around. "It's none of my business how you spend your Saturday nights. We have an agreement, remember?"

"I won the money playing poker."

"Well, we both know what a skilled poker player you are, Miz Honey."

"Please, Luke, let's not quarrel. I'd like for us to be friends."

After a long pause, he finally said, "I'd like that, too, but under the circumstances, I don't think that's possible." She detected an edge of remorse in his voice.

"Why not?" Honey implored.

A shudder jarred his broad shoulders and ramrod-straight back as he inhaled a deep breath. "It's gone too far. It's reached the point where I can't think of anything except having you. I'm beginning to hate the both of us because of it. We can never be friends until we settle that unfinished business between us."

"Not even for Josh's sake?"

He turned around. His steady gaze searched hers in a soul-searching probe. "Aren't we at this impasse because of our feelings for Josh?"

Suddenly she found herself fighting her own battle of restraint as much as he was. Lord, how she desired this man! Her body ached for his touch, for the thrill, the fulfillment of his lovemaking.

His gaze remained locked with hers, his whole being held in tight rein as he waited for her reply. This was not the time for coyness, for denial. This moment called for absolute honesty.

"If there were no agreement . . . no possibility of Josh coming out of that bedroom at any moment . . . I think we both know we could become *great friends*, Luke."

Now it was in the open! She had admitted that she desired him as much as he wanted her, only a question of honor prevented them from making love.

"Well, Miz Honey, it appears like we've both tossed our ante into a hand of dealer's choice."

He opened the door and departed, leaving her to the mercy of her own aroused passions.

Chapter 14

Sometime during the night, a light rain began to fall. Honey lay in bed listening to the patter of rain drops on the roof and thinking about Luke and the memory of his kiss. As much as she tried to tell herself he was no different from other men, her arguments fell short when she remembered the excitement his touch generated. She even allowed herself to wonder what it might be like married to him—without all the arguments and tension between them. What would it be like to have his love instead of his contempt? How lucky Sarah MacKenzie had been to have known the love of a man like Luke.

Then Honey realized the idiocy of her yearning, for the joys and tragedies of life were unpredictable. Sarah MacKenzie had been raped and murdered; Pop O'Leary's life had been destroyed by guilt. Her mother's ... No, even good people didn't escape the cruelties of life, she reflected before dropping into slumber.

The next morning she rose early to make breakfast and get Josh ready for church but again declined to go with them. Suffering from the effects of his own restless night, Luke did not attempt to hide his displeasure. "You should set an example for Josh," he grumbled.

"If *you'd* spend as much time setting examples for him, instead of expecting other people to do it, maybe he wouldn't have a problem." She folded her arms across her chest. "I figure I get enough disapproving looks from the *good people* of this town during my walks with Cynthia. I don't have to sit on a hard pew for an hour and suffer their collective stares."

"I'd say those stares are well warranted."

"Sure you would. You're as much of a hypocrite as they are. Besides, my going to church was not part of our agreement."

Abandoning the useless argument, Luke grabbed his hat. "Okay, Josh, let's go."

"Why do I have to go to church? Honey isn't," Josh said. " 'Sides, it's no fun."

Luke glared at Honey with another see-what-you-done-now look. "Josh, you can't expect everything in life to be fun. Besides, it's important that you learn about God."

"Then why can't Amigo come? It's 'portant he learns about God, too."

The toll of the church bell ended any further discussion. Sighing in exasperation, Luke clasped Josh's hand. "Let's go." When Amigo started to follow, Luke pointed a finger at him. "You stay here."

Amigo stopped on the stoop and stretched out with his head on his paws. Honey walked out on the porch and sat down on the stoop beside him. Lovingly, she began to scratch him behind the ears. He shifted over and put his head on her lap. Together, they watched the two figures walk up the street.

"Amigo, old friend," she said affectionately, "church is no place for outcasts like us."

When Luke and Josh returned an hour later, Luke headed back to the jailhouse. Honey decided the time had come to begin teaching Josh the alphabet.

The youngster soon became fascinated with the new game of copying her printed letters and pronouncing their sounds. After several repetitions, he was able to identify most of the letters from A to L without prompting from her. She smiled with satisfaction at his progress, and as a reward for his good work, she agreed to join him in a game of marbles.

A short while later, oblivious to the damp ground beneath her, Honey stretched out on her stomach, squinted with one eye, and took aim at the crimson agate marble within the marked circle. "Okay, sonny boy, my Black Beauty's gonna knock that big Blood Alley marble of yours right out of there," she boasted. Amigo hobbled over and sniffed at the large agate in the hastily drawn circle in the mud. "No fair, Amigo, get out of the way." With a flip of her thumb, she launched her marble.

"You missed!" Josh giggled with pleasure. He stretched out, took aim with a green marble, and knocked aside her black aggie.

Honey raised herself to her hands and knees. "Okay, you win, but you had Amigo's help."

She glanced up. A short distance away, four women watched them with disapproval. "Good morning, ladies. Care to join us?" Honey asked.

"Well, I never!" Clarabelle Webster declared. "Come, girls." The women marched off in a huff.

Grinning, Honey winked at Josh. "Okay, sweetheart, one more game, then we'll go down to the river and clean this mud off us."

Luke was standing outside of the Long Branch, talking to Pop O'Leary, when he saw the four women headed in his direction. It was too late to avoid them. "What the hell do they want?" he mumbled under his breath.

"Top of the marnin' to you, ladies," O'Leary said pleasantly as he doffed his hat. Clarabelle Webster drew back in disdain and looked down her long nose at him. "Mr. O'Leary," she acknowledged.

Luke touched a finger to his hat. "Ladies, what can I do for you?"

"Sheriff, we insist you do something about that woman," Clarabelle Webster declared.

"What woman, Mrs. Webster?" Luke knew damn well the mayor's wife was referring to Honey.

"She's over there now, wallowing in the mud like swine," Myrtlelee Quinn added.

"It's disgusting," the banker's wife interjected.

"What is disgusting, Mrs. Douglas?" Luke asked politely.

The four women exchanged knowing glances. "That woman's conduct," Helen Douglas declared.

"What woman?" Luke repeated patiently, which was enough to bring a chortle from Pop.

"That woman who is living in your house, Sheriff MacKenzie," Myrtlelee Quinn said. She crossed her arms over her enormous bosom. "Her conduct is a disgrace."

"And a bad influence on your son," Clarabelle Webster added.

Luke glanced at the fourth woman who had not said anything. "Do you also have a complaint, Mrs. Wright?"

"Well, Pastor Wright is concerned that she hasn't been in church for the past two Sundays," Nancy Wright said timidly.

Helen Douglas smiled triumphantly. "See, that's what we mean."

"There's no law requiring church attendance, ladies. If there were, the jails would be filled."

"Well, my husband said she frequents the Long Branch regularly," Helen Douglas piped in.

"And how would he be knowin' that, darlin'?" Pop O'Leary asked innocently. He wanted to add that the banker must have noticed Honey on his regular Saturday night visits to Miss Lily's room.

"Mr. O'Leary, this does not concern you," the mayor's wife said. "Although I think the town would be better off without you and that woman."

"Faith and begorra! So 'tis me that be annoyin' you, too. Would there be any others to be addin' to your

list, ladies? 'Twould make the good sheriff's job easier
to run all of us out of town on the same rail."

"Humph," Clarabelle Webster grunted.

"Ladies," Luke interjected, "Miss Behr intends to
leave Stockton as soon as I can find a housekeeper to
take care of my son. Until then, I can't see where she's
breaking any city ordinance."

"Mr. Grange at the general store implied she stole
merchandise from him," Myrtlelee said smugly.

"And don't forget, she threatened me," Clarabelle
added.

"She took a five-cent candy cane for Josh, and Jeb's
been paid for it. As for her threat to you, Mrs. Webster, it was made out of concern for the irresponsible
way you handled my son."

"Bravo, Sheriff," Pop O'Leary shouted.

Clarabelle's glasses dropped off her nose. O'Leary
reached out and caught them before they could fall to
the ground.

"There you be, darlin'," he said with a cherubic
grin as he centered them on the bridge of her nose.

"Well, I've never!" Clarabelle said, aghast. In tandem, each of the three other women drew a hand to
their mouths and gasped. "My husband will hear
about this." Shocked and indignant, Clarabelle pivoted and stomped away. Her three confederates followed.

"Well done, Sheriff," Pop commended with a slap
to Luke's back. "Will you be allowin' me to buy you
a small nip to toast the moment, Luke me boy?"

"I'd like to, Pop, but I'm on duty."

"Weel then, would you be considerin' buyin' me
one, an' I'll be doin' the toastin' for you."

"Later, Pop."

As Luke walked away, he thought about the four
women. Damnit, Flint was right, Luke reflected.
Women were nothing but trouble. He suddenly
stopped and shoved back his hat. *Wallowing in the mud
like swine! What in hell were they talking about?*

* * *

Hoping she would find a stone big enough to sit down on, Honey hopped from one to another along the muddy river bank. Occasionally she missed, and her foot sank into the soft mud. Finally, she spied a large rock and sat down.

Fed by a spring higher in the mountains, the river was one of a multitude of narrow waterways that crisscrossed the sprawling California countryside on their passage to the sea. Most of those same rivers and streams had been ravaged and fished out almost two decades earlier by the assault of the gold rush; however, this particular river, deep in the woods and less than a mile from his home, was a favorite fishing spot of Luke.

Honey removed her muddy shoes and hose, then leaned over and washed them off. "Josh, give me your shoes and I'll clean off the mud."

Josh ignored her. Barefoot, he was running up and down the muddy river bank with a barking Amigo.

Smiling, Honey leaned back on her elbows and watched them. Josh was having too much fun to stop him. Besides, what difference did it make anyway; it was only mud. It would always wash out later.

"Be careful, sweetheart. And don't allow Amigo so close to the water. If he fell in, he might not be able to swim because of his sore leg."

"Sure he could," Luke said suddenly from behind her. She turned her head in surprise; she had not heard him approach. "Everybody can swim."

"Well, I can't," she declared.

"I figured someone as slippery as you would take to water like a *bear* to *honey*."

"I thought you were through with your bear jokes."

"Yeah, I'm working on honey ones now."

"I've already heard them all."

"And you just can't bear another one," he mocked.

"That does it, Sheriff." She reached down, picked up a handful of mud, and let it sail. It hit him in the middle of his chest.

Luke looked down at the big stain on the front of his shirt. "Lady, that was a mistake."

Seeing the dangerous gleam in his eyes, she knew she was in trouble. She jumped to her feet and started to back slowly away. Luke shucked his gunbelt, pulled off his boots, then picked up a handful of mud.

"Don't you come near me, Luke MacKenzie," she declared.

"You asked for this."

She bent down and filled each hand with the oozing dirt. His pitch splattered the front of her gown. Honey scrambled to her feet and tossed each handful at him, hitting her mark both times.

Mud balls began flying in all directions as Josh gleefully joined the free-for-all, with Amigo yapping and racing back and forth from one person to another.

Finally, with mud on her head and face, her gown streaked from top to bottom, Honey threw up her hands in surrender. "Stop. I give up," she cried, and tried to scramble away.

Before she could bolt, Luke closed the distance between them and swept her up in his arms. "Put me down!" she cried as he waded into the river.

"That's exactly what I intend to do."

"No, please, Luke. I don't know how to swim."

"Then you'll soon learn," he said, reaching midstream.

"No, I don't want to learn. No . . . no!" she screamed but to no avail. He tossed her into the water.

Floundering, Honey came up for air. "Help me, I'm drowning!" she pleaded, struggling to keep her head above water. He didn't make a move in her direction, but quickly ducked his head in the water to get the mud off his own face and hair.

She discovered she could keep her head above water by vigorously splashing her arms and peddling her feet. "Good God! Are you going to let me drown?"

"Just stand up, Honey," he said calmly.

"Stand up? If I could stand up, I wouldn't be . . ." For the first time, she noticed that he was not moving at all. She stretched out her legs and felt a firm base under her feet. "Oh, you're insane," she fumed in anger, discovering the water was only shoulder high. "I could have drowned."

"How? The water isn't over your head. And I was here all the time. Now just relax, and I'll show you how to move your arms and legs."

"Go to hell, MacKenzie." She started to wade back to shore.

Luke began to laugh, which only angered her more. "Oh, shut up," she shrieked and shoved him backward, sending him sprawling. She enjoyed a fleeting moment of satisfaction when he went under. "How do you like a taste of your own medicine, MacKenzie?"

He disappeared. She waited for him to reappear. "Luke?" she called out after several seconds. When there was no reply, she felt a rising panic. Could he have hit his head on a rock? "Luke!" she repeated. She drew a deep breath and submerged herself in the water.

Suddenly she felt his firm hands grasp her waist, and he pulled her against him. She clung to him, and they surfaced, her arms clasped around his neck and her legs trapped between his. Only inches separated their mouths.

She was overwhelmed by his nearness and the strength of his arms. As water dripped from their hair and ran down their faces, she stared deeply into his eyes for a long moment. In their sapphire depths, she saw the intensity of his desire.

"This is madness, MacKenzie," she managed to mumble.

The hunger she saw in his dark-eyed gaze was his only reply as he slipped an arm under her knees and carried her back to the river bank.

Josh and Amigo were waiting for them. The boy

had done a credible job of washing the mud off the dog. "You're all wet," Josh said.

Honey began to shiver. "That's your father's fault."

"Better dry off," Luke warned. "Josh, you and I will hunt up some wood for a fire." Amigo started to follow them. "Son, tell your dog to stay behind with Honey."

"Stay with Honey, Amigo," Josh ordered. For a moment the dog looked from Josh to Honey and back again. She wondered if Amigo was confused or just disappointed. After repeating his command, Josh pointed to a spot near Honey. Amigo hobbled over to her and stretched out, but his head remained erect and his gaze stayed on Luke and Josh until they disappeared into the woods. Then he lowered his head and closed his eyes.

Shivering, Honey raised her skirt and removed her petticoat. After wringing out the wet garment, she vigorously rubbed her hair with the makeshift towel. If not as effective as she would have liked it to be, the effort helped to warm her. Modesty prevented Honey from removing her sodden bodice and skirt, so she wrapped the wet petticoat around her shoulders. Despite its dampness, the makeshift shawl helped; she stopped shivering.

Leaning back against the tree, she closed her eyes, and as she pleasantly recalled the passion in Luke's eyes and the thrill of his embrace, she felt a heated shiver of pleasure throughout her body. She opened her eyes when Amigo began growling.

The dog's head was raised, and his eyes seemed to be riveted on the woods. "What is it, boy?" She sucked in her breath with alarm when a rider emerged from the trees.

Lean but tall in the saddle, the man had a narrow face with several days' growth of whiskers. His thin lips were drawn into a mocking smile as he stared at her from under thick brows knitted together. "Well, how do, little lady." He shifted his gaze to her breasts. " 'Pears you had yourself a swim."

Honey pulled the petticoat tighter around her shoulders. "Yes, I did." She did not remember ever seeing him in Stockton and disliked him on sight. There was an aura of evil surrounding him. He reminded her of Jake Simmons. Amigo lowered his head and lay with his eyes still on the stranger. The man dismounted, and Amigo responded with another low growl.

"Can't you quiet that hound of yours, little lady? I don't cotton much to growlin' dogs."

"And he doesn't cotton much to strangers, mister."

The man laughed. " 'Pears to me like you might like some company."

"Well, you're wrong."

"Naw. A pretty little thing like you? Out here in the woods all by your pretty little self? I think you and me oughta get to know each other better." He stepped closer.

Amigo stood up and began to bark.

"You'd better tell that hound of yours to quit that barkin' or I might have to put a bullet in him," the man said.

The man looked evil enough to carry out the threat. "Quiet, Amigo," she ordered, fearful for the dog's safety.

Amigo ceased barking. With raised hackles, he stared at the stranger warily. "I'd say he's even less fond of you than you are of him," she said lightly. "And that would worry me some if I were you."

The man snorted and lowered his hand to the Colt on his hip. "I'm sure scared, lady."

"Well, there's something else about this dog I should tell you. The sheriff's son is mighty fond of it. So if you harmed his son's pet, I don't think the sheriff would think too kindly of you."

"And I think you're bluffin', lady."

With relief, Honey heard the sound of Josh's laughter nearby. "Sounds like they're returning." She smiled smugly. "Why don't you just stay around and you can ask him yourself."

As the sound of Luke's and Josh's voices grew louder, the stranger climbed back on his horse. "Maybe we'll have the pleasure again, little lady." He rode away just as Luke and the youngster emerged from the trees.

"Who was that?" Luke asked.

Honey shrugged. "Just some stranger riding through."

"You look as white as a ghost. What did he say?" Luke asked.

"Nothing. I'm just cold. Forget the fire, I'm going back to the house."

She picked up her stockings and shoes, then hurried ahead of them.

Chapter 15

Honey passed another restless night lying in bed, thinking about the pleasant afternoon she'd spent with Luke MacKenzie. They had actually gotten through the day without quarreling.

In the morning she introduced the second half of the alphabet to Josh. Once again, he grasped it readily. Before Honey realized it, Cynthia was at the door to begin their morning walk.

The two women stopped to examine the latest fashions from the east in the window of the Ladies Emporium.

"Oh my, isn't that a beautiful jeweled fan?" Cynthia exclaimed.

Honey's attention had been caught by a black lace peignoir. She shifted her glance to look at the pearl-encrusted fan Cynthia was admiring. "Oh, yes, it's lovely. Looks very costly, too," she remarked. She returned her attention back to the dressing gown.

The ornamental weave of the fine fabric appeared as if it would reveal as much as it would cover. She allowed her mind to wander capriciously and visualized herself wearing the gown while Luke held her in his arms. She felt a hot blush as she imagined his kiss, the feel of his hands with only the delicate fabric separating their bodies . . .

"Don't you wish it was yours?" Cynthia said with a deep sigh.

"Yes . . . yes, I certainly do," Honey said wistfully, unaware that Cynthia's attention was still riveted on the fan.

Absorbed in her fantasy, Honey was also oblivious to Luke's presence just a few feet away. As he studied the profile of her exquisite face, his hands clenched into fists, he wondered what thoughts were going through that fascinating mind of hers. Certainly not the same lascivious thoughts as his own. The demons of his carnal lust had run rampant at his first sight of the peignoir. He conjured up an image of Honey dressed only in the gown, her arms reaching out to him, while soft candlelight reflected on the silver blond hair that flowed to her shoulders. He ached to touch her ivory flesh and the dusky nipples shimmering through the black silk.

He glanced down to discover Amigo sniffing at his boots. *That damn dog,* he thought, annoyed. Shoving him away with the side of his foot, he approached the women.

"Enjoying your daily walk, ladies?"

"Good morning, Sheriff. Honey and I were just admiring that fan. I'm afraid neither of us has anything fetching enough to wear with it," Cynthia bemoaned.

He glanced at Honey. *She does,* he thought lewdly. He could imagine her blue eyes peering over the top of the fan while she wore nothing but her naked curves. Just then, she turned toward him, and for a brief moment, his eyes locked with hers. *But that's not what you were admiring, was it, Miz Honey Behr?* He saw the rise of color in her cheeks and guessed she suspected his thoughts, but she returned his gaze unflinchingly.

Dammit! She was too much woman for his or her own good!

"Hey, Josh," he said, "do you want to come to the

livery with me? I have to saddle up Alamo."

"Sure. Can Amigo come, too?"

Luke cast a disgruntled look down at two sets of eager eyes and a wagging tail. "I suppose so."

Honey smiled with pleasure as she watched the tall man match his strides to the small boy's, and the dog hobbled behind them.

After finishing their walk, Honey said good-bye to Cynthia and hurried back to the Ladies' Emporium to price the fan. It would be the perfect gift to give her friend when the baby was born. Upon leaving the emporium, she passed a man lounging against the front of the saloon and recognized him as the stranger who had spoken so insultingly to her the previous day at the river.

He doffed his Stetson. "Well, good morning, Miz Blondie," he said with a smirk. She sallied past him without looking at him or acknowledging the greeting.

After getting money from the house, she was about to return to the emporium when Luke arrived leading his dun mustang by the reins. Josh was perched proudly in the saddle. "Luke, I have a favor to ask of you," she said in a half whisper.

"Yeah? What is it?" He tied the horse to a hitching post.

"Will you watch Josh for a few more minutes?" She stepped closer to him to prevent Josh from overhearing her. "I want to go back to the emporium to buy Cynthia that fan she admired. I'm afraid if Josh knows, he'll tell her about it."

"All right. How much does it cost?"

"Seven dollars."

His mouth gaped open. "Seven dollars for a fan?"

"It's encrusted with pearls."

"Why don't you just buy a plain fan and paste some of your fake jewelry on it?"

Honey ignored the gibe. "Cynthia admired this one, so I'm sure she would love it."

"I hope you know what you're doing." He reached

into his pocket and started to extract some coins.

"I have my own money to pay for it," she said, stopping him.

"Oh, that's right. Easy come, easy go, right, Miz Honey?"

Her eyes flashed with devilment. "I've figured you out, MacKenzie. It embarrasses you to do something nice; that's why you hide behind nasty remarks."

"I've got nothing to hide. Sounds like more of that hogwash you've been reading in that magazine Doug Nelson gave you."

"I don't need any book to figure *you* out, MacKenzie," she said lightly.

Privately Luke admitted that the little vixen had his number, and the conversation was becoming too dangerous for comfort. "Well, hurry up. Matt's gone to Sacramento for a couple days, so I have to get back to work."

"I wouldn't want to distract you from your duty, Sheriff MacKenzie. The good people of this town are in need of guidance." She hurried away.

For a long moment, he watched her swaying hips and thought about the kisses they had shared. Lord, kissing her had been a damn fool thing to do! Now he had begun to do his thinking with what hung between his legs. He quickly untied the horse's reins. "Guess there's time for another short ride, Josh."

"Hooray! Did you hear that, Amigo?" Josh said to the dog on the ground. "Can Amigo ride, too?"

As he picked up the dog and handed him to Josh, Luke turned back for another long look at Honey's retreating figure.

The emporium's owner made no secret of her disapproval of Honey, but she had no qualms about taking her money. After the snooty-nosed proprietress agreed to keep the purchase of the fan a secret from Cynthia, Honey counted out seven gold dollars. "I would like it gift wrapped, please."

"If you want it gift wrapped, that will be an additional five cents," the woman informed her. "And I won't be able to do it now. I have other customers." She glanced at Myrtlelee Quinn, who had just entered the shop. The two women rolled their eyes.

Honey chose to ignore them. She put down another coin. "Gift wrap it please, and I'll come back for it later. Good day, ladies," she said saucily and sauntered out the door.

Smiling, Honey left the Ladies' Emporium and walked briskly down the street. She slowed her steps at the sight of the obnoxious stranger now lounging in front of the bank. Trying to avoid eye contact with him, she glanced into the plate glass window of the bank and gasped in alarm when she saw two men inside with drawn weapons pointed at the teller.

Suddenly, a hand was clamped hard over her mouth. She struggled against the powerful grip of the stranger's arm as he forced her through the bank door.

After whirling her around and seeing that his actions had been unobserved by anyone on the street, he kicked the door shut.

"You keep that pretty little mouth of yours closed, Blondie, or you ain't never gonna open it again. Understand?"

When she nodded, he took his hand away from her mouth, and she sucked in a gasping breath as he shoved her into the corner. "Now just stay there and mind your manners, Blondie." Turning to the two armed men, he grumbled, "What's takin' so long in here?"

"This yokel don't know the combination to the safe, and the guy in charge went to lunch. What in hell were you doin', Slim? You were suppose to be watchin' the bank."

"Well, I didn't see him leave. He musta gone out the back door," Slim said.

"I think we should ride out of here."

"Naw, we'll wait till he gets back. Can't be much longer."

The man offered no further argument, but the third outlaw picked up the dispute. "Oh, come on, Slim, what if someone decides to come in here before he gets back?"

"You've got a yellow streak up your back as wide as a skunk, Harry," Slim snapped. "You and Dallas hunker down behind that desk and stay out of sight." The two men did as ordered, and Slim turned to his hostages.

"Remember, if one of you makes a wrong move, it'll be all over for the both of you," Slim warned.

"Yes—yes, sir," the teller said weakly. Honey saw that poor Bernie Brewer was trembling so much he could hardly speak.

Then Slim cast his narrow glare on her, and snarling maliciously, he grabbed her arm in a painful grasp. "Did you hear me, Blondie?"

Honey nodded. She prayed that no one would come into the bank. If luck would have it, maybe the outlaws would get what they had come for and get out of town. With Luke's deputy gone, she didn't want him to take on the three gunmen alone.

Her hopes sank when she heard footsteps on the wooden planks outside. Slim released her arm, drew his Colt, and stepped behind her. "Remember, no dumb moves," he warned. She felt the pistol press against her back.

Laughing at a shared joke, the Calhoun brothers entered the bank. Randy hung back while Jess walked up to the teller.

"Howdy, Miz Honey," Randy said, tipping a finger to his hat.

"Good morning, Mr. Calhoun."

"Where's your manners, Jess? The lady was here before you," Randy said sharply.

"Oh, sorry, ma'am," Jess apologized. He started to step away from the cage.

"Go right ahead. I'm just waiting here for . . . Josh," Honey replied.

"What about you, mister?" Jess asked.

"I'm waiting with her," Slim said. "Got some business with Josh."

Randy looked perplexed, but Jess stepped back to the window. "Came to pick up this week's payroll, Bernie."

"Sorry, Jess, it's in the safe, and Mr. Douglas is at lunch," Bernie said nervously.

"Well, let's go have a drink and come back later, Jess," Randy said. "See you later, Bernie. 'Bye, Miz Honey."

As soon as the two young cowboys left, Slim sheathed his pistol. "You did real good, Blondie. You're as smart as you are pretty. Think I'm gonna take you along when we leave."

"Why you wanna saddle us with a female, Slim?" Harry asked.

Slim snickered. "If you can't figure it out, I ain't tellin' you."

"Yeah, a female's only gonna slow us up, boss," Dallas added.

"Not for long. Ain't that right, Blondie?" He fondled her breast. "If we had the time, I'd take you into that banker's office and try you out right now."

"Ah, come on, Slim, keep your mind on what we're doin'. You got time for that later," Dallas complained.

"Shut your mouth," he snarled.

Slim backed her into the walled front corner of the bank, pressing her against the hard stone as his hands cupped her breasts. "Been thinking of these milk cans of yours since yesterday. Can't wait to taste 'em," he mumbled.

When she turned her head away from his descending mouth, he grabbed her chin, twisting her head back. She began striking him with her fists, but he quickly wrenched her arms above her head, pinning them to the wall with one hand. As she tried to push her knee into his groin, he pressed her back tighter against the wall and said with a laugh, "I like a little fight in a woman. You keep it up, Blondie, and you could be around longer than I planned." Crushing his mouth over her clenched lips, he slammed her head against the wall.

Stunned and in pain from the blow, she was too dizzy to struggle against his savage grip. His mouth ground mercilessly against hers until she started to choke. On the verge of fainting, she bit his lip, drawing blood, and with a feral growl, he grabbed a fistful of her hair and cruelly wrenched back her head.

She stared into his eyes, narrowed to slits, and saw him curl his bleeding lip into a twisted smile. "Lick it off, Blondie," he ordered.

"No, I won't."

He yanked at her hair again until she wanted to scream. "Lick it, Blondie, or I'll break your neck. Lick it," he ordered.

Writhing in pain and near to gagging, she swiped his bleeding lip with her tongue. "I said you were a smart gal, Blondie. You see now who the boss is? Tonight you're gonna be lickin' a lot more than my lip." He grabbed her hand and pressed it to his arousal. "Feel that, Blondie? Tonight you're gonna suck it dry." She turned away from the malevolence in his eyes. "Tonight, hell! No time like the present, baby." He grabbed her arm and started to pull her toward the banker's office.

"For God's sake, Slim, forget it for now," Dallas said.

"I know what I'm doin'." Shoving Honey into the room, he slammed the door.

As soon as they stepped outside the bank, Randy Calhoun headed down the street. "Where you going?" Jess asked. "Thought we were gonna have a drink."

"I want to find the sheriff. Something funny goin' on at the bank," Randy said. "That stranger don't have no business with Josh MacKenzie—he's just a little boy. And ole Bernie looked scared to death. Miz Honey didn't seem right either."

Jess stopped and grabbed his brother's arm. "Well, let's go back and find out."

"Dammit, Jess, ain't you ever gonna learn? That's for the law to decide."

"Well, if you think there's some kinda trouble, by the time we round up the sheriff, it might be too late."

"Quit arguing, Jess," Randy said, hastening his steps. "There he is now."

Luke had just brought Josh back to the jail with him when the Calhoun brothers approached him. "Howdy, Sheriff MacKenzie," Randy said.

"Mornin', boys. What can I do for you?"

"Something's sticking in his craw, Sheriff," Jess said sheepishly.

Jess did not look him in the eye, and Luke could see the young cowboy was uncomfortable. This was the first time they had seen each other since their near fatal showdown.

"Ask Josh if he's supposed to meet Miz Honey in the bank," Randy said.

"In the bank? No, she went up to the emporium and was coming right back home."

Randy poked Jess in the arm. "See, whatta I tell you?"

"What's this all about, Randy?"

"We just saw Miz Honey in the bank with a stranger. They both said they were waiting for Josh."

"That doesn't make sense," Luke said.

"And I gotta tell you, Sheriff, I sure didn't like the looks of that stranger."

Luke knelt down and spoke to Josh. "Son, you and Amigo go over to Aunt Cynthia's house. Ask her to watch you 'til Honey comes to get you."

"Should I tell Auntie Cyntia to give me lunch?" Josh asked with childish innocence.

"If she's a mind to, son. Better if you wait to be asked. Now run along."

After he watched Josh skip down the street with

Amigo at his heels, Luke went into his office, checked his Colts, and added bullets to his cartridge belt.

"You think the bank's being robbed, Sheriff?" Randy asked.

That possibility was of no consequence to Luke at the moment. The sense of urgency he was feeling had little to do with being a lawman; he was thinking only of Honey's safety. Desperate to get to her, he knew that as a hostage she would be in greater danger than he.

"Sounds like I better get over there. Did you see any other strangers? Inside or outside?"

"No, but that don't mean there weren't any hiding. Bernie Brewer sure looked a mite uncomfortable. Could have been a gun to his back," Jess added.

"See any sign of Wes Douglas?"

"Bernie said he was out to lunch. Maybe Wes was being held in his office and Bernie was just coverin'. "

"Well, thanks, boys. I appreciate it," Luke said. "I'll check it out."

"Ain't you gonna find Matt Brennan first?" Randy asked.

"He's out of town."

"Then we're coming with you, Sheriff," Jess Calhoun spoke up. "No telling how many of them there are."

"Jess, I told you, I'm the law here. I don't want any citizen of Stockton getting hurt by taking chances that I'm being paid to take."

"Our pa's money's in that bank, Sheriff." Jess flashed a sheepish grin. "Besides, I owe you a favor."

"Well, I can't stay here arguing with you. Remember, no shooting unless it's absolutely necessary. Raise your right hands and I'll swear you in as deputies."

Moments later, the three men hurried up the street as Wes Douglas stepped out of the diner. "Well, that answers *that* question," Luke said. "Wes, hold up there," he called out.

Luke quickly related Randy's suspicions. The

banker mopped his brow. "Oh my, a bank robbery! You've got to stop it, Sheriff. There's a lot of money in the safe."

"Give me the key to the back door. I'll go in that way."

"You can't get in there without being seen or heard," Randy said.

"I sure as hell can try. They'll probably think it's the banker returning."

"They're expecting us to come back for the payroll, Sheriff," Jess piped in. "What if we go in the front door same time as you're going in the back?"

"That makes good sense, Jess. If you distract their attention, maybe I could slip in unnoticed." Luke hesitated, then said grimly, "It might get you killed, too—or anybody they've taken hostage."

He swept his glance along the street near the bank. "Two of those horses in front of the Long Branch are yours, aren't they?"

"Yep, the dun and the sorrel," Randy said.

"Don't recognize that black stallion. Any strangers in the Long Branch?" Luke asked.

Randy shook his head. "Not while we were there. And that black was at the hitching post when we rode in."

"And I don't remember ever seeing those two hitched in front of the feed store before or that gray in front of the doc's office either."

"Think I've seen Joe Carter riding that gray," Randy said, "but I won't swear to it."

"There's a couple more horses farther down the street that don't look familiar to me. I don't see any strangers lounging around on the street, so I make it anywhere from three to six of 'em, inside. I just wish we knew how many of them we're up against."

Chapter 16

⌒◯◯◯⌒

The Calhoun brothers casually entered the bank.
"I told you, Jess, one drink is enough. And
you sure slugged that one down," Randy said in
feigned irritation. "We gotta stick to business and get
that payroll back to the ranch."

"Ah, shut up, Randy, you're always—" Jess
stopped when he saw that neither Honey nor the
stranger were in the room. They looked at each other
then toward the closed door of the office.

"Douglas get back yet?" Jess barked.

"Not yet, Jess," Bernie said. Perspiration dotted his
brow.

Meanwhile, at the rear of the building, Luke drew
his Colt, then quietly turned the key in the lock and
carefully opened the door just enough to slip through.
Relieved to discover no one stationed at the back
door, he flattened himself against the wall and listened as Jess's voice carried to his ears.

"Goddammit, we ain't got all day to waste while
Wes Douglas fills his belly."

"Why—why don't you go to the diner and hurry
him along?" Bernie stuttered.

"Why the hell don't *you*?" Jess shouted, slamming
his fist down on the cage.

Peeking around the corner, Luke saw Randy and Jess but no sign of Honey or a stranger. Everything appeared normal. Then he tensed as he spied two gunmen crouched behind the desk. Their attention was fixed on Jess's performance.

Only two of them, Luke thought. He could take them easily. He shifted his worried glance to the office door, wondering if there were more men behind it. More important, where was Honey?

Damn those bastards! he thought in frustration, fearing for her safety. When he broke through that office door, he would have to go in with his guns blazing.

He shimmied along the wall, and when he reached the office door, he heard muffled sounds coming from the other side. Seeing that Jess's tirade continued to distract the outlaws, Luke made eye contact with Randy, nodded toward the desk, and held up two fingers. Then he drew his other pistol.

Inside the office, Honey had momentarily freed herself from Slim's grip, but he grabbed her arm and began to twist it. "Open my fly," he said.

"No, I won't," she said through gritted teeth as she struggled against his powerful grasp.

Increasing the pressure, he drove her to her knees. "Open it, I said."

"No," she screamed as loudly as she could just before the excruciating pain became too much to bear, and she felt herself being engulfed by blackness.

At the sound of her scream, Luke kicked in the office door, just as Randy reached for his pistol and yelled to Jess, "Two behind the desk, get—"

Before Randy finished the sentence, Jess's pistol cleared its holster. Instantly the sound of gunfire and splintering wood erupted simultaneously as he fanned several shots into the desk. Struck by two bullets, Dallas fell back mortally wounded. Harry immediately raised his hands in surrender.

Slim jerked around when Luke crashed through the door. The sight of Honey's slumped figure on the floor momentarily distracted Luke, giving the gunman enough time to draw and fire. Luke felt a searing pain as a bullet slammed into his shoulder. He dove aside, rolled onto his stomach, and fired several shots from both pistols. Slim was dead before he hit the floor.

With the return of light came a sense of tranquility; Honey knew the nightmare had passed before she even raised her eyelids and met a sapphire gaze.

"Luke." He was holding her in his arms on the floor of the bank office.

"How are you feeling, Jaybird?" The sight of his tender smile brought tears to her eyes.

"Oh, Luke." The memory of the pain and fright of her recent torment flashed before her eyes. "Did he . . . did he . . . ?" Unable to finish the question, she buried her head against his chest.

She felt the comfort of his hand on her head. "You're safe now. Nobody's going to hurt you."

Honey drew a deep breath and sat up. It was then that she saw the stain on his shoulder. "Oh, dear Lord! What happened to you?"

"It's just a graze. A bullet peeled off some skin, that's all."

"A bullet?" Her eyes were wide with distress. "You could have been killed!"

"Do you feel strong enough to stand up?" he asked.

"Of course." She winced when he took her arm to help her rise.

"What's wrong with your arm?" He looked so solicitous she wanted to hug him.

She tried to sound as casual about her injury as he had about his. "It's nothing. That Slim fellow twisted it a little."

"Apparently enough to cause you to black out. Well, he won't be hurting anyone again." She followed his glance to the other side of the room and saw the man she remembered as Harry now in handcuffs. Randy and Jess Calhoun were standing near a body lying on the floor.

"Is that . . . Slim?"

"*Was* Slim, you mean," Jess Calhoun said. "He ain't good for nothing much more than pushing up daisies now, Miz Honey."

She could only guess that the brothers had somehow helped Luke. She offered a weak but grateful smile. "I guess we all owe the two of you a debt of gratitude."

"We didn't do anything that anybody else wouldn't have done," Randy said.

"You'll get an argument from me on that one, Randy," Luke said. "Come on, Honey, let's get you over to Doc Nelson's."

"Before *you* bleed to death," Honey said, her spirits considerably buoyed.

As they passed through the bank, she was relieved to see that Bernie Brewer had not been harmed. Wes Douglas was sitting at the desk moping his brow. Dallas's body lay on the floor. "Will you boys take the prisoner and lock him up for me?" Luke asked the Calhouns. "Wes, I'll send Del Quinn to pick up these bodies."

Douglas stood up and came over to shake Luke's hand. "Thank you, Sheriff. The town's beholden to you."

"You're thanking the wrong man, Wes. If it hadn't been for Randy and Jess there, Lord only knows what might have happened."

Wes thanked Randy and shook his hand, then slowly did the same to Jess. It was apparent the banker had not forgotten the incident with the horses and carriage; Honey could see how difficult it was for the banker to give the young hellion his proper due.

"Your pa's going to be real grateful you saved his payroll," Wes said.

"Yeah, otherwise he might have started having second thoughts about keeping his money in this bank." Jess grinned broadly and doffed his hat. "Have a good day, Mr. Douglas."

Wes shook his head as he watched the young cowpoke saunter away. "You think that boy'll ever make something of himself, Sheriff?"

"Difficulty will lie in keeping him alive till he does." Luke winked at Honey. "Let's get you to the doctor, Jaybird."

The appearance of Randy and Jess Calhoun with a handcuffed prisoner between them had brought the citizens of Stockton outside, and they were now gathered on the street in front of the bank. As soon as Luke appeared leading Honey by the arm, the crowd closed in around them.

"She involved in the holdup, Sheriff?" Jeb Grange asked.

"Wouldn't that be more to your actions, Mr. Grange?" Honey responded to the storekeeper.

"Are you all right, darlin'?" Pop O'Leary asked with concern. Lily was standing beside him, looking just as troubled as Pop did.

Honey smiled at them. "I'm fine. Nothing to worry about."

In the meantime, Luke was besieged with questions from the curious spectators.

"Three men tried to hold up the bank. Miss Behr was a hostage," Luke said.

"Hostage, indeed!" Myrtlelee Quinn scoffed. "She probably planned the whole thing." Several in the crowd grumbled their agreement. Others just remained silent and curious.

"It's over now, so you all can go back to your homes or businesses," Luke announced.

"Luke, you're bleeding," Lily suddenly cried out. Honey glanced at the brunette in surprise. There was almost an intimacy to her tone.

"Just a scratch, Lily," Luke said. "Will you let us through please?" The crowd opened a path for them, then followed the short distance to Doug Nelson's office.

Just as they approached, Doug appeared at the door. "What happened? I was in the middle of stitching up the forehead of little Jenny Carter, so I had to finish."

"An attempted holdup at the bank. Couple of outlaws were killed."

"So, those legendary six-shooters of Sheriff Luke MacKenzie have blazed another tale of the West," Doug remarked as they entered his office.

"You here to heal or harp, Doc?" Luke replied with a long-suffering sigh. "How about checking out Honey's arm? One of those outlaws roughed her up."

Genuinely concerned, Doug said, "Let's check out that arm, Honey."

"It's nothing serious, Doug." Honey felt embarrassed even to be there.

"I'll have to ask you to step outside, Sheriff, until my examination is over."

Exasperated that the two grown men stood there making their usual banter while Luke might be bleeding to death, Honey said, "Doug, Luke needs attention more than I do. He's been shot."

"Shot?" Doug came over to them and saw the bloody arm that Luke had concealed since entering. "Jesus, Luke, looks like you've lost a lot of blood. Why in hell didn't you tell me! Sit on the examining table so I can have a closer look."

"Ladies first, Doc."

"Nonsense!" Honey declared. "I'm going home. Take care of him." She started to leave.

"Hey, hold up there. I want to examine that arm of yours as soon as I finish with Luke. How about helping him get his shirt off?"

"How come she doesn't have to leave the room when you examine *me*?" Luke demanded cantankerously.

"I like looking at her while I work," Doug replied.

Honey rolled her eyes and pulled the shirt over Luke's head. "You aren't modest, are you, MacKenzie?" She gently eased the garment off his wounded arm.

"I think he feels naked without that silver star. I'll pin it to your bare chest if that will help you relax,

Sheriff," Doug said as he began to clean the wound.

Standing in the background, Honey could not take her eyes off Luke: his wide, muscular shoulders, corded biceps, and bronzed chest covered with crisp dark hair were as magnificent as she had remembered.

"Looks like you were lucky, Luke. The bullet only grazed you," Doug remarked.

"That's what I said. Ouch!" Luke winced as Doug applied a disinfectant to the wound. "I think you're enjoying this, you sadistic bastard."

"I am. It's why I went into medicine." Frowning, Doug examined the wound, which had begun to bleed again. "The bullet chewed away a lot of flesh, Luke. I'm afraid I'll have to take a few stitches to close it up."

"Oh, for God's sake, Doc, I've been shot before. Just slap a bandage on it."

Doug ignored him and handed Honey the basin of water he had been using to clean the wound. "Sponge that blood off his chest while I get a needle and thread."

She stepped between Luke's thighs. Only the solid edge of the table prevented their bodies from touching. Her nostrils were tantalized by the smell of his bay rum shaving soap, and her heartbeat quickened at the feel of his warm flesh beneath her fingertips. She sensed the power in the taut muscles that contracted as she moved the sponge across his chest. Nervously she licked her dry lips and tried to stem the rising heat that had begun to suffuse her senses.

With his jaw clamped tight, his mouth in a thin-lipped slit, Luke sat immobile, his eyes fixed on a distant spot across the room. But despite his impassive mien, he was fighting his own inner battle for restraint. He ached to reach out and pull Honey into his arms. With the mere brush of her hips or casual slide of her fingertips, he felt his blood surge through him. Inhaling deeply, he tried to stop the harsh, erratic breath that caused his chest to ache. By the time she stepped away, he wanted her so badly that perspiration flecked his brow.

"You want it sitting up or lying down?"

"What?" Stunned, he looked at Doug, who was poised above him with a threaded needle in hand. "Oh, you mean the stitches."

Doug frowned. "Luke, are you sure you're feeling okay? You look like hell." He grasped Luke's wrist to count the pulse beats. "Dammit, man, your pulse is racing."

"I'm fine," Luke said uneasily. "Just stitch me up so I can get out of here."

"Then I want you to lie down and rest."

"Yeah, yeah, I will," Luke grumbled impatiently. He had no intention of going to bed. He knew damn well what had set his pulse to racing—the little blond temptress who was standing in the corner.

As soon as Doug finished, he took Luke's pulse again. "Well, thank goodness it's slowed down. I still want you to rest for the night."

"I'll do that, Doc," Luke said, pulling his shirt back on. "Why don't you check out Honey now?" He raised a hand to ward off Doug's next remark. "Yeah, I know. I'm getting out of here."

Outside, he found himself again deluged with dozens of questions from curious citizens. He was relieved when Honey finally joined him.

"What did Doug say?" he asked as they walked back to the house.

"He said my arm's fine. It's going to be sore for a few days and he gave me this balm to put on it." She held up a yellow tin. "Luke, Doug's very concerned about you. Are you sure you're all right? I think you should heed his advice and stay in bed. Take my bed and I can crawl in with Josh tonight. I'm sure he won't mind."

"My bed's larger, Jaybird," he said with a suggestive grin.

She blushed. "I believe Doug said you need your

rest, Sheriff. I suspect that would not be your intention if I did."

To Honey's relief, they reached the house, and Luke couldn't pursue the provocative subject further. Josh sat on the front stoop with his chin in his hands. Amigo barked in greeting, and Josh glanced up.

At the sight of them, his little face brightened. He jumped up and raced over to them. "Daddy! Honey! We heared all about the bank robbery."

Luke swooped him up in his good arm. "And just what did you *heared*?" he teased.

Josh held up five fingers. "I heared that this many mean men tried to rob the bank and you stopped them."

"Well, son, I'm afraid the story was slightly exaggerated. There were only three men. And I had a lot of help."

The front door slammed as Cynthia hurried out of the house. "Are you okay? When I heard about the robbery, I just had to bring Josh over to find out what happened," she said, all aflutter.

"Attempted robbery," Luke corrected with a trace of smugness. "This damn dog!" he grumbled, shoving aside Amigo, who was licking his boots. He bent down to set Josh on his feet. "Well, I must see to my prisoner. Ladies." Josh and Amigo followed him.

"Are you really okay, Honey?" Cynthia asked, still breathless. "When I heard you had been a hostage, I was afraid I'd have my baby on the spot."

Honey clasped her hands. "I'm fine. Truly I am." Frowning, she asked worriedly, "Cynthia, I thought Josh looked frightened when we first arrived. How did he react when he heard the news?"

"The little darling turned as white as a sheet when the Calhoun brothers came back to the jail without any sign of Luke or you. He sat on the stoop without saying a word until now. I was afraid he had kind of withdrawn again. Reminded me of old times, Honey."

"The poor sweetheart must have been afraid he'd

lose his father." Honey drew in a deep breath. "I've been considering leaving here soon, but I guess he's still far from being cured."

"Oh, Honey, the change in him is miraculous, and you can't blame him for being frightened at hearing his father was in danger. Any child would be." Cynthia smiled with relief. "But you're right, dear, he still needs your help. So no matter what, you can't leave Stockton yet."

Honey thought about the growing sexual tension between her and Luke. If she remained much longer, the outcome would be inevitable: she would end up sleeping with a man who desired her but obviously disliked her—she would become the whore he already believed her to be.

"Yes, I'm afraid you're right, Cynthia." She sighed, recalling the recent look of fright on Josh's young face. "No matter what I think, it's too soon to leave Stockton now." Slipping her arm through Cynthia's, she smiled, "Come on, dear, I'll walk you home."

After thanking Randy and Jess for their help and sending them on their way, Luke took Josh back to the house. Honey was subdued during the rest of the afternoon, and Luke figured she had begun to feel the aftershock of her harrowing experience. He left as soon as they finished supper and returned to the jail with a plate of food for his prisoner.

The prisoner offered no information other than his name. Luke planned to transport him to Sacramento the following day and turn him over to the U.S. marshal. At least he wouldn't have to worry about Josh's welfare while he was gone. He knew Honey would take good care of the boy in his absence.

After a short time, he started to make his rounds of the town. He encountered Doug Nelson, who was just leaving his office for the day. The doctor insisted Luke join him for a drink.

The two men entered the Long Branch and sat down at the nearest table. Carrying glasses and a whiskey bottle, the bartender shuffled over to them. "Good job today, Sheriff."

"Thanks, Sam. By the way, the next time the Calhoun boys come in, their drinks are on me."

"Gotcha." Sam filled the glasses and started to walk away.

"Leave the bottle, Sam," Doug said. Wordlessly, the bartender put the bottle down and returned to the bar.

Luke cast an ambivalent glance at the bottle of whiskey. "You figurin' on a long night, Doc? Don't expect much help from me. I'm on duty."

"Duty," Doug said, disgusted. "You just won't take your doctor's advice, will you?"

"Man's got to earn a living, Doc."

Doug's face had settled into grim lines. "What in hell are you doing with that badge on your chest, Luke? Hoping for an early grave?"

"Of course not. Never planned on being a lawman. My love's ranching. I ended up with this star because I followed a lead here to California."

"What kind of a lead?"

"Heard some of the gang who killed my wife and mother had headed to California. When the lead ran cold, I became a lawman. Thought I might be able to pick up some word about them that way."

"Yeah, well if you keep wearing that badge, you're liable not to pick up anything except a gunshot in the back."

"Appreciate your concern, Doug, but I can take care of myself." Luke hesitated, then asked, "Tell me, Doc, you ever take advice, or do you just give it?"

Doug shrugged. "Depends."

"It's getting late. Why don't you head home to that pretty wife of yours?"

Doug leaned across the table. "I'm putting it off as long as I can. It's rough, Luke. Cynthia's too far along for us to, ah, well . . . it's hard right now." He shook his head. "She's so beautiful, Luke. I have to force myself not to touch her. Do you have any idea what it's like not to be able to make love to your wife?"

"Yeah, I know just what it's like," Luke said bitterly.

Doug became the picture of contrition. "Ah, shit, Luke, I'm sorry. I forgot about Sarah . . . and all."

"Wish I could."

For a long moment the two men stared grimly down at their drinks. Doug finally picked up his glass and gulped down the contents. Then he poured himself a refill and shoved the bottle toward Luke.

"It's over, Luke. You're trying to follow a cold trail. You've admitted as much yourself. It's time to let it go."

"It's not over yet." Luke swallowed his drink and stood up. "I've got to finish my rounds."

"Yeah." Doug rose too and followed him outside. "Remember, take your doctor's advice. Go home and get some rest."

"Physician, heal thyself," Luke quoted. He slapped Doug on the shoulder and strode off.

Back at the jail an hour later, he was considering bedding down for the night when Delmer Quinn came into the office. "Here's the personal effects of those two bank robbers."

Luke started to sweep the items into a drawer but slowed his hand when a watch caught his attention. Curious, he picked up the timepiece and examined it more closely. The gold case showed signs of being well-used. Palming the pocket watch, he popped it open. His expression changed to incredulity. His face turned white, and he stared with pained disbelief at the watch.

"Which one had this?" he said in a hoarse whisper to Quinn.

The baffled undertaker shrugged. "I didn't give it much mind. Think it was the thin one."

Luke shoved back his chair. Grabbing the cell keys from a wall hook, he went back and opened the cell. Quinn followed him out of curiosity.

Luke snatched the sleeping prisoner off the cot.

"Wha . . . What?" the confused man asked.

"Who did this watch belong to?"

"I dunno," the man grunted.

Luke picked him up by his shirt front and slammed him against the bars. "I want an answer right now, you sonofabitch, or you're gonna find yourself in the same hole as those two friends of yours."

"All right, all right. It was Slim's."

Luke smashed him against the wall. "Where'd he get it?"

Terrified, Harry cowered in fear. "Said he won it in a poker game from some guy he rode with in Texas."

"A name. I want a name," Luke shouted.

"I don't know," the man whined.

Luke slammed him against the iron bars again. "I said I want a name." He pulled out a Colt and shoved it against Harry's temple. "A name, you little bastard, or I'll splatter your brains all over this cell."

The man began to whimper. "It was, ah . . . Charlie. Yeah, that's it. He said the guy's name was Charlie."

"Charlie what?"

"I don't remember," he said trembling. "I'm telling you the truth."

"Think fast, you sonofabitch. My finger's getting itchy on this trigger."

The outlaw trembled from fear and desperation. "It was Charlie . . . ah . . ." He looked Luke straight in the eye. "Charlie Walden. Yeah, that was it, Sheriff. Charlie Walden."

"You know where I can find Walden?"

"I never met him. Wouldn't know him if I saw him," the frightened man replied. "Honest, Sheriff, I've told you all I know. Only met Slim a couple of months ago."

"That's your bad luck." Luke released him, and the outlaw slumped to the floor.

Dumbfounded, Delmer Quinn followed Luke back to the office. He had returned to staring at the watch. "You recognize that watch, Sheriff?"

Luke nodded numbly. "This watch was my father's. He gave it to my mother shortly before he died." He stroked the timepiece. "She always wore it on a chain around her neck."

Chapter 17

$\sim\!\!\infty\!\!\sim$

Assuring Honey he would be back the following day, Luke left on the morning stage to take his prisoner to Sacramento. With the shocking events of the bank robbery still vivid in her memory, Honey decided to spend a lazy day just relaxing and nursing her aching arm. She hoped Luke's shoulder felt better than her arm did.

She told Josh there would be no lessons that day, and welcoming the idea of not "playing school" for a change, he thought it would be a good time for them to traipse off into the woods. Preferring to rest a day, she convinced Josh to put the walk off until the following afternoon when her arm would feel better.

By midmorning, she was already bored. Her usual walk with Cynthia did little to change her mood. Honey sat down at the kitchen table to analyze the reason for her bleak feelings and concluded that it all boiled down to Luke: she missed him. Whether they were laughing together or spatting with each other, time spent with Luke was never dull. And with him gone, she felt lonely.

She went over to Cynthia's in the afternoon, and while Josh played with Amigo outside, she and Cynthia made pomander balls for the forthcoming church bazaar.

"After all this work, it will be my luck that I'll have my baby on the day of the bazaar," Cynthia bemoaned as they sat at her kitchen table, sticking cloves into apples. "Then I'll miss all the fun."

"You better not. I don't think any of the good ladies would touch a one if they knew I had anything to do with them. But can you believe this, Pastor Wright asked me yesterday if I'd sell kisses for a dollar," Honey said. She held up a clove-encrusted apple. "Here, this one's done except for a ribbon."

Cynthia took it and began to attach a bright red ribbon to the ball. "Really! What did Luke say?"

"I doubt he even knows."

"Well, I bet when you tell him, he won't like it."

"He doesn't like anything I do. But Luke's not my husband, Cynthia. Furthermore, I don't intend to tell him. I'll just surprise him."

"Oh, you'll surprise him all right." Cynthia looked at her out of the corner of her eye, then continued, "Last year Miss Lily from the Long Branch sold kisses. You two ladies are the only single women in town. Underneath that cleric collar of Pastor Wright beats the heart of a businessman. He knows we made more money on that kissing booth than we did on these pomander balls."

"Do you disapprove of me doing it, Cynthia?"

"Not at all. Just as long as Doug doesn't buy a kiss. Like it or not, if he intends to donate to charity, it will have to be for one of these." Giggling, she held up the ball by its red bow. "Or a jar of Nancy Wright's pickle relish."

"I thought I'd read tarot cards, too," Honey said. "But don't tell Luke. I plan to disguise myself by dressing up like a gypsy."

Cynthia clapped her hands. "Oh, how exciting! I can just picture you. Let me help you with the disguise." Then she added thoughtfully, "You know, I've never had my fortune told." To Honey's surprise,

Cynthia suddenly sobered and took her hand. "Matter of fact, Honey, lately I've been worrying about the future."

"Oh, Cynthia, your baby will be fine if that's what you're thinking about. All mothers-to-be start having doubts when it gets close to birthing time."

"It's not about the baby, Honey. I know everything will be fine. After all, I have the best doctor in the world." Hesitating, she began to chew on her bottom lip. Honey had never seen her friend look so apprehensive. Cynthia was usually cheerful and had a positive attitude, two qualities that endeared her to Honey.

Honey treasured Cynthia's friendship because she had never had a female friend before—had never giggled over a shared secret, exchanged a confidence, taken a morning stroll, or made pomander balls. She suspected that some women in her past had resented her on sight because her looks appealed to men, and others, the snootier ones, liked her even less because of her background.

But Cynthia was a true friend. Since they'd first met, Cynthia had reached out a hand of friendship without ever questioning Honey's background or doubting her integrity. Now, seeing Cynthia's brow creased in a frown, Honey could not help but feel worried. "What's wrong, Cynthia?"

"It's Doug."

"Doug!" It was the last thing Honey expected to hear. "What do you mean?"

Honey watched appalled as Cynthia's eyes filled with tears. "I . . . I don't think he loves me anymore."

"Cynthia, why would you ever think anything that ridiculous? It's clear to anyone that Doug adores you."

"He never kisses me anymore, Honey." Cynthia dabbed at her eyes with her apron. "Oh, he'll give me a peck on my cheek, but he never . . . you know . . . *really kisses* me like he used to. I'm so fat and ugly, he probably can't stand looking at me."

Honey started to giggle, then stopped when she saw Cynthia's shocked expression.

"What are you laughing at?"

Jumping to her feet, Honey walked around the table and knelt down, grasping Cynthia's hands. "Dear Cynthia, do you really believe for one moment that Doug doesn't love you?"

Cynthia hung her head, then peeked up at her. "No, I know he loves me."

"And he's probably counting the days until your baby is born so he *can kiss* you—the way you would like him to."

Honey watched with pleasure as dimples reappeared in Cynthia's cheeks. "You really think so?"

"I certainly do." Honey went back to her chair. "I wonder, do all women in a family way get such dumb notions? I'm sure glad I won't be having any babies."

"Oh, don't be so sure, Miss Honey. I haven't given up on you and our handsome sheriff yet. And I'm going to remind you of this conversation when your stomach's all swollen and you waddle like a duck and Luke MacKenzie has to use a crowbar to pry your hips out of a chair."

"A crowbar?" Honey laughed. "Are you saying that's what Doug has to do?"

"Of course not. He's a doctor, so he surgically removes the arms of the chair."

They both burst into laughter. Then Cynthia suddenly stopped, and Honey smiled to see that her friend's brown eyes had been restored to their former bright luster. "You really think Doug's counting the days until we can—"

"I certainly do," Honey quickly interjected.

When they tired of making the pomander balls, Cynthia insisted Honey and Josh remain for supper. The hour was late when they finally returned home that evening. There was only time to get ready for bed and read Joshua two more chapters of *The Deerslayer*, another of the Leather-Stocking Tales, which were his favorites, before the youngster fell asleep in her lap. She carried him into bed and, with loving tenderness, stared down at his sleeping face. Then she kissed his cheek.

Glancing down, she saw Amigo staring up at her with an anxious look in his eyes and a fiercely wagging tail. "All right, you charmer," she whispered affectionately and lifted him onto the bed. The dog immediately stretched out against Joshua and closed his eyes.

Yawning, she climbed in her own bed and reflected drowsily that the effects from the previous day's bank robbery had taken a greater physical toll on her than she had thought. She closed her eyes and fell instantly asleep.

Eager to start off on the promised walk, Joshua was pesky and impatient the next day until it was time to go. After packing a lunch of sandwiches, fruit, and milk, they finally set off.

Finding a long, narrow stick, Josh said enthusiastically, "This is my long rifle." He pounded his little chest. "I am Natty Bumppo, the great scout. But I am called Hawkeye by my Indian friends."

He pointed to Amigo. "You will be Chiga— Chiga . . . ah, you will be Uncas, the last warrior of the wise Mohicans." The declaration was received by a bark and a tail wag.

"I think you'd be wiser to keep calling him Amigo, or you'll confuse him," Honey advised.

She smiled with amusement at the sight of his little brow creased in a frown of concentration. "And you can be Cora, the woman Uncas died trying to save."

"I think I would rather be Alice. She had a happier fate, Hawkeye."

"Very well, Alice." He raised his long rifle to his chest. "Hawkeye shall lead the way. And you must stay on the trail, for these woods are full of our enemy, the savage Earaboy."

"That's Iroquois, Hawkeye," Honey corrected, amused.

As she walked behind him, Honey considered making the youngster a buckskin shirt and pair of trousers. Although she would never count sewing among her skills, she had mended her own clothes enough times to know how to ply a needle and thread. Perhaps if she spoke to Luke, he would shoot a deer and cure the hide so she could make Josh the outfit.

A short distance farther she had second thoughts about the idea when they came upon an adorable tiny fawn, with a pert white tail, nibbling on some grass. As they came nearer, the animal raised its head and looked at them with gentle, glossy black eyes, then moved away on legs that looked too thin to support it.

"Isn't it darling, Josh—ah, I mean, Hawkeye?"

"I think it's lost its mother," Josh said worriedly, falling out of character. Fascinated, they watched the fawn step slowly into the underbrush.

"No, look." Honey pointed ahead to where a deer had come out of the trees. They watched as the doe nuzzled the fawn possessively. Then Amigo started barking, and the two animals bounded away.

They moved on and stopped on the edge of a bluff that sloped down to the river below. "Oh, what a lovely view. Let's have our lunch here," Honey declared. She laid out the food, and they sat down to eat.

After a while, Honey felt a cool breeze and noticed swiftly moving clouds coming from the north. Still munching on her apple, she said, "I've enjoyed the walk, Josh, but we better get back. It's clouding up for rain."

Scrambling to her feet, she hardly had time to collect her things before large drops started falling. "Let's get out of here."

Within minutes they were soaked to the skin. Honey stopped and glanced around hopelessly. "We have to find cover until the rain stops." The only shelter she could spy was the huge trunk of a fallen oak tree.

With the blanket around them, they huddled together with their backs against the trunk and the tree's limbs as a leafy, but damp, bower over their heads. Honey hugged the shivering boy to her side, with Amigo curled up on his lap.

Throughout the return stagecoach trip from Sacramento, one thought had been foremost in Luke's mind. He reached into his pocket and pulled out the watch that had belonged to his father. He stared morosely at it, remembering the many times he had seen his mother touch the timepiece that hung on a chain around her neck or raised it up to see the time.

Pressing the small catch, he popped it open and read the initials engraved on the inside lid. He traced the letters with a callused fingertip. Andrew Jackson MacKenzie.

Luke had been too young when his father died to remember his face, but he could recall his mother's tender smile when, thinking she was unobserved, she sat rocking and holding the watch to her breast.

He closed the lid, and clenching the watch in his fist, he felt his anger rising. Now he had a clue to the murderer of his mother and Sarah. He had a name: Charlie Walden, the same outlaw who had been harassing the area around Stockton. Luke now had a double reason for wanting to find the man. If Walden himself hadn't led the raid on the ranch, the fugitive probably knew who did. Unfortunately, Luke had only glimpsed the man from a distance and had no idea what Walden looked like—only that the outlaw now hated him for killing his brother and had vowed to seek revenge. The town would never be safe nor the people Luke loved until he succeeded in destroying the scoundrel.

A boom of thunder shattered his meditation, and he became mindful of rain pelting the coach. Luke returned the watch to his pocket and stared grimly out the window. He hadn't even been aware when the downpour had begun. However, the rising fury of the storm held his attention for only a short time before he dropped back into his deliberation. *Now I have a name.*

As soon as they reached Stockton, Luke jumped out of the stage, grabbed his saddlebags, and, with a quick good-bye wave to Will Hutchins, dashed for home.

His clothes were soaked by the time he reached the darkened house. Surprised not to find Honey and Josh there, he quickly changed into dry clothes and started a fire in the stove. Thirty minutes later he had coffee perking and his wet clothes strung out in front of the fireplace.

Finally, he sat down at the kitchen table with a mug of hot coffee. He began to feel uneasy about the whereabouts of Honey and Josh and figured they were holed up somewhere against the storm. He began to pace the floor nervously. After another quarter of an hour, he decided to go look for them.

Seeing Honey's cloak and Josh's poncho hanging on wall pegs in the bedrooms, Luke realized they must have gone out before the storm. After putting on his own poncho, he grabbed their coats and went to find them.

He checked the general store, the diner, the church, the hotel lobby, even the bank. A stop at the jail proved fruitless; Matt Brennan had not seen them since morning. Then Luke cursed himself for his own stupidity; the logical place to look would have been the Nelsons'.

Doug opened the door to his knock. "Luke, what in hell are you doing out in this downpour?"

The question shattered any hope Luke had retained. "They're not here."

"Who?" Doug asked. "Come inside, man, and get out of the rain."

"Thanks just the same, but I need to keep looking for Honey and Josh."

"What's that about Honey and Josh?" Cynthia asked, coming to the door. "For heaven's sake, Luke, come inside."

"I don't want to get your floor all wet."

"It's just water. I can wipe it up."

Reluctantly, Luke stepped inside the house. "I got back about an hour ago, and I've been looking for Honey and Josh. I was hoping they were here."

"Have you tried the general store?"

Luke nodded. "I tried all over town."

He felt even more uneasy when Cynthia's eyes widened in alarm. "Oh, dear! I wonder if . . ."

"What, Cynthia?"

"Honey mentioned this morning that they were going for a walk in the woods."

"Did she say which direction they were headed?"

Shaking her head, Cynthia threw her hands up in dismay. "No. Just that they were going for a hike." She clutched her husband's arm. "Oh, Doug, something must have happened to them."

He slipped his arm around her shoulders. "Now, now, Cindy, just relax. They've probably taken shelter somewhere from the storm."

"God! I don't know where to begin looking," Luke said. He turned to leave.

"Wait, I'm coming with you," Doug declared. "Sweetheart, don't you worry. We'll find them. Honey's got enough sense to get under cover during a storm like this."

"I guess you're right," she said. "But I'd rather wait at Luke's house than here."

Realizing it would be the line of least resistance to agree, Doug nodded. "All right. We'll go back there." He slipped her cloak around her shoulders and covered her head with a scarf. "Let's go," he said and from habit grabbed his medical bag.

With Cynthia huddled against the protection of her husband's body and Luke's firm grip on her arm, the three of them hurried back to Luke's house. But much to his disappointment, the place was still empty.

As he paced the floor, Luke struggled with a dozen possibilites of what might have happened to them. "You don't suppose they've merely lost their way, do you?"

"I don't think so," Doug replied. "I believe they're just waiting out the storm somewhere. After all, Amigo's with them, so he would find his way back here."

"That dumb dog!" Luke scoffed.

"Dogs aren't dumb, Luke. They're a species known as *Canis familiaris*, a domestic descendent from the *Canis lupus*, probably the greatest species of hunters and trackers there are."

"What the hell are you talking about?" Luke grumbled, irritated.

"Wolves."

"Then why not say wolves to begin with? Goddammit, Doc, this is no time for that Latin mumbo jumbo you're always spouting."

"Sorry, pal, just trying to take your mind off your problems." He cast an ingenuous glance at Cynthia.

"Well, I'm not going to stand around doing nothing. I've waited long enough," Luke declared. He grabbed his poncho and pulled it on. "One or both of them could be hurt and need help."

"Why don't you have more trust in our little four-legged friend? Be assured, Luke, he's not running around *crying wolf*."

"Dammit, Doug! I can't just wait out this storm. I'm going to start looking for them while there's still some daylight."

"In which direction?"

"I'll head west and follow the river. Maybe I'll get lucky and ..." He swung his head toward the door. "Did you hear that?"

They all paused to listen. A scratching sounded at the door, then a faint bark.

"Amigo!" Luke rushed to the door and threw it open. The bedraggled dog wobbled in, then shook himself off, sending a spray of water in all directions. Luke ignored the dog and peered through the rain.

He had already rushed outside when Honey staggered out of the trees carrying Josh.

"Is he hurt?"

"Just wet," she said, hugging the boy in her arms tighter.

"And you?" His eyes searched her face until their gazes met and merged for the brief length of an expelled sigh.

"The same." She shivered with cold and weariness.

"Give him to me, Jaybird." His look lingered on her face as he took Josh out of her arms. "Can you make it to the house?"

She closed her eyes when she felt the strength in the arm that slid around her shoulder, drawing her into the protective sanctuary of his embrace as he led her into the house.

Doug and Cynthia hurried to help. "Give Josh to me, Luke. I'll dry him off and get those wet clothes off him," Cynthia said.

Luke handed Josh over to her, then turned to Honey. His relief had yielded to anger. "Don't ever do a damn fool thing like that again! What the hell were you doing wandering around in those woods with my son? You could have both been killed. These goddamn hills are full of wild animals and that murderous Walden gang."

"Calm down, Luke. They're both safe and sound," Doug advised.

"Like hell I'll calm down! That was the goddamnest, dumbest stunt she's pulled to date," Luke ranted.

This sudden, unexpected attack shattered the fortitude that had sustained Honey throughout the ordeal. With head bowed and her shoulders slumped in wretchedness, she bore the viciousness of his tirade. Shivering and choking on her swallowed sobs, Honey managed to mumble, "I'm sorry. I guess I didn't stop to think of the danger."

"No, you never do. If just once you'd stop to think

beyond the moment's pleasure, we wouldn't have all these problems."

Cynthia came back into the room, carrying Josh dressed in dry underdrawers and wrapped in a blanket. "I'm putting this young man in bed."

"I'll do it," Luke said. Still angry, he carried Josh into the bedroom.

"Honey, get out of those wet clothes before you catch pneumonia," Doug said gently.

Tears mingled with the rain on her face. "I'm sorry. I'm so sorry." She rushed into the bedroom and closed the door.

"Oh, the poor dear. I'll help her," Cynthia said.

Honey glanced up when Cynthia slipped into the room. "I'm so ashamed, Cynthia."

"Honey, Luke's just blowing off some steam. He's been worried to death about both of you. You should have seen him. He was pacing the floor like a caged animal." She helped Honey pull the sodden dress over her head.

"No, it's more than that. He hates me, Cynthia. He really hates me. His hate is so tangible I can almost reach out and touch it," Honey said, stepping into her nightgown. She sat down on the bed and began to towel her hair dry.

"That's not true, Honey. I know Luke MacKenzie. He's got a temper, but he forgets his anger as soon as he lets it out." Cynthia began to gather up the wet clothes. "I'll spread out all this wet clothing on the fireplace. You climb in that bed and go to sleep. This will all be forgotten in the morning."

In the next bedroom, Luke finished drying off Amigo. The dog jumped up on the bed, and Josh opened his arms.

"You didn't have to worry 'bout us, Daddy. Amigo knew the way home even in the rain." Josh hugged his beloved pet and lay back. "Amigo's a better Hawkeye than I am." He giggled when Amigo licked his face, then the dog stretched out and closed his eyes. "I love him and he loves me. He loves Honey, too."

Josh yawned and closed his eyes. "And I think he loves you too, Daddy, even if you don't love him." His little voice trailed off as he began to succumb to slumber. "Amigo loves just 'bout everybody he knows 'cepting cats. Amigo don't like . . . cats."

Luke stared down at the face of his sleeping son. This precious child was his life. Earlier, he had been driven to despair at the thought that Josh might have been hurt or had fallen into the hands of Charlie Walden.

Honey had been right about one thing. For too long, he had shut himself out of his son's life. He'd lost cherished moments that could never be regained. In his blindness, he had not tried hard enough to reach the one person who gave his life purpose.

"I love you, son," Luke said softly and bent down and pressed a kiss to the boy's forehead.

Chapter 18

⌒◯◯⌒

She felt hot and sweaty; she was shivering. Honey opened her eyes and, despite the discomfort, finally managed to raise her throbbing head. Dazed, she peered into the darkness. Where was she? Trembling uncontrollably from pain and fever, she could no longer hold up her head. She slumped back, and shocked from the pain, she closed her eyes.

"Luke," she mumbled. Then she was spinning, spinning, spinning.

She felt so hot, so hot.

Honey heard the low hum of voices as she fought her way back to consciousness. Her eyelids felt weighted as she tried to raise them. They fluttered as she tried to focus on the nearest object, but her vision was too blurred to identify it.

"Doc, she's coming to. Come on, Jaybird, open those big blue eyes of yours."

Luke's voice! A wave of warmth swept through her. "Luke," she murmured with a smile. Then she began to spin again.

"She's out again, Doc, but she was conscious for a few seconds. She even recognized me," Luke said.

"Well, that's a good sign," Doug said. "Although

the way you talked to her last night, if I were Honey, I sure as hell wouldn't want to wake up and see your face. Okay, everyone out of here until I complete my examination. That goes for you, too, Cindy."

"Oh, Doug," Cynthia pleaded.

"Cindy, if you want to be helpful, put some water on the stove."

Twenty-four hours had passed since the storm. With Honey and Josh now under his watchful eye, Luke's previous anxiety had dissolved. He slipped an arm around Cynthia's shoulders. "It's clear we're not wanted here. Come on, Cynthia, I'll take care of the water; you read Josh a bedtime story."

By the time Cynthia joined him, the kettle of water on the stove was close to boiling. She sat down beside Luke at the table.

"How's Josh doing?" he asked.

Cynthia flashed her dimpled smile. "The little darling's sleeping like an angel. He's very precious, Luke. I love him, you know."

"I know that, Cynthia, and I'm really grateful for all you and Doug have done for us. Not just the last couple days, but ever since we moved here."

Cynthia knew Luke was a private person, and she could see how difficult it was for the reticent man to express his true feelings. He glanced worriedly at the closed bedroom door, then back to her. "It's sure taking Doug a long time with that examination."

"He's very thorough. But I believe in my heart Honey will be fine. And I think, despite being scared, Josh thinks so, too. He was just frightened when he woke up this morning and found Honey feverish and unresponsive. Particularly after what happened yesterday. Any child would be." She rose and headed for the stove. "Would you like a cup of coffee?"

"You bet." Reaching eagerly for the cup, he said, "Gee, thanks. This is a life preserver." He took several swallows. "You're a saint, Cynthia. If you weren't already married, I'd ask you to be my wife."

He had just touched on the subject to which she

was most dedicated. Cynthia sat down again at the table. "Heard you placed an ad again for a wife."

"No, this time I advertised for a housekeeper. I haven't had too much luck trying to find a wife." His face sobered as he thought of the letter that he had received that morning.

"Well, Sheriff, as long as you're looking for a wife"—she swung her glance to the closed bedroom door—"why buy a pig in a poke when—as they say—a bird in the hand is worth two in the bush?"

"Honey's not interested in getting married, Cynthia."

"How do you know until you ask?"

"I offered to marry her the day I brought her to Stockton." He didn't mention that Honey had said she was holding out for a rich man.

"Well, maybe she's changed her mind since then," Cynthia said hopefully.

He knew Cynthia wouldn't like what he had to tell her, but he saw no sense in postponing the news. He was on the verge of speaking when Doug opened the bedroom door. "Cindy, if that water is ready, I'd appreciate your sponging Honey off and changing her nightgown."

Cynthia jumped to her feet as quickly as her delicate condition permitted. "How is she, Doug?"

"She has a high temperature and some liquid on her lungs. When you bathe her, keep her out of any drafts. I don't want her lungs to get any more congested than they already are."

"You'll find a clean washcloth and towel in the top drawer of the hutch," Luke said. "I'll bring in the water and a bar of soap."

He filled a pitcher with warm water and carried it into the bedroom, while Cynthia poured some of the liquid into the basin. Luke took a long look at Honey. At the moment, she was asleep. Strands of her light hair were plastered by perspiration to her pale cheeks. When he brushed then off her face, he could feel her intense body heat. Cynthia shooed him out of the room, and he returned to the kitchen, poured himself another cup of coffee, and sat down at the table where Doug was sipping from a steaming mug.

"Are you sure she's okay, Doc?"

"I wish she were more alert. I'm concerned about the length of her exposure in that storm. The danger now will be if she contacts bronchitis or pulmonary pneumonia."

"And how do we stop that from happening?"

"Keep her warm and in bed. We'll continue with the antipyretic to control the fever. Tomorrow, we'll start her on salt baths: the salicylic acid has an analgesic and antipyretic, which will speed the healing process."

"Since I don't know what the hell you're talking about, I'll take your word for it."

"Well, it's about time. And it's also time for me to take my wife home. In her condition, she needs the rest. Send for me if Honey takes a turn for the worse. She'll probably be restless from the fever, Luke. Give her a spoonful of that tonic every three hours, and cool compresses will make her feel a little more comfortable."

"Well, she's all bathed, and I put a nightie on her," Cynthia said as she emerged from the bedroom.

Luke and Doug stood up and shook hands. "Thanks for everything, Doc."

"Let's get you home to bed, Cindy," Doug said, putting Cynthia's cloak around her. Then he slapped Luke on the shoulder. "Honey could be in for a couple of bad nights. The critical time will probably be tonight. But barring any setbacks, I think she'll be fine. I'll be back first thing in the morning."

Cynthia kissed Luke on the cheek.

"Thanks again, you two," Luke said at the door.

Luke lost his smile as soon as he closed the door. He went back to the bedroom. After emptying the ewer, he refilled the pitcher with cool water. When he finished, he put a hand on Honey's brow. She still felt very warm. Worriedly, he tucked the blanket around her, then left the room to check on Josh.

When Luke entered his son's room, Amigo opened his eyes, wagged his tail several times, and went back to sleep. Luke twisted his mouth into a half smile, half grimace. "You damn dog," he said with affection. He gazed tenderly at the sleeping child.

With Honey sick, you've been kind of lost in the shuffle the last couple of nights, haven't you, son? Tucking the blankets around Josh, he kissed his forehead.

Luke returned to the kitchen. He cleaned Doug's cup and sat down to remove his boots. Then, picking up the large parlor chair, he carried it into the bedroom.

It was going to be a long night.

He sat down in the chair and pulled a folded envelope out of his shirt pocket. The letter had been on his mind since he had received it that morning. For a long moment he stared at it thoughtfully, then he shifted his gaze to Honey.

Restless, he got to his feet and picked up the book laying on the bedside table. He glanced at the title. *Jane Eyre.* With a half smile, he shook his head. Honey sure loved those books of Abigail Fenton's. She read every chance she had, either to herself or Josh. Knowing Josh benefited from it, Luke was grateful to her.

Growing up on a Texas ranch, he'd had little time to enjoy books. His mother had educated them using a Webster's Blue-Black Speller and an old Johnson's dictionary. Even so, he and Flint hadn't cottoned much to reading; Cleve was the one who took to book learning. He read anything he could get his hands on, including the Bible from cover to cover. Luke smiled, recalling how pleased his mother had been that one of her sons had read the holy book. It wasn't until he went east during the war, Luke reflected, that he himself started to read for enjoyment. Books were more accessible there, and they helped to pass the time between battles.

He laid aside the book and glanced at the several

cartons containing more books in the corner of the room. Maybe he could build a bookcase for them. Struck by the absurdity of such a thought, he glanced quickly at Honey. What was he thinking of? She would be leaving Stockton soon.

He wandered over and stared at the battered cartons. The red-and-white gingham curtains were piled on top of them. Idly, Luke examined them. So she had finished them. He grinned fondly. She had actually finished something she had started. The least he could do was put up the rods for them. He'd do that first thing in the morning.

Luke went over and sat on the edge of the bed. Putting a hand on her forehead, he frowned at how hot she felt. He hurried over to the pitcher, poured water into the basin, and returned to the bed with a cool cloth for her brow.

For a long time he sat on the bed and studied the features of her lovely face—a face now flushed with fever. Picking up her hand, he traced her thin fingers with his thumb. "I'm sorry for all that's happened to you, Jaybird," he said softly. "Guess I never should have made you come here."

He shifted to the chair, settled back, and stretched out his legs, resting his stocking feet on the bed. Remembering Doug's instructions, he pulled out his father's pocket watch to check the time. She would need another dose of medicine at one o'clock in the morning. He cradled his head on his hand and sat looking at her until his eyes grew heavy with fatigue and drifted shut.

Honey's mumbling awoke him sometime later. She was thrashing in delirium and babbling incoherently. "What are you doing? Get away from me, Uncle George," she cried out.

Luke jumped to his feet and felt her brow. Her temperature had risen; she seemed to be burning up with fever. With a quick glance at the clock, he realized that she wasn't due for another dose of medicine for an hour.

"Don't touch me. Get away, Uncle George. Let me alone," she raved, striking out with her hands. He rinsed the cloth and put it on her brow again.

Suddenly, she began to sob. "Daddy, please don't drink any more. You promised you'd stop. Please stop, Daddy, please." Tears were streaking her cheeks, and he sponged them away.

She was shivering violently. Luke tucked the quilt tighter around her, then sat down on the bed and held her hand. She looked so tiny and helpless. "Don't cry, Jaybird," he said tenderly, brushing strands of disheveled hair from her flushed face.

To his relief, she quieted, so he returned to the chair. But within moments, her raving resumed. "You brought me here . . . Wanted this . . . Won't work . . . Can't be trusted."

With shock, he recognized some of the words she had said to him in an earlier argument. The thought that his past actions were contributing to her torment overwhelmed him with guilt.

"Such a fool . . . Easy mark . . . Hate you . . . Hate you, Luke," she sobbed.

Each word felt like a knife thrust into his heart. He clasped her hands between his own. Propping his elbows on his knees, he sat motionless with his bowed head pressed against their clasped hands. "I'm sorry, Jaybird. So sorry for how I've hurt you," he whispered.

"I love you, Mama. I'll never forget you." Her voice trailed off to a sob. Her condition seemed to be worsening, and he wondered whether he should summon Doug. Then he remembered Doug's warning that her condition might take such a turn for the worse during the night. He decided to wait awhile longer.

Finally, it was time for a dose of the antipyretic tonic. The medicine had a calming effect on her, but in the hours that followed, she shivered under sporadic attacks of chills. Luke continued to sponge her face with a cool washcloth and wet her dry lips to keep them from blistering.

By daylight, after another dose of the tonic, her trembling and delirium had ceased.

Honey opened her eyes and for several seconds lay motionless. She perceived that she was in bed back at the house. Then she sensed that she was not alone. Turning her head, she grimaced with pain; she felt as if thousands of needles had penetrated her skull. She waited until the pain passed, then, blinking several times, she focused on the figure in a nearby chair.

"Luke," she whispered. As her vision cleared, she realized he was asleep. She lay in silence looking at him until her eyes closed and she slept again.

When Honey awakened once more, Doug Nelson stood next to the bed, holding her wrist to take her pulse. The chair where Luke had been sitting earlier was empty.

"Well, good morning," Doug said cheerfully.

"Good . . . good morning."

"How are you feeling?"

"I don't quite know yet," she managed to murmur.

"Pulse is good and steady. Let's see what your temperature is." He stuck a thermometer into her mouth. "Luke said that last night you were so hot you brought the water to a boil when he tried to sponge you off."

So she hadn't just dreamed his presence.

Unable to speak, she raised her brows skeptically, which was a mistake; she flinched from the pain caused by the simple movement.

"Headache?" he asked.

She nodded. Even that gesture hurt her head.

When he read the thermometer, Doug frowned. "You're still running a high temperature. You can forget about any afternoon hikes today."

She could feel herself slipping back into sleep. "Josh . . . is he . . . ?"

"He's fine, Honey. Just rest now."

* * *

She felt weightless, as if she were floating through the air; then the feel of soothing, warm water closed around her.

"No," she mumbled. Her tongue felt thick and she could hardly talk. "I don't want to learn how to swim. Bed . . . I want to go back to bed." She started to struggle.

"Just relax, Jaybird." The sound of Luke's husky voice at her ear calmed her.

"You won't let me drown?"

"No. I won't let you drown," he said softly.

With great effort, she opened her eyes. After several seconds, she realized she was sitting in a tub of water. Kneeling beside it, Luke held her with one arm in a firm grasp to keep her head above water.

"What . . . what are you doing?"

"Doctor's orders. Just relax. The salt in the water will help your fever."

She tried to think through the haze surrounding her head. "Fever? What fever?"

"You're very sick, Jaybird. Feverish. Doug says these salt baths will help you."

She felt so strange. And she was totally confused by the incongruity of her surroundings: the tub, her nakedness, Luke. Suddenly, her head felt too heavy to hold up. She slumped back against the firm support of his chest. She didn't want to swim anymore. She wanted to sleep.

"Luke won't let me drown," she mumbled thickly and closed her eyes.

"Feeling any better, dear?" The sound of Cynthia's voice enabled Honey to cut through the cobwebs that enveloped her. When she felt a soft, cool hand on her brow, she opened her eyes. Smiling, Cynthia sat on the edge of the bed. The sight of her friend's warm, brown eyes drew Honey's gaze like a beacon.

"Yes, I feel much better," Honey said, although she was still somewhat confused. "What happened?"

"You were feverish."

"Feverish?" She closed her eyes and thought for a moment. "Oh, yes, now I remember. I was in the woods with Josh and it started to rain." She met Cynthia's gaze.

"That's right. You were soaked and took to a fever. You've been pretty sick, dear. We've been real worried about you for the past three days."

"Three days! You mean I've been sick for three days? I can't believe it!"

Cynthia patted her hand. "The important thing is that you're feeling better now. Are you hungry?"

"Matter of fact, I am," Honey said after some consideration.

"Good. I'll fix you some tea. And how about a dish of oatmeal?"

"I'd love that, Cynthia, if it's not too much bother."

Cynthia hurried from the room, and Honey closed her eyes, only to doze off. When she opened them again, Josh was standing by the bedside, his blue eyes wide and solemn. "Hi, sweetheart," she said.

"You all better now?" he asked in a trembling voice.

"I feel fine."

Amigo jumped up on the bed and began to lick her face. "Hi there, fella." She laughed and tried to pet him, but her arm felt too heavy to raise. "Guess I just need a little time to get my strength back."

"Amigo saved us," Josh said.

"He did? I don't remember much of anything after we got here. I want to know all that's happened while I've been sick."

Cynthia entered the room carrying a tray. "Okay, you can talk later. We have to let Honey eat now. Amigo, get off that bed," she ordered. The dog jumped down to the floor.

"Can we come back when you're through eating?" Josh asked.

"You sure can, sweetheart," Honey answered. "Remember, I want to hear what happened."

"Come on, Amigo, let's go see Daddy."

Cynthia sat down in the chair while Honey ate. "You're going to have to tell me what's been going on here for the past three days. I recall nothing but a few obscure impressions."

"Well, you were very feverish." Cynthia smiled slyly. "According to Doug, Luke has hardly budged from your bedside in the past three days."

"Apparently, I have Doug to thank, too."

"He is a good doctor," Cynthia replied matter-of-factly, "but Luke did all the work." Honey smiled as Cynthia's eyes gleamed. "And look, he hung up the curtains you made."

Honey glanced around in surprise. For the first time, she noticed the bright curtains at the window. "Well, I'll be sure and thank him," she said. Over the top of the cup, she smiled with loving indulgence at her friend. She figured that in Cynthia's determination to get them wed, she had exaggerated Luke's role in her recovery.

The act of eating the simple meal exhausted her, and Honey fell asleep shortly thereafter.

When she awoke, the bedroom was in darkness. Through the open door, she could see and hear Luke talking to Josh at the kitchen table. Josh cradled his head in his hand as he picked at his food with a fork.

"Josh, that's no way to sit at the supper table," Luke said. "Is there something wrong with your food?"

"Don't like it." His jaw jutted out petulantly. "Honey makes it better."

"I think so, too, son, but this is the best I can do."

Josh separated a piece of beef out of the stew on his plate and forked the bite listlessly into his mouth. "When will Honey be able to cook again?"

"Can't say, so you'll just have to make do with my cooking for a while."

"The biscuits are so hard even Amigo won't eat them."

Luke glanced at Amigo, who was busy gobbling the biscuit Josh had dropped down to him. "Don't look to me like he's having a problem."

"He's just being nice to you 'cause he don't like to hurt anyone's feelings."

"You could learn from him," Luke said. "I suppose you think you could do better."

"Yep, 'specially with biscuits."

"Okay, partner, you're on. We'll make some fresh ones for Honey."

Honey watched with amusement as they quickly cleared the dishes off the table. Then Josh pulled up the stool to stand on and waited as Luke mixed together the biscuit dough.

"All right, lead on, Chef MacKenzie," Luke said with a dramatic sweep of his arm.

"What's a chef?" Josh asked suspiciously.

Luke grinned. "He's a man who's, ah . . . a good cook."

That explanation seemed to please Josh, because he grinned broadly. He shook his finger at Luke. "Now you gotta roll out the dough till it's just right. I'll tell you when to stop."

"Gotcha, pal." Luke picked up the rolling pin and proceeded to follow Josh's instructions.

Concentrating intently, Josh leaned over the table. "Okay, stop," he declared when he decided the dough was thin enough.

"Now what?" Luke asked, putting aside the rolling pin.

"Now you take this glass, and you make these circles." When Luke started to follow the instructions, Josh stopped him. "No, that's not the way."

He took the glass out of Luke's hand to demonstrate what he meant. "It don't work if you don't wiggle your hips like this." Josh shook his little rear end back and forth like Honey had shown him.

"You mean like this?" Luke picked up a glass and began to shake his slim hips while he pressed out the dough. "I'd think it would work better with music."

"Daddy, how do you 'spect us to have music, 'specially when Honey's too sick to play her guitar?" Josh scoffed.

Lying in the darkened room, Honey's eyes moistened with sentimental tears.

Once the biscuits were baking in the oven, Luke put his hands on his hips. "Well, partner, what do you suggest we do about the stew?"

Luke suppressed a grin when he saw Josh's puckered frown of deliberation. "How 'bout more salt?" the boy suggested.

"Naw. Honey complained about too much salt when I made oatmeal."

"Can't we throw it away?"

Luke shook his head. "Waste not, want not, son. That's what my mother always told me."

Josh suddenly brightened. "I know! Let's feed it to Amigo. That's not wasting it."

"Good idea." Luke scooped the stew into a bowl and put it on the floor. Arms akimbo, Luke watched Amigo trot over and begin to devour the food.

Unconsciously emulating his father's pose, Josh put his hands on his hips and shook his head. "That damn dog will eat anything."

"Hey, I don't want to hear any more of that cussing," Luke said sternly.

"Well, that's what you always call him," Josh quickly piped up.

Realizing the truth of the accusation, Luke felt a trace of guilt. "Well, from now on, we'll *both* call him Amigo." The dog glanced up momentarily, then resumed eating.

"Whatta we gonna feed Honey when she wakes up?" Josh asked.

"There's still some of the soup left that Aunt Cynthia brought over yesterday."

As he looked up at his father, Josh appeared to glow with satisfaction. "Yeah, that's a good idea, Daddy. Honey can eat Auntie Cyntia's good soup and our good biscuits. I'm sure glad we thought of that."

As soon as the biscuits finished baking, they carried a tray of food into Honey. Joshua ran into his bedroom to get the pillow off his bed to put behind her back.

"Oh my, I'm not used to such service!" Honey exclaimed as Luke helped her sit up. Joshua sat on the foot of the bed, and Amigo jumped up beside him.

"Josh, get that damn—ah—tell Amigo to get down," Luke ordered.

"Oh, let him stay, Luke. He's not doing any harm," Honey said.

"In another moment he'll be up by you eating from that tray of food."

"I certainly wouldn't like that. Hmmm, this biscuit is delicious," Honey remarked. "Why, it's as light as a feather." She pretended not to see Josh grin broadly at his father or Luke wink back at him. Then, just as Luke warned, Amigo snatched the last bite of the biscuit from the plate.

They all laughed.

Later, after Josh was asleep and Luke had finished the dishes, he came into Honey's bedroom and sat down on the edge of the bed.

"How are you feeling, Jaybird?" he asked. The tenderness in his voice surprised her.

"I feel fine, truly I do."

Then he completely unnerved her by leaning forward and gently brushing some strands of hair off her face. "You gave us a scare for a while."

She swallowed with difficulty and gave him a shy smile. "I'm sorry to be so much trouble, Luke."

"I'm just glad you're out of danger and feeling better. Is there anything you need before I go to bed?"

"No. Nothing at all, Luke," she answered. A hot blush swept over her, and she thought she must look as red as a beet. "You've waited on me long enough. Tomorrow I intend to get out of bed."

"We'll see what Doug says."

Mesmerized by Luke's dark gaze, she fought the urge to reach up and throw her arms around his neck.

"I've got something to tell you that should make you feel even better," he added.

"I won't have to eat any more of your salty oatmeal?" she guessed.

"Yeah, reckon that's right. I've found a housekeeper. A mature woman recently widowed. Her name is Frieda Frick. At the moment, she's living with her daughter's family in Sacramento. She'll be arriving in a week. Then you'll be free to leave Stockton— the way you want to."

Honey felt numb. She had thought about it, had talked about it, had known from the first moment she arrived that this moment would be inevitable. Admittedly, at one time she would have willingly climbed on a stagecoach, ridden away without a backward glance, and erased any thought of Luke MacKenzie from her mind. But now . . . Now it was too late. He dominated her waking and sleeping hours. Faced with the prospect of no longer seeing him walk through the door or hearing the deep resonance of his voice or the warm chuckle that sent a shiver down her spine, she felt heartache and confusion.

She lowered her eyes, unable to look at him. "Are you saying I'm being pardoned before my ninety days are up?" She lifted her head and managed a weak smile. "I can't believe it's for good behavior. Sounds like you're anxious to get rid of me, Sheriff."

"I didn't expect to get such a quick response to my ad," he said.

"A week, you say. Looks like I won't have time to finish teaching Josh his ciphering." She was giving Luke an opening to ask her to remain. "He still needs more help with learning his letters, too."

"I don't mean to sound like I'm trying to get rid of you, Jaybird. I know your concern for Josh. If you want to stay, I could contact Mrs. Frick and ask her to delay her arrival."

"Well, do you want me to stay?"

For a long moment his dark gaze seemed to devour her. "Knowing how much you've looked forward to leaving, it doesn't matter what I want."

He was clearly trying to save himself the embarrassment of coming right out and asking her to leave, Honey thought. She felt the rise of tears and turned her head away so he wouldn't see her tears. "Yes, you're right," she said plaintively, groping for a response. "There's no reason to remain here when I'm no longer needed."

As anxious as she was to leave, Luke thought painfully, she would have stayed for Josh's sake. Funny how he had once believed she never thought of anyone's interests except her own. He had misjudged her as unjustly as most of the people in the damn town. For a moment he envied his son: if only he could win such devotion from her—but all he could provoke was her anger. He stared wistfully at her profile. She was so beautiful—even after the illness she had just suffered. Honey was all the woman any man could ever hope for. Her wit and intelligence matched her beauty. It was his fault they had started off on the wrong foot. Now it was too late to change her thinking about him.

When he rose to his feet, she turned her head and looked at him. "I'm bunking with Josh," he told her. "Call out if you need any help." He paused at the doorway. "Good night, Jaybird."

For a long time, she lay awake in the darkness, her tears dampening the pillow.

Chapter 19

Honey would not be deterred from getting out of bed the next morning. Although her legs were unsteady, she made her way slowly to the kitchen. The simple act exhausted her, so she sat down to regain her energy before attempting to start a fire in the stove.

Stopping frequently to rest, she finally got a pot of coffee brewing, and by the time she finished dressing she was feeling stronger. When Luke awoke, she tried to convince him that she felt much better and wanted to make breakfast. But he would not hear of it. So once again, she and Josh were subjected to a dish of salty oatmeal prepared at the hands of Luke Mac-Kenzie. When they finished breakfast, to make Honey's day easier, Luke took Josh with him on a ride out to the Calhoun ranch.

As she had done every morning since Honey had been ill, Cynthia Nelson came to spend the day. As the two women worked on pomander balls, Honey broke the news to Cynthia that she would be leaving Stockton soon.

Teary-eyed, Cynthia tried not to cry. "Does Josh know you're leaving?" she asked, dabbing at her eyes.

"No. Neither Luke nor I have gathered enough

courage to tell him yet. Maybe Luke will tell him today while they're alone."

"His little heart is going to break, Honey. You know that. He loves you so much."

Honey clamped her hands over her ears. "Don't say that. I don't want to hear it. We all knew I would be leaving one day. It's just a few weeks sooner than we thought."

"Why won't you stay? Luke told me he proposed marriage to you."

"Oh, good Lord, Cynthia! A business proposal. He asked me out of desperation to get me to agree to take care of Josh."

"Would marriage to Luke be so bad, Honey?" Cynthia pleaded.

Why was Cynthia putting such ideas in her head, leading her down this forbidden path? Honey shook her head to clear it of the thought. "Oh, Cynthia, I know you mean well, but if Luke can see that I've just been playacting another role, why can't you? I've been pretending to be someone I'm not. A home . . . a husband . . . a child, have no place in my life." With a sad smile, she hugged her grief-stricken friend. "I'll miss you, Auntie Cyntia."

For a long moment, Honey held the sobbing woman in her arms. When Cynthia finally got control of herself, Honey wiped away a tear from her own eye and smiled. "Let's finish these damn pomander balls! At least I'll still be here for the bazaar."

The bazaar officially began at high noon on Saturday. More than a dozen booths had been erected for the occasion, offering a variety of wares, from a five-cent hard-boiled egg to a ten-dollar quilt that the Ladies' Church Auxiliary had been working on since the close of last year's bazaar. Honey observed that the kissing booths had been set up at the far end of the fair, where a tent had also been erected awaiting the arrival of Mama Rosa, who, according to the sign, was a renowned astrological expert specializing in the reading of tarot cards.

Pastor Wright had kept her secret well, Honey thought in amusement.

The bazaar had not been in progress for more than a quarter of an hour when an irate Luke strode up to Honey's booth. "Just what do you think you're doing?"

She pointed to the sign. "I'm selling kisses for a dollar."

"What the hell are you doing that for? I thought you were selling those balls you and Cynthia have been working on for the past week."

Honey was annoyed by his objection. "Really, Luke, I don't understand what difference it makes to you what I'm doing. It's all for charity, you know."

"Yeah, and selling your kisses comes easy to you, doesn't it?"

She was stung by the remark. "Yes, about as easy as being nasty comes to you, Sheriff MacKenzie."

"Well, Lily always handled the kissing booth before," he said, somewhat contrite.

"Oh, I see, Sheriff. Are you here to complain on her behalf?" she asked sarcastically.

"I just don't think we need two of you doing it."

"Then I suggest you voice your objection to Reverend Wright. He's the one who asked me to do it."

"Either put up or shut up, Sheriff. You're holding up the line," Doug Nelson said.

Luke turned and saw the doctor standing behind him.

"Yes, I suggest you move on. You're scaring away my customers," Honey declared. She struggled to regain her composure, but Luke's remark had hurt her deeply.

He glared at Doug. "If you'd try kissing your own wife, Doctor Nelson, you could save yourself some money." He stalked over to Lily's booth.

Dismayed, Honey saw him put down a dollar. Lily embraced him, and Luke claimed her mouth in a long, torrid kiss. When they finally broke apart, Honey saw a slumberous look in the woman's green eyes. "Look me up later, Sheriff, and we'll pick up where we left off," Lily cooed seductively.

"I might very well do that," Luke murmured. He swung his glance to Honey, then walked away.

Chuckling, Doug handed Honey a dollar and kissed her on the cheek. "I think our sheriff's suffering a spot of jealousy, Honey." But she was not convinced.

By midday, she realized that Miss Lily's kissing booth was considerably more of a draw than her own. With a disgruntled glance, she looked at the long line of men in front of the other woman's booth. After kissing Lily fully on the mouth, some of the men would then move to her own booth and give her a chaste kiss on the cheek. Although she preferred their reserved kisses, she found their obvious preference rather humiliating—mostly because all along Luke was lounging against a nearby tree, watching the proceedings with his arms folded across his chest and a superior look on his face.

"Howdy, Miz Honey," Randy Calhoun said, doffing his hat as he moved over from Lily's booth. He laid out a dollar.

"Good afternoon, Randy," she said, raising her cheek to accept his kiss.

"Heard you've been sick," he said.

"Oh, I'm fine now."

"Glad to hear that, ma'am," he said, moving away.

"And it was nothing contagious," she called out for the benefit of every one within earshot, although she was convinced that Luke MacKenzie's towering, scowling presence had something to do with their lack of enthusiasm.

She looked over to see Jess engaged in a fervent kiss with Lily. When they broke apart, Jess emitted a long whistle.

"If you still got anything left after that, sugar, I want to see you later," Lily declared throatily, straightening her disheveled hair. The remark brought a round of laughter from the other men in line.

"Wait until I kiss you, Lily. Then you'll *know* you've been kissed," one of the men called out.

"You can quit that big-mouthin', Wally Boyd, 'cause I know better. Remember, I've been kissed by you before," she said, amused. "It would probably be more pleasing to Miz Honey here."

Honey was indignant. About to accept Jess's timid peck on her cheek, she turned her head, grabbed him by the ears, and kissed him long and hard on the lips. When she finally broke away, the startled young man blushed the color of a red rose and cast a nervous glance toward Luke.

"I wanted to give you a special thanks for saving my life the day of the robbery, Jess," she said demurely.

"My . . . my pleasure, ma'am," he said, flustered. He put down his dollar, and as he bolted away, she looked at Luke smugly. He smirked in return and doffed his hat.

"Damn you, Luke MacKenzie," she grumbled to herself.

Toward evening, she abandoned the kissing booth and was on her way to change into her gypsy costume when Luke stopped her.

"Don't tell me you're giving up so early, Miz Honey? I was just sending Josh over with a dollar. I noticed you seemed to have better luck attracting *boys*."

"Talk about boys! I'm surprised you didn't show up with *your* dollar, Sheriff."

"That bad, huh?" He chuckled warmly. "Guess I was being kind of childish. I'm sorry for what I said and the way I acted, Jaybird."

She couldn't help smiling at the sight of his engaging grin. "You really looked like a fool, standing around all day scowling at me. One would think you were jealous, MacKenzie."

"Maybe I was, Miz Honey." He winked, doffed his

hat, and walked away. For a long moment she stared at the retreating figure. He was just about the most exasperating man she had ever known.

Unobserved, Honey ducked into Mama Rosa's tent. Shortly after, Cynthia appeared and helped her change.

"In that black wig and in this dim light, no one will recognize you," Cynthia assured her.

Honey surveyed her image in the mirror. She now wore a brightly colored flowered skirt, a white blouse, and a black and red shawl around her shoulders. Her blond hair had been tucked under a wig of long black hair that fell over her shoulders. A large gold hoop hung from her right ear, and a red and black bandanna was tied on the crown of her head.

Cynthia helped to rouge her cheeks, then she lined Honey's eyes and darkened her brows with kohl. Honey had to admit she looked wonderfully mysterious, with little resemblance to her usual fair-skinned blondness.

"If I didn't know better, Mama Rosa, I'd never recognize you," Cynthia declared.

"Aha, zo you haf come for Mama Rosa to tell vhat za future holds for you," Honey declared in a deep voice as she rubbed her hands together. "Mama Rosa zees a baby boy vis za brown hair and eyes." She raised a finger to her temple. "Vhat is dis Mama zees? Zhere is a stetzoscope zhat is hanging from za baby's ears."

"Oh, you zany!" Cynthia exclaimed. "And to think you see all that without even a crystal ball or your tarot cards. Thou art truly amazing, Mama Rosa. I only wish I could be a little mouse in the corner and stay to listen."

Cynthia started to leave then paused to add, "Oh, if Doug shows up to have his fortune told, be sure to tell him how fortunate he is to have such a loving, dutiful, *and* beautiful wife." Giggling, she departed.

Honey spent the rest of the evening predicting good news and rosy futures for the venturesome townsfolk who paid the twenty-five cents to have their fortunes read, with two exceptions: Clarabelle Webster and Myrtlelee Quinn. She told Clarabelle that her husband was having an affair with her best friend, and then later, when Myrtlelee visited the tent, Honey told the undertaker's wife that her best friend was in love with Delmer.

"Just wait until I get my hands on that Clarabelle Webster!" Myrtlelee fumed as she stalked out of the tent. Honey savored a few moments of sweet revenge. Let them think about that for a while, she chuckled to herself.

When Honey could no longer ignore her hunger pangs, she decided that after the next reading, Mama Rosa would pack up her tarot cards.

Just then, much to her amazement, Luke MacKenzie entered. His tall figure seemed to fill the small tent, and he had to bend his head so as not to hit the ceiling. Honey quickly decided this was an opportunity to get even with him for his behavior at the kissing booth.

"Aha! Zo you haf come to Mama Rosa to learn za future. Pleaz zit down before you be knocking down za tent on top of her head."

Luke sat down, and Honey shuffled the deck of cards. "You vill cut, pleaz." When Luke reached for the deck, she slapped his hand. "No, vit za left hand."

"Mama Rosa should have said so," Luke said, smiling through gritted teeth as he divided the deck.

Honey forced back her grin. "Zo, big man, tell Mama Rosa vhat you vish to know."

"I'd expect *you* to tell *me*, Mama Rosa."

She cocked a brow and shook a finger at him. "Aha, you're a sly von, all right, but Mama Rosa reads cards, not minds."

She turned over a card. "Dis is your zignicator. I zee you haf many struggles, big man."

"You can say that again, Mama Rosa," Luke scoffed.

"Struggles inzide yourzelf." She leaned across the

table. "Alvays za spirit against za flesh, ya?"

He winked. "Yeah, I sure do have my share of that."

Honey studied the next card. "Dis card zays you von stubborn man, plenty tough vhen it be coming to vat is right. You be lawman or zomezing like zat?"

"I'm amazed, Mama Rosa. How did you ever guess? I bet this star on my chest gave me away."

"Mama Rosa is zuzpecting zhat you are not taking her zeriouzly." She glanced at the next card. "Dis card shows zere is a dark-haired child in your life."

Luke arched his brows in concession. Honey pointed to the next card. "And a myzterios voman."

"Oh, really? What does this mysterious woman look like?" Honey detected the tongue-in-cheek in his tone. "Mozt beautiful vit za fair hair. She be giving you pleazant news."

Turning over the King of Wands, Honey exclaimed, "Aha, you zee, comes here da mozt favorable card. It shows good marriage vith big, fat voman. Za marriage vill have zome difficulty but vill be zo good beyond your expectazions."

"Can't wait," he said drolly.

"Aha, jest as Mama Rosa feared. Za next card shows trouble. Mostly becauz za lawman is too zaspicious.

"Trouble?" he asked, leaning forward and squinting at her. Ignoring his insinuation, she continued turning the cards.

In the next several moments, she saw warnings of ill omens, hidden dangers, and enemies. With the next several cards, Honey frowned and quickly passed over them.

"What's the matter, is the honeymoon over?"

"No, no," she faltered. "I zee a fair-haired man. A man of arms." She flipped over several more cards. "Much conflict. And danger."

"To me or to this fair-haired man?" Luke asked.

"Mama Rosa does not know. But zhere vill be a time of much hardzhip, obstacles, and . . . much courage," she added, tapping two of the cards. "Aha, vhat is dis? Is dark-haired men. But I do not zense za danger. Zhey are vat you call rogues."

Alarmed at what she had read in some of the cards, Honey felt instant relief when the Ace of Pentacles appeared. "Aha, dis is mozt favorable card. All vill vork out. Mama zees triumph, pleazant news, and—" She looked up and smiled at him. "Big man, you vill find contentment vith your fat vife vith her chubby cheeks and knees." She reached out and playfully pinched his cheek.

"Well, I'm sure glad to hear that. Should we go and eat now? You must be pretty hungry, Jaybird—ah, I mean, Mama Rosa."

Incensed, Honey stood up and put her hands on her hips. "Oh, Luke! How could you lead me on like that?"

"Dunno. Must be the company I keep."

She wrinkled her nose. "So you didn't fall for my disguise?"

Chuckling, he shook his head. "Not for a moment."

Honey struck a haughty pose and resumed her gypsy voice. "Vhat gave me avay?"

He shoved his hat off his forehead. "Miz Honey Behr, that is the worst accent I've ever heard. Besides, I'd know those beautiful blue eyes anywhere."

Taken aback and embarrassed by the compliment, she answered defensively, "Oh really? I bet someone told you I was Mama Rosa."

"No. I just heard there was quite an act going on in this tent, so naturally I was . . . *zaspicious*."

Honey pulled off the bandanna and black wig. "Act? Beware, Luke MacKenzie, I really can read tarot cards." Shaking out her hair, she combed her fingers through its thickness. "Oh, it feels good to get that wig off. And you're right, I'm hungry. Give me a moment to get out of this gypsy costume. I'd hate for some of these people to discover Mama Rosa's true identity."

Chapter 20

When Honey joined Luke outside, she saw that the town now basked in the warm glow of moonlight and Chinese lanterns. Most of the booths were deserted: Lily had returned to the Long Branch, Cynthia Nelson had sold all her pomander balls, and the cakes and pies the Stockton ladies had baked the previous night were long gone.

The women sat talking in small groups, while the men stood in front of the booth offering five-cent glasses of tapped beer.

After Honey and Luke each finished eating a ham sandwich, accompanied by a glass of beer for him and milk for her, they strolled over to a deserted area by the river and sat down on the grass. Luke stretched out, leaning back on his elbows.

"This has been a fun day," Honey said. "Looks like they raised a lot of money for the church."

"Where'd you learn to read tarot cards, Jaybird?"

"I used to travel with a carnival."

"When was that?"

"Mama Rosa is truer to life than you think. I grew up in a carnival. We traveled the country like gypsies, never staying long in any one place. I learned a lot of tricks. By the time I was eight, I could pick pockets.

At twelve years old, I could read tarot cards."

Lying back, Luke tucked his hands under his head. "Didn't you have a home to go back to?"

"No. The only home I ever knew was a wagon in my uncle's carnival."

"Where were you born?"

"I don't know for sure. My mother said it was in Wisconsin, but my father claimed we had already crossed into Minnesota."

"Are your folks still living?" he asked, watching the shifting emotions on her expressive face. Funny how he never tired of looking at her, he thought contentedly.

"No. My mother died when I was twelve. My father drank himself to death six years later."

"No other relatives?"

"Only my uncle," she said.

He recalled her ravings about an uncle during her delirium. "Why did you leave the carnival?"

"Shortly after my father died, my uncle tried to . . ." He saw her eyes narrow with contempt. "Let's just stay he stopped thinking of me as his niece."

"You mean he attempted to—"

"He tried, but I fought him off and hit him on the head with a whiskey bottle. Then I ran away. I've never seen him since, and I never want to. It hadn't been the first time he tried to get familiar with me. After my mother died, he was always trying to touch me or kiss me. Then when my father died, my beloved uncle had considerably more in mind." She shuddered. "Oh, how I loathed that man."

Disturbed by what she had told him, Luke sat up. "Did you tell your father about your uncle's advances?"

"My father! He was always too pickled in alcohol to even notice. One time I did get up the courage to tell him, but I didn't get very far. He said I must have been mistaken, that we should be grateful to his brother for giving us a roof over our heads.

"A roof!" she scoffed. "A carnival wagon! Cold in

the winter and hot in the summer. When my mother got sick with influenza, we should have left the carnival and settled down where she could get a doctor's care and proper rest. Traveling around the country in a drafty, bouncing wagon was too hard a life for her. But my father didn't care as long as he had his bottle of whiskey," she said, unaware of the bitterness that had crept into her voice.

Luke wanted to stop her disclosure for, despite her mockery, he could sense that the memories were still painful to her.

"I'm sorry, Jaybird," he said. Moved by her sadness, he regretted he had encouraged her to talk about her childhood.

"Life would be a real pleasure if we could change all the bad times, wouldn't it?" she said in a lighter tone.

Amazed, he saw she had shrugged off her gloom. "So where did you go after you left the carnival?"

"By that time I was eighteen. The only education I had was the little bit of book learning my mother had taught me, so I couldn't become a schoolmarm or a nursemaid. Didn't have any skills except the carnival tricks my father and uncle had taught me: reading tarot cards and playing poker. You haven't seen anything until you've seen me stack a deck, MacKenzie," she added. "I worked on a farm in Minnesota for about six months. Then one morning, the farmer tried to trap me in the hayloft. Fortunately, the farmer's wife heard my screams, but of course, the farmer claimed I tried to seduce him. Although his wife knew differently, she sent me packing anyway. So I had to figure out what to do next. I started traveling the riverboats. Until that time, I felt my looks were more of a hindrance than a help, but I soon discovered how I could use them to my advantage. You'd be surprised how easy it is for a good-looking woman to get what she wants from a man."

Luke often wondered what had driven Honey to choose the road she had followed. The answer was becoming clear. "How old are you?"

"Twenty-four. Why?" He saw a flash of belligerence in her eyes.

"Twenty-four? And you have never found a man you could love? Or wanted to marry?"

He regretted the questions, for a wounded look had replaced the antagonism—the same hurt look he had seen in her eyes at the kissing booth. He felt remorse over the earlier cruel remarks he had made to her, but when he had seen her selling her kisses, he had lashed out in jealousy, just as she had suspected.

"Once. Just once I foolishly allowed myself to trust a man," Honey went on. "His name was Robert Warren. He was a lawyer. I met him on a riverboat. I was only nineteen. For one whole week he wooed me like a devoted suitor. I was so in love, and I believed that he loved me and wanted to marry me."

"What happened to make you change your mind?"

"He told me that as much as he wanted to marry me, he couldn't because he already had a wife. I should be flattered, though, because he did ask me to go to Chicago with him and become his mistress."

"And did you?" He didn't want to know. He was sorry he had asked.

"Did I what?" she asked, the belligerence back in her voice.

"Go to Chicago." *Dammit, MacKenzie, just forget it!*

"No, I didn't become his mistress if that's what you're asking."

He felt like a fool at his instant surge of relief.

"But I'm thankful for the lesson he taught me. No more illusions. Men only wanted one thing from me—and that wasn't marriage."

"That's pure hogwash!" Luke's sudden outburst splintered her mood of self-pity. "There were other options. Men out here are desperate for wives. You could have your pick of any man you want."

"Well, I guess I never thought about heading west before," she offered in her own defense. "And I guess, well, I guess I can't like or trust a man enough to marry him out of desperation."

"So what made you finally decide to head west?"

She arched a curved brow. "You want a romantic story or the truth?"

"The truth," he said solemnly.

Feeling a guilty flush, she glanced at him warily. "I was on a riverboat in Missouri and had picked out a gull named Peters to bilk by using my seduction con."

"The same one you tried on me in Sacramento?"

She nodded. "It was usually effective. You were suspicious from the beginning; that's why it didn't work on you."

Recalling that night, he chuckled. "Oh, I was tempted, Jaybird."

"There was a gambler on the same boat by the name of Jake Simmons, who suspected what I intended to do. He had already picked out Peters to swindle in a card game. Simmons came to my cabin and threatened to have me thrown off the boat if I didn't play along with him. He promised to split half of what he got if I helped set up Peters in a poker game with him. I knew Simmons had no intention of keeping his word to me, so I pulled my own swindle on Peters, and then—"

Honey dared go no farther. She knew she couldn't tell Luke the rest of the story because he was a lawman, dedicated to upholding truth and justice. If she told him about Peters's murder, he would have to report what he knew to the authorities.

"Well, when Simmons found out that I had double-crossed him, he came looking for me. He was a mean man, Luke; he would have seriously harmed me. So I fled from the boat at Independence, and that's when I met up with Abigail Fenton. When she asked me to take her place, I leaped at the opportunity to get as far away from Jake Simmons as I could."

Smiling, she raised her head. "You think this is far enough, MacKenzie?"

"Reckon so," he said, grinning.

"So," she said, "I've told you my life story, such as it is. Now it's time you told me yours. I know you have two brothers and you were raised in Texas. Begin by telling me how old you are."

"Thirty-four. My folks had a ranch near the Pecos River. In '36, when Sam Houston tried to rally an army to fight the Mexicans, my dad packed us up and we headed for the Alamo. I was only two years old then, Flint was one, and my ma was carrying Cleve. Well, according to Ma, when things really heated up down there, my father wanted his family out of danger. Ma didn't want to leave him, but my father wouldn't have it any other way. So Juan and Rita Morales, who had worked on the ranch and had come with us, snuck us through the Mexican lines."

"And your father?"

"He died at the Alamo. We went back to the ranch, and Ma gave birth to Cleve six months later."

"Your mother must have been a very brave woman."

"I was too young to understand what was going on at the time, but I could tell later how much she grieved for him."

"And she never remarried?" He shook his head. "It must have been pretty hard to raise three sons and keep a ranch going without a husband to help."

"Yeah, reckon it was, but Ma did it. It helped when me and my brothers grew up enough to help work the land."

"Working the land never gave you much chance to be a boy, did it, Luke MacKenzie?"

"Reckon not. Guess I was kind of hard on Flint and Cleve."

"You mean you had the most responsibility?"

"No, Ma was the one with the responsibility," he said thoughtfully. "Now that I've had a hand at raising Josh, I sure don't know how she did it. But one thing I do know for certain, I want my son to grow up knowing a mother's ways."

"What do you mean, Luke?"

"A little boy's gotta grow up knowing the comfort of his mama's arms closing around him when he's hurt or scared, the touch of her cool hand on his fevered brow when he's ailing."

Honey felt tears misting her eyes as Luke continued speaking, unaware of the poignancy that had crept into his voice.

"To fall asleep at night listening to her humming in the kitchen as she sets the next day's dough . . . and wake up in the morning to the smell of fresh bread baking on the hearth."

She had glimpsed this side of him before, the vulnerable core that he kept hidden beneath a hard shell of bitterness.

"His mama always has the answers to his questions . . . or the solutions to his problems." His deep, husky voice sent a ripple of desire through her. "And it doesn't matter what she looks like or how old she is. She's his mama . . . and she's beautiful to him." Deep in reflection, he paused momentarily. "Yep, a growing boy needs a mother."

"So that's why you're so determined to remarry," she said in a tremulous voice.

He nodded. "A father can teach his son the strength expected of a man. But only from a mother can he learn to appreciate a woman's sensitivity and quiet fortitude. Then, when the boy becomes a man, he discovers other needs—and other ways to appreciate a woman."

"You mean he falls in love? When did you get married, Luke?"

"I married Sarah in '60; Joshua was born in '62. I left then to join the army. Reckon you know the rest."

"And what happened to Juan's wife? Was she killed in the raid, too?"

He shook his head. "No, she died from a snake bite in . . . let me see . . . in '52." He lay back, slipped his hands under his head again, and closed his eyes. "Seems like a lifetime ago."

Honey shifted over to his side. Cherishing these

precious moments, she gazed lovingly at him, knowing she would never forget a single detail of his face. If only they could go on like this forever. But it was a foolish fantasy. Recounting her past had been a grim reminder of just how absurd the fantasy had become. She had allowed herself during her short stay in Stockton to be lulled into a false sense of security that must soon end. As if feeling her stare, Luke opened his eyes. "Did you know you have stars in your eyes, Jaybird?" he said softly.

"Do I?"

At the sight of her soft smile, he reached up and laced his fingers through her hair. "And silver moonbeams in your hair."

"That's very romantic, Sheriff MacKenzie, but somewhat out of character."

"So, maybe I'm feeling romantic."

"Oh, you're really out of character," she said lightly despite her pounding heart that seemed to be cutting off her breath.

As he slowly slid his hand to the back of her neck, she felt her pulses throb from the hot blood surging through her veins. He drew her head down until their breath mingled.

"What if I told you I'm seriously considering kissing you right now?" he whispered, smothering the final words against her lips as his mouth covered hers.

The feel of his firm lips and exploring tongue sent sweet sensations spiraling through her. She responded with reckless abandon to the divine ecstasy of the kiss, domineering in its possessiveness, exciting in its demand, yet so tender in its intimacy.

"So here you are! What a sneaky bastard. Too cheap to pay a dollar like the rest of us," Doug Nelson exclaimed. "Or are the two of you saying your goodbyes early?"

Reluctantly, they broke apart, ending the kiss too soon for either's satisfaction. Luke stood up and pulled Honey to her feet. "What do you want, Doc?" Luke grumbled.

"I want you to take your sleeping son off my hands."

"Oh, the poor darling," Honey said as she saw Joshua asleep in Doug's arms, his cheek resting against the doctor's shoulder. "Give him to me. I'll take him home to bed."

"No, I'll carry him back to the house," Luke said. He lifted Joshua from Doug's arms. With a weary trot, Amigo trailed after them.

The romantic mood that had existed on a grassy riverbank only moments before disappeared once they were under the roof of his house. As soon as Josh was bedded down, Luke said good night and left to maintain law and order among the more boisterous celebrants.

Exhausted, Honey fell into bed, but sleep eluded her. All she could think of was those shared moments, Luke's kiss, his tenderness. A side he had kept concealed from her. Why hadn't they ever been able to talk together like that before?

Damn you, Luke MacKenzie! Damn you! With only a couple days remaining before she left Stockton, why did she have to realize now how much she loved him?

Chapter 21

⟳⟲

Luke waited until Monday to tell Josh that Honey was leaving. Frieda Frick was due to arrive that morning, and Honey would be departing on the same stage, bound for San Francisco.

When Honey went into the bedroom to pack, Luke realized he couldn't put it off any longer. He sat down at the table where Josh was practicing writing the alphabet.

Grinning, Josh proudly held up the paper he had been working on. "See, Daddy, aren't I doing good with my printing? Honey says I must be the smartest boy in the whole world."

Luke tousled Josh's dark hair. "I think she's right, son." He glanced at the closed bedroom door. "Smarter than your old man, that's for sure."

After a moment's pause, Luke said, "There's something I have to tell you, Josh." Josh looked at him with round, trusting eyes. "Honey is leaving today. A Mrs. Frick will be arriving soon to take her place."

For a long moment Josh looked at Luke as though he had just struck him. Then he jumped to his feet, swept the papers and pencils off the table, and ran outside. Stunned, Luke gazed at the front door as it slammed shut on Josh's retreating figure. Then, feeling as if the weight of the world was on his shoulders, he buried his head in his hands. If only there was some way he could spare Josh this hurt. Finally, drawing a shuddering breath, he got up and followed his son.

Josh was sitting on the stoop, sobbing. Amigo lay beside him, with his head on his paws and a sad gaze fixed on the boy. Luke sat down beside Josh and put an arm around his son's trembling shoulders.

With balled fists, Josh swiped at his tears. "I thought she . . . she . . . liked me."

"Of course she does."

"Then is she mad at me?"

"She's not mad at you, son." Luke reached out and tilted up the youngster's chin. "It's not your fault, Josh. You've done nothing wrong."

"Then why is she leaving me . . . like my mama did? Is Honey sick, too, like Mama was?"

"No, Josh. You knew Honey would be going away some time," Luke said gently. "She only came here to help until I could find someone else."

"Can't you make her stay, Daddy?"

"I'm afraid not, son." Luke stood up. "The stage is due in, Josh. I have to go and meet Mrs. Frick. She'll be taking care of you now. Why don't you come with me?"

"No," he shouted. With tears streaming down his cheeks, he cried out accusingly, "I don't want to meet her. I never want to meet her. I hate you for letting Honey go. You don't like her, so you don't care."

"That's not true, Josh. I care very much. I want her to stay the same as you do." Luke didn't know how to explain to a six-year-old immersed in his own grief his feelings for Honey. How complicated the situation between Honey and him had become because of the goddamned agreement he had made. "I wish you would come with me now." After several seconds, he walked away, frustrated by his helplessness.

* * *

After she'd finished packing, Honey sat down on the edge of the bed to rally her strength. Earlier, she had said good-bye to the Nelsons, and now the worst was still ahead of her. Praying for the fortitude to get through the next few minutes, she picked up her carpetbag and guitar.

There was no sign of Luke in the house. With labored steps, she approached Josh, who was sitting on the front stoop.

"Josh," she said softly. He didn't look up. Her heart pounded against her constricted chest, and she didn't dare touch him. If she did, she would lose control. "Sweetheart, we both knew we would have to say good-bye some day."

"Don't go, Honey." His cheeks were streaked with tears. "Please don't go away."

Oh, dear God, please give me the strength to get through this, she prayed. She feared her aching heart would burst. "I have to, Josh." Despite her resolve, she pulled him into her arms, hugging him to her breast. "I love you, sweetheart. I'll always love you." She kissed him, then jumped to her feet. "I'll write you a letter, I promise." In desperation, she raced away.

Pop O'Leary was waiting at the stage. His white head was lowered, and the sparkle gone from his eyes. He took Honey in his arms and hugged her, and she slumped against him, allowing herself these few seconds of needed solace. Finally, she stepped back. A smile trembled on her lips. "At least I'm leaving without wearing tar and feathers," she said. "The good ladies of this town must feel cheated."

Pop cupped her cheek in his hand, his eyes sorrowful. "Good ladies, indeed!" he said bitterly. His tone softened, "Ah, colleen, those good ladies can only presume to be so by what they are taught, but few by what they are. You, darlin', are a *good lady*."

"Thanks, Pop. I'm going to miss you."

"Good-bye, darlin'." He squeezed her hand, then walked away with just a hint of a stagger.

Honey looked over to the stage office where Luke

was standing with a heavyset woman, whom he led to a seat on a bench. He said a few words to her, then turned and walked toward Honey. She drew a deep breath and fortified herself for this final, painful goodbye.

"Let me help you with that." He took her carpetbag and guitar and handed them to Will Hutchins on top of the stage.

She willed herself to smile, lest he see her trembling lips. "I'll send for the books as soon as I get settled."

"No hurry. Don't worry about them."

Honey felt a rise of tears and quickly turned her head, glancing over at the woman seated on the bench. Scowling in their direction as she tapped her foot, the older woman was dressed in black widow weeds and an unadorned black poke bonnet. She nestled a large tawny cat in her arms. "Mrs. Frick looks impatient, Sheriff. You'd better get going."

"Yeah," Luke said. He took off his hat. "Well, I guess this is it. Don't suppose you'll believe me when I say I appreciate everything you've done for Josh."

She thrust up her chin and produced a plucky smile. "Of course I believe you. I was great."

"I'm sorry about the way I've treated you . . . the things I've said. I reckon you got the worst of the bargain between us."

"I always said it was a bad arrangement, MacKenzie."

"I'm ready to roll, Sheriff," Will Hutchins called out, with the reins in hand.

Luke took Honey's arm and helped her into the carriage. For a prolonged heartbeat, their gazes locked, his sapphire eyes infused with tenderness. "Take care of yourself, Jaybird."

"Sure, I always do," she said gamely. "You best not keep Mrs. Frick waiting any longer."

"Yeah."

Her heart wrenched when he plopped his hat back on his head in the familiar manner she had grown to love. She watched his tall figure stride back to the woman on the bench.

As the stage rumbled out of town, Honey leaned out the window. Through a cloud of dust, she saw the tiny figure of Josh with Amigo beside him, wagging his tail.

Honey sat back and clutched her aching breast. It seemed the time had come to pay the piper for every sin, every wrong, she had ever committed. She knew the ache would remain for many months to come.

With each turn of the carriage wheels, she wrestled with her thoughts. *Why are you doing this, Honey Behr? Why are you breaking that precious child's heart as well as your own? You don't want to leave Josh. He needs you. Your life meant nothing before Josh. Always running whenever the going got tough. Slinking away in the night, one step ahead of the local sheriff or the likes of men like Jake Simmons.*

"Oh, damn you, Luke MacKenzie!" she cursed aloud.

And what does San Francisco have to offer that you can't find in Stockton? Does it have Josh? Cynthia? Pop O'Leary? People you've grown to care about? So what if Luke MacKenzie has no further need of you? What do you care if he thinks you're unfit? That he doesn't love you?

"I don't need you either, Luke—neither you nor any of those town biddies are going to drive me away!" Her heart soared. *Nobody* was telling Honey Ann Behr what she could and what she couldn't do. She'd face up to the best of them and give more than she took. She'd leave Stockton when she was good and ready to leave and not one minute sooner.

"Will!" she shouted at the top of her lungs. "Stop this stage, Will."

With a squealing brake and a cloud of dust, the stagecoach ground to a halt. Honey opened the door and jumped lithely to the ground.

"I ain't driving you back," Will grumbled.

"I'm not asking you to," Honey declared. "Just give me my things, and get on your way."

A few minutes later, her carpetbag in one hand and her guitar in the other, Honey raced back up the road to Stockton.

"Pssst." Amigo stood up, ears perked, and looked in the direction of the trees. "Josh," Honey called in a whispered voice. This time Josh lifted his head as Amigo trotted over to the trees. "Josh, come here," Honey said.

His face lit with joy. He jumped up and dashed over to the copse of oak trees where she was hunched down in concealment. She opened her arms, and he rushed into them, knocking them both off their feet. Laughing, she lay back hugging Josh, while Amigo jumped around trying to lick their faces in his excitement.

"You came back! You came back!" Josh cried as he rained kisses on her cheeks.

"I couldn't leave you, sweetheart," she murmured, hugging him tighter.

"I love you, Honey."

"I know you do, and I love you, too." She sat up, and he settled down next to her. She slipped her arm around his shoulders and hugged him to her side.

"Can we tell Mrs. Frick to go home now?"

"No, Josh. Mrs. Frick has to stay. I'm going to talk to Sam at the Long Branch and see if he'll hire me. Then I have to find a place to live."

"Why can't you stay here with us like you did before?"

"Because there's not enough room," she said hastily, hoping he would accept the explanation. "Now, this is what I want you to do. Until I get settled in, I don't want your daddy to know I've come back."

"Daddy's not here. He told Mrs. Frick that he had to ride to Colton on 'ficial business. He asked me to ride with him, but I was too sad to go."

"Well, don't say anything to anyone for now."

"Not even Auntie Cyntia? She's feeling 'bout as bad as I was."

"Okay, sweetheart. You go and tell Aunt Cynthia. But tell her not to say anything, not even to Uncle Doug. Then tomorrow, you go to her house for lunch. I'll come there."

"I wish you could stay here."

"I do, too, sweetheart, but we can see each other."

His face curved into a pout. "It's all Daddy's fault."

Honey cupped his cheeks in her hands. "Josh, you mustn't blame your father. He loves you as much as I do. And just because I won't be living here doesn't mean we can't see each other every day. Your daddy won't keep us apart. He doesn't want to hurt you. Now, do as I say, and I'll see you tomorrow at Aunt Cynthia's. Okay?"

He nodded reluctantly. "Okay."

Just then, the front door slammed. "Yoshua," Frieda Frick called out. "Yoshua?" She put her hands on her hips. "*Ach Himmel! Wo ist der Junge?* Vhere is dat boy?" She bent down and picked up the cat that was nuzzling her ankle. "*Kommt, Liebchen. Hast du Hunger? Wir haben Milch.*" She hugged the cat to her enormous bosom. "*Ja Vol, meine Liebchen,* I get you zome *gut Milch.*"

"You better go, Josh," Honey whispered.

He stood up and grinned. She felt the pull on her heartstrings. "Me and Amigo love you, Honey."

"I love both of you, too. Now go, you little scamp." Smiling, she watched as he ran to the house.

To avoid being seen, Honey skirted the main street and slipped into the rear of the Long Branch. At the sight of her, Sam Brazner drew back with a startled look. "Thought you left on the noon stage."

"I changed my mind, Sam. I'm looking for a job. Are you interested?"

"You mean every night or just Saturdays like before?"

"Well, I wouldn't mind one night off a week. Even the sheriff gave me that."

"You still not willing to work upstairs?"

"That's right, Sam. Same conditions as before. I'll

deal one of the tables, and I'll sing a couple songs.
What do you say?"

"I'd be a damn fool to turn you down, Honey.
You're good for business. 'Sides, I can't risk your going to the Alhambra in Colton and pulling away all
my business. So when can you start?"

"As soon as I find a room. Right now, I can't afford
the hotel."

"I've got a room upstairs that's not occupied. Used
to be worked by a redhead named Maggie. She ran
off and married up with some dirt-poor cowboy.
Needs a good cleaning up, though."

"Oh, Sam, it sounds like a lifesaver to me. But just
so there's no misunderstanding, I'll pay you rent."

"Damn right, you will," Sam said, swiping at the
bar with a wet cloth. "I ain't running no charity
house."

Honey spent the rest of the afternoon sweeping and
scrubbing the room. By twilight, she had the place
looking spick-and-span. It wasn't just another room
over another saloon, she thought with pleasure. This
time everything was different. *Everyday I'll be able to
see Josh — and Luke.* For the first time since climbing off
that stage earlier, she admitted to herself she could no
more leave Luke than she could Josh.

Smiling, she changed into her black dress.

Chapter 22

◦❯❯❮❮◦

Luke felt like hell. He had gotten home too late to say good-night to Josh, but according to Mrs. Frick, the boy seemed to have recovered from his earlier depression. Considering his son's attachment to Honey, Luke found it hard to believe. He'd have to judge that for himself.

Throughout the day, when his mind wasn't on Josh, he had been thinking about Honey. Helping her into the coach that morning had been one of the hardest things he had ever done. At the last moment, he hadn't wanted to let go of her.

Remembering their talk the night of the bazaar, he wondered about all she had told him. She sure had had a hell of a life. It was no wonder she had chosen the wrong road to follow. *Dammit, forget her!* he cursed to himself. *You gave her what she wanted. She's gone now. Out of your life.*

But there was no forgetting Honey. The little blond temptress had gotten under his skin.

He checked the door of the bank, then continued on his rounds. As he started past the Long Branch, he suddenly tensed. Instinct warned him that something was wrong. Reflexively, his right hand slid to the holster at his hip.

232

After several seconds, he sensed the cause of his uneasiness. It was too damn quiet! At this time of the evening, there should be more noise coming from the saloon. Where was that cacophony of sound—the clatter of chips, clinking of glasses, drone of voices? Quickly, he swung his glance to the hitching posts and saw a good half-dozen horses tied there. The saloon sure wasn't deserted, so why the unnatural silence? He lowered his left hand to the other holster.

As he cautiously approached the door of the saloon, he heard the soft tinkle of a piano and the melodic voice of a woman singing. Luke froze.

His legs suddenly felt too weak to hold him. In the few seconds it took him to enter the Long Branch, he broke out in a cold sweat.

The chandeliers were dimmed, and the room was obscured in hazy shadows. His gaze was drawn to one person in the room.

She sat in the center of the bar, looking even more provocative than when he had first seen her in Sacramento, more appealing than when he had said good-bye to her that morning.

Her black gown hugged the voluptuous swells of her breasts; her bare shoulders and arms shimmered like white satin in the muted glow from a wall sconce behind her.

He shifted his hungry gaze to where a slit in the gown revealed her beautiful, long legs. Sheathed in black mesh stockings, they were crossed in front of her and dangled over the edge of the bar.

He moved his gaze to her face. Her eyes were closed, and she appeared deep in reverie as she sang the lyrics of the romantic ballad "Santa Lucia." It seemed as if the haunting strains of the Neapolitan melody had been written especially for her mellow, husky voice.

The pit of his stomach was being squeezed in a vise.

Honey felt the intense stare. Before she even opened her eyes, she knew it was him. Her eyelids seemed weighted as she slowly raised them.

He stood in the entrance.

Her yearning gaze devoured the sight of his sun-toughened face and the tall, hard shape of him. She drank in his sensuality—even more magnificently virile than she had remembered. With pulse-pounding excitement, she felt the surge of blood from the top of her turmoiled brain to the toes of her trembling legs.

Like a magnet, his sapphire stare pierced the distance between them, drawing and holding her gaze. Her whole being filled with desire for him, a sexual urgency that unnerved her as much as it thrilled her. The male essence of him was an aphrodisiac that stimulated her passion even as it lulled her into euphoria. For the length of that hushed moment, the words of the song were forgotten, and in the aching intensity of their locked gazes, they breathed as one. All the craving and restraint of the past month merged into a swell of lust, flooding her senses.

Make love to me, Luke, she implored in a silent supplication. The intimate message in their eyes ignored the presence of all others in the room. She resumed the words of the ballad to keep the silent plea from bursting past her lips.

He drank up the sight of her, his revived thirst raging out of control. He wanted her so badly his body felt like it was going to explode. He'd never know another moment's peace until he felt her hands and mouth on him.

His whole being filled with waiting.

Reeling through a haze of cravings and emotions, Honey took little notice of the applause and whistles when she finished the song. Pop O'Leary swung her off the bar, and as soon as her feet touched the floor, she hurried upstairs to her room. Her hand trembled as she laid aside her guitar, then she went to the dressing table and removed the black plume from her hair.

She glanced up in the mirror when the door

opened. Luke came in, closed the door, and leaned back against it.

"Lose your way, Sheriff? Lily's room is down the hall."

"What are you doing here?" he asked.

"I work here. I've got a job singing and dealing poker." For the want of something to do with her hands, she began to brush her hair.

"Why here?" he said.

"I like the atmosphere. I'm checking out saloons before opening one of my own," she replied flippantly.

"I don't think so."

She turned her head when she heard the key click in the lock, laid the brush aside, and rose to her feet.

"Tell me why you come back, Honey. Wouldn't have anything to do with that unfinished business between us, would it?" His voice remained calm, his look implacable—his intention evident when he removed his gunbelt and hung it on the door peg.

She could feel her heart's palpitation as she backed up to the wall. "Why do *you* think I came back?" Her voice held the rasp of excitement that was surging through her.

Luke's eyes glowed with purpose. He closed the distance between them, standing so near she could feel the heat of his body, smell the intoxicating male musk of him. His arm clamped around her waist, drawing her into the curve of his hips. "I think we said all there is to say downstairs, Miz Honey."

She leaned back, her eyes large and liquid—blue pools of aroused passion. The invitation in their smoldering depths told him everything he wanted to know. "Then why don't we just cut to the quick, MacKenzie?" She snatched his hat off his head and tossed it aside.

His mouth covered hers hungrily, possessively. A sweet fire of passion ignited within her and swept through her body unrestrained.

Their long-contained desire for each other erupted into a lust that now demanded gratification. With reckless abandon, she returned the ferocity of his kiss, matching his urgency with her own unsated needs.

His tongue plumbed the chamber of her mouth as his warm palm swept the curves of her spine. He crushed her tighter against the wall and yanked up her gown until he could slip his hands under it. His warm palms cupped the cheeks of her derriere.

Impatiently he pulled the gown over her head and, in the space of her gasp, stripped the clothes off her. His smoldering gaze raked her nakedness as he stepped back and yanked off his shirt. Reveling in the lust she saw in his eyes, she felt her pulses pound with anticipation.

There was no subtlety or attempt at seduction. He moved with swiftness and urgency, expedient and singular in purpose.

His hard thighs rubbed against her soft flesh when he parted her legs and stepped between them. Gripping her under the arms, he lifted her effortlessly, crushing her bare breasts against his hair-roughened chest. The contact caused glorious shocks of sensation to ripple down her spine. She wound her arms around his neck and clung to him, reflexively locking her legs around him. Once again his warm palms cupped her rear as he slid her upward along the wall until his mouth found her breasts. His tongue teased the sensitive tips of her nipples into aching peaks. Clutching at the taut, corded sinew of his shoulders, she tightened her grasp as he took a nipple into his mouth and began to suck. She felt consumed by the exquisite heat that inflamed her.

Her heart hammered in her chest, and her nails dug deeper into his shoulders when he slid a hand to her parted thighs and covered the throbbing center with his heated palm. Her breath came in ragged gasps as he began to massage her. The gasps changed to moans of ecstasy when his callused, long fingers slid into the velvet moistness. Her body jerked in response, and her legs clamped tighter around him. She arched into him, seeking greater contact.

The fingers of his left hand fumbled at the belt of his jeans as the ferocity and tempo of his sucking and probing strokes increased. The sweet agony became unbearable, and just when she thought to plead for mercy, he drove into her.

There was no desire on their part for tenderness or patience. Their lust was too feral and raw—their urgency too severe.

He recaptured her mouth, crushing her lips in a bruising kiss. As the hot tide of passion raged through her, his tongue plundered her mouth with the same driving force as his male sex until that explosive moment of inundating sensation. She lost all hold on reality and yielded to mindless rapture.

As she slowly fought her way back to sanity, her mind swirled in a sense of weightlessness until she felt her feet touch the floor. Opening her eyes, she discovered Luke was staring at her, bemused.

"That was a long time past due, Jaybird."

Befuddled, she saw him begin to remove his boots. She could feel her heart still hammering at her chest, and oblivious to her own nudity, she walked over to the dressing table and leaned against it.

She sensed him behind her before he pulled her back against him. He had removed his pants, and now he was naked, too. His flesh was warm, the touch tantalizing. Closing her eyes, she leaned back against the solid strength of his body, as firm and unrelenting as the wall had been. Elbows extended, she raised her arms behind her and looped them around his neck, her fingertips pressing into the taut cords at his nape.

Filling his hands with her breasts, he began to caress them. She moaned with erotic pleasure and cradled her head in the slope of his shoulder. It was all the invitation he needed. He nibbled kisses down her neck, then his tongue traced a moist trail back up to her ear.

Flesh on flesh, she was aware of every spot where their bodies touched. Her knees weakened when he gently swept his hand down the flat plane of her stomach. The warmth of his hand closed over the core of her womanhood, and her whole being filled with renewed hunger as his lips continued to explore her neck and shoulders.

Overpowered with need, she turned and slid her hands up his bare arms, the feel of dark silky hair an added aphrodisiac. As she looked into his eyes, glowing with a renewed fire, an unspoken message as ancient as Eden passed between them. As though she were weightless, he swept her up and carried her to the bed.

Slowly, seductively, he embraced her nakedness with a dark-eyed gaze that stoked her internal fire. She remained silent, content for the moment to lay basking in the desire she saw in his eyes.

He lowered himself and pressed his lips to the satiny sheen of her stomach. Her nerves throbbed under the intense titillation. Arching her body against the arousing moistness of his mouth, she laced her fingers through his dark hair.

He trailed a line of kisses up to her breasts, and she felt them swell as his tongue toyed with the sensitive peaks. "Oh, God, Luke!" she groaned when his mouth closed around one of the nipples.

He raised his head to gaze into her slumberous eyes. "I've wanted you for so long, Jaybird. I didn't think I'd ever experience this moment," he murmured, covering her face with kisses.

He smothered her attempt to reply with a crushing, possessive kiss that sent divine shocks of pleasure to the core of her sex. Her head and body swirled with a sensation too exciting not to want more. Welcoming the heated sweeps of his plundering tongue, she savored every second in an uninhibited response. He showered light kisses on her lips, along her jaw, and down the slender column of her neck. Then he returned to crush her lips with a bruising intensity.

Arching against him, she locked her arms around his neck and fought to hold him even as she felt him pull away. "No, don't stop. Don't stop," she cried. "I want you. I want you, Luke."

He gripped her arms to free himself from her grasp, then stretched out on top of her. She reveled at the feel of his nakedness pressed to her own: his chest crushing her breasts, the long torso and powerful thighs that pinned her beneath him. Aching with escalating fervor, she felt the heated hardness of his arousal throbbing against the very center of her being.

She began to squirm beneath him, seeking satisfaction for the sensation coiling unbearably at the junction of her legs.

"I've been thinking about this moment ever since you walked through the door of that hotel room, wearing that damn white robe," he whispered, nibbling at her lips.

"I have, too," she confessed breathlessly, then gasped as his moist mouth closed around the nipple of her breast and began to suck.

Arching into his powerful body, she managed to roll over, stretching out on top of him. Now able to move with greater freedom, she covered his mouth aggressively and let her tongue duel with his. And in tandem with every thrust of her tongue, she rubbed herself against his hot, erect arousal now trapped between her parted legs. Groaning, he slipped his hands along the smooth curve of her hips and cupped her derriere.

Perspiration glistened on his chest when she lowered her head to the muscular plane. His body felt taut, and she could feel his heart pounding beneath her lips. As she laved his chest, she encountered one of his nipples with her tongue, and at the sound of his quick gasp, she moved her mouth to the other nipple. This time, she felt his body jerk in response. In a bolder exploration, she drew one of the hard nubs into her mouth and began to suck it as he had done to her.

Groaning, he rolled her over onto her back. "You're good, Jaybird. God, you're good."

He reclaimed her mouth in a hard, passionate kiss that devoured her breath, then he dipped his head again to her breasts and resumed the divine torture. Clutching his shoulders, she curved her hands around the corded muscles. She breathed in ragged gasps each time his teeth tugged on a pebbled nipple, and she groaned with rapture as undulating waves of exquisite sensation flowed through her.

He slipped his hand between her legs and parted them. Finding the warmth of the sensitive chamber, he cautiously probed the opening with his fingers.

He lifted his head but continued the exquisite massage as he straddled her. Increasing the rhythm of his hand, he sucked one of her nipples into his mouth.

Tottering on the brink of mindlessness, under wave upon wave of the ecstatic tremors that shook her body, she cried out breathlessly, "Oh, yes, Luke. Yes. Don't stop!" Her rasped breathing sounded like a drum pounding in her ears.

Grasping her trembling hand, he brought it to his extended sex. At the look in his passion-filled eyes, she knew what he was asking of her. Curling her fingers around it, she ran her hand along the length of the hardened shaft. She felt the throbbing organ in her palm pulsating with heat and energy.

He closed his eyes when he felt the flood of hot blood to it. "Ah, that's it. That's it."

He knew he had stretched his control to the breaking point. On the verge of climaxing, he rolled over and straddled her. Parting her legs, he began to massage her again until her body convulsed with tremors.

Then he eased himself into her. Moisture glistened on his forehead, and the cords of his arms and neck were taut with tension as he strained to control his ejaculation.

This time he moved gently within her. She tightened around him. Her excitement seemed to escalate in tandem with the increased tempo of his thrusts, and she cried out in the ecstasy of a rapturous climax at the same instant his hot liquid spilled into her.

Luke collapsed on her, and for a long moment they clung together, the sound of their labored breathing pounding in their ears. Finally he moved away, stood up, and began to dress.

Honey pulled up the sheet to cover herself, then lay silently, studying his chiseled profile. She would not have believed it possible, but after the glorious moments they had just shared, she knew her love for him was greater than before.

As Luke strapped on his gunbelt, he stood over the bed and stared down at her.

"The slate's washed clean. We're free and clear now—no more unfinished business. Right, Sheriff?"

His brow arched with amusement. "You leaving town?"

"I have no intention of leaving. I told you I have a job here."

He unlocked the door and paused in the doorway. "Then I'll be back."

She reacted instantly to the smugness in his voice. "What makes you think you're invited back?"

"Why toss in your hand just when the game's getting exciting?" He plopped his hat on his head.

Honey got out of bed and turned the key in the lock as soon as he'd left. Deep in reflection, she leaned her cheek against the door and thought about their incredible lovemaking. Now there was no doubt that he knew she was his for the taking.

But despite his cocky confidence, she savored the promise of his parting words.

Chapter 23

When Honey woke the next morning, she stretched and lay contentedly, thinking about Luke. Past grievances were forgotten as her mind and body blazed with the greater fire that had erupted between them last night. Shocked by her driving need in those blissful moments, she blushed, recalling her own boldness. She had never given herself so willingly and completely, even to Robert. But Luke would never have settled for anything less.

Shortly before noon, Honey started off to Cynthia's, anxious to see her friend again. She couldn't help but cast a wistful sidelong glance as she passed Luke's house. She came to an abrupt stop when she saw Josh sitting on the stoop, with his elbows on his knees and his head in his hands. As usual, Amigo lay beside him.

She hunched down in front of Josh. "Hey, what happened?" she asked gently. "Both of you look like you've lost your best friend."

"Can me and Amigo come and live with you?" Josh asked. "Frau Frick doesn't like us."

"Frau Frick?" Honey asked, confused. "Oh, you mean Mrs. Frick."

242

Josh shook his head. "She says she wants to be called Frau Frick, not Mrs. Frick."

"She told your father that, too?" Honey asked, amused.

Josh nodded. "And she won't let Amigo go inside the house."

"For Heaven's sake, why not?"

" 'Cause she don't like dogs. How come she don't like Amigo, Honey? He never did anything to her 'cept maybe chase her dumb cat one time."

"Maybe that was enough, sweetheart."

"But it's not fair. Amigo lived here 'fore her and her dumb cat did."

"Now, Josh, you mustn't dislike the cat just because of Mrs.—ah—Frau Frick."

"Don't like the dumb cat 'cause she spits and hisses at us like a snake."

"Well, you and Amigo are strangers to her. What's her name?"

"It's a dumb girl's name."

"You mean dumb like Honey?"

" 'Course not." He looked shocked that she would even say such a thing. "Honey's a beautiful name. The most beautifulest name I ever heared before."

Honey grabbed him and gave him a quick hug. "You little charmer! Well, tell me the cat's name."

"Sophie."

"Sophie's a nice name, Josh."

"Maybe for a lady, but not for a cat. A cat oughta be called Tiger or Kitty or some'n like that." He looked up at her with pleading eyes. "So can me and Amigo come and live with you, Honey?"

"Sweetheart, I live in a small room over the Long Branch. There just isn't enough space for all of us. Besides, you wouldn't want to leave your father, Josh. You know how much he loves you."

"I know." He hung his head. "I just don't know what I'm s'posed to do. Amigo loves me, too."

"Does your daddy know that Mrs.—"

"Frau Frick."

"That Frau Frick won't allow Amigo in the house?"

Josh nodded. "He said I should be patient and in a couple weeks he'll talk to her about it." He looked up questioningly. "How many days is a couple weeks, Honey?"

"Fourteen, sweetheart."

"Fourteen days!" He cradled his head in his hands again. "That's sure a long time."

"Well, let me talk to your daddy. Maybe something can be worked out so that Amigo can stay with me at night."

Josh frowned and slowly shook his head. "I don't think Amigo can sleep without me there."

Honey forced back a smile. "Hey, sport, are you sure it's not the other way around?" She stood up, clasped his hand, and pulled him to his feet. "Come on, let's go see Aunt Cynthia."

As they walked down the street hand in hand, Josh said to her, "Some'n else, too, 'bout that old Frau Frick. She's not a good teacher like you are, Honey. I heared her tell my daddy that I oughta be in school." He shook his head in despair. "Bad 'nough 'bout Frau Frick and her dumb cat. Now I'm gonna have that prune-face Mrs. Webster, too."

"Prune face! Shame on you, Joshua MacKenzie. Wherever did you hear an expression like that?"

"From you," he said, kicking at a stone in his path.

"It's no wonder the town thinks I'm a bad influence on you." She began to giggle. "Last one to Aunt Cynthia's house is a prune face." Laughing, she raced off with Josh and Amigo chasing her.

They found Cynthia on her knees scrubbing the floor. Her face changed from shock to joy. "Oh, Honey, is it really you? I couldn't believe Josh when he told me. And you couldn't have come back at a better time. I need you so much."

Concerned, Honey put her hand on Cynthia's shoulder. "What's wrong, dear?"

Cynthia glanced worriedly at Josh. "Darling, will

you quick run and bring back Uncle Doug? Tell him the baby's coming."

"Oh, dear Lord!" Honey said. She hustled Josh out the door. "Hurry, sweetheart." Josh raced away as fast as his legs could carry him.

"For Heaven's sake, Cynthia, why are you scrubbing floors in your condition?"

"My water broke, and I'm trying to clean it up."

As Honey helped her to her feet, she saw a combination of joy and fear in Cynthia's eyes. "You get yourself into bed," Honey declared, shooing her away. "I'll finish scrubbing up the floor." When she finished, she hurried into the bedroom to help Cynthia undress.

"I've put several kettles of water on to boil," Cynthia said. "I know Doug will want hot water to wash his hands and sterilize his instruments." Gripped with pain, she stopped to gasp, then continued as though nothing had happened. "The baby's crib is ready, and all those linens and buntings I've been sewing him for months are in the chest at the foot of the bed."

"Him?" Honey asked. "How do you know it will be a boy?"

"Of course it will be a boy. Mama Rosa told me so," Cynthia replied with a dimpled giggle. "Oh, just think, Honey, soon I'll be able to see my feet again," she exclaimed when Honey knelt down to remove her shoes and hose for her.

"I swear, Cynthia Nelson, I'm more nervous about this baby coming than you are."

Honey hurried out of the bedroom when she heard the front door open. Much to Honey's mortification, Luke entered the house. "Hi, Jaybird."

Her cheeks turned red. "Luke." She pivoted quickly and attempted to busy herself at the stove. She was too embarrassed to look him in the eye. After their passionate lovemaking the previous day, she was not prepared to face him unexpectedly—especially in the cold light of day. He appeared to be unaffected.

"I was hoping you were Doug and Josh."

"Josh is outside. He told me about Cynthia, but Doug's not in town. He rode out earlier to the Calhoun ranch. Ben Calhoun broke his leg."

Feeling a rise of panic, coupled with her embarrassment, Honey cried out frantically, "What are we going to do?"

"Hey, relax, Jaybird," he said gently. He tipped up her chin and forced her to look at him. "What else is bothering you, Honey?"

"Nothing." She jerked her head away and turned her back to him.

"Has it got something to do with last night?"

"What do you think?"

"Well, what about it?"

Exasperated at his lack of understanding, she turned back to him and lifted her chin defiantly. "Robert Warren was the only man I've ever let—"

"Robert Warren? Isn't he the man you fell in love with when you were nineteen?"

She nodded.

Remembering how passionately she'd responded to him the previous night, Luke emitted a long, low whistle. "The guy must have been one hell of a teacher!"

She shook her head in disgust. "Was that remark necessary?"

He chuckled with amusement. "I meant it as a compliment, Jaybird. But you're a paradox, Honey Behr! Makes sense now why you made such a lousy con woman." Shaking his head, he moved to the door. "I'm riding out to get Doug. I'll bring him back as quickly as I can."

She followed him outside. "What if the baby comes? I'm scared, Luke," Honey said. "I've never seen a baby born before."

"Not even an animal?" Luke asked her.

"No. I don't know what to do."

"Babies come natural, Honey. Just relax. I've got to get going." She watched with increased trepidation as

Luke swung onto Alamo and galloped away.

Returning to the bedroom, Honey told Cynthia the bad news. "Well, I just won't have this baby until Doug gets here," Cynthia said confidently.

"Will you at least get in bed?"

Cynthia still refused to do so. "We just had this mattress shipped in from San Francisco. I don't want to ruin it now," she announced. "I've put a pile of old towels in the corner for this occasion."

"I declare, you're worse than a general planning a battle," Honey censured as the two women proceeded to put a thick padding of towels over the sheet. "There, do you think you might be willing to get into bed now?"

"I suppose I must." Cynthia sighed and allowed Honey to help her into bed. When Honey started to cover her with a sheet, Cynthia grabbed her arm. For the first time since she had arrived, Honey saw tears glistening in her friend's eyes. "I'm glad you're here, Honey."

"I am, too." Honey hugged and kissed her, then hurried out to the parlor to dispose of the slop rags and bucket.

"Pull up a chair and tell me why you came back to Stockton," Cynthia said when Honey returned to the bedroom.

"I knew you'd have your baby today, and I sure didn't want to miss all this excitement."

"Oh, you zany," Cynthia declared. "Be serious."

"I just couldn't bear to leave Josh, Cynthia. I thought my heart would break when I saw him watching me ride out on that stage."

"What did Luke have to say about your return?"

Honey blushed, recalling what had transpired between them the night before. "He, ah . . . really didn't have too much to say about it."

Cynthia glanced at her with suspicion. "Why are you blushing? Is there something you aren't telling me?" She gasped again with pain. "Oh, I hope Doug gets here soon."

"I don't want to alarm you, Cynthia, but I don't know the first thing about birthing a baby," Honey said.

"Don't worry. I know Doug will get back in time."

"Maybe you should try and sleep," Honey suggested.

"With this pain?"

"Well, just try and rest then." Honey stood up. She wanted to get out of the room before Cynthia could ask her any more questions about Luke. "I better check on Josh. He's outside playing with Amigo. I'm not sure he understands what's going on."

"You'll come back, won't you?" Cynthia looked frightened.

Honey patted her hand. "Of course, dear." Realizing that Cynthia had been disguising her fears behind a brave front, Honey felt guilty for having sought an alibi to escape from the room. "Would you like me to fix you something to eat?" she said gently.

"No, but there's a fresh kettle of soup if you and Josh are hungry."

"I think I will give him some soup. And as soon as I finish, I'll tell you about Luke's new housekeeper— and just what Josh thinks about her."

"Oh, please do," Cynthia cried out. "And hurry, I can hardly wait to hear."

Honey spent the next three hours anxiously awaiting Doug's arrival. She had finished feeding Josh and had just washed up the dishes when Doug and Luke returned.

"I'm not too late?" Doug asked, wild-eyed.

"No. Not yet. Cynthia's in the bedroom, Doug."

He hurried into the room and closed the door behind him.

"Do you think we should stay?" Honey asked Luke.

He sat down on the floor next to Josh, who had fallen asleep in front of the fireplace. "Yeah, I think it would be a good idea. You at least. Doug can probably use your help. I'll take Josh home."

"You'd probably be more help to Doug than I could ever be."

Luke grinned. "Maybe not. Ma wouldn't let me in the room the night Josh was born."

"Why not?"

"She said it's not good for a man to see his wife suffering in labor. Might give him notions about not having any more children." His expression became downcast.

"What is it?" she asked.

"Josh is already six years old. Looks like he's gonna miss growing up with brothers or sisters. I sure can't imagine what it would have been like without Flint and Cleve."

"Were you and your brothers close, Luke?"

"Oh, yeah. With Pa gone, we kind of had to look after each other. You don't speak about it at the time or even think about it, but it's always there."

"What is?" she asked softly.

"Love. Loyalty. A kind of unity."

She thought of her own lonely childhood. She had never had someone her own age to talk to. Someone to bond with through good times and bad. *What good times?* she asked herself cynically, then shook aside the contrary thought.

"Didn't you ever fight amongst yourselves?" she asked and smiled tenderly at the sound of his warm chuckle.

"Hell yes! Punching and wrestling with each other all the time. But out of fun more times than not. Ma always said it was enough to drive her to distraction." Luke stared into space. After a long pause, he lifted his head and glanced over at Josh curled up asleep with Amigo snuggled beside him. "Yep, sure don't want Josh to grow up without any brothers."

"From the looks of him and Amigo, I'd say he's got one whether you want to admit it or not," she teased.

"That damn dog," Luke murmured with affection. He stood up. "Best get Josh home. Mrs. Frick—"

"Frau Frick," Honey hastily corrected.

Luke eyed her with surprise. "Yeah. She's probably wondering what happened to us. Tell Doug I'll be back."

Honey tried unsuccessfully to concentrate on one of Doug's medical journals. Luke had just returned when Doug came out of the bedroom and joined them. "Looks like it could be a couple hours yet," Doug said. He grinned at Luke. "Just think, pal, I'm gonna be a daddy. I'm sure glad I got back here in time. I'd hate to have missed the birth of my own daughter."

"Your daughter? Cynthia's convinced the baby will be a boy," Honey reminded him.

"I'd love to have a little Cynthia climbing up on my lap," Doug said. "Come to think of it, I'd enjoy the bigger one, too. But if we don't have a girl this time . . . we'll just have to keep trying."

"Reckon so." Luke grinned.

The afternoon stretched into the evening, and seeing Doug agonize as he watched Cynthia's suffering made Honey realize the wisdom behind Mrs. MacKenzie's words. Having to deliver his own baby had to make the situation twice as difficult for him emotionally.

Honey sat at her friend's bedside, holding her hand and gently sponging the perspiration off her forehead.

Cynthia closed her eyes, and smiled despite her pain. "Oh, I'm so glad you came back, Honey."

"I would have had to turn around and leave again if Sam Brazner hadn't given me a job at the Long Branch."

"You'll have to tell me all about it," Cynthia managed to murmur. "Just promise you won't leave us again." The last word came out in a scream as Cynthia jerked with pain.

"I promise, dear. I promise."

"Doug!" Cynthia cried. Honey moved aside, and Doug took her place. "Oh, God, Doug, how much longer?" Cynthia pleaded.

"Soon, sweetheart, soon," he assured her, stroking her cheek.

"I'm scared, Doug. Something's wrong, isn't it?"

"Everything looks fine. It shouldn't be much longer."

Her fingers dug into his arm. "Doug, if something happens to me, I don't—"

"Nothing's going to happen, sweetheart." He picked up her hand and kissed the palm. "I won't let anything happen to you or our baby."

Cynthia tried to smile through the haze of her pain. "I know. I've got the best doctor in the world."

Near tears, Honey wandered out of the bedroom. Emotionally exhausted, she slumped down on a bench at the table. *Dear God, please don't let anything happen to her.*

"You tired, Jaybird?" Luke walked over and sat down beside her.

"I imagine you are, too." She smiled at him. Funny how her previous embarrassment had vanished. Now she felt a warm glow at having him near.

"I've been dozing off and on in the chair," he said.

Honey yawned. "Poor Cynthia. She's in so much pain. How much longer can this go on? I never realized it could take so long to deliver a baby."

"I remember when Josh was born. Sarah labored for fourteen hours."

"Oh my, I hope it won't take that long. I don't think either Cynthia or Doug could bear it."

He turned his head and looked at her. Mesmerized, she watched his expression change to desire as their physical awareness of each other began to escalate. Her heart began to hammer at her ribs, pumping hot blood to her pulses. His hand cupped her neck and drew her slowly toward him.

He lowered his head, and she parted her lips.

The sound of Cynthia's excruciating scream jolted them apart. Honey jumped to her feet.

"Okay, Honey, this is it," Doug called out to her. "You want to come in and give me a hand?"

Honey hurried into the bedroom. Cynthia was gasping with pain, and a sheen of perspiration covered her forehead. She clutched Honey's hand.

"You're doing great, honey. The head's out," Doug said. "One more squeeze should do it."

Honey flinched as Cynthia's nails bit into her hand for that final push. At the moment of delivery, Cynthia fainted from the shock of the pain.

"Honey, open up one of those blankets and bring it here," Doug said.

Honey grabbed one of the tiny quilts Cynthia had worked on so lovingly. She stared with awe as he placed the infant in the blanket and laid it on the foot of the bed.

When Cynthia regained consciousness a few minutes later, Doug carried their newborn child, now cleaned and swaddled in a blanket, to his wife.

"Oh, Doug, is it a boy or a girl?" Cynthia cried anxiously.

"Sweetheart, I'm holding the most precious, rosy-cheeked little baby I've ever delivered," he said reverently, "with brown eyes, dark curly hair, and a dimpled chin just like her beautiful mother." He laid their daughter in her arms.

Cynthia wept softly as she peeked at the infant. "Oh, Doug, isn't she precious? She's just so precious." She smiled up at him through her tears. "Isn't she the most beautiful sight you've ever seen?"

Moisture glistened in his eyes as he looked down at the faces of his wife and newborn daughter. "No man could gaze upon a more beautiful sight." He lowered his head and kissed her gently. "Thank you, my love. Thank you for our daughter."

Cynthia fell asleep almost immediately, and Doug handed the baby to Honey so he could finish administering to Cynthia. Honey trembled as she stared with wonder at the newborn child; she felt overwhelmed by the miracle of birth.

She carried the infant from the room. "It's a girl, Luke."

He bent over the child in her arms. Gently he picked up one of the little hands, and the tiny fingers immediately curled around his thumb. Grinning, he gazed at Honey.

Honey carried the baby back into the bedroom. While Doug thoroughly checked out the infant, Honey removed the soiled towels off the bed.

When he completed his examination, Doug laid his daughter in her cradle and slipped his arm around Honey. "What we have here, Miss Honey Behr, is a perfect child in body, beauty, and—irrefutably—in soul."

"Of course, Dr. Nelson." Honey grinned. "And I'm certain you're speaking clinically and not out of bias."

"I always base my medical opinions on clinical observations, my dear."

Looking not unlike a strutting peacock, Doug joined Luke at the table. "Well, now that you've gazed on perfection, old man, what have you got to say?"

"Only that you're one doggone lucky, undeserving son of a—" Remembering Honey's presence, he stuttered, "Ah—son of a gun." Then he laughed and grabbed Doug in a handshake. "I'm happy for you, buddy."

"This calls for a toast." Doug went to a cupboard and pulled out a bottle of whiskey. "Are you a drinking woman, Honey?"

"No, I'll pass, Doug."

He filled two glasses, handed one to Luke, and raised his own in a toast. "To my daughter."

"And thank goodness she has her *mother's* beauty," Luke joshed.

Doug quickly raised the glass again. "And to my daughter's mother. The bravest and most wonderful wife a man could hope for." Turning serious, he said solemnly, "Isn't this a remarkable night!"

"That's right, Doug," Luke said. "I don't think any of us will forget it."

* * *

Honey and Luke left the new parents a short time later. Luke insisted on walking her back to the Long Branch.

"Really, Luke, that's not necessary," Honey protested.

"Yeah, it's late."

Sam was just closing up when they reached the saloon. "Boy or girl?" he asked after Honey explained the reason for her absence.

"A girl." Honey beamed.

"Remind me to buy Doc a drink the next time he comes in. Good night," Sam said and headed for his room at the rear of the building.

For a moment Luke and Honey stared awkwardly at each other. Then she said, "Well, good night, Luke, and thank you for walking me home."

Luke's gaze never shifted from her face. "Good night."

She walked up the stairs, stopped at the landing, and looked back. He hadn't budged. "Good night, Luke," she repeated softly. "It has been a remarkable night, hasn't it?"

Honey entered her room and closed the door. She did not light a lamp but walked to the dressing table and turned slowly when she heard the door open.

Luke crossed the room to her. For the length of several shared heartbeats, he stared down into her serene face. Reaching out, he curled several strands of her hair around his finger. It felt like silk. It smelled like Honey, that intangible scent that permeated his senses day and night.

"Yeah, a remarkable night, and it's not over yet, is it, Jaybird?"

In the glow of moonlight, her eyes seemed to glimmer like calm pools of blue water deep enough to drown in.

He dived in.

Wrapping an arm around her waist, he drew her into his embrace. Her unresisting body curved into him, and he felt her response even before he covered her mouth and devoured her soft lips.

He slipped his tongue past her lips and explored the warm recess of her mouth. As the kiss deepened, he could feel her passion rise. She slipped her arms around his neck, and he savored the crush of her breasts. Her hard nipples stabbed at his chest. Unhurried, he opened the buttons of her gown and pushed the gown and camisole aside. Then he grasped her shoulders, lowered his mouth to her breasts, and began to feast on them.

Passion rose in him like a fire, fueling his appetite. He wanted more, and the fierceness of her response told him she did, too. Under the bruising pressure of his mouth, her tongue dueled with his until breathlessness forced them apart.

"God, I want you," he rasped as he kissed the pulsating hollow at the base of her throat. He could feel himself tighten, and he raised his head, trying to gauge her wants.

The desire he saw in her smoldering eyes flamed the intensity of his own cravings, but unhurried, he stripped the clothes off her and caressed her breasts. Lowering his mouth, he sucked on one of the nipples. No one tasted like Honey. He needed to taste more of her. Sinking to his knees, he trailed his lips and tongue down her stomach to the junction of her legs. She was trembling now, and he clutched her hips and brought her to his mouth.

Her breath came faster, and he felt the contraction of the muscles beneath his mouth. Gripped in a spasm, her body arched, thrusting her hips to meet him. Her body continued to shudder with tremors and she threw back her head, his name an incessant groan on her lips. As he continued to probe the sweet center with his tongue she whimpered for mercy, but he gave no quarter; he was hard, hot, and hungry.

And ready to explode.

He stood up, and her groping fingers helped him shed his clothes. He thought he would climax when her fingers began to stroke him. With a hoarse growl, he swept her into his arms and carried her to the bed.

He stretched out on top of her and kissed her, releasing her only long enough to draw a much-needed breath. Then he smothered her lips with a hungry, demanding kiss, his tongue ravishing the chamber of her mouth. When he reached down to part her legs, she took him by surprise by shoving him to his back. She drew away from him and glanced down at his hardened organ.

He could feel the rise of gooseflesh on his body as he guessed her intent. He lay back, and she palmed him, her fingers fondling, stroking, caressing. Then she lowered her head and took him into her mouth.

Hot blood coursed to his temples, pounded in his ears, blinded his vision. It felt like raging fire as it swelled his member to even greater proportions. Moaning, he thrashed out of control.

He knew he was going to ejaculate and pulled her across him. Cradling her head in his arm, he flipped her over. Without a second to spare, he drove into her and spilled his hot release.

For several minutes, he lay, trying to calm his labored breathing. Then he raised his head and gazed down at her. He saw bewilderment in her flushed face and blue-eyed stare.

His feelings toward her were becoming more confused each time they were together. Cupping her check in the palm of his hand, he leaned down and kissed the tip of her nose, then gently covered her lips in a tender kiss.

"Reckon you're right, Jaybird. This has been a remarkable night."

Chapter 24

The next morning, Honey hurried over to the Nelsons' to check on Cynthia and the baby. She met Josh on the way.

"What are you up to so early this morning?" she asked.

"I went to see the baby," he said.

"That's just where I'm going."

"She sure is little. Auntie Cyntia said it was time for the baby to eat, so Amigo and I had to leave. Don't see why. Don't bother me if somebody sees me eat. Girls sure are different."

Honey hugged and kissed him. "It's not girls, sweetheart. It's babies."

"I'm gonna be a godfather to the baby," he piped. "Isn't that 'citing news, Honey?"

"My yes! That's quite an honor, Josh."

"Honey, what's a godfather?"

"Well, it means you're entrusted to make certain the child will carry on her religion."

Josh scratched his head. "You mean I have to take her to church?"

"Only in the event that something should happen to Aunt Cynthia and Uncle Doug."

"You mean like if they get sick and die like my mama did?"

"That's right, sweetheart."

"How could they die? Uncle Doug's a doctor and knows how to make people better when they get sick."

"Well, people have accidents, too, Josh. Like falling off horses or even down stairs." She intentionally avoided the mention of gunshot wounds.

"Oh," he said sadly. "I sure wouldn't want them to die just so I could be a godfather."

"That's not going to happen, so let's not even think about it. After I see the baby, we'll go to the general store and you can buy the baby a doll."

"A doll! Why not a wooden horse like I have?"

"Little girls like dolls, Josh. Now, you go back to your house and wait for me. As soon as I finish visiting with Aunt Cynthia, I'll come and get you."

She continued on to the house. Doug opened the door at her knock and greeted her with his usual cordiality. "Good morning, pretty lady. Have you eaten breakfast?" She nodded. "I'm just finishing mine, but my wife and daughter are in the bedroom."

Looking refreshed and beautiful, Cynthia was sitting up in bed, nursing the baby.

"You've got visitors, Cindy," Doug said, following Honey into the room. He leaned over the bed and kissed the top of the baby's head. "I wish I had the convenient eating arrangement my daughter has."

"Well, your daughter has fallen asleep again. Apparently she doesn't appreciate the arrangements like her daddy would."

"No, she doesn't, brown eyes," he said devilishly, lightly passing his hand over the bodice of her gown.

"Doug!" Cynthia glanced with embarrassment at Honey.

"Oh, Honey is family," he said. Then he kissed Cynthia on the end of her nose and took the baby from her arms. "Come to Daddy, sugar plum."

"Sugar plum! Do you believe it? Who would call anyone sugar plum?" Cynthia giggled.

Honey arched a brow. "My dear, you are asking someone cursed with the name Honey." They both burst into giggles.

Doug laid the sleeping baby in her cradle. "Honey, would you take care of my girls while I go to my office for a couple of medical journals that I haven't had time to read?"

"Of course."

"I'll be right back."

Honey sat down at the bedside. "I just saw Josh. He's thrilled that you've asked him to be the baby's godfather."

"And we want you to be her godmother."

Honey was astonished. "Cynthia, I'm a bad example for any child."

"Doug and I don't think so. We can't think of a finer example."

Honey felt the rise of tears. "But I'm shunned by the citizens of this town. You and Doug have a position to maintain here."

"You're our friend, Honey. That's more important to both of us than maintaining any position. Confidentially, Doug has been offered a surgical position in Seattle's hospital. He's considering taking it, but he hasn't made up his mind."

"How would you feel about leaving Stockton?"

"I'd hate the thought of leaving the MacKenzies and you. I love all of you so much. But I would be nearer my father, and the baby, her grandfather. So I guess I would have to consider that, too. Of course, you could always come to Seattle to live."

"What about other family members? Are you sure you won't offend any of them by not giving them this honor?"

"My mother died five years ago in a carriage accident, and my father remarried the following year. Now I have a three-year-old half-sister. But my step-mother, Catherine, is . . . rather difficult. I'm afraid Doug doesn't like her at all."

"Doug? With his bedside manner? I can't imagine him not getting along with anyone."

"Doug says Catherine's too uppity, and he thinks that she married my father for his money." She shrugged. "I hope not. I'd hate to think my father isn't happy." Then she chuckled devilishly. "Wait till Daddy hears he's a grandfather. I hope Doug remembers to send him a telegram. I should have reminded him before he left." She clasped Honey's hand. "But you will agree to be our baby's godmother, won't you? Luke and Josh will be the godfather—or godfathers, I should say."

"I would be honored to be your daughter's godmother, Cynthia." Honey smiled through her tears.

"And will you sing a song at the christening? Doug heard you sing at the Long Branch. He says you have a beautiful voice." When Honey started to protest, Cynthia quickly added, "Please do, Honey. We'd be so thrilled."

"All right, I will. But you and Doug will probably be the only two who will think so."

Cynthia folded her hands and smiled. "Well now, let's get to planning the christening."

"Speaking of christening, I brought a baby gift—even though it's really meant for you." She dug in her pocket and handed a brightly-wrapped box to Cynthia.

Honey smiled at Cynthia's obvious pleasure when she opened the gift.

"Oh my! It's the fan I admired in the window of the emporium," she squealed. "Oh, Honey, I love it. And I'll be sure to carry it at the baptism."

"Well, I thought you could always pass it down to—" Honey suddenly stopped. "Cynthia, what are you going to name the baby?"

"We thought we would call her Melissa Diane. That was my mother's name. It's sure not going to sit well with Catherine, though."

The subject of their conversation chose to wake up at that moment, so while Cynthia tried to feed the baby again, Honey washed Doug's breakfast dishes. He returned shortly after, and Honey left so Cynthia could rest.

The following Sunday afternoon, most of the citizens of Stockton crowded into the church to witness the christening of Melissa Diane Nelson.

As Pastor Wright baptized the baby, Honey heard whispered comments about her own presence there. She stood with her head high and tried to ignore them. Pop O'Leary squeezed her hand in a sign of support when she returned to the pew and sat down beside him.

Soon, the dreaded moment arrived for her to get up and sing her solo. Squaring her shoulders, she walked to the piano. Nancy Wright did not even glance at her. The pastor's wife struck the opening chord to "Beautiful Dreamer," the song Cynthia had requested.

Honey had just finished the first line of the song when Clarabelle Webster said loudly, "Hiram, it's very stuffy in here. I would like to go outside for some fresh air." The mayor and his wife got up and walked up the aisle. Myrtlelee and Delmer Quinn followed. The undertaker cast a sheepish look as he passed Luke.

Luke clenched his fists and tried to maintain an impassive expression as several others followed Clarabelle's example. *You've insulted a lot of the people in the town, Honey,* he thought in defense of the rude townspeople. But he couldn't help but admire Honey's spunk as she continued to sing over the mumbling voices and shuffling feet of the departing parishioners.

Nancy Wright halted playing but was stopped from leaving by a stern look from her husband. She sat back down on the piano bench and resumed, but the instant the song ended, she stood up and marched up the aisle.

Only the Nelsons, Josh, and Pop O'Leary remained in the pews. Even Frau Frick had left. After a cursory thank you to Honey, Pastor Wright hastened up the aisle, offering a quick nod to Luke.

Honey refused to cry. She would not give the town hypocrites the satisfaction. "I'm sorry I spoiled Melissa's christening."

Cynthia hugged her. "That's nonsense, Honey, and you know it. You didn't spoil it; you sang beautifully. The song was perfect for the beautiful little dreamer right here in my arms."

"Aye, darlin'," Pop O'Leary exclaimed. "I'm thinkin' this church has never heard anything sweeter."

She felt the comfort of Doug's arm around her shoulder. "That's right. Cindy and I appreciate what you did for us, Honey. It took a lot of courage to stand up to this town, and you did it. Believe me, this is a story we'll be proud to tell your godchild one day."

"Well, I'm not going to drive away your guests. This is too important a day in the baby's life. So I'll be going now, and you get on with the celebration."

"Don't go, Honey," Cynthia pleaded. "Stay and join us for punch and cake. We'd rather celebrate it with friends instead of those hypocrites outside."

"I have to get to work," Honey lied glibly.

"No, you don't, Honey. This is Sunday, don't you remember?" Josh piped up in his innocence.

"I know, but I promised Sam I'd work today. I have to go." She bent down and kissed the baby's cheek, then hugged and kissed Josh.

"I'll be goin' with you, darlin'," Pop said.

As she passed Luke, she paused and looked up at him. "How come you hung around here, Sheriff? You, more than any, know what a sinner I am." She stepped past him.

* * *

"I'll see you and raise you five dollars," Honey said later that evening to the remaining player in the hand. For several seconds the man tapped the chips in front of him. His hands were beautiful: tanned and long fingered with clean, clipped nails. *Looks like he hasn't done a lick of hard work his whole life*, she thought.

He shoved a chip to the center of the table. "I'll call you, ma'am." His voice was low, with a hint of southern honey.

She had noticed the stranger earlier when he had first entered the Long Branch. Small boned and of medium height, he hadn't appeared to have a speck of dust on him. With a suave and confident air, he had sat down and joined the game.

Honey looked into silvery eyes rimmed with gold-tipped eyelashes. His features were so delicate and symmetrical they bordered on being ethereal. His hair was thick and silky and lay in tawny gold waves on a head held with patrician grace. Were it not for the neatly trimmed moustache above his generous and sensuous mouth, he would have been too pretty to pass for a man.

"Aces full," Honey said, turning over her hand.

The smile remained on his flawless face. "That beats me, ma'am." He pocketed his remaining chips, picked up his Stetson, and shoved back his chair. "It's been my pleasure, Miss . . . ?" He arched an aristocratic brow.

"Honey," she said. "Just plain Honey."

His wide grin revealed dazzling white teeth. "My pleasure, just-plain-Honey." She felt uneasy under his fixed, silvery stare. "I hope I'll have the pleasure again. Now if you'll excuse me, I have an appointment."

Honey watched him walk over to Lily. Taking her arm, they climbed the stairs.

A short while later, Honey decided she'd had her fill of poker. "I'm cashing in, boys." She went over and sat down at a table where Pop O'Leary was sitting alone. "I think I've had enough of this place for tonight."

"Why are you workin' anyway?" he asked. "This is your night off."

"I just didn't feel like sitting up in my room."

"I'm hopin' you're not allowin' those town biddies to be causin' you heartache, darlin'."

"Of course not, Pop. I don't care what they think."

She knew she hadn't fooled him for a moment. His eyes saddened. "You're more of a lady then the whole passel of them put together. What are you doin' in a place like this? You don't belong here."

"I'm alone in the world, Pop. I have to make a living."

"Aye, but this is no place for the likes of you."

Honey patted his hand. "Please don't lecture me, Pop. I get enough of that from the sheriff."

"Whatever it is you want, child, you won't be findin' it behind the doors of the Long Branch."

"Yeah, I know that." A tone of yearning had crept into her voice. "I want what's on the other side of that door, Pop. I'm getting tired of being snubbed by the so-called decent women. Of being told I'm unfit. Of being stared at and pawed by men cheating on their wives. I want a home . . . a child."

"Then get out while you're still young enough to get those things, darlin', or one day you'll end up like Lily or at the bottom of a bottle like me."

She sighed, her voice hardly above a whisper. "But you see, Pop, I want it all: the love of the man who can give it to me. But no matter how much I might love him, I can't make him love me. He has to do that on his own."

"And when, to your thinkin', will the sheriff agree to the doin' of just that?"

She gave him a sidelong glance of surprise. "Who said anything about the sheriff, Pop?"

His eyes twinkled. "Isn't that who we've been talkin' about, darlin'?"

"Whatever gave you that idea? You know, Pop

O'Leary, I'm thinkin' there's a bit of the dev'l in ya."

"And speakin' of the dev'l, darlin' . . ." He nodded toward the door where Luke had just entered.

He came over and sat down at the table with them. "Did you enjoy the punch and cake with the good citizens of your town, Sheriff MacKenzie?" she asked with sarcasm.

He shoved back his hat. "Don't start jawing on me, Honey. You asked for it. It's too long a walk from the Long Branch to Our Savior's Church to try and make it in one day."

"Hear that, Pop? I do believe the good sheriff is a philosopher."

Pop winked in reply.

Just then, Honey saw Lily and the stranger come downstairs. Lily looked pale and shaken. She walked away from him without her usual lingering smile.

Honey got up and went over to her. "Are you okay?" she asked Lily.

"Yeah, I'm fine," Lily said bitterly. She picked up the drink Sam put in front of her and gulped it down. "You know, no one knows a man like a woman who goes to bed with him." She glanced to the table where Luke and Pop were sitting. "Count your blessings, Honey gal."

Still disturbed, Honey returned to the table. "Luke, do you know that blond man who just sat down over there at the poker table?"

Luke glanced in the direction she indicated. "No. Why?"

"I don't know. There's just something about him I don't like."

"What'd he do, win a pot from you?"

"No, I guess you'd call it woman's intuition. He's just too smooth. Besides, you ought to know by now, MacKenzie, when Honey deals, Honey wins. That's the only way to play the game." She stood up. "Time for my song."

The two men watched her walk over to the piano and take the guitar Fingers handed her.

"Why are you so hard on the lass, Sheriff?" Pop asked. "She's got the heart and soul of a saint."

"Not any saint I've ever heard of," Luke scoffed.

"I'm thinkin' you don't know much about women, Sheriff MacKenzie."

Luke shrugged good-naturedly. "I won't argue with you on that point, Pop. But I sure would be happy to find one I could call my own."

Pop's eyes twinkled with amusement. "Tell me, lad, have you ever heard the term 'a diamond in the rough'?"

The question was forgotten as Honey began to sing "Jeannie with the Light Brown Hair." Within seconds, she had mesmerized her audience.

Luke sat silently, his enigmatic gaze riveted on her face as she sang. When the song ended, he waited for her to momentarily close her eyes, like she always did after finishing a song. That was the moment that always knotted his groin.

Honey looked up and smiled. Raising her hand to silence the applause, she said, "Boys, let's try one a bit more livelier. How about 'The Yellow Rose of Texas'?"

The response came in a chorus of cheers and whistles.

"I've got to get to my rounds," Luke said. "See you later, Pop."

Luke paused at the door and looked back at Honey. As she sang, she moved gracefully among the tables. She glanced up, and their gazes locked for a breathless beat as a tangible, sensuous message passed between them. Then he pushed open the doors and walked out.

Chapter 25

After Luke's departure, the men clamored for another song. Relenting, Honey declared, "All right, but this is the last one."

"Sing me favorite, darlin'," Pop called out.

"Okay, Pop, just for you." With a nod to Fingers, she began to sing "My Old Kentucky Home."

As Honey strolled among the tables, she glanced casually at the sharp profile of a man seated in the corner. Then he turned his head, and the words of the song momentarily froze in her throat as she stared into the beady eyes of Jake Simmons. His mouth narrowed into a thin slash as he recognized her. She felt an instant jolt of fear. Her initial instinct was to run, just as she had done on the *Delta Princess.* She quickly turned her back to him and forced herself to take one step at a time. His fixed stare seemed to bore into her back.

She managed to finish the song, then without turning or waiting to acknowledge the applause, she hurried up the stairs and sped down the hall toward the sanctuary of her room.

"Hold it, sister." The remembered voice sent a chill down her spine. Simmons stepped out of the shadows. "Figured you'd be dumb enough to come up here instead of staying down in the crowd where you'd be safer."

"What do you want, Simmons?"

He squeezed her arm. "Which is your room, sister?"

"Let go of me or I'm going to start screaming."

"One sound out of you, and it'll be your last one. You and me are goin' for a walk."

"I'm not going anywhere with you, unless it's down to the jailhouse. There's a cell waiting for you."

Just then Lily's door opened, and the blond stranger came out of her room.

"I've got a knife in my other hand," Simmons whispered. "You start something, sister, and you'll die before he does."

"Well hello there, just-plain-Honey," the man said in his pleasant voice.

"Move on, pal," Simmons growled.

The stranger dropped his gaze to Simmons's grasp on her arm. "May I be of service, ma'am?"

"As a matter of fact you can," Honey said boldly. She felt the pressure of the knife at her back. "Very shortly, I'm expecting a visit from the sheriff. Will you tell him I'm occupied at the moment?" She knew when Luke heard that message he would be curious enough to come looking for her. She smiled sweetly. "I never did catch your name, Mr. . . . ?"

The stranger flashed his dazzling smile. "You can call me just plain Charlie."

As soon as he left, Honey told Simmons, "I'd advise you to get going while the going's good. I don't want any trouble, Simmons. I've got a good arrangement here, and I'm not planning on losing it. So ride out of here now, and I'll keep my mouth shut."

"What's to stop me from killing you here and now?"

"You're not that stupid. You'd never get away with it. The sheriff doesn't take kindly to killing in his town."

"Nobody cares if a whore ends up dead."

"The sheriff might. He happens to be sleeping with me."

Simmons smirked. "So that's what you mean by a good arrangement."

Honey could tell he had begun to falter. "I saw you kill Sheldon Peters, but I kept my mouth shut, didn't I? I mind my own business and look after my own interests. Live and let live is my motto."

His mouth narrowed to a slit. "Okay, sister. I don't need any more trouble than I've got already. I gotta get some quick money, so I'll play a few hands and then ride out of here tonight." He lowered his arm. Relieved, Honey drew a deep breath. "But I don't want you sneaking off somewhere. You stay where I can keep an eye on you."

"Simmons, I'll be in plain sight all evening."

"Then get back downstairs," he said.

He followed her down the stairway and took a seat at one of the poker tables. Honey sat at a table with Pop O'Leary. As he played cards, Simmons constantly shifted his glance over to her. There was no question in her mind that no matter what Simmons said, he would try and kill her before he left town. She could only hope that Luke would drop by again, and she could seek his help.

As she watched the game, she saw how Simmons was setting up the other players. He would lose several hands in a row, then win when the pot was larger. After watching him win a pot with four aces, she saw him palm them and knew he was getting ready for the big pot.

As she expected, he opened the pot, and the betting proceeded until only Jess Calhoun and the blond stranger remained in the game. Finally Charlie folded, and after Simmons raised, Jess called his bet. Simmons turned over the four aces.

"Mister, that hand looks kind of familiar," Jess said. "Same one you held the last hand."

"Coincidences happen," Simmons said and started to pull in the chips.

"I wouldn't be so fast in raking in that hand, sir," Charlie said with his soft-spoken drawl. "I think my young friend here has expressed my sentiments exactly."

"I didn't deal the hand," Simmons snarled.

It was the opportunity Honey hoped for. "You didn't have to, Simmons. I saw you palm that winning hand."

The gambler's eyes dilated with fury. "You lying little bitch! I should have killed you when I had the chance." Jumping to his feet with a drawn pistol, he aimed it at Honey.

"Look out!" Pop shouted. He lunged and knocked her to the floor just as three shots rang out simultaneously. Simmons's shot hit Pop in the chest; both Jess's and Charlie's bullets slammed into Simmons. He was dead before he hit the floor.

For a second Honey lay stunned from the fall, then she crawled over to where Pop sat slumped on the floor. "Pop," she cried, gathering him in her arms.

The old man's face had turned ashen, and his once-bright eyes were glazed. Lily and Sam knelt down beside her. After a cursory examination, Sam looked at her and shook his head.

"I'm thinkin' I could use a wee nip, me good man." Despite his condition, Pop's grin didn't waver.

"Sure, Pop, I'll get you one," Sam said. He grabbed the bottle on the table, quickly filled a glass, and handed it to the dying man.

"Put it on me tote, Sam."

"It's on the house, Pop," Sam said gently.

"Let me help you, Pop," Honey said.

" 'Twoud be a sad day, indeed, if Dan'l Webster O'Leary couldn't raise a glass to his lips." He drank it down and began coughing violently.

His breathing became more labored, and he lay back, cradled in her arms. "Well, darlin', I'll not be dyin' of the drink after all."

"Oh, Pop, you'll be with us for a long time yet," Honey said as tears streaked her cheeks.

Pop grinned. "Aye, but what sweeter way of passin' than the sight of your lovely face." He raised a hand to her cheek. "Sing it for me one more time darlin'. Weep, no more, my lady," he began in a shaky voice.

"Oh, weep no more today," she began in a whispered sob. "We will sing one song for my old Kentucky . . ." His hand slipped from her cheek, and he closed his eyes. "Pop! Pop!" she cried frantically.

"He's gone, Jaybird."

Dazed, she looked up at Luke. He took her by the elbows and gently drew her to her feet. Sobbing, she leaned against him, and he held her as she gave way to her tears.

"Come on, Honey gal, I'll help you to your room," Lily said, slipping an arm around her shoulders.

Luke relinquished her to Lily and walked over to where Simmons lay on the floor. "Will someone tell me what happened here?"

As she climbed the stairs, through the depth of her despair, Honey heard Jess Calhoun begin to relate the events of the last few minutes. Honey paused at the top of the stairway and glanced at the scene below. Those present were gathered around Luke. The bodies of Pop and Simmons lay on the floor.

There was no sign of the blond stranger.

A short time later, Luke tapped on her door and entered. Honey was in her nightgown and robe, with her arms folded across her chest, staring out the window.

"How are you feeling?"

"I'm okay. Pop saved my life."

"I know."

"I keep thinking, I should have said something sooner. I might have prevented Pop from getting killed."

"Honey, nobody has control over who will live or die."

"But that was Jake Simmons who killed Pop. I

knew him. He's the one I was running away from. I told you about him before."

"Everything happens for a reason. I had to learn to accept that when Sarah and my mother were killed." After an awkward moment, he said in a lighter tone, "You mind if I bunk with you tonight, Jaybird? A leg broke off the cot in the jail."

She looked at him in surprise. "Luke, I'm not in the mood tonight, so you better go back and repair the leg of the cot."

"It's too late. I had to shoot it."

She grimaced and shook her head. "That's really a bad joke." She started laughing, then suddenly without realizing it, her laughter turned to tears.

Luke went over to her, carried her to the bed, and gently laid her down. After stripping off his clothes, he climbed in and gathered her into his arms. He held her until she cried herself to sleep.

Then he continued to hold her until he, too, fell asleep.

The following morning, Pop O'Leary was laid to rest under a bright sky as blue as his eyes. Before Delmer Quinn sealed the plain wooden coffin, Sam Brazner slipped in a bottle of his best Irish whiskey; Lily, a red garter; and Honey, the sheet music to "My Old Kentucky Home." She vowed she'd never sing that song again.

Cynthia and Josh joined Honey and Lily at the graveside, and the small group huddled together and watched as Sam, Luke, Doug, and Fingers lowered Pop to his final rest.

Later that day, Honey was dressing to go to work when Luke tapped on her door and entered her room. Seated at the dressing table, she glanced up with a smile. "Hi."

When he didn't respond, she looked more closely. With his hips leaning against the foot of the bed, he stood staring at her. "What's wrong, Luke?"

He pulled a folded paper from his pocket, walked

over, and tossed it on the table. Puzzled by his actions and prolonged silence, she looked up at him. She saw his stare was still fixed on her face. Confused, she put aside her hair brush and picked up the paper.

Honey felt his eyes on her as she unfolded the document. It was a wanted poster. The name of Jake Simmons seemed to leap off the page. With a sinking feeling in her stomach, she read the poster offering a reward for the apprehension of or information as to the whereabouts of the gambler wanted for the murder of a shipline detective in Missouri. In a blur, she scanned the list of several more victims he was suspected of having murdered.

Unable to hold up the poster any longer, she dropped her trembling hand to the table and stared in despair. "I told you about Simmons, Luke."

"Did you read the whole poster?"

She heard no sign of forgiveness in his tone, only accusation. Hesitantly, she raised the paper and continued to read.

"The poster says Simmons and the victim were both seen with an attractive blond woman who is believed to have been Simmons's accomplice," Luke said.

"I told you about Simmons," she repeated tonelessly.

He approached her and leaned over the table. Grasping her chin, he tipped up her head, forcing her to look at him. "Just tell me you didn't know anything about this murder." The accusation in his voice had changed to a desperate plea. Suddenly she knew she couldn't lie to him. She lowered her eyes. The gesture was the same as a confession. Slowly, his fingers slipped from her chin, and he walked over to the window, where he stood staring out in silence.

"Surely you can't believe I had anything to do with Peters's murder, Luke. If I even suspected Simmons intended to kill the man, I would have tried to stop him."

"I understand. Then it was too late, of course, to

tell the ship's captain about it." There was an undertone of sarcasm in his voice.

"I was scared, Luke. Can't you understand that?
Simmons knew I saw him kill Peters, and I knew he
would try to kill me, too. All I could think of was
getting off that boat and getting away from him."

"You witnessed the murder of a lawman, and you
couldn't even stop to report his murder to the local
sheriff."

She stared at the stiff set of his shoulders. "I suppose I could have if I hadn't been scared sick and not
thinking right at the time. Of course, I didn't have a
way of proving my innocence. All Simmons would
have had to do was deny the murder. I would have
been the one under suspicion. A con woman with no
money—and the last person to be seen with Peters."

Luke continued to stare out the window.

Her nerves felt raw, and she could feel her composure slipping away. "Why would you expect the
ship's captain to believe me anymore than you do
now?"

He wheeled around angrily. "I didn't say that I
don't believe you."

"Oh, you don't have to say it, Luke," she lashed
out, close to tears. "Your actions speak louder than
words."

Luke struggled with his emotions. He resented the
inference that he was being unfair when she was the
one who hadn't been honest.

"My actions? That's the pot calling the kettle black.
What about your actions?"

She could no longer control her hurt and shock.
"Oh, I wondered when you'd get around to bringing
up my past. You can sleep with me, even pretend to
care about me, but the self-righteous Sheriff Mac-
Kenzie can't forget that I'm a con woman. An *unfit*
woman. That's it, isn't it?"

"No, that's not it at all. I can't understand why you
didn't tell me the whole story. You witnessed a mur-

der! My God, Honey, Peters was a lawman just like me."

Torn apart by anger and heartache, she felt numb and had no further heart for the argument. "I suppose I was wrong in not telling you the whole truth, but you know what, Luke? I can see it wouldn't have made a damn bit of difference. The outcome was inevitable. If you believe I was involved in Peters's killing, then arrest me. Otherwise, get the hell out of here and leave me alone."

She didn't turn around when she heard the door close behind him. She willed herself not to cry. The fantasy had had to end sometime. Why had she ever allowed herself to think otherwise?

Desolate, she finished dressing.

After leaving the Long Branch, Luke returned to the jail. Bombarded with doubts, he sat down at his desk and put his head in his hands. *God, what a mess!* Of course he believed Honey had had no part in the murder. How could she think otherwise? But why hadn't she been honest with him? That was the issue. Why wouldn't she expect him to be shocked at discovering she was a suspect in a murder? And how could she say telling him wouldn't have made a difference? Knowing about it in advance instead of reading about it in a wanted poster would have made a hell of a difference. It would have created a trust between them.

Frustrated, Luke jumped up and started to pace the floor. He crumbled up the poster and tossed it into the wastebasket. *Damn you, Honey!*

He slumped back down in the chair. Then, reliving the argument once again, he began to feel the misery of remorse for his actions.

The rest of the week, he avoided the Long Branch, but by Saturday night, Luke couldn't stay away from her any longer. Grabbing a wrapped parcel from his desk, he headed for the saloon. There was no sign of her in the barroom, and he climbed the stairway and went to her room. He tapped lightly and entered when she unlocked the door.

"Hi," he said with a contrite grin.

She didn't reply. Turning away, she sat down at the dressing table. Luke entered the room and closed the door. He watched as she pulled the pins out of her hair. Released from its restraint, the hair dropped to her shoulders like a mantle. His fingers itched to dig into it.

"You still angry at me?" She continued to ignore him, so he walked over and put a package down in front of her. "For you."

She glanced down at the brightly wrapped box. "Beware of sheriffs bearing gifts," she said mockingly.

"Will you open it?" he asked.

She hesitated momentarily, then she removed the paper and lid from the box. By the light glowing from the table lamp, she saw the black lace peignoir she had admired in the emporium window. "It's lovely," she said softly.

"It will be on you."

Honey stood up and went over to the window. Folding her arms across her chest, she stood in silence and stared out of it. Luke walked up behind her and put his hands on her shoulders. A shiver skimmed down her spine. She closed her eyes and sucked in a deep breath.

"I know I hurt you, and I'm sorry, Jaybird," he whispered, his breath a tantalizing warmth against her ear.

She remained rigid in his arms, conscious of the sweet sensation that rippled from the touch of the hands. She swallowed past the suffocating lump that had formed in her throat and drew in a shuddering breath. "It was raining that night . . . thundering and lightning," she began in a wooden tone. "Peters told me he was a detective for the shipline and left my cabin to get the captain to arrest me."

"Jaybird, you don't have to explain."

"I want to," she said. She took several more deep breaths until she felt strong enough to continue. "All I could think of was getting away before he could return. When I started to leave, I saw him and Simmons arguing. I couldn't hear what they were saying, but when Peters started to walk away, Simmons pulled out a knife and slit Peters's throat. I was paralyzed with fright. I couldn't even scream. By the time I was able to move, Simmons had dumped the body over the railing. It was then he saw me and knew I had seen him murder Peters. I knew he intended to kill me, too. Terrified, I ran. He followed, and I managed to hide. I was so scared I didn't know what to do. As soon as he was out of sight . . . I ran."

The pressure of his hands tightened on her shoulders. "Honey, I understand."

She turned in his arms, her eyes imploring. "Do you, Luke? Do you really understand what a person will do in desperation?"

"It's over, Jaybird. I wired Independence and told them Simmons was shot and killed when he was caught cheating in a card game. It's all over now, Honey."

"It's not over between us, Luke. I know now that I should have told you the whole story the night of the bazaar. But I knew I would be leaving Stockton in a couple of days, so I didn't see what could be gained by it."

"I never believed for a moment that you had anything to do with Peters's death, Honey. I was disappointed that you didn't trust me."

"And I was disappointed you didn't trust me," she said with a woeful smile.

He cupped her cheeks in his hands, his grin tugging at her heartstrings. "Will you put it on for me?" At her confused look, he took her hand and led her over to the dressing table. "The peignoir."

A hot flush of excitement swept through her. With trembling fingers, she lifted the lacy garment out of the box. She grinned shyly at him. "I've never owned anything this elegant in my life."

While she changed into it, Luke sat down on the bed and removed his gunbelt and boots. Honey slowly turned and met his gaze. Barefoot, he had shed most of his clothing except for his white shirt and trousers. The shirt front was hanging open, and the sleeves were rolled up almost to his elbows. The sight of his virile manliness, raw and sensuous, flamed her already-aroused hunger for him. The past few nights without him had been a living hell. She felt mounting desire lick at her loins as his dark-eyed gaze moved down her in a slow, provocative perusal.

Their passions drew them toward each other until they were only inches apart. "I fantasized how you would look in that gown," he said in a voice heavy with emotion.

She raised her head, and her heart lurched wildly; she tore her gaze away from the powerful intensity of his dark eyes. Nervously, she turned away.

He turned her gently and tipped up her chin. "What's bothering you, Jaybird?" he asked tenderly. "Are you still angry with me?"

"No. I feel as if this is our first time, Luke."

"I feel like that every time we make love," he said softly. The rich timbre of his voice seemed to stroke her spine like a caress. When he turned her to face him, she closed her eyes and enjoyed the slide of his lips up to her mouth. The kiss left her feeling as shaky on her feet as she suspected he was.

When she opened her eyes again, she met his gaze. He began to stroke her back. "I won't rush you. We can just sit and talk until you feel more comfortable."

"I think I'd like that, Luke." She felt so foolish. She was acting like a blushing and hesitant virgin on her wedding night. In truth, her desire for him was anything but reluctant.

"Or we could always play cards," he said light-heartedly to cover her embarrassment.

Amused, she arched a brow. "Cards? You mean another game between us?"

"No, I mean actually using a deck of cards."

"Do you actually believe you can beat me at my own game, MacKenzie?"

"Won't know until I try, Miz Honey."

"Okay, MacKenzie, cards it will be."

He sat down on the center of the floor as she got a deck of cards. Returning, she sat down opposite him and rifled the cards adroitly.

"All right, what's it going to be? Name your pleasure, Sheriff."

"You know my pleasure," he intoned drolly. Suddenly, she saw his eyes light with a dangerous gleam. "Let's make it strip poker."

She glanced down at the single garment she wore. "Rather lopsided, wouldn't you say?"

He simply shrugged. "What about all that 'beating you at your own game' talk?" he challenged. "And I vaguely remember you mentioning how skillful you are at stacking a deck."

"Aren't you afraid I might cheat?"

His dark eyes appraised her boldly. "Cheat then, my dear. I'll come out a winner either way."

"Okay, strip poker it will be, MacKenzie. Five card showdown."

She slowly dealt each of them five cards face up. His pair of eights lost to her pair of aces, one of which she dealt from the bottom of the deck.

"Looks like I lost," he remarked.

"The shirt, MacKenzie."

He slipped off his shirt and tossed it aside. The sight of his broad, muscular chest with its swath of dark crisp hair was a disturbing distraction.

"Would you like the deal?"

"No, you're doing just fine," he said pointedly.

In the next hand, Luke got nothing—not even a pair. Glancing at her winning cards, he said complacently, "Amazing! That's the same pair of aces you had last time." He pulled off his trousers. Now only his drawers remained.

Her long fingers masterfully rippled the cards as she reshuffled the deck. When she was about to deal, he reached over and covered her hand. "My deal."

He picked up the deck and slowly began to deal. Her first card was a nine; his was one of the familiar aces. He continued the deal and her fifth card turned up another nine. Slipping the bottom card off the deck, he turned up the other ace. "Well, up popped the devil, Miz Honey," he murmured with a wolfish grin.

She released the tie on the peignoir, and the front gaped open, giving him a very provocative view.

"Allow me to clear the table," he said and shoved aside the cards.

He cupped her face in his hands and gently kissed her. Then he raised his head and for a long moment stared deeply into her eyes. "Feeling better?" he asked kindly.

Desire gleamed in his eyes. Possessed by a sublime feeling of headiness, her body throbbed with need for him.

"If feeling better means I ache from wanting you so badly, then Lord yes, I'm feeling much better, Luke," she said, lacing her fingers through his hair.

He lowered the peignoir off her shoulders and gently laid her back, then he stood up to remove his drawers.

She closed her eyes, waiting to savor the return of his tantalizing, hot touch. After several seconds, she opened her eyes. She stared transfixed at him standing naked before her. He looked like a bronzed Greek god: tall, dark-haired, his powerful shoulders and muscular chest in perfect symmetry to the rest of his beautifully proportioned body.

She tore her eyes away from his nakedness and saw that he was staring intently at her. "What were you thinking right now?"

"I was thinking that . . ." She cast her eyes downward, too embarrassed to finish.

Luke eyed her with uncertainty. "Please, Jaybird, tell me what you were thinking," he repeated.

Swallowing her pride, Honey raised her head and looked into his troubled gaze. "I was thinking what a beautiful body you have."

Luke felt an overwhelming flush of love for her. Barely able to keep from going to her, he said in a hushed tone, "Will you stand up?"

She somehow sensed the importance of this moment to him. Clutching the peignoir to her breasts, she rose and waited for him to move or speak.

"Drop the gown."

She released her hold on the gown, and it slipped past her hips and dropped to her ankles. She stepped out of the crumpled pile and stood before him.

His gaze moved from her eyes to her breasts, then slowly lowered down her body to her bare feet. The tide of hot blood washed through her as his dark eyes swept back up her trembling body in the same, seductive perusal until he looked directly into her eyes once again.

In answer to the curiosity he saw there, he said huskily, "I think your body is beautiful, too, Jaybird."

Then he walked over and lifted her into his arms.

Chapter 26

Drifting slowly back to wakefulness in his office, Luke sensed he was not alone. He raised his eyelids and saw two blue eyes staring down at him.

"Are you sleeping?"

"What do you want, Josh?" Luke swung his legs over the side of the cot and sat up. Yawning, he buried his head in his hands. "What time is it?"

"Time to get up. I already ate my breakfast. You said you would teach me how to ride a horsie today."

"Oh, yeah, that's right."

"Can Honey come with us? It's Sunday, and she doesn't have to work on Sundays."

Luke stood up and stretched. "Let's go back to the house. I need a cup of coffee. We'll talk about it after church."

From the time Josh had run up to Honey in the diner that morning on his way to church and asked her to join him and his father, she had been on pins and needles thinking about Luke. Now, as she dressed, she thought of their lovemaking last night. It had been different from before. Not that it hadn't been just as remarkable, just as soul shattering. This time there seemed to be a quality that had never been present before. This time they made love not only physically, but emotionally.

She stepped back to take a longer look at herself. The swell of her uncorseted breasts above the plain white bodice was a tantalizing reminder that she was a woman. The voluptuous body of a woman who had known ecstacy at the hands, the mouth, the mastery, of a man. Luke.

She closed her eyes, recalling his manliness and his strength: the muscle, the heat of his powerful body; the unsurpassed thrill from the touch of his hands and mouth; the mindless ecstasy of their shared orgasms.

Opening her eyes, she saw that they no longer seemed to sparkle with excitement. Instead, she saw sensuous desire shimmering within them, and her blush had been replaced by the fever of passion.

Shocked, she brought her hands to her cheeks. "Oh, God, Honey Behr, what's happening to you? Just the thought of Luke excites you!" she admonished her flushed image. She quickly pulled back her hair, tied it with a ribbon, and turned away.

Sitting on a blanket in the shade, Honey tried to concentrate on the book she was reading, but her attention strayed constantly to Luke and Josh nearby.

For the past hour, the rich timbre of Luke's voice and laughter had carried to her ears as he instructed Josh how to ride the rented pony. His rugged profile appeared swarthy in the shadow of the hat brim carelessly shoved up on his forehead, but she was acutely aware of his tall, superbly proportioned body. His bronze face and arms were a sensuous contrast against the white fabric of his shirt, opened at the neck to reveal a swath of dark hair. Faded jeans molded his narrow hips and long, powerful legs.

She smiled as she watched the emotions on Josh's face. The youngster was thrilled, and his little face seemed to glow with pleasure.

Amigo limped over to the blanket, and Honey put aside the book, gathered the dog into her arms, and began to stroke him. According to Doug, Amigo would always walk with a limp, but it didn't stop him from keeping up with Josh. Amigo's devotion to Josh was so indisputable that even Luke had ceased complaining about the animal.

"You poor little darling," she cooed. "You got kicked out of your house the same way I did. I guess strays like us will never find a home." Together, they watched the man and boy.

"That's enough for now, Josh," Luke finally said. As he swung Josh off the pony, his shoulders strained against his shirt, and she watched the ripple of muscle under the fabric. Her pulse quickened in response.

Josh came racing over to her and threw himself into her arms. "Did you see me, Honey? Didn't I ride good?" His little body trembled with excitement.

"You sure did, sweetheart." She hugged him to her breast.

Josh scrambled from her arms, sat down, and grabbed Amigo. "Did you see me, Amigo? I rode the horse just like Daddy." The dog responded with several eager licks to the boy's face, then settled his head in Josh's lap.

Luke sat down, wiped his brow, and tossed his hat on the blanket. He leaned against the tree, stretched out his legs, and studied the back of Honey's head. Her long blond hair glistened in the afternoon sunshine filtering through the tree. He had an urgent desire to lean over, slip his arms around her waist, and pull her softness against him, then bury his nose in the sweet scent of her hair. He had to touch her.

She felt his eyes on her. She felt her own quickened heartbeat, the exciting rush of heated blood she always experienced whenever she fell under his intense stare. Luke's kiss, the feel of his arms, his nearness, were the most exciting sensations she had ever known. She wondered how much longer this irresistible physical attraction could last between them. She closed her eyes, and despite the temptation, she willed herself not to turn and look at him.

Luke stood up and walked over to Alamo. "You're next, Jaybird."

"Me? Not on your life, MacKenzie. I have no intention of learning how to ride a horse. My legs have always gotten me where I have to go."

"How do you expect to live in the West without knowing how to ride?"

"I figure you don't need a horse as long as there are stagecoaches and trains," she insisted, though she allowed him to pull her to her feet.

"Come on, you're not scared, are you?" he dared as he led her over to his gelding.

"Yes, I am. Look at him. He's too big."

"How can you be afraid of horses when you drove a wagon all the way from Missouri? You weren't lying about that, were you?"

"No, I was not lying," she declared, "but I was sitting on a wagon seat, not a horse's back. And they were mules, not horses."

Tentatively, she reached out and patted the horse. The animal turned its head, eyed her, then turned away again. "What does that mean?" she asked warily.

"I don't know, he didn't say," Luke said.

"Sometimes actions speak louder than words." She started to walk away.

He grabbed her arm. "Hey, hold up there."

"I don't think he likes me."

"He likes you, or he would have shied away when you came near him. Get as close to him as you can."

"I'm as close as I intend to be," she informed him.

"Now, you gather both reins in your left hand and grab the saddle horn, or the horse might try to move away from you as you mount."

"I thought you said it liked me. Why would it move away?"

"Because horses are unpredictable."

"Which is why I have no desire to learn how to ride one," she mumbled as he put the reins in her left hand.

"Okay, now grab the saddle horn, and since you're not real tall, you have to kind of hop into the stirrup with your left foot and swing your right leg over the saddle."

"With this skirt on?" she asked, aghast. "It's not full enough."

"I can fix that." Kneeling down, he grabbed the back hem of her skirt.

"What are you doing?" she cried, startled.

"Just relax," Luke said. He pulled the skirt between her legs and tucked it into the front of her waistband.

"This looks ridiculous," she exclaimed, staring down at her bare legs.

"Not from my view. You've got great legs. Don't tell me you've never tucked your skirt between your legs to go wading," he scoffed.

"Certainly not!"

"Oh, I forgot. You don't swim either."

"That's right, MacKenzie. That's what boats are for," she remarked.

"Okay, here we go. Grab the saddle horn, left foot in stirrup, and swing right leg over the saddle," he repeated. It was a stretch for her, and she felt two firm hands on her derriere giving her a helpful hoist. She shot him an annoyed backward glance.

Luke grinned. "That wasn't so hard, was it, ma'am?" He adjusted the length of the stirrups. "How do they feel?"

"Okay, I guess. I don't know how they're supposed to feel," she said shakily. He swung himself up behind her and straddled the horse's haunches. "Okay, now I'll take the reins." His arms enfolded her.

Honey had been clutching the saddle horn with both hands. She released her left hand long enough to hand him the end of the reins, then quickly grabbed the horn again.

"Now lightly nudge the horse with your knees. Both knees," he said.

"Can't I just say, 'Go, horsie,' or something like that?"

" 'Fraid it's not in Alamo's vocabulary," he replied with a chortle. "Alamo responds to the pressure of the legs or the reins. Just apply some light pressure with both knees."

When she did, the horse moved forward. "That's good. Now take the reins in one hand and hold them lightly. Don't jerk or pull up on them."

"Don't you let go of the end of them," she said nervously.

"I won't."

"Which hand should I use?"

"Use the left to keep your right hand free."

"Free for what?"

"To draw your pistol, rope a steer, or whatever. Use both hands if that makes you feel more confident right now."

"I'm not going to feel confident, no matter what hand I use," she said. She took the reins in both hands.

After several moments, she began to feel less uneasy. "Now we want to turn left, so tighten up on the left rein and nudge him with your left knee." She grinned broadly when the horse obeyed the command.

"How am I doing, cowboy?"

"Good," he said. "Now do the same with the right knee and reins."

When the horse turned to the right, Honey felt positively ecstatic. "This isn't as hard as I thought it would be."

"You want to try it alone?"

She felt a quick loss of confidence. "Well, don't get off the horse."

Luke released the ends of the reins and slipped his arms around her waist. "Just don't lose the reins, because 'whoa, horsie,' won't stop him," he cautioned.

Honey didn't much care. She felt as if she were floating on a cloud, and all because Luke's arms were around her. "What . . . are you doing?" she said when he slid his hand up and began to fondle her breast.

His warm breath tantalized her ear. "See what I mean about keeping the right hand free?"

Her eyes widened with shock at the glide of his other hand under her bodice. A warm palm cupped her breast. "Stop it, Luke."

"God, you feel good, babe." He nibbled the words at her ear. "And your hair smells like a flower garden."

Her breath started to come in quickened gasps when he began to rasp her nipples with his thumbs. "Don't, Luke."

"You don't like it?"

"That's not what I mean." He increased the pressure and began to massage her breasts. She sucked in her breath and leaned back into him. "Josh might see us."

"If he happens to look this way, he won't see anything but my back." He ran his tongue from her ear down to the hollow of her throat.

The sensation sent a fiery jolt through her, and she inadvertently pulled up on the reins, causing the horse to stop. The unexpected movement caught Luke unprepared. He slipped off the rear of the horse and ended up on his backside. Honey gripped the horse tighter and in so doing, nudged the animal with her knees. The horse started off at a fast trot in response to the command.

"Luke! Help me!" she screamed. Dropping the reins, she grabbed the saddle horn with both hands.

Luke gave a sharp whistle, and Alamo came to an abrupt halt that almost tossed her out of the saddle. "I told you not to let go of the reins," he said, running over to her.

"How do I get off this animal?" she asked, relieved but breathless.

"Slip your feet out of the stirrups, put your hands on my shoulders, and I'll lift you down."

When she felt his strong hands spanning her waist, she practically collapsed in his arms. She slipped her arms around his neck as he slowly lowered her to the ground. For a long moment, she continued to cling to him, and he made no effort to release her.

"You're okay, Jaybird." His breath was warm and moist against her cheek, and the husky tone in his voice set her already racing pulses to pounding. The feel of his hard body intensified her swirling emotions.

She raised her head and looked into his warm sapphire eyes. "Am I, Luke? Am I really—?"

His mouth drank her final word.

When they drew apart, Honey glanced up at him and blushed under his intense gaze. He had looked at her the same way last night.

"You look beautiful." His voice was deep and husky.

"So do you," she blurted out.

He grinned and blushed. She couldn't believe it, but Luke MacKenzie had actually blushed. " 'Fraid you're mistaken, ma'am. Nobody ever accuses a little ole Texas boy of being beautiful. Could get a body shot, you know."

"Well then, this body says you look very handsome, Sheriff MacKenzie." *Devastating would be more accurate*, she thought to herself as she walked back to the blanket and sat down.

"Daddy, when can I ride Alamo?" Josh asked.

"In a few years. I'm afraid you're a mite too young right now."

"Can I ride the pony then?" he asked impatiently.

"Give him a little more rest, Josh. He's just a pony. You don't want to overtire him."

"Then me and Amigo are gonna go and look for pretty stones by the river."

"Well, don't get too near the riverbank. And don't stray away too far," Luke ordered. He plopped down beside Honey.

"Luke, I'm glad we have this time alone, because I promised Josh I'd talk to you about something that's bothering him."

"What's that?"

"Josh is very upset that Amigo is not permitted in the house. Good Lord, Luke, Amigo's the boy's pet. Can't you convince your housekeeper to change her mind?"

"Mrs. Frick—"

"Frau Frick," she corrected.

"Frau Frick is no longer a problem."

"Oh, then you did get her to change her mind."

"I don't think anybody could do that."

She looked confused. "I thought you just said you did."

"No, you said that. I said that she was no longer a problem. I put her on the noon stage and shipped her back to Sacramento."

Honey tried not to show her elation, but she couldn't help smiling. "I'm surprised Josh didn't tell me."

"He doesn't know yet."

"Well, let's call him back here and tell him the good news."

"Oh, let him play. He's having a good time. You'll just have to settle for my stimulating conversation for a while."

"Stimulating conversation! You, Sheriff MacKenzie, are not noted for your stimulating conversation."

"How about if I talk indecent?"

She gave him a haughty look, then smiled in spite of herself.

"All night I've been thinking about how you looked last night standing naked in the glow of that lamp. Your skin looked like satin, and I—"

"Is this some of your indecent conversation, MacKenzie?" She pressed her flushed cheeks between her hands.

"Stimulating indecent conversation, Miz Honey Behr," he corrected with a mischievous grin. "Let me finish, because I soon have to think about getting back to relieve Matt."

"He's a nice young man, Luke."

"Sounds like you're changing the subject. But I agree, Matt'll make a good sheriff."

"You plannin' on turnin' in your star, Sheriff?" she mocked in an exaggerated drawl.

"Matter o' fact, I am, Miz Honey Behr. That's what I want to talk to you about. Been puttin' my mind to goin' back to runnin' cows and bustin' broncos."

"Oh, so you're joining a circus," she remarked.

He chuckled warmly. "You always get the last word, don't you, Jaybird? I've been thinking about going back to Texas. Reckon Josh would enjoy growing up on a ranch."

"I'm sure he would. Do you miss ranching, Luke?"

"Yeah, I do. It's a lot of hard work, but it's a good life. You've got a lot of room to stretch your legs, and there's no describing the sense of freedom when you're out riding the range."

"Then why didn't you go back to ranching after the war?"

"After I tracked down Josh, I couldn't very well leave him, so I thought if I became a lawman, I'd have a better chance of picking up news about outlaw gangs. You know, wanted posters and word of mouth from other lawmen and bounty hunters. I figured something might turn up that would give me a lead. Unfortunately, Josh kept me too occupied to finish what I started."

"You seem such a dedicated lawman that it's hard to believe you intend to give it up."

"Oh, I'll never stop believing in upholding the law, with or without a badge. My family would all be alive today if it weren't for those who won't live by the rules of law and order."

"I hope all this isn't leading to your lecturing me about my wicked, wicked ways," she said, trying to sound lighthearted.

When she saw the solemn look in his eyes, her spirits dissolved along with the smile on her face. Forcing a breezy tone, she said, "So it is, isn't it?"

"No, Honey, that's not what I have to say."

Since he rarely used her name, she had a sudden feeling of foreboding. She didn't believe for a moment that their lovemaking had meant the same to him as it had to her, but maybe he even regretted it had ever happened. Maybe he was preparing to tell her the time had come for her to leave Stockton again, this time for good. That he was through with her now. The thought set her head to reeling, and the ground seemed to spin around her. She reached out a hand to steady herself.

Instantly, she felt a firm grip on her arm. "Are you okay?" His arms folded around her protectively as she leaned against him.

"It must have been that horseback ride."

"Just lie back, Honey."

"No, that's not necessary." She sat up, freeing herself from his embrace. "I just felt dizzy for a moment. It's already passed."

"Well, just sit still until you feel better."

"I feel so foolish. Usually I have the constitution of a horse."

He leaned back on his elbows and glanced up at the sky. "It's too nice a day for you to be taking ill."

To her eyes he looked more handsome than ever. His long, lithe body was stretched out in relaxation, and she yearned to touch him. She loved him so much, the very thought of leaving had become unbearable. She felt the retribution for all her past sins was being manifested in the pain of knowing the day was coming when she would never see him again.

"You said there was something you wanted to discuss." Despite her brave attempt to remain calm, the words quivered on her lips.

When he turned his head and grinned, the thought of never seeing his cherished expression devastated her. She feared that in another moment, she would burst into tears.

"It can wait until you're feeling better. Tomorrow's soon enough."

"Let's get it over with, Luke. I don't want to lie in

bed thinking about it all night." She closed her eyes and drew a deep breath, rallying strength for the moments to follow.

Luke sat up, brushed off his hands, and simply said, "I think we should get married."

Chapter 27

Honey's eyes popped wide open. Prepared for the worst, she was overwhelmed by the astounding declaration. "What did you say?" she asked shakily.

"I said I want to marry you."

Her thoughts remained focused on his first remark. "No, Luke, that's not what you said. You said, 'I think we *should* get married.' Not long ago, you were prepared to lock me up in your jail. I was a scourge in your eyes. Unfit. A liar. A cheat. Now you're saying you think we should get married. I'm the same woman now that I was then."

"Dammit, you're making this as difficult as you can, aren't you?"

She offered a nervous smile. "I don't know what you're talking about."

"You damn well do. For one thing, we've been sleeping together, so it's the proper thing to do," he said righteously.

"That may sound proper to you, but it's hardly a reason to convince me you'd want to spend the rest of your life with me."

"Well, then, there's the way Josh feels about you. He'd be real upset if you left."

"Go on."

"And you're a good cook and housekeeper."

"I also work in a saloon. Have you forgotten that, Luke? I don't think the good people of Stockton would appreciate your choice of a bride."

"I don't give a damn what they think."

"Well, I do. Not for my sake, for Josh's. He's the one who'll suffer for it."

"Suffer! Jaybird, he worships you. Look at him." They turned their heads, and in the distance saw Josh skipping stones into the water. "You've taught him how to be a boy. How to lift his head and walk tall. How to laugh. The good people of Stockton had two years to do that and didn't come near."

"But my past, Luke. The Long Branch. Even if it doesn't matter to Josh, it does to you."

"Honey, your past isn't important. We'll get married, go back to Texas, and make a fresh start."

Not one mention of love. "Well, no one can accuse you of not shooting from the hip, Sheriff MacKenzie," she scoffed. "Your proposal gets more romantic by the minute. Maybe I'm not proud of everything I've done in the past, but that doesn't mean I'd marry a man just because he needs a cook, a mother for his child, or . . . or a woman to share his bed. "

"You know damn well there's more to it than that. You know how I feel about you."

"Yeah, you've made that quite plain; we're good together in bed."

"I love you, Jaybird."

Her heart started to pound. She couldn't have heard him right. Her wishful imagination was playing tricks on her again. "What did you say?"

"I said, I love you."

"Oh, Luke, don't lie to me now! That would be the cruelest thing you could do. At least be honest with me."

He put his hand over her mouth to cut off her words. "You're bound and determined to make this hard for me, aren't you? I've never been one for sweet talk, but if you want me to tell you that I think you're beautiful, I do. I like seeing you in my kitchen, like the lingering scent of lavender when you pass by. I can't keep my hands off you. I think about making love to you when my mind should be on business. Is that what you want to hear?"

Surely she was fantasizing the whole conversation. "Not quite in that manner, MacKenzie. Is that so difficult for you to understand?" She turned her head away.

"Is it so difficult for you to understand that I love you?"

"Yes, considering all the cruel things we've said to each other." Irritated, she swung her gaze back to him. "What do you expect me to say?"

"Either yes or no. You wanted honesty, I've given it. Why won't you be honest now with me and your-self?"

"Honesty? I don't possess that virtue, remember?" she snapped, then regretted the hasty reply, for it re-vealed more to him than she wished.

And as she feared, he didn't miss the implication. "So that's what's at the bottom of this. Look, Honey, I'm sorry for the things I've said to you. We both have to put our pasts behind us."

"That's easier said than done. To me, putting my future into the hands of a man is riskier than running a con game. I have good cause not to trust men."

"Maybe I've given you reason not to trust me, but I'm not a drinking man, so don't compare me to your father. And even though I'm not wealthy, I can make your life comfortable. I know starting up the ranch again will involve a lot of hard work, but I don't ex-pect you to carry any more burden than being my wife and a mother to Josh. And—"

When he stopped, she looked at him questioningly. "And what?"

"And I know that you wouldn't be marrying me out of love, but I love you, and I'd try to make you happy."

"And what makes you think I wouldn't be marrying you out of love?"

"If you don't want to marry me, just say so and we'll drop the subject. So let's not be beating around the bush—" He stopped as the meaning of her words sank in. "You mean . . . ?"

She slipped her arms around his neck. "I love you, Luke."

He pressed her to the ground as he claimed her mouth in a slow, leisurely kiss. She parted her lips in a sigh, and his tongue explored her mouth in tantalizing probes that shocked her body with tingling sensations.

The pressure of the kiss deepened, arousing in its intensity, devouring her breath in its hunger. She drew a shuddering breath when he feathered light kisses along her neck.

His moist mouth centered around the hollow of her throat. "We'll get married right away?" he whispered.

"Yes. Oh yes, Luke." She breathed the acceptance through parted lips.

He raised his head, and she watched his sensuous gaze rove over her face and settle on her eyes. Gently, he cupped her cheek in a warm palm. "You know I'll try to make you happy, Jaybird."

For a long moment, she was mesmerized as his compelling dark eyes held hers. He lowered his head and kissed the tip of her nose, then her eyes, and finally his tongue traced her parted lips before he covered them with his mouth in tantalizing persuasion.

Inundated with emotion, she felt her aching heart would shatter in her breast. *Oh God, Luke, I love you so much. Only you can make me feel this way.*

Seeking closer contact, she arched toward him, and as her tongue gamboled with his in an erotic dance, she was rewarded by the feel of his hand closing around the curve of her breast. He lifted his head and released her.

She lay back, waiting with anticipation, her hands still clinging to the hard bulge of his biceps. The lust evident in his sapphire eyes locked with the bold, unconcealed invitation in her passion-glazed gaze. Unconsciously, she moistened her dry lips. Desire instantly flared in the glance he swung to her mouth, and his firm fingers slipped into her bodice.

He fondled her breast. "Your breasts are beautiful, you know."

She sucked in a breath when he lightly stroked the hardened nubs.

The corners of his mouth curved with the traces of a smile. "I love watching your expression. You like this, don't you?"

"You're . . . you're not being fai—fair," she managed to mumble.

His heated palm continued to toy with the swollen peak. "You want me to stop?" he asked, sliding his hand over to pay homage to the other quivering breast.

She could not reply; not one word would pass the breath of expectation suspended in her throat.

His eyes were dark with passion and held hers in a fixed stare. "I'll stop if you really want me to."

He shoved up the bodice and camisole, then lowered his head. His tongue caressed her swollen nipples. The contact jolted the nerve ends of her body with exquisite currents. Sighing a moan of pleasure, she pressed his dark head tighter to her breasts.

In a sensual feasting of his mouth and tongue, he wove a sublime web of ecstasy around her until she writhed helplessly, enmeshing herself deeper into the carnal snare.

When his lips returned to reclaim hers, she slipped her arms around his neck. Clutching him nearer, she could feel the thud of his heart against her own. Then he slid his lips in a moist trail along her jaw until his warm breath ruffled the hair at her ear, sending shivers down her spine.

He tipped her chin up toward him. His eyes were warm with sincerity. "I love you, Jaybird. This can be a new beginning for us. No more lies between us.

We'll lay to rest all the mistakes of the past," he whispered between erotic nibbles at her earlobe.

"Oh yes, Luke. Yes," she cried out in mindless acquiescence. Then once again she breathed her concession into his mouth as they sealed the agreement in a hard and passionate kiss.

He sat up and adjusted her bodice. "Dammit, I wish we were married already. Trying to steal kisses like a schoolboy behind the barn is beginning to take its toll on me." He stood up and reached out a hand to assist her. "I'm looking forward to the privacy of marriage."

Honey still felt light-headed from the "schoolboy" kiss, but she slipped her hand into his and allowed him to pull her to her feet.

"I can hardly wait to see Josh's face when we tell him," Luke said.

"I can't wait to see Cynthia's," Honey replied with a laugh. She felt her heart wrench in her breast when he grinned down at her.

"Josh is gonna be so happy. You know that, don't you?"

"I only hope we will be too, Luke."

He tenderly brushed back some strands of hair from her cheek. "We'll probably fight like hell, but think of the fun we'll have making up."

He drew her into his arms and claimed her lips. Sweet sensation flooded her body. Tightening her grasp around his neck, she matched the hungry demand of his kiss with the unleashed fervor of her own need.

For the long seconds of the kiss, they drifted in the throes of aroused passion that obliterated an awareness of everything except the urgent sensations swirling through them. Then Josh's shout brought them crashing back to earth.

"Look how fast I can go, Daddy!"

Luke broke the kiss and turned his head to see Josh atop the pony. The youngster was racing across the clearing. "Slow down, Josh, that's too fast." He stiffened with alarm when he saw the decayed trunk of a fallen tree directly in the pony's path.

"Pull up, Josh!" Luke shouted. To his horror, he saw Josh drop the reins. They flapped along as the pony continued to race forward, apparently oblivious to the obstacle in its path.

Releasing Honey, Luke ran to the gelding and leaped on its back. But he knew he was too far away to catch the pony before it would reach the fallen tree.

Amigo had apparently also sensed the danger. Barking furiously, he raced into the path of the pony. The frightened little horse veered away from the terrifying animal, and within seconds, Luke caught up with the speeding pony. He snatched Josh from the saddle, and the riderless pony dashed on for several more yards before finally coming to a stop.

Breathless, Honey raced up to them. Luke sat in the saddle clutching Josh to his chest. "Don't ever do that again, son. You could have been killed."

"It was fun, Daddy," Josh declared.

"I think we've had enough riding lessons for one afternoon," Honey said, reaching up for him. Luke handed Josh down to her, then climbed down himself. Leading the horse, he followed Honey back to the blanket. Puffing, Amigo limped beside him.

Luke stopped and scooped up the dog with his free hand. "You damn dog," he mumbled.

When they were all seated on the blanket, Honey made eye contact with Luke and signaled him to begin. "Josh," he began slowly, "we've got some good news for you. I sent Frau Frick back to Sacramento."

"Hooray!" Josh shouted.

Luke cleared his throat. "And Honey and I are getting married, son."

Both Luke and Honey stared at Josh to capture every nuance of his reaction. His face puckered in concentration. Finally, he looked up at Luke.

"Does that mean Honey'll be my mama now?"

Luke looked at her and winked. "That's right, son."

"Oh, boy!" He threw himself at them and flung an

arm around each of their necks. All three fell back, laughing.

Josh kissed their cheeks, then asked Honey, "Should I call you Mama 'stead of Honey?"

"I'd like you to do that, Josh," Luke said.

"But you don't have to if you don't want to, sweetheart," Honey quickly interjected.

"Hmmm," Josh said. "Think I will." He jumped up. "Did you heared that, Amigo?" The dog had been trying crazily to jump on the pile with them. "Honey's gonna be our mama now, so we can call her Mama 'stead of Honey. And that old Frau Frick and her dumb cat's gone, too. You'll never have to sleep alone again."

Luke slipped an arm around Honey's waist. "And neither will your daddy."

Chapter 28

⌒⌒

Luke and Honey were married the next morning in a quiet ceremony attended only by Cynthia, Doug, Matt Brennan, and a beaming Josh.

The joyous event was saddened by the knowledge that following the ceremony, the two couples would be separating: Cynthia and Doug were leaving on the stage for Seattle. As Cynthia had hinted, the hospital's offer to Doug had been too good to ignore.

"This trip is just to check out the hospital," Doug said when the moment of good-bye arrived.

"Yes, but by the time you return, we'll be gone," Honey said sadly.

"Who knows, if I don't like what I see, we might end up staying in Stockton after all."

"You could always move to Texas, pal," Luke said as the two men shook hands.

"Don't be surprised if we do," Cynthia quickly interjected. "Because if we don't move to Seattle, I'm not raising my daughter here. I don't like most of the citizens of this fair community."

Honey turned away, unable to watch when Cynthia said good-bye to Josh. Then, tearfully, the women embraced.

302

"I'll write to you as soon as Luke and I get settled," Honey assured Cynthia.

"Be sure you do," Cynthia replied, dabbing at her eyes. She climbed into the stage.

Honey kissed Melissa and handed the baby to her mother. Then Doug hugged and kissed Honey, climbed into the stage, and closed the door.

Cynthia reached out the window and Honey clasped her hand. "I love you. I'll miss you."

"I love you, too," Cynthia said. "Remember, you promised to write." Honey's hand slipped from Cynthia's as the stage began to move.

Luke slid his arm around her shoulders as they watched the stage rumble down the road. "Will we ever see them again, Luke?"

"Of course we will." He grinned. "After all, Texas isn't that far from Washington."

Honey glanced up at him with a frown of confusion. "Not far!"

"Jaybird, in a couple more years, there'll be so many railroads crisscrossing this country that nobody will be more than a couple days away from each other."

He lifted Josh high, then slipped an arm around Honey's shoulders. "Come on, we've got some packing to do ourselves if we're going to pull out of here tomorrow."

The following morning, by the time Luke returned from turning in his badge, Honey had everything packed and ready to load onto the wagon. Since the house, furniture, and most of the household effects belonged to the city, Matt Brennan, as the newly appointed sheriff, would move into the house as soon as they vacated it. Honey left the red and white curtains on the windows as a special thanks to Matt. Other than the Nelsons, he was one of the few people who had ever shown her any respect.

What with her books, their clothes, and the personal belongings Luke had acquired in the past two years, they had a wagonload by the time he finished loading. Once Josh and Amigo were settled in a snug spot near the front of the wagon, Luke swung Honey up on the seat. "You ready to head out, Mrs. Mac-Kenzie?"

"Texas, here we come," Honey exclaimed, laughing gaily.

Unobserved, Charlie Walden slipped into the copse of trees that bordered the sheriff's house. For several moments, the outlaw watched the family's preparations to depart. His eyes glittered with malice as he fixed his gaze on Luke MacKenzie. He despised lawmen, but he hated Luke MacKenzie with a vengeance. The sheriff had killed one brother, Beau, and had seen that his other brother, Billy Bob, was sent to prison. Just because they had killed a gambler in a poker game!

His temper flared some more, recalling the three members of his gang who had been shot down by the same bastard. Hell, the damn town was lucky he didn't burn it down, like he used to in the days when he rode with Quantrill and along the Texas border during the war.

He hadn't figured on the sheriff getting married and leaving town. It had forced him to change his plans. Now there wasn't time to carry out the slow and painful death he had planned for the sheriff—after he made the bastard watch him kill his son. Now he'd have to kill him fast and miss seeing the lawman's expression as he tortured him to death. After all, hadn't his brother Beau been like a son to him? he thought bitterly. An eye for an eye.

He watched the sheriff climb up onto the wagon. Drawing his lips into a thin line, he raised the pistol in his hand, took aim, and pulled the trigger.

Honey's heart seemed to slam into her throat as several gun shots exploded. Then she saw Luke's face change to shock, and his eyes glaze with pain. "Jaybird," he mumbled before he fell to the ground.

"Luke!" she screamed. Jumping down from the wagon, she knelt beside him. Horrified, she stared at the blood streaming from wounds in his back and leg. "Somebody help!" she cried.

Reverend Wright came running down the street. "What happened?"

"Luke's been shot," she cried frantically. "He needs help."

"There's no doctor in town," the pastor said.

She rested Luke's head against her breast. "Luke, Luke, can you hear me?" He was unconscious, and his breathing was labored. In near panic, she slipped her hand into his shirt and felt a faint heartbeat. Pressing her cheek to his, she held him in her arms. "Please, somebody help him."

She jumped when she felt a hand touch her shoulder. Matt Brennan's voice sounded gently near her ear. "Move aside, Mrs. MacKenzie."

Feeling as if she were in a stupor, she stared at him. "He's been shot, Matt."

"I know. Let me look at him."

Honey laid Luke's head down on the road and shifted to one side. Matt turned him enough to check the bullet wounds. "A bullet went clean through his leg. It don't look busted up any. But he's got another in his back. Let's get him inside the house, where we can try to stop the bleeding."

Honey looked up and realized Matt wasn't speaking to her, but to a ring of familiar faces surrounding them. He moved over and helped her up. "Did you see who shot him, Mrs. MacKenzie?"

She shook her head. "It all happened so quickly and unexpectedly. Luke had just climbed up on the wagon . . . then there were these shots . . . and he fell."

"I'm going to see what I can find." Drawing his Colt, Matt headed toward the trees nearest the house.

Still feeling dazed, she heard Pastor Wright give instructions to several men, who carried Luke into the house.

Honey cast a worried glance toward Josh on the
wagon. The poor child was pale and trembling, his
eyes wide with shock. She lifted him down. "Come
on, sweetheart, we'll go back inside."

"My daddy's gonna die, isn't he?" The young boy's
voice sounded solemn with acceptance.

She felt tears sliding down her cheeks. "I don't
know. We've got to pray and try to be very brave,
sweetheart."

Josh shook his head. "No, my daddy's gonna leave
me just like my mama did. Like you will, too."

"I'm not going to leave you, Josh, I promise. I won't
ever leave you." She slipped her arm around his
shoulders, and Josh cuddled closer. The crowd that
had gathered parted for them.

"Sit down on the stoop and stay outside, sweetheart, until we help your daddy," she said hurriedly.
As she rushed into the house, she saw Amigo jump
up on Josh and lay his head in the boy's lap.

They had laid Luke on his stomach on the kitchen
table. Delmer Quinn was bent over, checking him out.
"Yep, he's been shot in the back near his right shoulder, and a bullet went clean through his right thigh
just like Matt said. We need something to stop the
bleeding."

"I'll cut up a sheet," Honey said. She ran back to
the wagon and dug out a sheet and her sewing kit.
Returning to the house, she tore the sheet into strips.
Delmer folded several of them into neat square wads.

"You're very orderly, Mr. Quinn," she said. "The
bullet in his shoulder has to come out. Will you help
me?"

"I ain't no doctor, lady."

"You're an undertaker. Surely you've removed bullets before," Honey said.

"Sure, from somebody dead. I ain't never took a
bullet out of somebody who's alive." He started to
walk away.

Honey reached for one of the Colts in Luke's gunbelt. "You're about to, Mr. Quinn." She cocked the

hammer of the gun. "And you'll do it now or someone will have to dig a bullet out of you." Delmer turned around and blanched when he saw the pistol pointed at him. "I want everybody out of here." There was a mad scramble for the door. "Sam, take Josh with you and send a bottle of whiskey back here with him."

"Sure, Honey, sure," Sam said, hurrying to leave.

"Now, Mr. Quinn, how about you put a kettle of water on to boil so we can sterilize the instruments."

"What instruments?" he asked.

"I've got a pair of sewing scissors, and Luke's got a knife."

By the time Josh returned with the whiskey, they were ready to begin. Delmer poured some of the liquor into the leg wound to clean it, covered it with a compress, and bound the wound with a strip of sheet.

"I ain't making any promises, lady," Delmer mumbled as he removed the compress on Luke's back.

Honey thanked God that Luke was unconscious when the undertaker began to probe the wound with the scissors. He finally located the lodged bullet. The attempt set the wound to bleeding again, and Honey tried to wipe away the blood.

Delmer picked up the whiskey bottle, brought it to his mouth, and took a deep draught of liquor. With a disgruntled look at Honey, he dug into the wound with the sewing scissors and managed to get a hold on the bullet.

Despite her effort to wipe away the blood, the bleeding became more profuse, and Delmer could not hold on to the bullet. He tossed the scissors aside in disgust.

"How do you expect me to get out a bullet without the proper tools?"

He picked up the knife and pried at the bullet until he finally managed to work the piece of bent metal to the mouth of the wound. He grabbed the scissors and lifted it out.

"There's your damn bullet."

Honey wanted to cry with relief. As Delmer went to the sink and washed the blood off his hands, Honey poured whiskey into the wound and applied a compress and bandage.

Delmer put on his hat and slipped his arms into the sleeves of his coat. "I'll be leaving now, and don't expect me back," he said with a dark glare at her.

"You're not leaving until we get him in bed," Honey said. She picked up the Colt and waved it at him again.

"How do you expect me to carry him into bed?"

"I know a way. We can push the table into the bedroom and lift him onto the bed."

With Delmer cursing under his breath every step of the way, they pushed and shoved the table across the floor and finally lifted Luke onto the bed.

"Thank you, Mr. Quinn. You did marvelously," Honey declared.

"Thank you, indeed! I intend to tell the sheriff that you pulled a gun on me, lady. My Myrtlelee was right when she said you were crazy." Delmer stomped out of the house.

Honey removed Luke's bloodstained clothing, then she bathed him and put clean drawers on him. She assigned Josh the task of watching Luke while she scrubbed the bloodstains out of his clothes.

In order to keep her mind off the seriousness of Luke's condition, she forced herself to stay busy by unloading the wagon. She checked Luke frequently, hoping for a change, but he remained unconscious, his breathing labored.

By nightfall she felt both physically and emotionally exhausted. After putting Josh to bed, she dragged the parlor chair into the bedroom and sat down. She leaned back and closed her eyes.

Honey awoke with a start. Luke still lay motionless on his stomach. She looked at the clock and saw that she had slept for only fifteen minutes. Rising from the chair, she moved to the bed, and as she had done repeatedly ever since Delmer Quinn had removed the bullet, she felt Luke's brow. He was burning up with fever, and she had no medicine to give him. Slumping down on the floor next to the bed, she laid her cheek on the mattress to study him. He looked so peaceful. As if he were sleeping.

A tear slid down her cheek. Wiping it aside, she reached out and tenderly brushed the dark hair from his forehead.

"Please don't leave me, my love," she said softly. Smiling wistfully, she continued to stroke his head. "You don't know how often I've wanted to call you that, my love. That's why you can't leave me now. I've got so much to confess to you. I've loved you, Luke MacKenzie, from the first moment I met you."

She picked up his hand, which no longer exuded its customary strength and energy. Lovingly, she kissed the tip of each firm, long finger. "And I love your hands . . . their touch. I've never told you that either, my love." She smiled. "But I think you figured that out for yourself."

She pressed his hand against her tear-streaked cheek. "Oh, Luke, there's so much I love about you. Please, my love, please don't die."

Throughout the night, she sat on the floor holding his hand.

At the sound of a rap on the door early the next morning, Honey kissed Luke's palm, then gently laid his hand on the bed. Wearily, she rose to her feet and moved to the front door.

"Come in, Matt."

Matt Brennan entered solemnly, doffing his hat. "Good morning, Mrs. MacKenzie. I'm just getting ready to ride out, and I thought I'd stop to see how the sheriff—I mean, how Luke is doing."

"About the same, Matt. He hasn't gained consciousness yet, and he's feverish."

"Well, we finally found a trail leading into the mountains. I've deputized Jess and Randy Calhoun.

We're gonna follow it and see if we can catch up with the man who shot him."

"Be careful, Matt," she said sadly as he left.

Woodenly, Honey went into the kitchen. She poured a cup of coffee, sat down, and laid her head on the table. A short time later, she looked up with a forced smile when Josh wandered out of the bedroom.

"Well, Josh MacKenzie, what do you want for breakfast this morning?"

"I'm not hungry." He cast a nervous glance at Luke's bedroom door. "Is Daddy better today?"

"No, Josh, but at least his condition's not getting worse. That's an encouraging sign, sweetheart."

"He's been asleep yesterday and all night. My daddy's gonna die and you know it."

Honey closed her eyes and tried to control her quivering chin. "I know no such thing, Joshua MacKenzie. And I don't want to hear you talking like that again." Then regretting her harshness, she reached over and covered his hand with her own. "Look, sweetheart, he's lost a lot of blood, but he's holding his own. And if anyone can pull through something like this, your daddy can. He's strong and in good physical shape. Mr. Quinn removed the bullet from his back; that's the important thing."

"Mr. Quinn's no doctor. He buries people. Like he buried Mr. O'Leary."

Oh, Pop, she thought sadly, *I miss you so much. I wish you were here now. I sure could use your shoulder to cry on. I've got no one, Pop. Even Cynthia and Doug are gone.*

The misery she was feeling must have shown on her face. "I'm sorry if I made you feel sad, Mama. Please don't cry."

"I know you're scared, Josh. So am I. But both of us have to be brave right now. That's what your daddy would want." Wearily, she got up to return to the bedroom.

Josh followed her and stood next to the bed with Amigo at his feet. As the youngster stared at his father's motionless form, his little chin quivered, but he didn't cry. She glanced at Luke, then back to Josh, then at the devoted dog at his feet.

Funny, she thought, for the past six years she'd had the responsibility of looking out for only herself. Now she had a wounded husband, a heartsick child, and a lame dog depending upon her. She prayed for the strength not to let any one of them down. Swallowing the lump in her throat, she put her arm around Josh's shoulders.

"I wish my daddy would open his eyes."

Honey seated herself on the chair and lifted him onto her lap. Looking into his somber blue eyes, she tried to find words that would ease his fears.

"Sweetheart, often when people are seriously hurt, they become unconscious. It's like a sleep. I think it's the Lord's way of protecting them from thrashing around and possibly injuring themselves worse."

"Is that why Daddy has to sleep on his tummy now?"

"Yes, to protect the wound in his back."

"But Daddy don't like sleeping on his tummy. Daddy likes sleeping on his back. I knowed that 'cause I sleeped with him already."

"Well, that's why it's good he's unconscious, because he doesn't know he's on his stomach."

"Will Daddy wake up pretty soon?"

"I'm sure he will, sweetheart. Now, why don't you go to your room and get dressed? Then I'll read to you." Obediently, he climbed off her lap and, followed by Amigo, left the room.

When Josh returned a short time later, Honey sat slumped in the chair. "If me and Amigo are quiet, can we stay and watch Daddy?"

"Of course," Honey said kindly. "Just don't let Amigo on the bed."

Moments passed like hours to her. She mended the rips in Luke's shirt and pants and tried to keep Josh occupied. Only the Reverend Wright and Sam came to check on Luke's condition.

Finally the sun set and she put Josh to bed.

* * *

Luke opened his eyes and for a long moment lay disoriented, aware only of an unusual silence. His vision was blurred, and he focused on a large, bulky object near him. Slowly his eyesight cleared, and he realized the object was a chair. With concentrated effort, he recognized the figure in the chair.

"Jaybird."

Honey opened her eyes to discover Luke awake and looking at her. "Luke!" She dropped to her knees at the bedside.

"What . . . what happened?"

"You've been shot, Luke," she said anxiously. "You've been unconscious since yesterday."

"Unconscious . . . yesterday." He tried to shake off the wave of blackness engulfing him.

"Oh, darling, how are you . . . feeling?" The sentence trailed to an end when he closed his eyes. "Luke. Luke," she whispered, shaking him lightly.

He opened his eyes again and struggled to see through the haze. He was in bed—on his stomach. He lifted his head. His arms tingled with numbness, as if thousands of needles were being driven into his flesh. He braced himself to turn over.

"Don't move, Luke, or you'll open your wounds."

He gave up trying and collapsed.

Honey felt encouraged. At least he had regained consciousness. She settled back in the chair. Just hearing his voice again gave her renewed hope.

Chapter 29

⌒◯◯⌒

Startled by a light tap on the door, Honey looked up. It was almost ten o'clock, and she couldn't imagine who would be calling at such a late hour. Then she remembered Matt Brennan. She figured he must have gotten back and wanted to check on Luke.

Honey opened the door, but not to Matt: Lily LaRue stepped in hurriedly and quickly closed the door behind her.

"How is Luke, Honey?" The woman's eyes were wide with fright.

"Not good," Honey said.

"You've got to get him away from here."

"As soon as he's well enough to travel."

"No, I mean right away."

"What's wrong, Lily?"

"Charlie's the one who shot Luke. He's been at the Long Branch bragging that he got Matt Brennan out of town on a wild goose chase. He just rode out of town to bring back some of his gang."

"Charlie?" Honey stared at her, astonished. "You mean that smooth-talking blond-haired stranger that was hanging around the Long Branch?"

Lily nodded. "Yes, that's him. Charlie Walden."

Honey was astounded. "You mean the same man

who's been shooting up this town? According to Luke, Walden was one of the gang that raided his ranch and killed his wife and mother!"

"They'll be back tonight to finish Luke off, and Charlie's threatened to kill anyone who tries to help Luke."

"Oh, God, Lily! Luke has just regained consciousness. But he's feverish and much too weak to fight back. Why didn't you tell Luke sooner who Charlie was?"

"I just found out myself. He never mentioned his last name. And I'm in a business where you don't ask if it's not offered."

"I've got to get some help. I can't leave Luke and Josh alone. Will you wait here for just a few minutes?"

"All right, but hurry. If anyone sees me here, the word will get out. And that bastard Walden will probably kill me too," Lily replied.

Honey ran next door. The jailhouse was dark. She pounded on the door, but to no avail. Obviously, Matt had not returned. Seeing a light in Quinn's mortuary shop, she hurried over there.

Delmer opened the door. When he saw her, he tried to close the door but Honey shoved it open. "Mr. Quinn, we need your help. Charlie Walden is riding in tonight to kill Luke. He's too weak to protect himself. Will you help me?"

"I've got no intention of becoming involved in any gunfight. I've done enough for you folks. Now get away. I've got work to do."

"Work? At this time of night?" She glanced over and saw a partly finished pine box. Suddenly, the implication struck her with horror. "You knew, didn't you?" She stared at him with disbelief. "You're building that pine box for Luke!"

"I'm a businessman, lady." He shut the door in her face.

She raced up the street to the Long Branch. Sam would help her. She realized she should have thought of him sooner. Breathlessly, she entered the barroom, but it was deserted. Then she sighed with relief when Sam came out of the rear room. "Oh, thank God! Sam, I need your help. Charlie Walden's coming back into town to kill Luke. And he's too feverish and weak to defend himself."

Sam shook his head. "Sorry, Honey. A bartender's gotta stay neutral in these kind of fights."

"But Luke's your friend, Sam," she said, aghast. "How can you stand by and let him be killed?"

"Sure, I like Luke, Honey. He's a good man. And I sure as hell don't want to see him killed. But this is a tough land, kid, and there'll always be a Luke MacKenzie and a Charlie Walden at odds. There's no preventin' it. The secret of survivin' is to keep your nose out of it. Just look around you. This place is empty. The word's out. Once it's over, this place'll fill up, and Walden will probably be buying everyone drinks. Truth is, kid, a Charlie Walden's good for business; a Luke MacKenzie scares it off."

"Oh no, Sam," she said. "No." Stunned, she backed out of the door.

Out on the street, she looked around in desperation. She felt a rush of hope when she saw Reverend Wright and Stockton's mayor in front of the church. She ran down the street to them.

"Mr. Webster, I'm sure you've heard about Charlie Walden's threat. And Matt Brennan is out of town. Will you raise some of the townspeople to help Luke?"

The two men exchanged wary glances. "Mrs. MacKenzie, as the town's mayor, I can't ask my constituents to risk their lives to defend Luke MacKenzie. That would have to be an individual's choice."

"But Luke's been your sheriff for the past two years. How often did he jeopardize his life defending this town?"

"That's what he was paid to do, Mrs. MacKenzie. And need I remind you, he is no longer the sheriff here. When he up and resigned, his concern was clearly not for the people of this town. Thank goodness young Mr. Brennan was willing to step in to protect the citizens of Stockton."

She felt sick in the pit of her stomach. "You mean you won't help him?"

"I am truly amazed that you would presume to ask help from the very people whom you have personally threatened and maligned with your name calling."

"So that's it! You're doing this just to get even with me—Luke's life doesn't matter to you. Mr. Webster, I'll apologize to your wife. I'll get down on my knees and beg if that's what you want. But please don't take your resentment toward me out on Luke. Don't you understand? He's helpless, unable to protect himself."

"Once again you have insulted the citizens of Stockton. We are not narrow-minded or spiteful people, Mrs. MacKenzie, but we have no personal obligation to risk our lives for your husband."

She glanced in desperation at the pastor. "I suppose you feel the same way."

"I have the greatest respect for Luke, Mrs. MacKenzie," Reverend Wright said.

Honey looked at him hopefully. "Then you'll help him, Pastor Wright?"

"I certainly will."

"Oh, thank you, sir. Maybe the two of us will be enough to fight them off."

"Fight? Oh no, Mrs. MacKenzie, I'm afraid you misunderstood me. I am a man of the cloth; my weapon is the Holy Bible. I'll pray for Luke's safety."

"Don't bother," Honey said with scorn. "Pray instead for the good citizens of this town, Pastor," she lashed out angrily. "They need it!"

Disheartened, she ran back to the house. "Did you find help?" Lily asked as soon as she returned.

She shook her head. "No one, not even Sam. I thought he, at least, was my friend." Her eyes were pleading. "Lily, will you take Josh with you?"

"You can't stay here, Honey. They'll kill you, too."

"I'm not leaving Luke."

"Listen, I've been thinking while you were gone. If

we can sneak Luke into your old room at the Long Branch without being seen, you can hide there."

"How will we get him past Sam?"

"If you can get him on his feet, you can sneak in the back door. I'll unlock it and keep Sam occupied."

"Oh, God, yes! It's a chance. I'll hide the wagon, and maybe they'll think I've left town with Luke."

"It's better than sitting here waiting for them. Let's go, Honey gal," Lily said.

"Why are you doing this, Lily? You're risking your life."

"Luke MacKenzie's a good man. Too good to die at the hands of an animal like Charlie Walden."

Honey hugged her, then hurried into the bedroom and began to shake him. "Luke, please, if you can hear me, open your eyes. Fight it, darling. Please. Open your eyes."

"What . . . ?"

"Luke, I have to get you on your feet. Can you stand up? We have to get out of here. Charlie Walden's on his way here to shoot you."

Luke was too feverish to ask questions or resist her, but her urgency got through to him. She managed to get him into his trousers and shirt, but he could barely stay on his feet. "Lean on me," Honey said. She grabbed his arm and looped it around her shoulders. She thought her knees would buckle under his weight.

Lily grabbed his gunbelt and boots and tossed them onto the wagon. Both women shoved him bodily as they helped him to climb up on the seat.

When Honey drew her hand away, it was spotted with blood. To her dismay, she realized his wounds had opened. But there was no time to worry about it now. She ran in and woke up Josh. Within minutes, Josh and Amigo were tucked in the wagon, too.

"Good luck," Lily said. "I'll have the door unlocked by the time you get there."

"Thank you, Lily." Honey grabbed and kissed her. "I'll never forget what you've done for us."

The streets were deserted. Avoiding the main street, Honey drove the wagon along several back roads to the rear of the Long Branch. She reined up the horses.

After lifting Josh down, she put a finger to her lips. "Listen, sweetheart, we have to play a game. You must pretend you're Hawkeye and we're surrounded by Iroquois. We'll pretend that they're the bad men who shot your daddy. We're in grave danger, so we can't make a sound or they'll discover us. You carry Amigo and he mustn't make a sound either. Do you understand, Hawkeye?"

Josh nodded. He picked up Amigo. "You can't bark, Amigo, or them mean Earaboy will find us and scalp us," he whispered.

Cautiously, she tried the back door. True to her word, Lily had unlocked it.

Honey helped Luke down from the wagon. "Luke, we're at the rear of the Long Branch. I have to get rid of the wagon. Can you make it upstairs to my old room? You must be quiet because we can't let Sam hear you. Do you understand me?"

Despite his fever, he understood the danger. "Yeah. Give me my gunbelt."

"No. It's too heavy, and you'll need both hands to get yourself up the stairs. Please, just go. I'll be back in a few minutes."

She waited until he started to climb the back stairway, then she got back on the wagon and concealed it in a clump of shrubs behind the livery. Tethering the horses, she grabbed Luke's gunbelt and boots, then dashed back to the Long Branch. Honey snuck in the door and locked it.

She paused for a moment to listen. She could hear Lily and Sam laughing together at the bar, but nothing seemed amiss. She climbed the stairs and opened the door of her old room. Luke had passed out on the bed, and Josh was sitting on the floor in the corner of the room, Amigo cuddled in his arms.

When she closed the door, the room became pitched in darkness. Groping, she managed to lock the door but knew she dared not light a lamp. After several moments, her eyes adjusted to the darkness, and she moved to the bed. Pulling off one of the pillow cases, she folded it and stuffed it under Luke's shirt to stem the bleeding. She pulled down his pants. The old bandage on his leg was saturated with blood. After ripping a strip off the bottom of her slip, she tied a clean compress and bandage to his leg.

There was no more she could do for him at the moment, so she pulled up his trousers and readjusted them.

Honey walked over to Josh. "Sweetheart, I want you to get on the bed with your daddy. We're going to stay here until morning."

In a short time, Josh had fallen asleep next to Luke. Honey settled down where she could watch the street without being seen. In the still of the night, she heard several riders approach the Long Branch. When she heard them enter the saloon, Honey reached for Luke's gunbelt. She lay one of the Colts on the floor beside her, cocked the other, and waited. The sound of male voices filtered upstairs, but she was unable to understand what was being said.

Soon she heard the sound of hoofbeats riding away, and the Long Branch became silent. Honey still didn't close her eyes. She waited, alert and listening.

In a short time, she heard a scratching at the door and a whispered, "Honey." Recognizing Lily's voice, she unlocked the door.

"They're gone," Lily whispered. "Walden and his boys were downstairs. They were madder than hell. Just as we thought, when they found the house empty and your wagon gone, they figured you left town. Sam locked up and went to bed, too, so you can relax for now. How's Luke doing?"

"His wounds reopened. He passed out, but from what I can tell, he's sleeping now."

"Well, you better get some sleep, too."

"Thanks, Lily. I know Luke will thank you, too,

when he's able to. I don't know how we'll ever be able to repay you."

"I didn't do it for money, Honey gal."

"I know you didn't," Honey said. She hugged and kissed her again. Then Lily slipped away.

Honey locked the door and stretched out on the very rug where she and Luke had once made love. She closed her eyes and fell asleep.

Will Hutchins reined up the horses in front of the Wells Fargo office in Placerville and set the brake of the coach. He began to toss down parcels from the top of the stagecoach to the clerk who had come outside.

"Howdy, Will," the man greeted him.

"Zeke," he acknowledged. "Hear 'bout the sheriff in Stockton gettin' bushwhacked? Shot in the back."

"Who shot him?" the clerk asked.

"Charlie Walden."

Grunting, the clerk put down a heavy carton and wiped his brow on his arm. "Is the sheriff gonna make it?"

"Don't know yet; he's still unconscious."

"Shame if he don't. Sheriff MacKenzie's a good man." He toted one of the parcels into the office.

The conversation had carried to the ears of a man lounging against the wall of a nearby building. He walked over to the coach. "When's this stage heading to Sacramento?" he asked.

Will eyed him with curiosity. The man had a beard and drooping mustache that covered most of his face and a scar that ran from the beard almost to the temple on his right cheek. The long black hair under a battered Stetson was tied back with a piece of rawhide.

"You got business there, mister?"

"If I do, it'd be my business, not yours," the stranger said in a low voice.

Will felt the hair rising on his arm from the underlying threat in the tone. He saw a look of irritation in the man's dark blue eyes and realized the stranger was holding his temper in check.

Dressed in buckskin pants and a fringed shirt stained with dust and sweat, the stranger was tall with the lean build of a man who spent most of his time outdoors. He wore a Colt low on his right hip and a sheathed knife on the other hip. *And probably another pigsticker in his boot,* Hutchins thought.

The man's boots were run down at the heels and as dusty as his clothing. *Lean and mean,* Will concluded. *And as dangerous as an angry sidewinder in the hot sun.*

"I lay over here tonight, then I head back down toward the coast in the morning," he said warily.

The stranger nodded, then turned abruptly and strode to a nearby hitching post. He walked with the long, loping strides of a man who felt more comfortable on horseback than on foot.

Will watched him enter the telegraph office. A few minutes later, when Will had almost finished unloading, he saw the stranger come out, swing up effortlessly on the back of the dun mustang, and rode south at a full gallop.

"Wonder why he's in such a dadblasted hurry," he grumbled as he tossed down the last parcel.

A cloud of smoke swirled above the heads of the four men seated at the poker table in Sacramento. The bartender wiped at a stain on the mahogany bar as the clink of poker chips and murmurs of the card players were accompanied by the low strains of "Shenandoah" coming from the piano in the corner.

Mordecai Fisher stepped into the barroom, and for a long moment the wagonmaster swept his glance around the room. Then he walked over to the bar.

The bartender automatically placed a shot glass on the bar and filled it. "Ain't seen you around for a spell. Whatta you been up to, Mordecai?"

"Been down to Frisco. You remember that Stockton

sheriff that was here a month or so ago?" Mordecai asked.

"You mean the one that brought in one of them Walden brothers?"

Mordecai downed the drink and wiped his mouth on his sleeve. "Yeah, that's the one. Shot one of 'em, too, if I remember."

"Well, what about him?" the bartender asked.

"He's been backshot."

The piano player stopped playing. "You talking about that Sheriff MacKenzie?" he asked.

"Yeah," Mordecai said.

Arnie got up from the piano and walked over to the bar. "Who done it, Mordecai?"

"Word's out that Charlie Walden's been boastin' about it."

"Goddammit!" Arnie cursed. "I liked that man. Sorry to hear he's dead."

Mordecai downed another drink. "He ain't dead yet, but might just as well be. Charlie Walden's declared that he and his gang are gonna go back and make sure they finish the job."

One of the card players had listened with interest to the exchange at the bar. Dark haired, with an open, friendly face, he shoved his chips to the center of the table. "Buy me out."

"Pulling out kind of early, ain't you, stranger?" the dealer asked.

The man shrugged nonchalantly. "Happens sometimes."

The dealer eyed the stranger with hostility. He had lost a lot of money to him and didn't like the idea of this stranger leaving without giving him a chance to win it back.

Compared to the others at the table, the stranger could have passed as a dandy. His cheeks were clean shaven except for a dark mustache. Tall and well muscled, he was wearing a white shirt, black cravat, a black fitted frock coat that hung to his thighs, and fawn-colored trousers. On neatly clipped hair, he wore a low-crowned black hat set at a slight angle.

Observing the man's nose, which clearly had been broken more than once; the wild recklessness in his dark blue eyes; and the holster that appeared to set as comfortably on his hip as a worn boot on the foot, the dealer was discouraged from messing with him. He handed the stranger the cash.

With a congenial smile, the man shoved the money into a vest pocket, then tipped his hat. "It's been my pleasure, gentlemen."

The man's smile shifted into a worried frown as soon as he left the bar and entered the hotel lobby. The desk clerk called him over. "This telegram just came for you, sir."

Picking up the envelope, he tossed the clerk a gold dollar, then quickly read the cryptic message.

Arriving first thing in the morning.

He crumpled up the telegram, tossed it into the wastebasket, and climbed the stairs.

Chapter 30

~~~~~~~~~~ೕ ⁀ ೕ ~~~~~~~~~~

With the threat of Charlie Walden temporarily behind them, Honey felt it safe to return to the house. Luke's wounds had stopped bleeding, and he felt strong enough to be moved. They managed to sneak out of the Long Branch without anyone being the wiser, thus ensuring Lily's safety from the wrath of Charlie Walden.

Nevertheless, Honey was surprised that afternoon when Lily showed up at her door to tell her she was leaving Stockton.

"Where will you be going, Lily?"

"Probably to San Francisco. I just don't like this town anymore. It seems to be losing the only people worthwhile."

"I had always thought of going to San Francisco, too, until I fell in love with Luke."

"I've never been lucky enough to find a man like Luke. And even if I did, no man wants to marry a woman with my shady past."

"Why don't you give it up, Lily? You're young and lovely. Surely, you could find a man who would be willing to overlook your past. I found one, didn't I?"

"Honey gal, there aren't too many men around like

Luke MacKenzie. And since I can't sing or deal poker, I don't know anything but what I've been doing."

"Why not come to Texas with us? You can find work there, I'm sure."

"No, I'll stay with the big cities. But who knows, maybe some day I might work my way down to Texas. Good-bye, Honey gal, and say good-bye to that husband of yours. Get him out of here before he's killed," Lily added.

"I will as soon as he's well enough to travel," Honey said, hugging her. "Good luck, Lily, and God be with you."

Honey stood at the door with a sense of melancholy and watched Lily climb on the stage. "Good luck, Lily," she repeated sadly.

The next day, Luke was well enough to eat a little soup. The wound on his back seemed to be healing. Although it no longer bled, moribund tissue had begun to form around the mouth of the wound. Fearing the start of infection, she began to bathe it with hot compresses.

Due to the effect of the fever, Luke slept most of the day, but at least she no longer felt a need to spend the night at his bedside. That night, for the first time in four days, she laid down and shared a bed with Josh.

Two men rode slowly into town. Sitting straight in the saddle, their faces solemn and their gazes steady, they drew curious glances from several townspeople hurrying home after a late night. Amber lights glowed from the window of the jail at one end of the street and from the Long Branch at the other. The sound of a tinkling piano drifted through the open doors as they rode up to the saloon. One of the men cast a sideways look at the bank clock that indicated the hour of ten. Dismounting, they tied their horses to a hitching post. One of the men took off his hat and brushed the trail dust off it. The other man checked the Colt on his hip, then ambled ahead and stopped in front of the entrance of the saloon until his companion joined him. With a cautious glance around them, they entered the Long Branch.

Within minutes they were back outside and climbed on their horses. At a slow trot, the two strangers rode down Main Street and reined up in front of the jail. Only a faint creak of leather sounded as they dismounted. Matt Brennan jumped to his feet when they entered.

A short time later they left the jail, their eyes darting right and left, then they moved stealthily to the house next door. Soundlessly, they mounted the porch stairs. The grizzled one turned and watched the shadows as the other rapped softly on the door. Receiving no reply, he turned the door handle. With a faint squeak, the door swung open.

Honey wasn't certain what woke her. Had Luke called out to her? For several seconds she sat motionless, listening for any sound. Finally, satisfied, she settled back in bed.

The next moment, a slight creak from the parlor sent her bolting to her feet. Someone had just stepped on the loose floorboard near the entrance to Luke's bedroom. She glanced at Josh, who was sleeping soundly. Amigo lay with a lifted head and perked ears. She raised a finger to her lips and cautioned him to remain silent. Fearing the gunmen had returned, she started to tremble.

She slipped out of bed, picked up the Colt on the night stand, and moved cautiously to the door. With her racing heart pounding in her ears, Honey feared the intruders could hear her loud breathing. Drawing a deep shuddering breath, she rallied her courage and peered around the door.

The dimmed lamp burning in Luke's bedroom cast the darkened room in an amber glow. A quick glance showed the parlor and kitchen to be empty. Then her breath lodged in her throat when she saw a reflection on the wall—a shadowy outline was leaning over Luke's bed.

Desperate to protect Luke, Honey lost all fear for herself. Clutching the Colt in both hands, she moved to the doorway of Luke's bedroom. "Get away from him," she ordered.

There were two men standing over Luke, one on each side of the bed. She quickly concealed her shock. "Get your hands up in the air. One false move from either of you, and I'll shoot you both."

"Yes, ma'am," one of the intruders said, raising his arms. He was clean shaven, and he looked younger and less dangerous than his grizzled companion, who was eyeing her with a wary scowl. The scar running along his right cheek added to his menacing appearance.

"One warning is all you get, mister," she bellowed as she extended her arm and took direct aim. Reluctantly, the man raised his arms.

Honey was running the bluff of her life. She had never fired a gun before and doubted she could hit anything if she tried, even at this close range. Before they discovered her con, she had to get them as far away from Luke as possible.

She backed up slowly. "Just step out of this room real nice and easy. And don't try any fancy steps, or you won't be dancing for a long time."

She felt dwarfed by the two tall men, who seemed to crowd the small parlor. "Now close the door."

"My pleasure, ma'am," the younger man said and quickly did as ordered. "I'd say you're one tough lady for your size. I sure don't want to tangle with you."

"Yeah, well I don't cotton to tough ladies—and tough ladies playing with Colts even less," the bearded man said in a malicious tone.

"All right, unbuckle those gunbelts. You first," she said to the scar-faced man, whom she perceived to be the most dangerous. She countered his scorching glare with determined, unflinching eyes. "Now you,"

she ordered the other. He smiled obligingly, unbuck-
led his belt, and let it drop to the floor.

She backed up to the front door. Keeping the gun
trained on them, Honey opened the door. "Hello,
anyone out there?" she shouted.

"There's no one out there, ma'am; we've already
checked. Something *we* can help you with?"

Irritated, she glared at the cocky young man, sus-
pecting he was having a laugh at her expense. "Then
the three of us will just have to march next door to
the jailhouse, won't we?" she said.

"I'm willing if you are, ma'am. 'Pears like a pleasant enough night for a walk."

His cavalier attitude did not fool her one bit; he was
trying to catch her off guard so his mean-eyed cohort
could rush her.

"Of course, it'll get real interesting to see the stir
you cause if someone sees you in that nightgown,"
he said, shifting his glance down the length of her.
" 'Specially if you're standing in a light like you are
right now."

Honey gasped in shock and looked down at her
thin nightgown. Too late, she realized she wasn't in
the light. As quick as a striking snake, the other man's
hand slipped around her wrist.

"You've plumb irritated me, lady," the bearded
man growled. He lifted the gun out of her hand.
"Next time you point a Colt at someone, you best
have it cocked." He released her, then strapped on his
gunbelt and headed back to the bedroom.

"No, stop!" she screamed. "Don't you touch him. I
won't let you hurt him." She rushed at him and
started to pummel him with both hands. To avoid her
fists and keep the gun from her reach, he looped an
arm around her waist and lifted her feet off the floor.
Held in his viselike grip, she kicked and struggled as
she dangled in midair.

"Goddammit, Cleve, get this she-cat off me 'fore
someone gets shot."

The younger man burst into laughter. "Looks like you've got your hands full, Flint."

Cleve? . . . Flint? The names were like a blow to the head. Honey immediately ceased her struggles and hung limply, staring mutely at the floor in utter astonishment.

Strapping on his gunbelt, Cleve hurried over to them. "What the hell did you do to her?" he asked worriedly. "You didn't hurt her, did you?"

"Sure didn't mean to if I did. She probably hurt herself, kicking and scratching the way she was," Flint said. He lowered her until her feet touched the floor. "You okay, little lady?"

"You're Flint!" she exclaimed. She quickly swung her glance to the younger man. "And you're Cleve!"

"Yes, ma'am," Cleve said.

"Oh, thank God," she cried joyously. "You're Luke's brothers."

"That's the first thing you've said tonight, lady, that makes any sense," Flint said.

Giddy with relief and happiness, she threw her arms around his waist and, as much as she could, bear-hugged the man who seemed to be twice her size. "Oh, Flint, you're just as cantankerous as I suspected you would be."

Perplexed, he patted her shoulder awkwardly and glanced over the top of her blond head to his brother. Cleve's eyes were filled with amusement.

Turning to Cleve, Honey gushed, "And Cleve! Oh, Cleve, you're just as pleasant as I imagined."

Anticipating her next move, Cleve opened his arms to receive her, and she eagerly embraced him. "Well, that's right nice of you, ma'am." Once again the two men exchanged mystified glances over her head.

"Reckon we owe you an apology for popping in and scaring you the way we did, ma'am," Cleve said apologetically. "We knocked several times, and the door was unlocked."

"I know. The key's lost, and there's no bolt on the door."

"When we heard about our brother getting shot, we just hightailed it down here as fast as we could," Flint added.

"And I can't tell you how relieved I am that you did," Honey assured them.

Cleve grinned. "Well, we sure are thankful that he pulled through. After fearing the worse, it was downright heartening to see him in there sleeping like a baby."

"And sawin' wood like a choked bull in a sandstorm," Flint added.

"Sawing wood! Luke doesn't snore in his sleep," she quickly denied. "I certainly would know if he did."

An awkward silence followed her declaration as the two men exchanged quizzical expressions.

Clearing his throat, Cleve was the first to speak. "Ah . . . I apologize, ma'am, but I'm afraid you kind of have us at a disadvantage. Just who are you?"

Honey raised her hands and clasped them together. For a moment it appeared as if she was about to lead them in prayer. "Oh, of course!" she exclaimed. "How stupid of me!" Then she bowed her head on her hands. "I'm so sorry. The two of you must think I'm deranged." From the sudden glint in Flint's eyes, she suspected the thought had crossed his mind.

She raised her head and looked at them. "I'm Luke's wife."

The two men gaped at her with astonishment. "Luke's wife!" Flint exclaimed.

"That sheriff next door never said anything about Luke having a wife," Cleve said, astonished.

"I think we should all sit down and have a cup of coffee," she said to the flabbergasted men. "Soon as I get a robe, I'll put a pot on to brew."

"I can make the coffee if you tell me where I can find the makings, ma'am," Flint said.

"Honey," she corrected.

"Not for me, ma'am. I just take my coffee strong and black."

"Whoa! If I remember rightly, Brother Flint, your coffee is so strong it coats your throat with sludge, then mudslides into your stomach. I'll make the coffee," Cleve commented, lighting the parlor lamp.

Honey hadn't moved. "No, I meant my name is Honey."

The two men, who had started for the kitchen, stopped to look back at her. She prepared herself for the worst, especially from Flint. Flashing the whitest teeth she had ever seen, he grinned broadly. "That's a mighty sweet name."

"Well, I've heard worse," she said, referring to past comments relating to her name.

Cleve thought she was offended by the remark and quickly said, "He meant it's a lovely name, Honey. Fits you, too, especially with that long hair of yours all tawny and goldlike. Kind of reminds me of the fresh honey Ma used to pour into jars, doesn't it, Flint?"

"Reckon it does," Flint said, staring solemnly at her.

Instinctively she put her hand to her hair, feeling unexpectedly touched by their expressions and ridiculously sentimental. Something within her seemed to conjure up images of love, family, and devotion—images that she had always longed for but had never experienced. She had to get out of there before she burst into tears.

"I take that as a compliment, gentlemen," she said softly and escaped into the bedroom, closing the door behind her. Smiling through her tears, she glanced heavenward. "Thank you, God," she said faintly as she reached for her robe.

By the time she freshened up, brushed her hair, and went out to join them, she found Cleve alone. He was lighting a log in the fireplace, and already had set the coffee pot on the stove to brew.

"Where did Flint go?" she asked.

"To get the horses." He sat down on the floor,

stretched out his long legs, and leaned back against the wall.

"Wouldn't you be more comfortable in the parlor chair, Cleve?"

"This is just fine, ma'am—ah, Honey." He grinned at his slip of the tongue. "Takes a mite getting used to."

She sat down near him on the floor. "You mean my name?"

"No, I guess . . . just having a little sister again." His expression darkened, reminding her of the bitter grimness she had seen so often on Luke's face whenever he spoke of his wife's tragedy.

Flint came in and tossed the saddlebags on the floor, then settled down next to Cleve.

"What about you, Flint? You'd probably be more comfortable in the chair."

"Don't worry about me, Little Sister. Any time I've got a roof over my head, I'm content just to sit and enjoy it." He removed his gunbelt and laid it beside him.

Suddenly remembering her manners, Honey exclaimed, "Oh my, how thoughtless of me! Would you like something to eat?"

"Just coffee'll do for me," Flint said.

"Me, too," Cleve agreed.

"Are you sure? It wouldn't take long to fry up some bacon and eggs. They're fresh too. I just bought them today. I'm going to try and get Luke to eat a couple in the morning."

"That'll be soon enough then," Cleve said. He grinned at Flint, who was stretched out with his hands tucked under his head. "It'll be like old times, having the three of us sit down at breakfast together."

"Yep, it's been a long time, Little Brother."

"Six years," Cleve said, soberly.

"I'm afraid Luke's not ready to sit at the table yet. He's still very sick." Alarmed, Cleve instantly swung his glance to her. "Luke's okay, isn't he? He's gonna pull through?"

"He's . . ." She couldn't speak past the lump in her throat.

"He's what? Goddammit, tell us," Flint shouted, springing to his feet like a huge cat. "Is he gonna die?"

"No. He's just had a serious relapse, because his wounds reopened and there's no doctor here in town. Please, let's sit down at the table, and I'll tell you what happened."

Once they were seated, Honey explained the circumstances under which Delmer Quinn had removed the bullet and then Lily's subsequent help. Not once did either of them interrupt her during the painful discourse.

"Well, it appears we owe this Miss Lily our thanks." Cleve glanced at Flint. "I'll be sure to pass on your gratitude, too, Brother Flint."

"It's too late, Cleve. Lily has already left town."

"Shame. We could have celebrated together."

"I'll hold my celebrating until we know Luke's pulled through," Flint grumbled, casting a critical look at his brother.

"You always did tend to look on the black side of things. Remember, Ma always told us to look up."

"I've tried that a time or two and landed on my backside for the effort. I've learned to depend on my instincts." He looked at Honey. "What's your feeling on it?"

She looked him squarely in the eye. "I believe Luke's going to be as sound as ever in about a week."

Twitching at his beard, Flint stared at her for a long moment, then he nodded. "Reckon I'll trust your instincts, too, Little Sister."

Sensing the importance of being honest about everything, she drew a deep breath. "There's more you should know." Once she started, the words seemed to spill out of her unchecked. She didn't withhold anything from them: her shady past, Jake Simmons, the murder of Sheldon Peters, Abigail Fenton, and her taking a job at the Long Branch.

When she was finished, she waited for their censure, for their words of disapproval. Instead Flint stood up and stretched. "Don't know about the two of you, but I'm gonna get me some shut eye."

"Yeah, sounds like a good idea," Cleve said. "You best get some rest, too, Honey. From what you say, 'pears like you've been under a big strain lately."

Woodenly, she watched as they removed their boots and then settled down before the fireplace. She felt confused, bewildered by their reaction. Hadn't they listened to what she had told them about Luke and her? About her past? "Don't either of you have anything to say about what I've just told you?"

"Little Sister," Flint said, "if our big brother loves you, that's all we have to know. You're a MacKenzie now."

"And I'd say you sure as hell proved it the last couple nights," Cleve added.

Suddenly Luke called out, "Is that you, Jaybird?"

Honey hurried to the bedroom. "I'm sorry we woke you, Luke," Honey said, peeking in. "There's a couple of people here who are anxious to talk to you."

Flint got up, threw back his head, and issued the famous Rebel yell as he came through the door.

Flabbergasted, Luke jerked up his head and stared. "Flint? My God, Flint, is it really you?" he exclaimed.

Cleve stepped in beside Flint. "And what the hell are you doing in bed? That's plain unsociable, Big Brother. Whatever happened to that Texas hospitality Ma taught you?"

"Cleve! Goddammit, I don't believe it!" Luke looked incredulous. He tried unsuccessfully to shift himself into a sitting position, and Honey felt her heart ache when his brothers hurried over to assist him.

After a series of handshakes and backslaps to cover up the awkward moment, they sat down on the chairs Honey carried in from the kitchen.

"Where in hell did you two come from?" Luke asked.

"From up north," Flint said. "When we heard about you getting shot, we hightailed it down here. Goddammit, Luke, how the hell did you let yourself get backshot? Don't sound like any MacKenzie I ever knew."

"That's smart talk coming from a man toting a scar the length of his face. Some Comanche get his knife into you?"

"Naw, picked this up at Fredericksburg."

"Stuart?" Luke asked. Flint nodded. "Might have known you'd end up in Stuart's cavalry."

"Then, after he was killed, I served under Pelham's command. He was a good officer, but there sure wasn't any of 'em like Jeb Stuart."

"What about you, Cleve?" Luke asked.

"Served under General Jackson for awhile. Then after Chancellorsville, and the general's death, I was transferred to Lee's command."

Luke glanced at him, surprised. "Lee's command! Were you at Appomattox Courthouse the day he surrendered?"

"Sure was," Cleve said.

"Hell, Cleve, so was I. I was with Longstreet."

"Dammmit, we were in spitting distance of each other," Cleve bemoaned. "Reckon we kept missing each other. When I got back to Texas, I found you'd been there already."

Honey had stood forgotten throughout their reunion. Despite their light banter, the camaraderie and love that flowed between them was clear to see. Now, at Cleve's mention of Texas, she decided she would not intrude upon this private moment. Unobserved, she left the room and closed the door.

"When we got back to the ranch and found out about Ma and Sarah . . . I'm sure sorry about Sarah, Luke," Cleve said solemnly.

"Yeah, I know," Luke said grimly. "You two find any leads?"

"We split up to follow a couple of 'em. I tracked down one of the Comanche who took part in the raid," Flint said. "Had to kill him though before I could get anything out of him except that the gang had broken up and a few had headed for California. Didn't pick up any clues farther south in this state. Cleve and I had agreed to meet in Sacramento about the same time we heard about you being shot."

"What about you, Cleve? You have any better luck?" Luke asked.

"I trailed you to Mexico, talked to Juan, then thought you might have gone back to Texas. So I went back to the ranch. That's when I met up with Flint. After we split up, I met this fella in Laredo who rode with the Rangers at the time of the raid. Got the same story as Flint did. He said the gang had headed to California. I'd just gotten to Sacramento when I heard about you."

"Well, I've got something to show the two of you," Luke said. He reached for the watch on the night stand and handed it to Flint.

Flint looked at it and glanced at Luke. "Pa's watch!" He handed it to Cleve.

Luke watched as his brothers examined the watch. Memories of the last time they had seen the watch their mother always wore around her neck became painfully etched on their faces.

"Where'd you get this, Luke?" Cleve asked.

"Took it off the body of a man called Slim, who tried to rob the bank here. The bastard that rode with him claimed this Slim had won it in a card game from a guy named Charlie Walden."

"The Walden who backshot you?" Flint asked.

Luke shrugged. "My guess is as good as yours. But he said Walden rode with a gang in Texas."

Flint shifted his glance to Cleve. "We've got a name . . ." He grinned. "And now a place—right here in these hills."

Cleve slapped Luke on his good shoulder. "Tell you what, Big Brother, time we got out of here and let you get back to sleep."

"Hope you two aren't planning to ride off until I'm

well enough to go with you," Luke said meaningfully.

"We'll be here, Big Brother," Cleve assured him.

"Yeah, we all have a stake in this fight. When the time comes, we'll ride out together," Flint said.

Flint left, but Cleve stopped at the doorway on the way out. "By the way, Big Brother, you've got yourself one hell of a wife." He grinned at Luke, then went out and joined Honey and Flint at the table.

"How is he?" she asked hopefully.

"He's fine, Little Sister," Flint assured her. "You best get some sleep now."

She nodded. "I guess you're right." After a quick good-night to them, she headed for Josh's room. Pausing at the doorway, she looked back at the two brothers, settling down before the fireplace.

"Flint . . . Cleve." Both glanced up from what they were doing. "I'm glad you're here," she said shyly, then slipped into the room.

Chapter 31

I n the morning a still-sleepy Josh emerged from his bedroom and stopped abruptly at seeing two strange men sleeping on the parlor floor. Amigo had no such qualms; he trotted over to the nearest figure.

At the first touch of a wet snout on his face, Flint grabbed his Colt and bolted upright. Man and dog eyed each other suspiciously.

Yawning, Cleve sat up groggily. "What's going on?" Seeing, the dog, Cleve grabbed Amigo and began to scratch him behind the ears. "Hey, boy, where did you come from?"

"He's mine," Josh declared, stepping forward.

"And just who are you, kid?" Flint asked gruffly.

"I'm Joshua MacKenzie. Whatta you doing in my daddy's house?"

Cleve eyed him more closely. "So you're Joshua. I'm your uncle Cleve. And this mangy critter beside me is your uncle Flint."

Flint grinned. "Howdy, Josh."

"Why's my mama still in bed?"

"You'd have to ask her, kid," Flint grunted, pulling on his boots.

"She don't stay in bed in the morning. Mama gets up early, 'fore I even do. And I already got up and

338

got dressed." With curiosity, he studied them. "I seen two horses outside my window. Are them horses yours?" Josh asked.

"What kind of horses are they, Josh?" Cleve asked, amused.

"Same kind as my daddy's."

"Reckon they're ours then, Josh," Cleve replied.

"How come you guys got the same kind of horses as my daddy?"

"We all like the same kind of horse, kid," Flint answered.

"How come you didn't put them in the livery like my daddy does his?"

"Our horses like the outdoors, Josh," Cleve told him.

"Kid oughta become a Pinkerton detective," Flint commented aside to Cleve.

Just then Honey hurried out of the bedroom, tucking her blond hair into a snood. "Good morning, sweetheart. I see you've met your uncles."

Joshua scrambled over to the table and climbed up on a chair. She smiled at the delightful sound of his laughter. "Mama, I got up 'fore you did."

"Well, your uncles arrived late last night, so we were all up past our bedtime."

"Can I go in and see Daddy now?" Josh asked.

Honey capped the coffee pot and set it aside. "As soon as I light the stove and get this coffee to brewing, we'll go in and see him. But you know how he is about his morning coffee."

"I could run over to the jail and get some from Matt, Mama."

"Well, maybe Matt's still sleeping. Let's wait and see," she advised.

Cleve came over and tousled Josh's hair. "Honey, Flint and I are going to the public bath to get rid of some of this trail dust."

"Can I go with you?" Josh asked eagerly.

"You need a bath, kid?" Flint asked.

"Don't need one for three days yet, but I'll take one

again if you want. By the time we get back, maybe my daddy will have his coffee."

"Well, come along, kid," Flint said. "Does that dog come with you?"

Josh stretched his neck to look up at the tall man. "Amigo goes everywhere I go. He loves me. He'll never leave me."

Flint patted him on the head. "You've got a good friend there, kid. Just keep him out of the bathtub."

Honey went to the door and watched the little figure walking down the street between the two tall men.

She couldn't help smiling.

As soon as the coffee was ready, Honey carried a breakfast tray into the bedroom. Luke had been sleeping but woke when she entered.

"Good morning," she said brightly and kissed him on the cheek.

"Hi, Jaybird. Was I dreaming last night, or are my brothers really here?"

"They're here all right."

"Well, where is everybody?"

"They've all gone over to the public bath." She leaned over and ran her hand along his chin. "You could use a shave, MacKenzie. I think I'll do it."

"Not on your life," he snorted.

"We'll see about that. Eat your breakfast," she said as she left the room. As soon as he finished, she returned to remove the tray, carrying a basin of water and his shaving cup and brush.

"What do you think you're gonna do?" he asked.

"Here, hold this." She shoved the basin into his hands, sat down on the bed, and tucked a towel under his chin.

"Looks like I'm not the first man you've shaved," he said as she worked up a soapy lather in his shaving cup. He managed to close his mouth before she swabbed the soapy brush across his face.

"Now keep your mouth shut and hold still. I'd hate to cut you, MacKenzie."

Concentrating intently, she tried to ignore his steady gaze as she carefully scraped the razor over his cheek. Dipping the razor into the water, she glanced at him.

"Who else have you shaved?" he asked when she made eye contact.

"My father when he was too drunk to shave himself." She curled her tongue over her upper lip as she maneuvered the razor over his chin.

"Anyone else?" he asked as she wiped away the excess soap.

"Why, you worried, MacKenzie?" She leaned back to study his face. "You know, I did a good job. Never nicked you once." She took the basin away from him and put it on the table, then turned toward the door.

He grabbed her arm and pulled her to a quick stop. "Don't run off so fast." He patted the bed beside him.

She sat down, resting her hands on his chest. "You must be feeling a lot better this morning," she teased.

"I am." His eyes never wavered from hers. "I love you, Jaybird."

"I love you, too, Luke." She leaned over and lightly kissed him.

"I was afraid with all that's happened you might have had second thoughts."

Astonished, she looked at him. "Whyever would you think something like that?"

"Women have been known to change their minds, you know."

"Either you've been talking to Flint or you're still feverish." She put her hand on his forehead. "You're still feverish."

"Oh, don't take it off, babe. Your hand feels good. If I ever get out of this bed, we've got a wedding night to celebrate."

"Is that what you've been thinking about? No won-

der you're hot. All this time you had me believing
you were sick."

The sound of his chuckle set her heart to thumping
wildly. Riveted, they stared into one another's eyes,
then he dropped his gaze to her mouth. The prolonged moment became almost unbearable for her as
her heart pounded and her pulses throbbed.

She felt the slide of his hands up her forearms, then
he drew her to him and kissed her. His mouth was
firm and searching, his tongue sending sweet sensation spiraling through her. As the kiss intensified, his
grasp tightened and he pulled her across him, cradling her neck in the curve of his powerful arm.

His mouth released hers only long enough to draw
a much-needed breath, then he smothered her lips
with hungry, demanding persuasion as his tongue
ravished her mouth. He cupped his hand around the
fullness of one breast, and she felt the heat through
all the layers of her clothes.

"Luke, you're too sick for this," she warned with
regret and drew back from him, swamped by a sense
of loss as his hands slipped away from her.

His dark-eyed stare remained fixed on her face. "As
soon as I'm healthy again and back on my feet, we'll
have that wedding night, Jaybird. And until we do,
you're damn right I'll be thinking about it."

She kissed him hurriedly, then picked up the basin
and sped from the room. Her heart was beating so
fast, a warm flush colored her cheeks. And she
couldn't help smiling. She was thinking about it, too.

There was a spring to her step as she disposed of
the shaving items and returned to the bedroom. Luke
was lying on his stomach, with his cheek resting on
his hands.

"Those muscles of yours must be beginning to ache.
Do you want me to massage you?"

"You don't have to ask twice," he mumbled.

Honey got the tin of balm and started to rub salve
into the taut cords across his shoulders, carefully
avoiding his wound. Gradually, she felt his muscles

relax. She continued the massage down to the small of his back, then she kneaded the muscles of his long, powerful legs, checking the wound on his leg, she saw it was healing satisfactorily.

"Now the arms," she told him. Luke dropped his arms to his sides. She applied the same rhythmic pressure to each of them. When she finished, she didn't want to stop; she wanted the excuse to continue touching him. She wanted this moment with just the two of them to go on forever.

Hearing voices at the front door of the house, she left the room in time to see Josh arrive on the wide shoulders of his uncle Flint. Now, after his bath and change of clothing—but unfortunately not a shave—she couldn't help but notice how she had been deceived by Flint's tall, rangy physique. On closer inspection, she realized he was also very powerful: his chest wide, his legs long and firm. His broad shoulders strained against his shirt as he swung Josh to the floor. She decided his beard tended to make him appear older, when in truth she knew that Flint was a year younger than Luke. One of his features was identical to that of his brothers: he had wide-set sapphire-colored eyes tipped with long, thick lashes.

"Mama, we're back!" Josh shouted.

He ran to her with outstretched arms, and she scooped him up. After a hug and kiss, she put him down and stepped back to study him. "Well, from the looks of that wet head of yours, you must have had a bath, too."

"Yep, we picked all the fleas off him," Flint said with a wink.

Josh giggled. "Oh, Uncle Flint's fooling, Mama. I don't have no fleas." Her heart leaped to her throat when she saw the flash of devilishness that she had witnessed so often in his father's eyes. "Bet they were yours, Uncle Flint."

"Must have been that dog's."

"Oh, no!" Honey groaned. "Amigo didn't take a bath with you, did he?" she asked, aghast.

"Just for a little time, Mama. Amigo don't like baths. Can I see my daddy now?"

"You sure can, sweetheart. He's been waiting for you."

Josh grabbed Flint's hand. "Come on, Uncle Flint, let's go see Daddy."

Cleve came into the house before she could follow them. "I stopped to talk to the sheriff. Seems like the town's considering not hiring extra help until after Luke leaves. I told Matt that Flint and I will spell him any time he wants us to."

"That's nice of you, Cleve. He's a fine young man. Luke feels he'll make a good sheriff."

"I don't know why anybody is fool enough to become a sheriff," he said.

Since the statement was rhetorical, she didn't bother to answer, asking instead, "How about something to eat?"

"Oh, we ate at the diner."

Wide-eyed with shock, she stared at him. "Whyever did you do that?"

"We didn't want to put you out, Honey."

"You're Luke's brothers, all right! I'm more put out that you'd even consider going elsewhere to eat. Can you imagine how much worse Luke would feel if he heard what you did?"

Cleve grinned engagingly. "No offense intended, Little Sister, and don't you go batting those big blue eyes at me to try and make me feel guilty. Flint and I figure you've got your hands full with our brother and little nephew. You don't need any more Mac-Kenzies crowding you."

She put her hands on her hips and faced him boldly. "Well, there just better be MacKenzies crowding around that dinner table tonight."

He snapped to attention, clicked his heels, and whipped out a crisp salute. "Yes, ma'am."

Once in the bedroom, Cleve picked up the teasing with Luke. "Tell me, Big Brother, how'd you happen to marry such a sassy Yankee?"

"You noticed," Luke mumbled with a mock derogatory glance at Honey. "At least you don't have to lie here and take it." He sat up, and Honey tucked an extra pillow behind his back.

"Stop fussing over me, Honey. I'm not an invalid."

"You best cut some slack, Big Brother," Flint spoke up. "We're all kin in this room, and we look after our own. Reckon you'd be doing the same if it was one of us in that bed."

"I hate to see her wearing herself thin waiting on me," Luke said with contrition. "I've caused her enough problems in the last couple of days."

"Oh, long before that," Honey said, winking at Flint.

Josh was sitting on the foot of the bed, staring up at his two uncles with awe. "Wow, you guys must be 'bout the tallest men I ever seen," he murmured. "Bet you're even taller than my daddy."

"Well, Josh," Cleve replied, "years ago your grandmother once measured us, and your daddy stood two inches above six feet; your uncle Flint over there stood an inch taller than your daddy, and I stood an inch taller than your uncle Flint."

At the sight of Josh's puzzled look, Flint said, "That means your daddy's the shortest and your uncle Cleve's the tallest, kid."

The explanation appeared to confuse Josh further.

"So what's bothering you now?" Flint asked.

"Well," Josh replied, his brow creased in a frown, "then why do you call my daddy Big Brother and Uncle Cleve Little Brother?"

Flint exchanged an exasperated look with Luke, who couldn't help grinning. "Think you should have your mama explain it to you, kid."

Honey's face was still flushed with laughter as she hurried to answer a steady knocking at the door. Matt Brennan stood on the stoop. From the seriousness of his mien, she sensed something was wrong and immediately lost her light humor.

"Morning, Mrs. MacKenzie," he said solemnly. "Thought you should be told."

"Come in, Matt."

Cleve and Flint had come out of the bedroom to join them and everybody waited expectantly.

"Well, ma'am, Will Hutchins just drove a stage in from up north. He said he was in a waterfront bar when a gang of about a dozen men came in. One of 'em was Charlie Walden. The gang was drinking pretty heavy, according to Will, and making all kinds of big talk, so he hung around to listen. Will heard Charlie say that they were heading back to Stockton to finish the job they had started, killing the sheriff."

"And this Will says there were about a dozen of 'em?" Cleve asked.

Matt nodded. "I thought you'd want to know."

"Yeah, Matt. Appreciate your telling us," Cleve said.

After seeing Matt out, Honey turned to the two men; both seemed in deep thought.

"Well, at least the odds aren't bad," Cleve said.

"How can you say that?" Honey asked in disbelief. "Will said there were a dozen members in the gang." With rising hysteria, she turned to Flint.

His eyes were hard and cold as he replied, "The sun don't rise on a day that three MacKenzies can't take on a dozen men, Little Sister."

Chapter 32

Having been told of the latest threat on his life, Luke got out of bed the following morning. Without knowing for certain when the gang would hit them, there was no time for recuperating slowly. His mobility was essential.

"You should stay in bed," Honey argued. "What if your wounds break open?"

"I'll be fine, Honey. I'm just trying to get some strength back in my legs."

"Well, if you think you're well enough to get out of bed, why don't we head for Texas the way we intended?"

When Luke refused, the issue became a running argument between them.

"You were prepared to leave when there wasn't a threat. Why stick around now?"

"We'll leave when this is over, but I'm not running away," he declared.

"You mean you're going to stay here just to draw them out?"

"That's right. I'm letting Charlie Walden come to me." He cupped her face in his hands and kissed her gently. "But if he doesn't show in another week, we'll head for Texas, Jaybird. I promise."

Another tense day passed uneventfully. Flint and Cleve had agreed that one of them would stay in the house at all times. Bored with watching Luke and Flint play chess, Cleve decided to walk up to the Long Branch for a couple hands of poker. After several hours had passed, with the approach of nightfall and supper ready to be put on the table, Honey decided to go get him.

Josh followed her outside. "Can I go with you, Mama?"

"Sure, sweetheart."

Hand in hand, they walked up the street, Amigo trotting behind them.

As they passed the general store, a figure stepped out of the shadows. "Well, this is an unexpected pleasure, ma'am."

Alarm slammed through her as she recognized the honey-sweet voice. "Oh, you startled me," she said, pretending a calmness she didn't feel.

Charlie threw back his head in laughter. "I didn't expect such luck."

She put a hand on Josh's shoulder to shove him away. "Josh, you run home now."

"No, Josh, you come with us," Charlie countered in his usual pleasant voice. The youngster looked confused.

Charlie took her arm. "Let's get going, ma'am."

She started to struggle. "I'm not going anywhere with you."

Suddenly, he pulled a pistol out of his coat. "That's what you think. Move. You come too, Josh. You wouldn't want me to hurt your mama, would you?" He tightened his grasp on her arm, forcing her to go with him.

He led them into the shadows near the livery to where a mounted man waited with a saddled horse. "All right, just-plain-Honey, climb on," Charlie ordered. "Blackie, you take this young boy here." He tousled Josh's hair. "Ya'll like riding, Josh?"

"What's goin' on, boss?" Blackie asked as Charlie lifted Josh up to him.

"Change in plans. When MacKenzie finds out we've snatched his wife and kid, he'll come looking for them. We'll catch him and his brothers in the open. Much easier than trying to take them in town here. They could have a whole arsenal in that house."

Honey had just climbed on the back of the horse when Matt Brennan appeared a short distance away and glanced in their direction. "Mrs. MacKenzie, is that you?"

Charlie spun around and drew his pistol.

"Matt, look out, he's got a gun," she cried.

Matt started to draw, but Charlie fired, and she screamed as she saw the young sheriff fall to the ground. Charlie jumped on the horse and goaded the animal to a run. Amigo chased down the road after them.

Luke and Flint were still at their chess game when Cleve returned from the saloon. "Where's Honey and Josh?" Luke asked, glancing up at him.

"Why ask me?"

"They walked up to the Long Branch to get you. Didn't you see them?"

"No. Maybe they stopped off to talk to someone."

"Yeah, maybe," Luke said, but he felt uneasy. "How about checking it out, Cleve?"

Flint stood up. "I'll go. Need to stretch my legs anyway." He was cut off by the sound of a gunshot. Instantly, Luke grabbed his gunbelt off the wall peg.

"What the hell are you doing?" Flint asked. "You're not the sheriff any longer." Luke ignored him and snatched up a nearby rifle.

"You can't go out there, Luke. This is probably an ambush," Cleve said.

"If it is, then Honey's in trouble," Luke said.

"Goddammit! We're probably walking right into a trap," Flint growled, grabbing his Winchester. Reaching for his own rifle, Cleve followed on his heels.

Outside, Luke saw that people were rushing over to where a crowd had formed around a figure on the ground. Flint and Cleve dashed ahead of him, and Luke followed as fast as his wounded leg would allow him. He was instantly relieved to see that the figure on the ground was not Honey. But his relief was short-lived when, clutching his bleeding thigh, Matt Brennan sat up.

"There were two of them, Luke. They rode off with your wife and son."

"Which direction, Matt?"

"Toward the north."

"We'll get the horses," Flint said grimly. He and Cleve hurried away.

"Let a posse handle this, Luke. Sounds like they're just trying to get you in the open," Matt warned.

"Haven't got time, Matt. My brothers are waiting for me," Luke said as he limped away.

As Delmer Quinn helped him to his feet, the frustrated young sheriff shouted, "Listen to me, Luke. You were able to get patched up the last time; you won't be that lucky again."

Flint and Cleve already had the horses saddled by the time Luke got back to the house. Painfully, he climbed into the saddle, and the three men rode north.

"You got any destination in mind, Big Brother?" Cleve asked.

"Reckon they'll let us know. They must have figured there'd be too many guns against them in town, so they snatched my family to get us to follow. They're gonna see to it that we find 'em."

After nearly a thirty-minute ride, they reined up when they came upon Amigo in the road. Puffing vigorously, he lay with his pink tongue hanging out.

Cleve dismounted and knelt down. "Hey, boy, are you okay?" After checking the dog for a wound, Flint looked up and shook his head. "He's just winded. Probably chased the horses as long as he could."

Flint and Luke climbed down from their horses,

and after a few minutes, Amigo stood up. "Where's Josh, boy?" Luke asked. The dog started off in a run again. "Maybe he can lead us to Josh," Luke said. "He must know the boy's scent as good as his own."

"He ain't no bloodhound, Luke," Flint scoffed.

"Neither are you, but that never stopped you, Brother Flint," Cleve joshed. The three men hurried to remount.

In a short time, moonlight revealed a fork in the road: one trail continued to head straight north, and the other swerved east into higher ground. "Looks like this is as far as we go until daylight," Cleve said. "It's too dark to see which way they headed."

Amigo was chasing around zealously sniffing the ground. He finally raced off on the high road.

"Goddamm!" Luke exclaimed. "I always said that dog was worth his weight in gold." They galloped in pursuit.

After a short distance, Flint pointed to a red glow in the hills. "There's the sign we've been looking for. 'Pears to be a campfire." Amigo doubled back and was sniffing the ground again.

"Except you know we won't find anyone around that fire," Cleve said. "That's the oldest ploy in the world."

"That's right, so let me scout around here a little bit. You two just sit tight under that boulder there. It'll spell the horses and give you a chance to rest your back and leg, Luke."

"You expect me to just sit tight, knowing my wife and son are at their mercy?"

"I know how you feel, Luke, but you won't do Honey or Josh any good riding into Walden's trap," Cleve advised.

Flint sat down and changed into a pair of moccasins. "And keep that dog with you. I don't want him chasing into the middle of that campfire."

"But he can lead you right to Josh," Luke said.

"Let me get the lay of the land first. Just give me about fifteen minutes."

"That's all you're getting," Luke warned. "Come here, Amigo." He picked up the dog, went over to the boulder, and sat down.

Honey could feel the stares of the dozen or more men gathered around the campfire. She hugged Josh to her hip.

"Who are they, Charlie?" one of the men asked.

"MacKenzie's wife and kid." Charlie threw back his head in a laughter that sent chills down her spine. "We'll tie them to those saplings over there. I want both of them in full sight when MacKenzie comes sniffing around here. If we can take him alive, boys, that's even better. Just killing his brothers isn't going to even the score for him killing Beau and locking up Billy Bob. There's a few things I want to do to that ex-sheriff before he dies. Time's wasting, so let's get going."

One of the men wrestled Josh out of Honey's grasp. Politely, Charlie took her by the arm and led her over to a tree. "If you'd be kind enough to sit down, ma'am." A firm hand on her shoulder directed her to the ground, her back against the tree. "Sure hate to do this to you." He yanked her arms around the trunk and tied her wrists together, then he stuck his face right up to hers. Squeezing her chin in his hand, he forced her to look into his silvery eyes. "Comfortable?" His touch repulsed her as he slid his hand to her neck. "I'm sure going to hate cutting this pretty little throat of yours, just-plain-Honey." His voice had returned to sugar. "That is, if you're still alive when we all finish with you." She turned her head and saw that Josh had been bound in the same fashion.

"If he's not back in the next two minutes, I'm going up there," Luke said, impatient to be underway. "Lord knows what that gang might be doing to Honey."

"Relax, Luke. I don't think they'd try anything right

now, knowing we'd be following. Just sit tight the way Flint asked us to."

"Two more minutes," Luke declared.

Suddenly, Flint appeared out of the darkness. "Goddammit, Flint!" Cleve cursed. "Do you have to sneak up on a person like that? You're worse than one of those goddamned Comanche."

"I've scouted the camp. It's empty, just as we thought it would be," Flint said. "They've got Honey and Josh staked out as decoys. The rest of them are scattered throughout the rocks and trees. I make it thirteen, maybe fourteen of them all together."

"Which is it?" Luke grumbled. "You talk about Cleve getting careless."

"It's thirteen."

"Thirteen, that's unlucky," Cleve said, grinning.

"For them," Luke mumbled ominously.

"We'll have to split up when we get there. Most likely, they've got rifles trained on Honey and Josh. Ah . . . don't suppose you'd let *me* cut them loose?"

"That's right, Brother Flint," Luke replied.

"Luke, it's a bit of a climb to get there," Flint warned.

"Don't worry, I'll make it," Luke said grimly. "I can always crawl on my knees if I have to. Let's go."

"You best tie up that dog with the horses. We don't want him to show our hand." When Luke tied him to a tree, Amigo appeared unhappy and began to chew on the rope.

For a long moment the three men exchanged an unspoken message in their glances to each other. Luke wondered if, so recently reunited, all three of them would survive the fight that was about to follow. "I'll see you two when this is over."

Flint and Cleve nodded, then they all moved out.

Honey continued to fidget with the rope binding her wrists, but her arms were beginning to feel numb. Concerned for Josh, she turned her head, and from what she could see in the darkness, he appeared to be okay. Her heart ached for him, knowing how frightened he had to be.

"Are you okay, sweetheart?" she called out softly to him.

"Why are they hurting us like this?"

"They're mean men, Josh. Just don't do anything that will make them mad. I know your daddy and uncles will get us out of here. So don't be scared, sweetheart. Just try and go to sleep. That's the best thing to do."

"Is that what you're going to do, Mama?" he asked in a frightened little voice.

"Yes, sweetheart, that's what I'm going to do. So you do it, too."

Honey wished it could be that easy. Sitting in plain sight of the fire, she felt like a sacrificial lamb. A dozen stuffed blankets were placed around the campfire to give the impression that the gang was asleep. She knew that they had spread out and were now hiding in the rocks. Surely, if Luke and his brothers had followed, they wouldn't be foolish enough to fall for the trap. She wondered if Luke was even strong enough to ride a horse. For the first time since his injury, she prayed he was too weak to move.

Finally, realizing her effort was useless, she gave up trying to free her wrists.

"Jaybird, don't move!" Luke's whisper came from the darkness somewhere behind her.

Instantly, she felt the surge of blood to her head from her quickened heartbeat. She bit her lip to keep from crying out with relief.

"We figure that they've got rifles aimed at you and Josh, so don't make a move until I tell you." Within seconds she felt a tugging on the rope, then the tension eased, and her wrists were free. "I'm crawling over to free Josh. When I tell you to, run like hell for the bushes behind this tree," he whispered.

She stared ahead and remained motionless.

After cutting the rope on Honey's wrists, remaining in the shadows to avoid the light from the campfire,

Luke slithered over to the tree where Josh was tied. He knew this would be the most difficult, because the young boy would be sure to react when he heard him. As dangerous as it might be, he dared not free Josh until he heard Flint's signal. From the layout of the land, there appeared to be only one angle from which the bastards could get a sure shot at Honey and Josh. Flint should be up there now scouting it out.

Luke's fingers tightened on the knife in his hand as he waited for Flint's signal.

Flint drew his knife and crawled along the ground toward the man hunched behind the rock ahead. Not a leaf rustled or blade of grass stirred as he crept stealthily forward. When he was within striking distance of his quarry, he saw that there was only one man. He held a rifle trained on Honey in the clearing below. In a smooth, lithe leap, Flint sprang at him and clamped a hand over his mouth as he slit his throat. Then he cupped his fingers to his hand and emitted the cry of a whippoorwill.

Luke heard the signal, then glanced up toward the answering cry that sounded from the rocks above. That would be Cleve. He responded with the same cry and started to slither forward.

Suddenly, barking joyously, Amigo dashed across the hearing toward Josh. There was no longer any time for stealth. "Run, Jaybird," Luke cried out.

As Honey dashed toward the bushes, Luke jumped up from concealment to cut Josh loose. The darkness was ripped by gunfire as Cleve and Flint opened up with their rifles and return flashes of gunfire erupted from all directions.

Cleve's first two shots took out the two men below him. Bullets whizzed around him, ricocheting off the rocks as he scrambled to the rock below. Meanwhile Flint returned the fire from several gunmen targeting him, and two more of the outlaws pitched to the ground.

Luke slashed the ropes binding Josh, picked him

up, and ran in a crouch to the bushes. He scampered over to Honey as quickly as his legs allowed him and shoved Josh into her arms. "Head for the cover of that rock."

Bullets from one of the gunmen in the rocks above kicked up the dust at their feet. Luke fired several shots in the direction of the gun flashes.

At the sound of Honey's scream, Luke spun around. A gunman had jumped from concealment and grabbed her. Too close to shoot for fear of hitting Honey, Luke charged him. Knocked off his feet, the attacker lost his hold on Honey as the two men fell to the ground.

The fall slammed the air out of Luke's lungs. The outlaw got to his feet and grabbed his rifle. Luke drew his Colt and fanned the hammer of the pistol. The shock threw the outlaw backward as three bullets tore into his chest. The rifle dropped from his hand as he doubled over and fell to the ground.

Slipping his Colt back into its holster, Luke struggled to his feet and picked up his rifle. "Let's get out of here." He grabbed Honey's hand, and in a low crouch they hurried toward the cover of the rock. A bullet kicked up the dust at Luke's feet. He spun and fired, and as the man toppled to the ground, Luke dived behind the rock. Honey had Josh and Amigo in the circle of her arms, and they huddled together as gunfire flashed like lightning in the rocks above them.

Within minutes, the gunshots became sporadic. Then they stopped.

For a long moment, Luke paused and listened for a sound. An eerie silence descended over the small area, which only moments before had been shattered with the blast of gunshots. The pungent odor of sulfur stung his nostrils, and wispy trails of gunsmoke drifted through the air.

Luke sucked his tongue behind his teeth and emitted two short whistles. From the rocks above, Cleve repeated the sound, then stood up and waved at them. Luke waited expectantly, but there was no third whistle. No sign of Flint.

He felt his chest constrict and his stomach tie in a knot.

"Flint?" Honey whispered and clutched his arm.

Suddenly, they heard two short whistles, and Flint appeared in the clearing.

"Oh, thank God," Honey sighed.

His leg ached so much, Luke wanted to sink to the ground. But he painfully limped to the campfire and joined his brothers.

"Where the hell were you, Flint?" he asked. "You scared the hell out of us."

"Just checking on our friends. Four of 'em snuck away and rode off."

Exhausted, Luke sat down and watched as Cleve and Flint collected the bodies in a pile. There were nine in all.

"I wonder if any of them is Charlie Walden," Cleve said.

Revolted by the carnage, Honey walked among them and studied the faces of the dead men. "None of these men are him."

"So that damn bastard escaped," Flint swore, frustrated.

"We'll get him some day, Brother Flint," Cleve said, slapping Flint on the shoulder.

Angrily, Flint kicked at a log in the fire and suddenly uttered a long string of expletives. Glancing at their startled faces, he grinned sheepishly. "I plumb forgot I was wearing moccasins."

They couldn't help but laugh.

Cleve walked over for another look at the bodies. "What a sleazy assortment they are," he commented in disgust. He suddenly bent down and removed a beaded chain from around the neck of one of the dead men. After studying it for a moment, he glanced surreptitiously at Luke.

"What is it, Cleve?"

"Well, maybe it's just a coincidence."

"What is?" Luke asked.

Flint walked over and took the chain from Cleve. He studied the object, then swung his gaze to Luke. "Coincidence, hell!" He handed it back to Cleve.

Curious, Luke stood up. "What?"

Cleve cleared his throat. "Didn't Sarah make a blue beaded chain with a red heart in the center?"

"Yeah, she gave it to Ma the first Christmas we were married," Luke said, sensing the inevitable. "Let me see what you've got in your hand, Cleve."

Long after Cleve handed it to him, Luke stared numbly at the blue necklace.

"Reckon there's no doubt this is the same gang we've been looking for," Flint mumbled and turned away with renewed anger. "What are we waiting for?" He walked away.

"I gotta get Honey and Josh back to town. I'll catch up with you," Luke said. Cleve nodded and followed Flint.

Honey glanced up at him. "What do you mean, you'll catch up with them? Aren't they coming with us?"

"No. They'll stay on the trail."

The first rays of the rising sun filtered through the bedroom window and began to creep across the floor. Honey watched in despair as Luke hurriedly shoved several boxes of rifle cartridges into his saddlebags. "So you're determined to just ride off and leave us?"

"Jaybird, this is the hottest trail we've ever had. Flint is sure to track them down in a couple of days. A week at the most. Then I'll be back."

"You told me we were going to Texas, Luke. Instead, you're chasing off after these outlaws."

"Honey, please be reasonable. This is an obligation I can't ride away from."

"What about the obligation to your son? To me? You have an obligation to the living, Luke, not to the dead," she pleaded.

"You don't understand, Honey. You're not trying

to understand," he said. Cramming in a shirt, he tied the saddlebags.

"I understand this has nothing to do with obligations; if it did, you wouldn't leave. This is about revenge, Luke. Why can't you see that?"

He paused long enough to look solemnly at her. "You can call it what you want, but I consider it my duty."

"Your duty? You consider it your duty to ride off and get killed? Do you actually believe that's what Sarah and your mother would want you do?" she shouted, appalled. "Oh, Luke," she pleaded in a softer tone, "I'm sorry about Sarah and your mother. But I have to think about Josh and me, too. We love you. We don't want to see you killed over something that you can't change."

She drew a shuddering breath. "Luke, if you're lucky enough to return, it'll be because you didn't catch up with Charlie Walden. And as long as he's alive, you'll be searching for him."

The onus of this declaration became even more of a reality to her for having said it aloud. In a voice heavy with regret, she continued. "I don't have your mother's strength, Luke. I don't intend to raise my children without their father. I've just finished helping to dig Charlie Walden's bullets out of you, sitting at your bedside, praying that you wouldn't die. I won't do that again. I won't bear your children to sit at that bedside with me and Josh. So if you ride out now, don't expect to find us here when you get back."

For the briefest second, there was a glint of anger in his eyes. "There's nowhere you can run to, Honey, that I wouldn't find you." Then he grasped her shoulders and pulled her to him. "Sweetheart, as soon as I get back, we'll talk this all out; there's just not time now." He cupped her cheeks in his hands. "I love you, Jaybird. Please don't quit on me now, babe." He kissed her fervently, tasting the salt from the tears sliding down her cheeks. Then he grabbed his saddlebags and left.

With a feeling of hopelessness, Honey went to the door and watched him gallop away. He left her no choice.

Weary from seven days in the saddle, Luke slowly climbed the porch steps. He sensed the house was deserted before he even opened the door. Nevertheless, he went into the bedroom they had shared, then walked into his son's room. Slumping down on a kitchen chair, he rested his head in his hands. First, they'd lost Walden's trail. Now he'd lost his wife. Would she have headed to San Francisco or north to Sacramento? The damn little fool might have been determined enough to even go all the way up to Seattle to try and find Cynthia and Doug.

Well, there was one good chance of finding out. Rising to his feet, he strode past his brothers, slammed out the door, and headed for the stage office.

Flint and Cleve exchanged baffled looks, then followed.

Chapter 33

The three tall men caught Ethan Pomroy's attention as soon as they entered the lobby. Newly arrived in Sacramento, the desk clerk felt apprehension at their intimidating size.

When one of them walked over to the desk, Pomroy noticed that the man walked with a slight limp. He was relieved when he glimpsed a badge under the man's vest.

"Do you have a Mrs. MacKenzie registered here?"

"No, sir," Ethan said politely.

"How about a Mary Jones? Abigail Fenton? Ah . . ." Luke struggled to dredge up the name from the back of his head. "Becky Sharp?"

The clerk carefully checked the register. "No, none of them."

Flint shoved his hat to his forehead. "Who the hell are all those ladies, Luke?"

"It's a long story. I'll explain it later." He turned back to the desk clerk. "Let me see the register."

Glancing at the signatures, his gaze locked on one name. He knew he had seen or heard it before, but it slipped his memory just where. "Has this Jane Eyre checked out yet?"

"No, Mrs. Eyre is still registered."

"Does she have a child with her?"

"Yes, a young boy."

"Which room is she in?" Luke asked curtly.

"Room number 6."

Six! The same room she had had before, Luke thought ironically. "Is number 7 available?"

"Matter of fact it is, Sheriff."

"Good, I'm renting it tonight." He slapped down a dollar. "And give me the key to the door of the connecting room."

The desk clerk cleared his throat. "But that's Mrs. Eyre's room." His uneasiness was evident.

"I know," Luke said. "The keys," he repeated impatiently.

"This is very improper, sir," the clerk said with haughty disapproval.

Casting a quick glance at his name plate, Luke said, "This is official business, Pomroy."

Agitated, the clerk handed him the keys.

Followed by Flint and Cleve, Luke hurried up the stairway and unlocked the door to room 7. "Light a lamp and wait in here," Luke said as he unlocked the connecting door. He opened the door slightly and was met by the sound of a low, feral growl.

Peeking in, he saw that the room was lit with a dimmed lamp on the table. With bared teeth and ears upright, Amigo stood on the foot of the bed like a sentinel on duty. At the sight of Luke, though, the dog's tail began wagging. He jumped down, trotted over, and began to sniff Luke's boots.

"Hi, boy," he said, bending down to pat Amigo's head. "Never thought I'd be glad to see you." Luke shifted his glance to the bed. Josh lay asleep with his hand tucked under his cheek.

Luke moved quietly across the room and sat down on the edge of the mattress. For a long moment he stared at the sleeping boy. He felt overwhelmed with emotion, and his eyes moistened with unshed tears.

Tenderly, he reached out and stroked his son's

cheek. Josh turned over and opened his eyes. "Hi, Daddy," he said sleepily.

"Hi, son."

Josh's eyes drooped and he fell back to sleep. Luke leaned over and kissed his cheek, then he stood up. Amigo jumped up on the bed, stretched out, and laid his head across the lap of the sleeping boy.

"Take care of him, pal," Luke said, patting the dog's head.

He returned to the other room. "Josh is in there, but Honey isn't. I wonder if she went back to the Golden Palace and got a job there again. Let's check it out."

Returning to the lobby, Luke stopped at the desk. "I found the boy, but he was alone."

"Had you asked, I could have told you that Mrs. Eyre wasn't in her room," he said smugly.

"You know, Pomroy, you're beginning to get on my nerves," Flint interjected.

"Where the hell is she at this time of the night?" Luke demanded.

"Mrs. Eyre is in the barroom."

"Barroom? Singing?"

"No, the woman deals cards," Pomroy said with distaste. Luke spun on his heel and headed for the barroom, but Flint and Cleve hung back.

"Don't you mean the *lady* deals cards, Mr. Pomroy?" Cleve asked pleasantly.

"Lady!" he snorted. "I doubt she's much of a lady."

It was the wrong thing to say. Flint hauled off and landed a punch in Pomroy's face that sent him flying. The hapless clerk ended up on the floor on his backside. Wordlessly, Flint turned and walked away.

Shaking his head, Cleve looked down at the shocked clerk, who was now clutching an aching jaw. "Should of warned you, Ethan. Brother Flint doesn't take too kindly to anyone making nasty remarks about our little sister." He offered a broad grin, then followed Flint.

* * *

After a quick glance around the crowded room, Luke saw Honey seated at a corner poker table with four other players. He didn't like that sight any more than he liked the gown she was wearing. That damn black dress she had worn at the Long Branch. Her bare shoulders and breasts, which were meant to be for his eyes only, were in plain view for any god-damned lecher who wanted to ogle them. Long black gloves reached almost to her underarms, and it appeared to Luke that she had more of her arms covered than her body.

As Luke charged across the room to the corner table, he nodded a greeting to Arnie. The piano player shifted a toothpick to the other side of his mouth and began to pound out a spirited rendition of "Dixie" on the ivory keys.

"You'll have to find a new dealer, gentlemen," Luke declared.

Startled, Honey glanced up in dismay.

"New dealer? What are you talking about?" one of the players grumbled.

"This woman is my escaped prisoner. She is a notorious cardsharper. Travels around the country using several aliases: Becky Sharp, Abigail Fenton, and Mary Jones to name a few. She has even been known to assume the disguise of a Gypsy fortune teller by the name of Mama Rosa. Her latest crime involved abducting a young boy from his father's house," he said with a meaningful glance in her direction. "Lucky for you, gentlemen, I have caught up with her. No doubt, I have saved you a great deal of money."

"Abducting a child? Lady, you ought to be strung up," one of the players complained. "It's no wonder you was winning. Didn't figure you could be that lucky. Well, I want back the money you cheated me out of, or I'm gonna start smacking the hell out of you."

Luke grabbed a fistful of the man's shirt front and yanked him out of his chair. Nose to nose, he glared into the man's startled eyes. "You want to try smacking me around instead, loud mouth?" He shoved him back down so hard the chair crashed to the floor.

"I didn't cheat you," Honey declared, glaring down at the astonished man on the floor. "I wouldn't have to. You're the worst poker player I've ever dealt a card to." Angrily, she pulled out some currency from between her breasts. "Here's your damn money." She tossed it down on his chest.

Luke grasped Honey by the arm and lifted her out of the chair.

"Take your hands off me," she cried, kicking at his shins.

"Lady, I'd advise you not to add kicking a lawman to your list of offenses," he warned.

"You're not a lawman anymore."

Luke flashed his old star. "Matt deputized me for the occasion."

"Even if you are, you have no authority here. You told me that yourself. I'm not going anywhere with you."

"I'm afraid you force me to take more drastic action." He pulled her arms behind her and locked handcuffs on her wrists.

"You can't do this to me, Luke MacKenzie! I haven't committed any crime," she declared as he picked her up and slung her over his shoulder. She raised her head, and her desperate glance fell on Cleve and Flint standing at the bar. "Help me! Stop him!" she cried out.

The two men just shrugged.

Luke strode into the lobby. He ignored the desk clerk, who stood holding an ice pack to his swollen jaw, and carried her up the stairs.

"I haven't done anything wrong. Put me down at once, Luke MacKenzie, or I'm going to scream loud enough to bring down the rafters!"

Ignoring her threats, he unlocked the door of his room and kicked it shut behind him. "You want to get down? You've got it, baby." He threw her on the bed, her cuffed hands trapped under her side.

By the time the bed stopped bouncing, he had tossed aside his hat and removed his gunbelt. She tried to get up, but he shoved her back down. Hands on his hips, he glared down at her.

"You better have a good excuse for kidnapping my son, lady."

"He's my son, too," she snapped. "And since his father is determined to get himself killed, I figured I have the right to take Josh someplace where there's less chance of his getting killed just because his name is MacKenzie."

"Have you forgotten that's your name, too?"

"Not at all. More reason to leave. I have no desire to get caught in the cross fire again. By the way, did you carry out your vengeance with Charlie Walden?"

"No. He managed to slip away. But let's not change the subject. What did you have in mind? Raising my son in a room over a barroom?"

"Is that where you found him now?" she lashed out defiantly.

"That doesn't mean he wouldn't end up in one," he accused.

"It couldn't be any worse than subjecting him to Frau Frieda Frick!"

"Abducting a six-year-old is a serious offense, lady, whether you make light of it or not."

"That's how much you know about the law, Sheriff MacKenzie. I didn't force him. Josh came willingly, so it's not abduction."

"Well, kidnapping then."

"Wrong again, Sheriff. No ransom note," she said mockingly. "So don't worry about us, Sheriff. You MacKenzies can go off on your manhunt and get yourselves killed. As long as you've made revenge your goal, you can sleep with *it* instead of me for as long as you remain alive. I made up my mind I'm not staying around just to bury you when they bring me your body slung over the back of a horse."

"You sure you don't mean you're running away as

usual? Every time the going gets tough, you run, lady."

"I was willing to scrub your floors, cook your food, and grub in the dirt if I had to. There's only one thing I'm not willing to do for you, Luke MacKenzie, and that's bury you."

She turned her head aside. "So unlock these handcuffs and get out of here, or I'm going to start screaming."

Before she could guess his intent, he grabbed her ankles and pulled off her shoes.

"Stop that. What are you doing?" She tried to kick herself free but only managed to shove her skirt above her knees.

"Love these legs of yours, Jaybird." Still grasping her ankles, he leaned down and kissed each dimpled knee that had come into view.

She stared up wide-eyed. "What . . . what are you doing?"

"Seems plain enough to me." He moved a hand slowly up her leg, unhooked the stocking from her corset, and slid it off her leg and foot. He never took his eyes from hers as he slowly removed the other stocking. Grasping her legs by the ankles, he ran his tongue along the sole of each foot.

"Stop that! What are you going to do?" she cried out, alarmed.

He plunked down a hand on either side of her head and leaned over her. "Now, just what do you think I'm going to do, dear wife?" He placed a quick kiss on her gaping mouth.

She tried to shimmy away but got no farther than the edge of the bed when she felt his hands grasp her around the waist and pull her back. He slid his hands to her breasts and cupped them in his palms.

Lowering his head, he licked the swell of her cleavage as he tucked a thumb under each narrow strap of her gown and ripped them loose. Vainly, she thrashed to get free when he slipped his hands beneath her and released the buttons of the gown.

"What a wild cat you are," he whispered, nibbling at her ear. "But it's not gonna do you any good."

He manipulated the dress past her hips and off her legs, then quickly removed her petticoat and corset. Hungrily, he swept his gaze over the flimsy drawers and camisole to the pointed peaks of her breasts.

His warm breath fanned her heated flesh. "And I love these breasts of yours, Jaybird. But I think they should be for my eyes alone." He closed his mouth over one nipple through the thin fabric. Then, shoving down her camisole, he rasped his tongue across the dusky nubs.

"Don't—don't do that," she demanded in a shaky voice.

"Now you know you like that, baby." He lightly pulled the camisole back in place, then dipped his head and sucked on her breasts until the delicate fabric clung damply to the turgid peaks.

She squirmed to free herself, hairpins flying in all directions. The long strands of her hair, freed from restraint, flared out on the counterpane.

"No, not like this, Luke. Please, not like this," she pleaded.

Cupping the back of her head, he raised her face to his. For a long moment, he held her head suspended as he stared into her terrified eyes.

"Why are you doing this to me?" she asked in a frightened whisper.

Shifting her so her head lay on the pillow, he stood up. "If you remember, dear wife, I told you that as soon as I got back to Stockton, you and I would have a long talk."

He freed her left wrist, but before she could pull away, he locked the loose cuff to the brass headboard. "If I have to keep you chained to this bed for a week, we will get this settled once and for all." He walked around to the other side and sat down on the edge of the bed. Quickly pulling off his boots, he thrust his jeans down his legs and over his feet.

"I'll never forgive you for this," she threatened.

Tugging at the cuff on her wrist, she tried to sit up, but the firm pressure of his hands at her shoulders gently forced her back.

"You leave me no choice, Jaybird. We'll settle this either here or with you locked in a cell back in Stockton. If you'd been willing to sit down and discuss our problem intelligently, all this wouldn't be necessary. But instead, you ran off, Mrs. Jane Eyre. By the way, when did you give up on Becky Sharp?"

She glared at him. "I think the story of an orphan girl who becomes a governess and falls in love with her sardonic employer parallels my life even better."

Grinning, he leaned over her. "You just admitted that you loved me, Jaybird."

She felt the rise of tears and tried to choke them back. "I've always loved you, Luke."

His grin dissolved, and his wounded gaze locked with hers. "Then how could you run away?"

Her eyes glistened with tears. "I just told you why. I can bear leaving you but not burying you."

Smiling tenderly, he caressed her cheek. "Then come with me, sweetheart. We'll do as we planned. We'll go to Texas. Build up the ranch again. You were right when you said the time had come to consider the living, not the dead. We've both been hanging on to our pasts. It's time to think of the future. And you're my future. Let me be yours."

He kissed her gently, tenderly. "I love you, Jaybird." She heard the words repeated in a husky timbre at her ear. "Please come with me to Texas. We'll have a new beginning, free of every dark side of our lives."

"Do you really mean that, Luke? What about Charlie Walden."

"There's nothing as important to me as you and Josh. I love you."

"And I love you, too." She slid her hand to the nape of his neck, the pressure of her fingers propelling his mouth down to hers. "I love you so much, Luke MacKenzie, I ache with love for you." She kissed him.

"Make love to me, Luke." She whispered the words into his mouth.

His mouth covered her hungrily, devouring its softness. Shivers of desire raced through her, curling in a heated swirl at the junction of her legs. The kiss intensified, and she moaned with ecstasy under the firm pressure of his lips and heated sweeps of his probing tongue. His hand splayed her stomach and slid under her camisole, and as his warm palm massaged her breasts, intimately and possessively, she felt them swell to fill his hand. She wanted more. She forced his head lower. Following her lead, he sucked a nipple into his mouth and, lowering his hand, palmed the junction of her legs.

Mindlessly writhing under the rapture of his mouth and hands, Honey tried to slip her arms around his neck. She gasped with pain when the handcuff on her left hand pinched her wrist.

Luke raised his head and immediately saw her plight. "Oh, Lord, I'm sorry, sweetheart. I forgot—"

"I did, too," she quickly whispered, caressing his cheek with her free hand.

He hopped off the bed and grabbed his jeans. "Key's in the pocket," he said apologetically as he groped for the key. "I didn't really intend to keep you chained to the bed. I was just running a bluff."

A knock on the door sounded before she could tell him just how thoroughly convincing his bluff had been.

"Now who the hell is that?" He tossed the key on the table and quickly pulled the bed sheet over her near nakedness. Then he leaned down and gave her a quick kiss. "Promise me you won't move until I get back?" He hobbled over to the door as he pulled on his jeans.

As soon as Luke opened the door, Cleve MacKenzie glanced down with disdain at Luke's open pants. "May we come in?"

"Ah . . . this isn't the best time, Little Brother. You two got a problem?" Luke asked, glancing at Flint.

"Yeah, we sure do." Flint snorted gruffly.

"Okay, come on in. But make it quick." Luke turned and walked back to the bed. Cleve and Flint stepped into the room and closed the door.

As she waited with one wrist still chained to the bed, Honey felt ridiculous. She was utterly shocked when Luke agreed to let them in the room.

Mortified at the embarrassing and compromising position she was in, Honey clutched the sheet to her neck with her free hand, but she knew they couldn't help but see her hand shackled to the headboard as well as the discarded clothing tossed on the floor.

"What's wrong?" Luke asked, sitting down on the bed. The move partially blocked her view of them. He glanced at Cleve, who looked uncomfortable, then at Flint, who was scratching at his beard. "Well what is it? What the hell's going on with you two?"

"We've been wondering the same thing about you, Big Brother," Cleve said.

"What are you talking about?" Luke asked impatiently.

"We're talking about our little sister there, chained to your bed," Flint broke in. "It just don't set in our craw, Luke. It don't seem a proper way to be treating your wife. I'm thinking Ma wouldn't take kindly to it either."

Honey peeked around Luke's shoulder and saw that all three men were staring at her.

On a single flush of hot blood, Honey was swept from the depth of mortification to the height of anger. Having barely recovered from believing her husband intended to ravage her, she was now being subjected to his brothers' leering eyes. She loved them all dearly, but for the moment she had had all she could bear of anyone named MacKenzie.

Rising to her knees, she glared at them over the expanse of Luke's broad shoulders. "All of you get out of here, or I'm going to start screaming. Right now. Do you hear?" she shouted, looking like a crazed vixen with her blond hair wild and disarrayed.

She yanked furiously at the handcuffs. "And if you don't unchain me from this bed, I'm having you all arrested."

"Calm down, Honey. I'll get rid of them," Luke said, trying to soothe her.

"Like hell, I'll calm down!" she shouted. "Get out of here. All of you, dammit!"

"Now you don't have to start cussing," Flint censured.

"Then get the hell out of here."

"Since I don't cotton to listening to screeching women talking vulgar, you don't have to ask me twice, little honey bear," Flint said.

With a snort of contempt, Honey tossed her head and further disheveled the mass of blond hair hanging in disarray around her shoulders. "You already *have* been asked twice, so why in hell are you still standing there like a leering idiot? Get out of here. And take your big brother with you."

"I'm not going anywhere," Luke shouted back. "Goddammit, Jaybird, you're my wife and you can't order me out of this room."

Cleve, who had been uncharacteristically silent since entering the room, strode forcefully over to the bed. "I'll settle this here and now. Where's that goddamned key to those handcuffs?"

Seeing it lying on the table, he picked up the key, unlocked the cuff, and pulled it off the bed. Before Luke or Honey could guess his intent, he grabbed Luke's left wrist and snapped the cuff around it.

"What are you doing?" Luke asked, jumping to his feet. The quick move yanked Honey with him, since her right hand was now chained to his left hand. She frantically clutched at the sheet and managed to hold onto the cover and her maidenly modesty but not before exposing a fetching leg.

"Flint and I have been chewing this over, Luke, and we figure it just isn't your way not to be fighting fair." He tucked the key into his vest pocket. "So this kind of evens the odds."

He paused at the door and flashed a roguish grin at the two stunned people on the bed. "Have a good night, Big Brother." He winked at Honey. "And you too, Little Sister."

Laughing, Flint whomped Cleve on the shoulder as they walked down the stairs. "Ain't seen nothing like Luke's face when you put that cuff on him. And that there little honey bear's madder than all tarnation and screeching like a plucked jaybird. Luke sure named her right. Hate to be in his drawers right now."

"Trouble with you, Brother Flint, is that you don't understand the finer subtleties of romance," Cleve informed him as they entered the barroom. "I'll bet you the next drink our big brother is already *out* of his drawers."

Grinning, Flint put his arm around Cleve's shoulder. "Yep, more I think on it, more I reckon I owe you a drink, Little Brother."

Throwing back their dark heads in laughter, the MacKenzie brothers bellied up to the bar.

Avon Romantic Treasures

*Unforgettable, enthralling love stories,
sparkling with passion and adventure
from Romance's bestselling authors*